A BEAUTIFUL NOISE

SAM COLLINS

First Published in Great Britain in 2024
by Mostyn March Publishing
www.mostynmarch.com

www.samjcollins.com

COVER ILLUSTRATIONS BY UKRAINIAN ARTIST, ROKSOLANA TKACH

A NOTE ABOUT DECIBELS

A decibel (dB) is a measure of the intensity of a sound.
30dB is a whisper; 95dB is an underground train;
120dB is the threshold of pain;
and a nuclear explosion at 250dB is enough
to kill you by sound alone.

But sometimes it's not what you hear
it's how you listen that counts...

PART I

BATTLE CRIES

A rat... 40dB
An opera singer at full pelt... 100dB
A drum kit in a Folly... 110dB
A backfiring petrol lawnmower... 120dB

1

MATTHEW
THE BANKRUPT EARL

Matthew Roundell Wolstenholme, 7th Earl of Bedingford, emptied his wallet and searched through every pocket for the odd pound coin that might mean a decent lunch that week. Somewhere in the back of his mind he knew he ought to widen the search to the drawers and furniture, but the back of his mind was where he resolutely wished it to stay. Since his exam results at Winchester as a boy, Matthew refused to open, let alone answer, any correspondence addressed to him. Letters would be found by staff and family piled in drawers, stuffed behind sideboards, and in all corners of his car. Small hidden spaces that Matthew could no longer see.

He found a couple of old pound notes behind the radio in the kitchen and wondered if he could still take them to a bank. The thought shamed him. He was well aware of the ridiculousness of living in a place like Bedingford Manor and being penniless in ready cash to buy the most basic of necessities. A ridiculousness he continued to obscure with a veil of largesse and good humour that was becoming as threadbare as his carpets.

Matthew sighed and considered a rare foray into the village centre. Perhaps if he lingered long enough and rattled off a few stories to the walkers visiting The Huntsman's Arms, they might stand him a pie and a pint on the pretence of 'having left his wallet in the glove compartment of the Roller'. His stomach turned. *Free lunch*, he had always hated the concept, dished out as it usually was to those who least deserved it.

A rat scuttled along the skirting board, a stale Twiglet gripped between its teeth like a lacquered moustache. Sauntering around the dresser, it stopped, nose in the air, interrogating, eyes fixed on him as if to say, 'you're not getting this one, mate.' Matthew could have sworn the rat raised an eyebrow. He was sharing his house with the Roger Moore of vermin. Not to mention the rest of the cast. Every day he walked around the Manor accompanied by the insects that freely came and went through the broken windows. He could no longer hear the tick, tick, tick of the various creatures behind the skirting, under the floorboards and in the eaves. But then, he no longer noticed the bare floors, rotting sills and frames, the damp, peeling wallpaper and holes in the walls. Half the house was under dust covers and was becoming little more than an antique theme park for wildlife. But that made it no less his home; and no less his desire to preserve and share it as much as he ever had.

Matthew's stomach rumbled so loudly his ribcage rattled. Or at least he thought it was loud. These days, he was not sure what was hearing and what was feeling half the time. A thought that would have interested him if he wasn't quite so frightened of silence.

But as he gazed out of the library window at the chaos all around him, his tightened lip twitched into an enlightened smile. *Ah yes, the festival crew facilities!* Beryl, his beloved golden retriever, was growing fatter by the hour, spending the last few days begging round the catering van. He could surely try something similar. Perhaps with a little more decorum and a little less drool.

He wandered out to the terrace. Five days ago, the front of

his house had been as it always had – a set of grey stone steps dipping before an expanse of lawn, rising up towards the flower gardens and beyond to the orchards of the estate; an overgrown gravel path leading to the crumbling Palladian archway of the stable courtyard on the right. But now the place was alive with activity; workmen banging and crashing over the flower beds and lawns, incongruous structures appearing in their place. A hotch-potch of stage and scaffolding, which could loosely be described as 'constructed', stood at one end of the courtyard, the wood panel floor still exposed to the elements, but a huge translucent canopy swinging ominously overhead, with a fifty-fifty chance of fitting on top or searing through the coach house roof.

They had all said he was mad, of course, opening the Manor to hundreds of strangers like this again. There were moments – like this one – when Matthew agreed. Particularly with the almighty furore the whole thing had created in Bedingford over the last eighteen months. Of all the Wolstenholmes' restitution schemes over the years, it was the plan to stage an opera festival that had finally split the village. Matthew could not begin to fathom the intensity of it. The main reason he had opted for opera in the first place was to find local support within the village. Just the 'class of activity befitting such a place as Beding-ford,' he could hear them all say (and probably even claim it as their idea in the first place). But apparently his efforts were just a noise nuisance and 'interfered with the legitimate enjoyment of their front gardens on a summer's evening.' Or something like that.

The pendulous stage canopy swaying precariously in front of him was too much of a metaphor for Matthew to bear. He turned his back, held his breath and gazed up at the Manor wall instead. With a flash of violet blouse and bone white bun, Victoria appeared in an upstairs window, throwing her thumbs in the air and beaming. She had been doing that a lot lately and Matthew was reminded, as he tentatively followed her pointed finger to see the successfully roof-capped stage, that despite it all, this thing had lit a touch paper to both their waning spirits and brought them back to life.

Within moments, she had joined him on the steps.

Twelve years his senior, Matthew's widowed sister-in-law, Victoria Wolstenholme, was a substantial woman. Tall and broad, she walked with an alert and upright stance that belied her eighty-six years. It was all in the neck, she maintained throughout her life. If that was in the right place, everything else would follow.

'Matthew, dear, the phone is ringing *again*. Barely stopped all morning. Might one dare hope that it be answered before Christmas? Or have we developed some kind of allergic reaction to it lately?'

'Oh, is it?' Matthew's brow furrowed before he decided it would be better to claim it as deliberate. 'Yes, I know,' he corrected, 'but I really am most awfully busy.'

'Clearly.'

'I'm just about to take a wander up to the stables, actually. Care to join me?'

'Hmm, finally noticed that Beryl is the only one getting fed around here then?' Victoria smirked. 'Sounds delightful dear, but Mrs Burlington is kindly sending her nephew to pick me up at the gate and take me into Winchester for luncheon.'

'Hmmmph,' Matthew pursed his lips. It was the only thing he disliked about his sister-in-law – she still got invited to lunch.

'And, as an added bonus,' Victoria continued regardless. 'She's discovered a new shop just out of town that she thought I might like. It's called Lidl. She loves it, says it reminds her of the war. Anyway, I'll see what I can find for our tea, shall I?'

'Well, that would be very nice, thank you...' Matthew hesitated. 'And I'm sor—'

'No, Matthew. Please, not again. If I have to hear one more apology emanating from that dear little mouth of yours, I swear I will get on that stage myself and do the Can-Can for money. Now please, it is a very fine day,' as she almost always said, whatever kind of day it was. 'Let us do all we can to keep it that way.'

Matthew forced his mouth shut. He knew she was right, but still felt he had so much to apologise for that he would never outrun the compulsion. His unfortunate mishap at Newbury Races last year, which saw off the remainder of the family purse as well as most of the old woman's jewellery, was just the last of it.

Victoria stepped back to unhook her cavernous handbag from the coat stand and re-appeared rummaging.

'Marvellous, two doggy bags.'

'You're not taking Beryl, surely?'

'No, of course not! Her table manners are atrocious, Mrs Burlington would have a pink fit. For the leftovers, Matthew dear, of course.' Matthew opened his mouth to speak, but she cut him dead. 'What did I just say?'

Victoria strode down the path towards the main gate, pulling an umbrella from her bag. 'Ah, excellent!' she waved it spiritedly in the air.

'The forecast is very good, Victoria. I don't think you'll need it,' he called after her.

'Not for the rain, dear boy. For the fucking protesters!'

Matthew's mouth twitched, not knowing whether to smile or weep. Victoria's grim determination had served many a time to both show him the way and show him up. She had certainly coped far better at losing Robert as a husband than he had at losing him as a brother all those years ago. She became the Dowager Countess and he became the Earl. Neither of them was quite sure which was worse. And it was Victoria, of course, who had talked him back from the docks at Southampton when he lost Edward, his only son, ten years ago.

Well, Australia. Lost enough.

Like tumbleweed, Matthew's most recent dark recollections, full of protests and bureaucracy, were rolling down the pathways of his mind picking up more distant memories he had no wish to revisit. He gazed back at the Manor, sun-bathed in a cloudless sky, his jaw tightening with resolution. He would *not* be the one to lose it all. Changing tides, that's all, he persuaded himself (he was good at that), a little choppy of course, but sure to wash them all up on a more peaceful shore. At least now, with the marvellous Fat Stat taking charge of the festival, all the arrangements appeared to be coming together for once. Matthew just needed this new spell of sunshine – in every sense – to last just a little bit longer.

He also desperately needed a sandwich.

The stable courtyard was heaving with a true motley crew. Matthew ducked as two men went by carrying 'scaffolding' scavenged from an old barn. Everywhere, bits of this and that – begged, borrowed or stolen – were being lifted, prodded or stared at. Men stood scratching their heads and pointing at spaces and objects that might make likely pairings, as if embarking on the world's biggest game of Perfection. A group of stagehands, who Stat had bribed from a three-day layover during a Metallica tour, stood discussing whether a dismantled flatbed lorry could provide some 'premium seating' somewhere. And would people pay more for sitting in the disused stables running along the sides of the courtyard, or the scorched grandstand seating rescued from a fire at Gosport Football Club?

They parted to let Matthew through, nodding cheerfully as he strolled up to the stable gate, and into the arms of the biggest man he had ever seen.

'Oh, terribly sorry,' Matthew quickly offered, although truth be told he quite enjoyed it.

'Pass,' the man barked.

'Yes, thank you, I certainly will— Oh, I say!'

'No pass, no access, got that?'

'Ah,' Matthew nodded, wriggling a little in the big man's arms. 'Um yes, of course, doing your job and all that, splendid.'

The grip was getting tighter and Matthew's ubiquitously charming babble did not seem to be encouraging any prospect of release. 'Right, I see, now then, um... Manor House,' he extracted his arm sufficiently to wave toward the side walls of his residence. 'Venue, Earl of Bedingford, Matthew – any better? Wolstenholme. Owner. That sort of thing...'

The giant loosened his grip but was clearly not getting it.

'Morris, let go of Lord Bedingford, would you?' A fat man in a stained white shirt, chewing on a cigar, appeared by their side. 'He's had a hard life and it's not particularly good for business. Here...' Lester Berkeley-Staten thrust an egg mayonnaise roll into Matthew's hand, fished in his pocket and unceremoniously draped a lanyard around the Earl's neck. And once again, Matthew gave silent thanks for the intervention of this powerhouse of a man, known simply as 'Stat' or 'Fat Stat' to friend or foe alike. Matthew was well aware that Stat loathed opera (and he had a point) but difficult times in the rock business had found him under-bidding for a few of them lately, and Stat's intervention, Matthew suspected, might just have saved the event altogether. As well as providing a welcome breath of fresh air. Well, perhaps not that fresh. From the moment they first met, when Stat had just smiled, farted, and asked if he had any Jack Daniels, Matthew found the man's complete lack of sycophancy utterly breathtaking. That and his weighty, authoritative voice. Something Matthew feared was becoming an increasing bonus to his own failing ears.

He fingered the laminated pass that now hung around his neck. 'Access All Areas,' he read aloud and his eyes sparkled. 'Good heavens, that actually exists! How utterly marvellous! Thank you so much!'

But Stat was off. 'Sorry, calls to make. Horace Harper has finally confirmed he'll headline the opening concert. Announcement in *The Telegraph* tomorrow and a big feature on him in their Saturday magazine. That should put the final bums on seats.'

'Oh splendid, that is good news! I hoped a little arm-twisting might pay off.'

'And I'm optimistic of other coverage. He's not been in Britain for years, apparently.'

'Indeed. Double splendid, give the village something else to get aerated about. What will he be giving us?'

'He's proposed a retrospective – Verdi to Vegas, his life in opera, or something like that. Suppose it's some kind of greatest hits? Do they have that sort of thing in this ghastly music? Apart from *Just One Cornetto*.'

'Come now, Lester, we've talked about this. We must attempt to at least keep an appearance of *some* appreciation.'

'Hmm, a toughie. But if you will, I will... Oh, and more good news, I had this valued in Soho like you asked.' Stat pulled a Second Edition copy of *On the Origin of the Species* from down the front of his shorts. 'Worth eight to ten grand, apparently. Hundred and fifty quid to get the Smurf stickers off the front cover, then they'd expect the upper end. So we should be OK to pay the Acousticians, yes?' Matthew nodded blindly, looking down at the book, his pass, and the egg mayonnaise roll, and feeling a little light-headed at the riches being bestowed this morning. 'The valuers wrote it all down on that slip of paper in the front,' Stat concluded. 'Maybe show it to the sound guys when they come on Monday, persuade them that the funds to pay them are on their way. Oh, and if you happen across a *First Edition Darwin* in your dusty old attic, let me know and we can both give up this merry-go-round, OK...?'

When Matthew returned to the Manor, sated and whistling, two burly men stood at the door, one in a cheap suit, the other in shorts and a T-shirt. Matthew giggled, still heady from this morning's good fortune, and a double hot dog. Remarkable how all these crew sorts looked the same.

'Good afternoon, Lord Bedingford...' The suited one was clearly saying something, but over the noise of construction to the side of the house, Matthew had little hope of deciphering what. His lightened heart sank again. It was getting worse. Even if this event was a success, would it be his last chance to hear it?

A familiar stab of fear caught his breath at the thought. He swallowed and painted on the equally familiar smile. 'I am so sorry, what were you saying?'

'Yes, it is very noisy out here. Mind if we pop inside for a moment?' The man raised his voice as a power drill charged the air.

Matthew opened the door, his smile securing at the prospect of more company. 'Oh indeed, please do. It's a frightful din, isn't it? I don't know how you cope with it all the time. A couple of weeks is quite enough for me!' He stepped aside to let the two men pass, which they seemed quite eager to do – shorts and T-shirt was already in the library. The other man stood silent at the door. Matthew knew that look well. The interior of the Manor was always a surprise to the uninitiated. The entrance hall was impressive enough, with the obligatory heavy wooden staircase dominating the room, but the floor was bare and what carpet remained up the stairs you could grow cabbages on.

'Good afternoon, again, Lord Bedingford,' the visitor finally regained his voice. 'Thank you for letting us in. As I was saying, we represent Delaney and Sorrell, insolvency solicitors. We wrote to you ten days ago and have not had a reply. I trust you received it.' Undoubtedly he had, but in which particular orifice of the Manor it was currently residing, Matthew had no idea. 'But here is a copy, along with my identification and a statement of account from your creditors, Aubrey Estates.'

The colour drained from Matthew's face. How could he have been so stupid? Especially as he had been caught in exactly the same way two years ago, letting in that 'maintenance man' who asked to use the toilet.

Matthew knew the score. No, he didn't have £15,000 on him and no, he wouldn't be able to find it, plus the man's astronomical fees, in five days. But it appeared that had already been assumed, as his colleague headed back towards the door with one of Matthew's ancestors under each arm.

'Oh, but not—'

'All the details are in the paperwork, sir,' the suit said, scribbling his makeshift inventory. 'You'll have a little time to reclaim your possessions, on payment of the fees, of course.'

Matthew nodded slowly. There seemed little point in any further objection, as the other man returned and left again with another painting and a Queen Anne stool.

The suit eyed the book with the valuation slip sticking out of the top and whipped it from Matthew's hand. 'That should do it for the moment. If there's any left over, we'll let you know in the next fourteen days.' He peeled off his receipt, touched his forelock like a Dickensian undertaker, and followed out of the door.

Matthew sank onto the terrace steps, his head in his hands, where it seemed to have taken residence lately. Once again reflecting on the fragility of his grip on his heritage and how easily the marks of history could be removed.

2

PIP

THE BROKEN DRUMMER

'Breakfast, Pip.' Ma Godfrey switched on the strip light and placed a tray just inside the allotment shed at the bottom of her garden. The door softly closed and Pip watched through his tiny window as her aproned rear padded back up the path towards the house. He knew that the old woman was developing a discretion in her later years that was quite alien to her, and he felt a pang of affection and regret. The same kind of affection and regret he saw in her face every morning.

Margaret Godfrey, or 'Ma' (for obvious reasons), had been fostering for over thirty years, taking charge of fifty-two children in that time. Occasionally officially, but more often than not, children just seemed to appear. It did not seem to matter to them, no more than it did to her, that the tiny old estate workers' cottage on the east side of Bedingford had only two bedrooms and never more than a pencil-width of spare space anywhere. Stuffed full as it always was with bits of this and that, which Ma insisted would 'come in handy' sometime, for some child or other.

Pip nevertheless doubted that even she would expect her

husband's allotment shed to be coming in quite so handy for one of them at thirty-one years old.

Bill Godfrey was outside now, having to make do with the lean-to at the other side of the allotment until Pip emerged each morning and attempted to find some occupation for his day.

'Alright, son?' Bill mouthed through the window, with his broad gappy smile and thumbs in the air. Bill called everyone under the age of forty either 'son' or 'my girl'. Depending on your point of view, it was either irritating or endearing. But, Pip supposed, with fifty-two foster children over the years, it was only that Bill could never be quite sure.

Pip put his pillow over his head and could almost feel the old man's sigh through the slats in the shed wall. He did not want to be reminded that he was not just another one of those random lost children. But in the light of every new day, it rehearsed itself on a loop over which he seemed to have no control anymore. Reminding him, with relentless monotony, that of all the fifty-two children Ma and Bill Godfrey had taken in over the years, he had always been different.

Special needs, they called it, at first. Ma just told him that was ridiculous. All their needs were special.

Pip fingered the drumstick that lay, as always, under his pillow. Like a severed limb returned to his body, its intense familiarity gave him momentary comfort. Until the reality kicked in. The reality that the sticks remained the most potent reminder that he had lost the battle that nobody, except Ma and Bill, had ever thought he could win. Now they were just another symbol of the modest endurance of these two uncomplicated, genuine people; how hard they had worked to accept an inquisitive, boisterous boy and help him hold on to the only thing that made sense when his world changed so completely all those years ago.

And he had repaid them with only desertion and disappointment.

The flame ignited then, from his feet to his head, as it did every morning since his release six weeks ago. Pip had promised himself in prison that as soon as he was out of there, he would give up the burden of anxiety. As soon as he could see more than grey, hear more than the echo of banging metal, smell more than men and cottage pie. But worry would not be traded like that. It gave him a few moments sometimes, like a heavy theatre curtain temporarily parting to reveal the light and colour of the world behind. But it slid back in the early mornings and he lay with it wrapped around him, prodded in and out of fitful sleep, waking like clockwork between four-thirty and five, his body jolted on a cliff edge, the heat rising until he had to push away the covers, even in the cold crisp air of the early dawn.

It seemed out of proportion to anything Pip could ever have done, or not done, to deserve it. But deserve it, he had decided, he must have.

He thrust the drumstick back under the pillow and swung his legs over the mattress on the workbench. The heaviness pressed down on him to stay there, smothered and hidden, but he knew that movement was the only thing that worked. *Just keep moving*. Wherever he was going, it at least gave his body something else to do while his mind might be persuaded to leave it alone.

He sat for a moment, his breathing deep and deliberate, legs swinging over the side of the makeshift bed; metronomes counting his progress. *Keep moving, keep counting...* Dressing was another rhythmic affair, marking his progress slowly and methodically, bargaining with himself that he'd just get to the next bit; today would be different; the afternoons were usually better, weren't they? Constantly negotiating his release with a body refusing to contemplate leaving this cloistered enclosure.

Pip scanned the modest shed. All his belongings neatly stacked on shelves and in any spare corner amongst the garden tools, the floor remaining empty, with an unobstructed path to the door. Keeping a small space tidy and always having a clear route to exit were the only things of value he had learned during his short spell in prison. Other lessons about human nature remained rather less easy to stomach.

Bill was sitting on his beloved bench, reviewing his bean seedlings, as Pip finally emerged. He shuffled up his belongings as if he were on a packed bus making room for the last desperate passenger.

'Glad you've surfaced, son. I could really do with another trowel.'

'Sorry,' Pip muttered. 'I'm trying. I mean, I'm thinking. I tried again yesterday, but— I'll be out your way as soon as I can, Bill.'

'You know that's never been the problem, Pip.' Bill patted the seat beside him. Rotted by years of sun and rain, the old bench creaked and moaned but was holding on through endless fixes. A patchwork testimony to a diligent man; a man focused entirely on 'making good' with whatever resources were available to him.

Pip gave in and sat down. Despite the momentary sadness in the old man's eyes, he knew Bill would never dwell on *such things* and would soon be telling him about the vegetables. Bill's conversation, his whole presence, had always been comforting. As he generally said and did the same thing day after day, Pip never had to pay too much attention to what he was actually saying to know exactly what was going on. It gave him a break from the effort of more interesting people.

But there was one subject to which Bill returned with a monotonous regularity that was not welcome. 'Bob Tandy's been eyeing my new compost bin again.' He nodded towards the charred bass drum, upended and filled with withering vegetation. 'Reckon he thinks it's some new-fangled gadget to get one over on him in the Flower and Produce this year,' Bill chuckled, but his smile quickly faded. 'Such a waste though, son. I'll never fathom why you had to set fire to it like that.'

'Yeah well, you wouldn't let it go, would you?'

'Useful son, even half-knackered and smoking!' Bill's smile returned, even as he looked down at his hands, still faintly blistered from his efforts to rescue the smouldering remains of Pip's manic bonfire two weeks ago.

One sleepless dawn, he'd built a funeral pyre behind the runner beans and set fire to his drum kit. Awoken by the smoke, Bill had rushed from the house, but there was little to be saved by then, least of all Pip's reason.

'Look, I know it weren't much to have left, and it weren't no patch on your proper kit,' Bill acknowledged. 'But we could've made do, you know, built it up again. Like the old days!'

'No, Bill! How many times?' This came out rather more forcefully than Pip intended. His voice lowered to a whisper. 'That's all over now. I have to accept it was never going to work. I have to move on.'

'I'm not having that!' Bill protested. 'You were—'

'Stop it!' Pip pitched the remains of his coffee into his mouth, stuffing toast in his pockets as he got up from the bench. 'Please, Bill. I have to.'

'Oh Pip, son, don't just— Hey, look at me when I'm talking to you!' This was one of Bill's stock phrases throughout Pip's teenage. But he had already turned away down the path. It was never any use then.

Pip set off towards the village centre. It was impossible to admit the horror of his days and nights, least of all to Ma and Bill. Rounding the corner of the allotments into the bottom of Trefusis Lane, the sun shone modestly over the fields and hedgerows, posts, gates and traffic signs of rural Hampshire, and it was hard to see the world as a dangerous place. Yet Pip's day ahead was filled with danger, as real to him as any. His mind eternally on guard against some vaguely formed opponent with whom he was trapped in battle, or fleeing escape, for most of his waking hours.

He shoved his hands into his pockets to stop them shaking and started to count. Ninety paces and he was allowed to look behind him. Yesterday it had been eighty. Progress had to be made.

As always, the walk into the village both fascinated and appalled him. From the tiny terraces, through open country, to near mansions within fifteen minutes, each step more muted than the last. Six times winner of the Noise Abatement Institute's award for 'The Quietest Village in England' (nobody bothered competing with the Welsh), the village sign welcomed him with its accolades. Here, Trefusis Lane became a portal, narrowing the gentle tranquillity of the open countryside to a different kind of hush as it wound its way towards the village centre, where the quiet and order became a commodity, an object of pride and competition.

It was one reason Ma suggested he try the big houses in the village first when he had finally emerged from the shed a couple of weeks ago. They would always need help with their gardens and he'd get on alright there, wouldn't he, in the quiet places? Might help calm him down a bit?

'Tell them you're one of Bill's sons,' she said. 'Everyone knows how handy he is. It's sure to help.'

Somehow Pip doubted it. The apple had fallen a long way from the tree on that one. Besides, there had been a little too much trouble with one or two of Bill's 'sons' over the years. Villagers still whispered outrage about the Delaney brothers caught chipping lead off the church roof in 1997. Then there was Ryan Bates last summer, running a protection racket at the local primary. And their most recent (and possibly last) official charge, Nathan Thomas, who was 'sent on' just before Christmas after seven village bikes in a row turned up in the window of Cash Attack in Winchester.

Pip knew, like most things, he'd just have to do it for himself.

The best job prospects were further up Trefusis Lane and

into Yarnside Drive, where the properties became really 'aspirational', vying with each other for the largest, most orderly front garden, closest cut lawn and biggest driveway-parked vehicles. The highest honour was reserved for Glebe House on the corner of Yarnside Bridge, the 'country seat' (as some villagers dubbed it) of Sir Henry Pordage and his family. Being neither ennobled nor in politics, the Pordages dismissed this notion, of course, but were delighted with it nonetheless. Naturally, Ma suggested that be his first port of call. After all, they had over an acre and she'd heard from the Reverend Blythe that 'their man' Donald was struggling to cope these days. But Pip thought he might work up to that, try the slightly less intimidating ones on Trefusis Lane first.

He hadn't quite managed that yet either, hovering around outside their gates every day like some rudderless prick, or worse...

One, two, three, four... The count of his footsteps ticked in his head like an invisible abacus, adding up his progress...

Eighty-seven, eighty-eight, eighty-nine, ninety. Look behind, nobody there, keep going...

He stopped at the first house on Trefusis Lane (well, the second, the first had solid bolted gates and an intercom that frightened the life out of him) and stared up the long drive to the front door. His heart started to race. He tried to breathe it away, tapping his foot on the gravel to the precise rhythm of his heartbeat, willing his leaden legs to *finally* make the journey to a front door. He checked behind him one last time. Dr and Mrs Page were coming down the road, in full combat Nordic walking gear for the rigours of the Hampshire countryside. Pip raised his eyes, and a smile flirted at the edge of his lips. But they kept their attention firmly on each other and their conversation. It was another minefield, Pip considered, knowing who to attempt to be pleasant to these days. It wasn't that long ago he would just have smiled at anybody.

It was the briefest of thoughts. It had barely reached his consciousness before his foot began to tap again, faster and faster and faster. Until it turned and took him swiftly away.

He ran across the road to count along the Bedingford Estate wall instead. No doors to remind him that he was about to spend another day avoiding knocking on any of them. And he'd always loved this wall. The sustaining antiquity of the lichen-covered grey stone immediately induced a hint of calm; a sense of gentle strength and optimism, that whatever crawled over you and got into the cracks, it was possible to endure, to remain grounded with grace and solidity. The stillness here was the real quiet of this place, Pip reflected, not the competitive hush of the village gardens. He stood with his palms resting on the cool, damp stone and studied it. And for a few short moments, his attention stilled his body and slowed his thinking, and he felt a small sense of himself solidifying. Imagining disappearing into the wall and reappearing on the other side into a harmonious space and quiet, where he could hear himself again...

He walked on slowly, his breathing steadying as he counted the stones. The Bedingford Estate wall stretched on towards the village centre, broken only by the solitary arch of the Main Gate up ahead. A dense overgrowth of bush plants usually obscured the view beyond, but today the gate was wide open and Pip could see swells of movement from the other side. On the grass verge in front stood a slim, polished woman in her sixties, holding a clipboard in professionally cared for hands, gesticulating to two elderly gents carrying upside down placards.

Harriet Pordage had a loud voice and an expensive face. Although only the latter was being employed this morning, even her mouthed words and sweeping gestures were powerful and voluminous. Behind her, half a dozen villagers gathered by the gate, as if they were waiting for a school bus outing under the beady eye of the Headmistress, leaning into each other to mime and whisper.

Bedingford had a long history of conducting protest in silence. It somehow made it all the more effective. In the 1990s, villagers had successfully diverted the M3, and blocked the expansion of an ex-MoD airfield on the outskirts of the village. In an unholy alliance with tree-camping environmentalists, the Greens had claimed the victory, but it was the medal-wearing pensioners and recreational gardeners of Bedingford who really won the day, with their quiet, stealth tactics. Relocating endangered snails the size of breadcrumbs in mysteriously appearing colonies along the proposed motorway route; obscure American scientists popping up to confirm the delicate growth of a rare Amazonian orchid in Timothy Smollett's front garden; and Sir Henry Pordage's discovery of an 18th century covenant on the Orchard Cottages, which prohibited them from ever being sold out of the Bedingford Estate. The fact that the investment company to which he was a silent partner had been trying to buy them from the Earls of Bedingford since 1955 was a minor detail he omitted from the Public Inquiry. Instead, he pulled the document from a black box in the dying hours of the Inquiry like a Victorian showman, and closed the show.

Bedingford, with its small, silent protests, had a habit of getting what it wanted. And what it clearly did *not* want this summer was an opera festival on its doorstep.

Pip stopped on the grass verge long enough to decipher that something was expected to happen fairly shortly. Even so, it seemed to take the group by surprise when two minibuses of orchestral musicians drew up the road, igniting a flurry of activity around the gate. Thermoses were hurriedly discarded, lines drawn and banners raised, tupperware dishes cracked open and stale scones inscribed with the words, 'GO HOME, WE DON'T WANT YOU HERE!' were hurled at the vehicles as they blundered off the road onto the driveway between them.

Out of nowhere sprung two shirtless heavies, swinging the huge gate shut behind them. And that, it seemed, was that. The demonstrators fidgeted and shuffled, exchanging glances that served both to communicate and obscure a shared understanding that this may not have been their finest hour. But Pip was fairly sure that the Southampton Philharmonic would never have been treated to anything quite like it before.

A couple of the demonstrators turned towards him on the verge, as if they couldn't quite work out if he'd jumped out of the minibus. They nudged their compatriots and more gazes joined until they were all standing, staring at him in unison. It instantly reminded Pip of prison scrutiny, which always ended somehow with his head being kicked in. And it occurred to him that there were iron bars in front of him and, once again, he was on the wrong side of them.

The thought reached his feet before he had a chance to avoid it, or reason with it. His ribcage plummeted, a pain thumped his breastbone and a frightening dizziness blurred the grass verge and swayed him. He put his hand to the wall to steady himself. From nothing, he despaired, his body had decided to dial up the misery. It seemed so nonsensical and unpredictable, the things that set the panic soaring. A random stealth thought that he had not been alert enough to notice, a moment of inactivity, the jolt of wakening in the morning. Or was it just being too visible, culpable, disappointing, failing expectations? Whatever the *expectations* were supposed to be. Pip's mind raced with questions and demands for explanation that he could never answer, and he stood silently screaming to run, but caught frozen and nauseous in the headlights of someone else's attention.

'Ahoy, you! You there!' The vortex was interrupted by Marilyn Harper from Number 7 scuttling down her driveway in the distance. Pip squinted at her as she stood on the pavement, frantically waving a copy of *The Daily Telegraph*. The protest group turned their gaze to stare at her too. She was at least a hundred metres away and she was shouting. *In Bedingford!* Clearly, they could not fathom what she was thinking any more than he could. His mouth dropped, but no words came out. He touched his chest and raised his eyebrows and could almost feel the wind thrust of her exasperated sigh from here.

'Yes, you! Come along now!'

Pip looked between her and the group by the gate. He began to count; he was moving. Across the road and up to her front garden was 147 paces. He didn't look backwards once.

'I know who you are and I know what you're doing,' Marilyn said, at an acceptable volume since he was now only a couple of metres in front of her. Pip stopped, the alarm rising again, and a billow of Estee Lauder sticking in his throat. 'Do you know anything about lawnmowers?'

'Lawnmowers?' he squeaked, eventually. Marilyn looked to the sky as if she were dealing with an imbecile.

'Yes, yes, yes, lawnmowers! I can't get a peep out of mine and it is most important that I do.' No response. 'So, do you know anything about lawnmowers?'

'Uh... yes?' Pip said, as if experimenting with Mandarin.

'You can stop gaping, then. We've got work to do!' Marilyn ushered him around the back of her house to the shed door, a huge and ancient petrol lawnmower standing sentinel in front of it. 'There, dead as a dodo. See what you can do. I'll be back in ten minutes!'

Pip stared hopelessly at the machine. As far as he was concerned, mechanical things had private lives of their own and it was much better for everyone if they were left to lead those lives without any interference from him. Nine minutes of staring were followed by thirty seconds of frantically scouting the shed for inspiration as Marilyn re-emerged from the house. Pip screwed his eyes shut as they began to prickle, despairing that it took so little these days. But the moment felt momentous somehow. He'd been given a chance, however small and ridiculous, and here he was standing on the edge of another cliff of disappointment.

In desperation, he grabbed the carton marked 'petrol' from

the top shelf, hurriedly stuffed it in the tank and turned the ignition. The mower coughed and spluttered into life.

'I knew it, thank you!' Marilyn Harper stood still by the shed door and smiled at him.

It was a delight that Pip had not seen on anybody's face for so very long.

And he'd only had to tell a *tiny* lie this time to get it.

3

SHELLEY

THE SUPER-HEARING PEOPLE PLEASER

Another backfire echoed through Pip's breastbone and he could still feel the tiny vibrations speed through his upper body. An unwelcome electricity, but not entirely unusual when he spent most of his days feeling as if he was plugged into a socket. He stared down at his clenched fists and counted each finger as it uncurled from the lawnmower handlebars. Persuading himself that the slow release of tension was deliberate, that he was in control, and capable of sufficient calm to deal with this crazy woman coming towards him waving a pencil case and a wooden spoon.

His life right this moment: Tragedy and Farce.

'Getting there!' Marilyn Harper called over the thunderous roar of the mower's engine. 'Much better than this morning. A few more hours and I'm sure we'll be approaching satisfactory.'

It had been like this all day, Mrs Harper standing on the sidelines of her front garden drop-kicking disapproval. For the last hour, her insistent commands had been doing battle with a spirited counterattack by that awful man from the Council, prowling up and down the embankment in front of the house, measuring wind speeds and demanding the immediate return of the traditional Bedingford silence.

'Mrs Harper, I really must insist,' Graham Tweedle, the local Environmental Health Officer, whined. 'Please tell your chap to stop this instant!'

Pip watched the man's lips flapping, trying to make out the gist of the continuing war between the two. Desperate for a bit of rest from the incessant vibration himself, he would have been quite open to any suggestion to stop – if it had been addressed to him. But, of course, it wasn't; he was used to that. Besides, Mrs Harper had made her demands quite clear: there would be no let-up in her quest for perfection-in-grass until the place was fit for visiting royalty – which, in effect, was exactly the outcome on her horizon.

Marilyn Harper was 62, wore a brooch with everything and more perfume than anyone had any right to. And now she was on her hands and knees, measuring the lines in her lawn with a child's school ruler. Pip knew this attention to detail was not in the least bit unusual in this part of Bedingford. All the residents were absolutely obsessive about their front gardens. What set Marilyn apart at the moment was her newfound willingness to have hers exposed to a season of public opera at the Manor across the road. The much more representative group of villagers was marching from the Manor gates now, interrupting their protest to throw silent daggers at him every time the mower ignited. As if he really wanted to be creating this much noise, particularly in such a place so passionately devoted to quiet. And more particularly, as it had been his mission since his release from prison to be as inconspicuous as possible.

'Oh, for heaven's sake, look!' Tweedle jabbed a pudgy finger at the screen of his sound meter. 'It's ruining the readings. That last one might as well have been an explosion. Look, look, look!' He stormed up the drive and thrust the device under Marilyn's nose with an incredulity that only the truly passionate can display.

'There are some numbers and a dial, Mr Tweedle, do you—?' Marilyn stopped, a smirk flitting her lips. 'Oh, yes, it *does* seem rather high.'

'Quite!' Tweedle snapped. 'How on earth am I supposed to get a baseline reading when you insist on making such a racket? It's far louder than the planning conditions would allow for the festival itself!'

'Really?' Marilyn turned, the smirk blossoming towards the group on the pavement.

The poisonous glares of the protesters, still directed at Pip, twitched with incomprehension. The Quietest Village in England trophies were apportioned throughout the village in recognition of outstanding contribution. Harriet Pordage had two; the last one, awarded in April, sat on Marilyn's kitchen dresser. Pip concluded that it was far more difficult for the perplexed group on the pavement to fathom her spectacular about-turn than to simply assume it was his fault.

'Right, that's enough. Stop that at once!' Tweedle clicked his fingers in Pip's direction. He looked between them, his hand hovering over the ignition.

'You will do nothing of the kind,' Marilyn hissed. 'Back up to the fence this minute!' Her accompanying gesture was even clearer. Pip sighed, but went where the money was, following her immaculately painted finger to steer the mower back down the side of the house.

He had had this job (if that is what it could be called, he wasn't sure yet) for four and a half hours. *Just another half an hour,* he'd bargained with himself nine times already. *Just keep going, keep moving... Today's the day... You can do it...* repeated in his head, over and over. But the other voices – the ones that told him otherwise, the ones that said he couldn't – were getting louder and louder, chiming mercilessly in step with the disturbances rattling all around him. Pip fixed his eyes on the edges of his lawn trimming and began to count.

'Want to measure something, do we, Tweedle?' Marilyn Harper shouted from the kitchen door. 'See how some proper music fares on your mechanical toys, eh? Try this!' Within seconds, she had thrown open every window and Verdi was blaring out down the whole road.

Pip could feel the windows shake. He really thought he could not take much more of this.

Until he reminded himself that choice was a luxury he had not yet earned...

Shelley Harper looked at her mother warily, as she so often did, hanging out of the window, dressed in a preposterous flowing gown held closed only by the most gregarious six-inch brooch. A peacock, like its owner, its glory displayed. But it was the beak that Shelley focused on. As if, despite its flamboyance, it would tear you to shreds any moment now.

She put down her rucksack in the utility room, pushing down with it her reluctance to venture into the kitchen, where her mother was now rooting through the cutlery drawers.

'Hello...'

'Not now, Sheldon dear. You can see I am rather busy.'

Indeed, she could: all the kitchen cupboards were open, their contents spilling onto every surface; five different recipes for Hampshire Rasher Pudding sprawled over the counter; the rattle and hum of utensils drowned only by the industrial volume opera booming from the old ghetto blaster on the windowsill, the sound of which had assailed her from the other side of Yarnside Bridge.

'Aha!' Marilyn shrieked, brandishing two long wooden spoons and heading for the front lawn as if about to conduct a symphony orchestra. And as if her only daughter's first appearance in the house since Christmas was not in the least bit worthy of competition.

It had been with very mixed feelings that Shelley had made this journey this morning. A courageous leap of faith over fear, back to her roots, back to the village, back to the... *motherland*. Oh, God. She had even allowed herself a tear or two on the train from Waterloo. If she had allowed any more, she felt sure they would have drowned her face in waves of panic and regret. She could see it in the murky train window. Her reflection was younger than she was. Behind the welling eyes, a worried child on high alert, shrinking in the seat, holding back the flood. And the only sound in her ears: Verdi.

Even as she had approached her old home on Trefusis Lane, Shelley could see that something was wrong. Well, that was ridiculous; where her mother was concerned, there was usually something wrong. But today the *something* had been elevated to new heights of *wrongness*. A District Council van parked outside; two men erecting a mast by the side of the patio; the front wall lined with bits of garden machinery; and four crates of caterers' suet on the driveway. But perhaps the oddest of them all was the music. All the ubiquitous opera records that had dominated Shelley's childhood had been banned from the house since her tenor father disappeared to Las Vegas with a Big Band five years ago. With the whole of Trefusis Lane now being treated to Rigoletto, so far in advance of the actual festival beginning at the Manor at the end of the month, Shelley had been quite chilled by the implications.

She tentatively followed her mother to the door just as a lawnmower, sounding as if it had its exhaust ripped out, roared into view from the side of the house at a volume with which Pavarotti himself would have struggled to compete if he was parked in the kitchen.

Pushing the lawnmower, wearing the biggest pair of ear defenders Shelley had ever seen in her years in Acoustics, a man, a stranger, going at it as if the lawn was a mutant life-form in need of total and immediate annihilation. She could not see his face, just the curl of his ruffled hair falling over the collar of a crumpled white T-shirt; his body hunched, arms rigid, demanding the mower go faster, louder, deeper; the grip of his hands, knuckles white, as if he was trying to wring the very life out of the thing.

'Monstrous, Pip! Hurrah!' Marilyn screamed from the other end of the garden, raising the conducting spoons once more. 'That really might give them something to record!'

Graham Tweedle hugged his sound meter to his chest, grabbing his tripod but dropping the microphone to the lawn as Marilyn chased him off down the path.

Shelley stood still by the open door. She could not begin to fathom the situation but was aware that she might be beginning to dribble. She clamped her mouth shut, just as the man behind the lawnmower headed towards the rhododendrons in front of her. He didn't seem to have noticed the dancing red light of the dropped microphone in the longer grass before him. Shelley was well aware of the value of such things. She'd been using something similar for the last two years with her students at South Bank Technical College. In fact, there was one in her rucksack in the utility room. She hoped they wouldn't miss it. Or her.

'Hey!' Shelley hastily attempted to rescue the microphone from man and machine's inevitable approach. 'Stop!' It was useless, of course, nothing could be heard. 'Oi!' It was meant to be a tap on the shoulder but it landed like a punch. He inevitably jumped, but his startle was quickly overtaken by the same expression of intense focus that he had been directing at the lawnmower. She still couldn't see much of his face, hidden as it was by a generous expanse of unruly caramel beard. He flicked a switch on the handlebars but made no attempt to take off the ear defenders.

'*What?* Who are you?'

It seemed to Shelley that this stranger was displaying a level of abrasion quite inappropriate for a first encounter, so her instinctive apology for unwittingly thumping him remained in her throat. But there was something else coming to his eyes now, clearing the pointed agitation to a calmer hint of relief.

'Oh, it is, innit? You must be the daughter. Thank God.'

'Excuse me?'

'Mr Smollett next door said things always calm down a bit when you're around.'

'Did he?' Shelley was still having to shout. Even without the mower, Verdi was providing more than enough competition. 'Can you take those off, please?'

'Makes no difference,' he sniffed, removing the huge ear defenders anyway and hanging them on the handlebars.

'Why are you wearing them, then?'

'Because *she* thinks they do, and manages to talk ever so slightly less when I've got them on.' He gestured towards Marilyn, who was now hauling a crate of suet up the drive.

Shelley laughed, which surprised her. She hadn't had one of those scheduled for today. It clearly surprised him, too. She bent down to pick up the microphone and noticed his foot tapping rhythmically on the grass, and by the time she had straightened herself to agree, he was staring right through her with an expression as if he could hear a juggernaut coming but had no means of getting out of the way.

'Sorry, I... I gotta go,' his breath tugging in his throat, he set off running full pelt across the driveway and down the road.

Marilyn was bellowing after him. The protesters were booing him. It seemed hardly fair to join in over a bit of a dent in a microphone casing.

Besides, as Shelley knew so well by now, when everyone else's volume was turned up so high, she would never be heard...

. . .

31

Pip ran until he'd reached the allotment at the edge of the village, the exertion making sense of his breathlessness and the pain in his lungs. He flung open the door to his shed and flopped down on the makeshift bed on the counter. Comforted by the familiar smallness, safe from anybody or any more expectations, slowly his breathing returned deeper into his body, and the insurrection of his muscles began to subside.

Not today then. Perhaps tomorrow. He'd feel better tomorrow. It was obvious – he felt better already with only the thought.

Tomorrow was always a safer place, where he had not yet tried, so he had not yet lost.

4

THE MEANING OF SUET PUDDING

'I don't know why you bother, Sheldon. I know you're smoking. I always did.'

Shelley had finally steeled herself to come downstairs, removing what traces she could of both emotion and cigarettes. It was only the second day since her return to Bedingford and she was already having a crafty smoke out of the bathroom window. Reverting to type, as her mother would say. Of course it was no pleasure at all after six months without, tasting as revolting as the very first one, and so unaccustomed these days that the rush was quite alarming, leaving her feeling dizzy and nauseous. Not to mention every drag bathed in self-reproach. It was never just the one. Risking herself back on this leash, a slave to doing something, the same thing, ten, twenty times a day. And for what? Because she did not want to be here, did not really know why she was, but did not know how not to be.

Her mother sat in the kitchen on her third cup of coffee.

'You are thirty years old, Sheldon. There really isn't very much I can do about it, even if I wanted to.'

'Really?' Shelley could not hide the peevishness in her tone.

Although, to be fair, her irritation was directed at herself as much as her waspish mother.

'Yes really, when are you going to grow up? You smoke, so what?'

'Well, I don't, actually.'

'Oh really, Sheldon,' Marilyn tutted, 'I can smell it. Disgusting habit.'

'I thought you didn't care.'

'So you do?'

'No!'

'Sheldon! I will not row with you before eleven o'clock in the morning.'

'Is that a new rule?'

Marilyn Harper fixed her daughter with a silent glare, as if to prove her point, and then followed it with a dramatic sigh, a sniff in the air, and an incongruously immediate smile. She slid this morning's *Telegraph* over the table.

'You see, it is a good day, Sheldon, and I will not have you ruining it again, like yesterday.'

'Oh,' Shelley said, glancing at the newspaper with the practised interest she had learned over the years. 'Well, I suppose that's another extension to the pool house for Harriet then.' She scanned the text below a smiling photo of their near neighbours, Sir Henry Pordage KC and his princely son Russell, outside the Houses of Parliament with the Chair of Wessex Retail Consortium and the Secretary of State for the Environment. They were marking – the small front-page piece read – a 'landmark case', finally allowing a stretch of land in Mid-Hampshire to be excluded from the South Downs National Park, and therefore fair game for the largest shopping centre in the south of England. The planning case had gone on for eight years, with the celebrated lawyer eventually bringing it to a conclusion on a legal technicality discovered by his son, Russell. According to *The Telegraph*, this alone could secure Russell's elevation to the ranks of King's Counsel to join his illustrious father. And that, if it happened within the next eighteen months before his 35th birthday, would make him the youngest ever to take silk in the UK.

Even more of an achievement, Shelley thought – missing from *The Telegraph* but sure not to have been missed by a single person in her current vicinity – the plans cleverly moved the National Park boundary to put the whole of Bedingford *inside* it.

'Yes indeed, Russell has again achieved the recognition he deserves. Harriet will be cock-a-hoop, which is always good news. She's so much more agreeable when Henry or Russell win their cases.'

'They always win their cases.'

'Not like this one, though! Just think, we might get one of those huge Marks & Spencer only fifteen minutes away, with no additional traffic through the village! Ooh, goodness me, perhaps even John Lewis!'

'Oh well,' Shelley attempted to match her mother's brightness in a way that was clearly expected but which didn't indicate she had left herself completely on the doorstep yesterday, 'if Russell does get his KC at 34 it would be the only thing he could do in the law that his father couldn't. I'm pleased for him.'

'I think you could be rather more than that, Sheldon.'

'Well, of course I am pleased for you too,' Shelley added, experimentally, sensing that she had not grasped the point of this exchange. 'If it's made you so cheerful?'

'Oh, it's not that,' Marilyn snapped. 'It's that! Are you quite blind? Or just deliberately provoking me as always.' She jabbed her finger at the topline preview of the forthcoming weekend magazine.

Verdi to Vegas – On his 60th birthday and long-awaited return to the British stage, Arts Review profiles veteran opera and variety star, Horace Harper.

'Oh,' Shelley concluded, and a short silence followed.

'Oh?' Marilyn demanded, unable to take any more of this torture. 'Oh? Is that all you can say?'

Shelley was at a real loss now. In truth, yes, that was all she had to say. Nothing else was coming to mind at all.

Marilyn snatched the paper. 'Look, there! "Long-awaited return to the British stage" in print. It's official now, isn't it?'

'Yes, but I thought you knew that. That's why I'm here, because Dad wanted me to help Matthew with the sound at the festival.'

Horace's letter had actually said that if she 'made sure the conditions were befitting a star of his stature' in this 'garden fete of an endeavour', he would take her back to Las Vegas with him as his sound engineer for his next residency. It was such an unexpected offer, it had prompted Shelley to hand in her notice at the college the very next day. She'd been in a bit of a panic at the impulse ever since, pouring petrol on the flames by admitting any of that to her mother right now seemed foolhardy at best.

'He *is* coming back,' Marilyn ignored her, as if only by being in *The Telegraph* it was real anyway. 'So Harriet can say what she likes. I'm not speaking to her in any case. You know she's been making an awful fuss about this festival thingy, very nearly scuppered it altogether with all those people in Yarnside Drive.'

'You mean the "protest group" you were Secretary of before this wee—' Shelley's breath caught. Of course! How could she have been so stupid?

A dark cloud descended over Marilyn's face. 'You really know how to wound me, don't you, Sheldon? It's just an art, isn't it, that you continue to perfect?'

In the end, all Shelley could think of to say was, 'I'm sorry.' And she genuinely was. She had not taken much notice of any family anniversaries, least of all her father's birthdays, for many years. Neither did she pay much attention to the odd (infrequent and very small) appearance in print, on TV and radio. But she was acutely aware of the effect such things had on her mother.

The apology, however, just seemed to irritate Marilyn even more. 'You're sorry? *You're sorry?*'

Shelley's heart sank in step with her mother's rising tone.

'Oh yes, you're always sorry, aren't you? Miss-know-nothing-about-anything. You can be sorry all you like, just so you can pretend it's nothing to do with you that he's not here in the first place and everyone can go on thinking how lovely you are just because you're sorry!'

The venom spiralling, Shelley had been here so many times before, but had still never worked out an adequate response. A response that didn't leave her shaky and unsure and generally less than she was before.

She opened her mouth to form something that would not leave this day totally overshadowed by yet another maternal fallout.

'No, do not say anymore,' Marilyn stopped her. 'I said I would not row with you and I will not have you spoiling that resolution too. I admit, I may have been... *wrong*.' The unaccustomed word twisted in Marilyn's throat. 'This festival is clearly going to be something special and might just be what we all need. Less than three weeks to go, Sheldon. Please do not try to spoil my good mood!'

'But—'

'No, I know what you are going to say – the house is not ready.'

Shelley looked blankly across the table. It always astounded her how a mother could know so little about her own daughter; this could not be further from anything she would remotely think of to say.

'But I will just have to make the best of it. As I always do. At least by the time your father comes home – now that I have persuaded Pip back – he is sure to be pleased with the state of the lawn, and I have time to be experimenting with plenty of new recipes… Now, I can't sit here nattering to you, I have to locate some lambs' kidney for the suet puddings. They only had pigs' in Tesco. Pip will be able to take one for his tea if I start this afternoon. He will deserve a treat. Assuming you and that clown from the Council don't scare him away again!'

Shelley sat, hardly able to process this about-face. So now it would appear that the deep trauma of Harriet's betrayal, and the blatant disrespect of her wayward daughter, were far less important than the teatime of her mother's new gardener.

'And while I am gone, young lady, you can make a start by shifting all that awful junk you had delivered yesterday out of my utility room. And then perhaps you can explain why there is quite so much of it for a temporary stay!'

The door slammed, leaving Shelley wondering exactly the same thing.

She idly fingered the newspaper. Below it was an open copy of *The Stage*, and there too was a photo of a smiling, round, silver-haired man reclining on a couch at Caesars Palace. Shelley looked at it longer than she expected. She had not heard from her father in over five years until his letter last month. She knew he had made a couple of fleeting visits to Bedingford in that time, between gigs. The last time he had gone 'for good' fourteen years ago – or rather the last time he admitted that was what he was doing – set off a train of events that had enchained his daughter from that moment on.

Shelley doubted whether any of that would be in *The Telegraph* magazine this weekend.

She scanned the short piece in *The Stage* instead. And yes, the list of things Horace said he missed about England was remarkably short. But Marilyn had double ringed 'bowling green lawns', 'dahlias' and 'suet pudding' in red biro and written simply, 'Yes!!!'

Shelley sat back in her chair and closed her eyes, beginning to write the script of how this was going to play out. *The Telegraph*, the red biro, the garden maintenance, the suet puddings... Realisation dawning that once again Marilyn had constructed a fantasy that her husband still loved her, and was coming home to her, that was as strong as any fortress.

Only Shelley knew it was made of sand, and one more tide of truth and it would dissolve as quickly as it had been built...

'Oh, sorry,' Pip withdrew from the door, travel kettle in hand. Mrs Harper had told him he could come in whenever he needed to. At least as far as the utility room.

'It's quite alright. Do you want some coffee? There's still some in the pot, if you don't mind it industrial strength.' Despite looking straight at her, Pip remained fidgeting at the door. Shelley faltered, but smiled. 'It's OK, really.' Perhaps they hadn't got off to the best start yesterday and she really could do with something else to think about.

Eventually, he shuffled forward and sat down. She poured him a cup, attempting another polite smile, watching his chest visibly inflating and slowly deflating, before this curious man spoke again.

'Look, I'm sorry, it was rude of me yesterday,' he said. 'Was I rude? Yes, I think I was. I was just... well, a bit stressed, you know.' He attempted a small laugh, but it seemed entirely without humour. He was now making breakfast out of the side of his thumb, his darting eyes continually returning to her face, as if willing her to say something else.

'It's OK, really,' she repeated, offering milk. 'It's no surprise with my mother.'

'Oh, yeah.' His smile unexpectedly twinkled with mischief, but he quickly withdrew it. 'Oh, no, no, I didn't mean— Your mum has been very kind, you know, taking me back, giving me work and that. No-one else seems much inclined to.'

'Really? I can't see why. Everyone round here wants lines in their lawn like that. You're obviously a very good gardener.'

Pip snorted. 'Oh, I ain't a gardener.'

'Could have fooled me. What are you then?'

'So, you're Sheldon?' The diversion was as swift as a switchblade.

'Shelley,' she corrected.

'Alright, Shelley,' he repeated the name like a question as he held out his hand. 'Pip Berry. *Not* Philip. This time, nice to meet you.'

Despite his outstretched arm, Shelley doubted it. His hand was shaking slightly. She took it and it stilled a little, which seemed to unlock his voice.

'Short for Philip, obviously, but what with the Berry thing, you know, and apparently I used to have a bit of a thing about the speaking clock, and then there's the— Well, that's probably enough, isn't it?' He clamped his mouth shut.

'No, go on,' she laughed.

'So, are you staying in Bedingford long?' he veered off again, but as if he was hauling concrete. 'Your mum said something about you being a big shot academic up in London.'

'Did she? Well, not quite,' Shelley smiled wryly. Her mother was always much better at being proud of the accomplishments her daughter *hadn't* achieved. 'I teach at South Bank Technical College. Acoustics.'

Pip's direct eyes widened, and his mouth twitched. 'Acoustics? Really?'

'Yeah. My father's singing at the Opera Festival. He's asked me to help with his sound. I'm a sound engineer. Well, I... anyway...'

Pip was still looking intently at her. He had a very unmediated gaze, she noticed. She couldn't work out if it was flattering or slightly unnerving. But as if he sensed the dilemma, he looked

40

away, with no further response and, as it turned out, a prolonged and resolute concentration on his coffee cup.

'Ah well,' she laughed again. 'Perhaps neither of us knows what we are, eh?'

In the quiet that followed, Shelley realised she had not said that out loud for years. She had held silently to her dream of being a sound engineer for so long, the words were so familiar, so often heard caged in her head. It seemed her father's offer had picked the lock to let them out, however tentatively given where she was, in her mother's house.

'Did you hear that?' Shelley turned to the kitchen window, but there was nothing there.

'Uh, no,' Pip replied, still a little cagily.

Shelley shrugged. It was not unusual. As far back as she could remember, she had heard things that other people couldn't. It was one of the earliest bones of contention with her mother. When she was six years old, tearful that she could hear an owl in distress over the Bedingford Estate wall, Marilyn had told her she heard things because she was possessed, and shut her in her room until midday the next day. Shelley never mentioned the owl again, and from then on, her small acts of nurture and observation were always, like so much of Shelley's life, conducted in secret.

'Ah, see what you mean now, isn't that the bloke from the Council?' Pip nodded towards the window. Shelley turned as a red and cream Council cap disappeared under the sill. She got up and opened the window.

'Is she there?' A voice hissed from below.

'Graham, what are you doing?'

'Is she in?' Graham Tweedle repeated, his eyes joining his ears in surveillance as he crouched between the hydrangeas.

'You've just missed her, but please do come in and wait, Graham,' Shelley teased. It had been over ten years since she'd been this close to Graham Tweedle, since A-level physics, and she was delighted to have the upper hand this time. 'My mother seems to be *so* enjoying your company at the moment, I'd hate for you to miss her.'

'No, no! Have you got it?'

'What?'

'Come on, Shelley, throw me a line here. I know you won't have missed my microphone— Oh, God...' Both of them had heard distant footsteps on gravel at the other side of the house, despite Graham's instinct to do so first. Shelley finally relented and darted into the utility room, grabbing her (undented) college microphone from her rucksack. She ran out of the door, thrust it into Graham's hand and led him round the back to the old coal shelter.

'Wait here for a moment until she comes in, then you can get out through the side gate.'

'Thank you, Shelley,' Graham panted, appreciating the shared exertion a little too much. 'Will I see you—'

'Got to go now, Graham. Good to catch up, bye... Twat,' she muttered, as she heard him clattering into the wheelie bins.

'You know each other, then?' Pip ventured.

'Afraid so. We were at school together. Oh, he's alright really, but let's just say in the hearing stakes he's always been quite competitive. He's rather precious about it, for some reason. Listening though, he never seemed half so interested in.'

A warm grin spread over Pip's face, washing away any trace of unease for a moment, but then as quickly pulled back like an ebbing tide as Marilyn swept into the kitchen, dumping a squelching bag of lambs' kidneys on the counter.

'Oh,' she said, the moment's pause before the practised smile was a clear enough indication of its disingenuity. 'Pip, you've joined us. How delightful. And I can't really blame you, with all my daughter's frightful rubbish cluttering up the utility room.'

'You mean my luggage?' Shelley protested. 'I haven't had a chance—'

'Swanning back here with all these complications.'

'Complications?'

'You know full well what I mean. What is it all doing here, anyway? Oh, my God!' Marilyn's hand flew to her mouth. 'Don't tell me they've sacked you from the university!'

'I haven't swanned anywhere, it's not complicated, they haven't sacked me, and it's a technical college.' Shelley knew the last would be the most wounding and regretted it immediately. It never did to try.

'We'll talk later,' Marilyn hissed. 'Just get it out of here. That box of junk hardly creates the right impression for indoors, does it?'

Pip looked at Shelley as if she might provide some clue to all this and 'indoors' might be some kind of code for polite society. She crossed her eyes and wrinkled her nose, which seemed to be all the code that was required. He nodded.

'Plenty of room in the shed, isn't there, Pip?' Marilyn continued. 'Pip is something of an authority on the capacity of sheds, Sheldon. Aren't you, dear? The poor boy is living in one at the moment.'

'Really?'

He looked away.

'Yes indeed, so perhaps you could attempt to be a little more grateful for the luxuries afforded to you once in a while. And don't keep raising your eyebrows at me like that, young lady! Now, get that rubbish out of my house!'

'I can help if you like,' Pip mediated unexpectedly and Shelley was impressed by the unusual interruption, risky as it was.

'Ahem,' Marilyn was having none of it. 'I'm quite sure you've got more than enough to do, Pip dear. Now if you wouldn't mind, I did notice a rather nasty kink in the last strip by the Japanese Acer.' She cocked her head sharply towards the door.

'Oh yes, of course...'

'That was rude,' Shelley objected, as Pip shuffled out to the utility room with his coffee cup.

Marilyn checked the closing door. 'I just wanted to say, out of earshot, not to get too familiar, that's all. He might be good on grass, but he is a jailbird. Something to do with music and drugs, I heard.' Marilyn fixed her daughter with a knife point stare. 'Your favourites.'

The wound was as inevitable as it was deliberate, and Shelley felt an immediate pressure behind her eyes. Her chair scraped back and she left the room, mouthing something that she thought was inaudible as she slammed the utility room door behind her. But Pip burst out laughing. His deep blue eyes danced, and the melancholy was completely obliterated for a moment. It was quite startling. And so were they.

Then he stopped and turned away.

'Are you going to help me, then?' Shelley called after him as she lifted a box of equipment.

But he kept on walking.

5

REX TRENTON & THE EDGE OF
DARKNESS

It was with some regret that Lester Berkeley-Staten returned from Bedingford Manor to his London office the next morning. His feet dawdled as he wandered towards Soho Square from the betting office in Wardour Street. Stat was unaccustomed to dawdling. Most mornings he faced the world with a brisk stride, more often than not on the first of his thrice-daily visits to Ladbrokes. Every day, people looked at him askance, in his string vest, baggy shorts and carpet slippers, whatever the weather. The fattest Cuban cigar hung perpetually from his open mouth, the girth of the cigar reflecting the girth of the man, which spilled out beneath the frays of his vest. The colour of Stat's vests depended on the day of the week. Since he imagined it bad luck to have more than one in circulation at any one time, and laundry was strictly for a Sunday, from Monday onwards white would gradually be replaced by Jack Daniels and egg mayonnaise stains. An elfin art student from St Martin's College had once offered him a shag in exchange for a Friday vest. Stat had naturally accepted, but ended up with the two models she was sketching at the time.

Those were the days...

This day, however, his feet were without their natural strident rhythm. Irritating, Stat thought, how feet could register reluctance so far in advance of a JD-addled consciousness. That kind of clarity usually took two morning espresso shots, the first perusal of the *Racing Post* and the second cigar to materialise. But it was doing so now. He had bad news. And bad news imparted to Rex Trenton and The Edge of Darkness meant only one thing. More bad news.

It was there, right in front of him. Their beloved Lumpwood Club, closing notices plastered across the doors. How was he going to break this to them? As if the loss was not enough in itself, it was here that it had all began. And it was here that The Edge of Darkness were to achieve their 'secret' comeback this summer. (Secret in the sense that it would be the most heavily promoted event in Stat's life).

Judging by the chew marks on his cigar, it didn't seem to be making it any easier that Stat's co-existence with this lot had been characterised by a steady stream of bad news over the years. From their very first meeting, in fact. Standing staring at the bolted doors of the club, Stat was instantly and wistfully transported. *Could it really have been forty-five years?* That day on the dingy roadside of the A1, five young Afghan-coated long-hairs sitting huddled beside a steaming Bedford van. Well, four of them were huddled, passing around a single plastic cup from an empty thermos of tea. The fifth had his head beneath the open bonnet, removing his clothes, dowsing them with a can of cider and wrapping them around the hissing radiator. Stat had pulled up behind them just as the underpants were being lost to the business of vehicle maintenance. It was then that he realised he had seen that backside before – in the latter pages of the *Melody Maker*. Rex Trenton. A tiny eighth of a pager, six sentences and a passport-sized photo of a microphone stand, a puff of purple dry ice and an arse. *That* arse.

1978, when the earlier pages of the *Melody Maker* were rife with bands making a name for themselves by the elaborate nature of the make-up and clothes they put on, Rex Trenton was bucking the trend by taking them off. Making his name flogging round the grungiest venues across the country, ripping his shirts and dropping his trousers.

That day on the side of the A1 was to be Stat's very first lesson in the delivery of bad news to The Edge of Darkness. Rex had used all the cider supplies drenching his discarded clothes, so that there was no liquid left to replenish the engine itself; the radiator had a hole in it the size of a melon; and wouldn't the exhaust pipe that had narrowly missed Stat's Capri, clanking down the carriageway, have fit nicely into the conspicuous emptiness of the back of the van...? This last disclosure only resulted in the evident tension between Rex and the rest of the band escalating into a full-blown roadside fist-fight. And although he was a little less portly in his carriage in those days, Stat had had a fight of his own to prize Rex's head from the guitarist's stranglehold.

What would he have done if someone had told him that day on the roadside, that forty-five years later, he would still be here, rescuing Rex Trenton? But in the moment, Stat had felt an unusual exhilaration, something quite indefinable, and within the hour he had delivered them to the door of this very building, outside which he now stood paralysed. And if he had caught just a hint of exhilaration on that roadside, Stat was positively pulsating with it by the time The Edge of Darkness dripped off stage after their twenty-five minute support slot that night. They were awful, of course. The tension of the afternoon was clearly not a one-off. Benny, the keyboard player, had decided he was stressed enough to smoke himself to sleep. The bass player's lead barely stretching two feet from the PA had him completely deafened by the second number, until he just wrenched it out in frustration and pretended that nobody would notice. The main act's drummer, everyone had neglected to mention, was left-handed, and thus Alan – clearly under the influence – thundered over the kit for twenty-five minutes completely the wrong way round. And, the pièce de résistance, guitarist Damon Dark, having been content for ten minutes merely to exchange murderous looks with their stripping singer, responded to a dig in the ribs with the microphone stand by refusing to play at all. Whilst Rex wailed and threw off clothes, Damon just stood there for the rest of the set cleaning his fingernails with his guitar pick.

But there *was* something. Indefinable. Stat supposed that 'indefinable' was just one of those ridiculous descriptions so beloved of lazy journalists. But if he could define it, and God knows he had tried, he would have given up years ago and joined a monastery. Because this lot were work. Bloody hard work.

It had been a teeter in and out of the red, the charts, public favour, and rehab, for the last forty-five years. Forty-five years, three name changes, four guitarists, two bass players, seven drummers (in their heyday famously two at once) and half the time no keyboard player at all. And Rex. Always Rex. Finally bankrupting himself on bribes, loans and detox and desperately in need of a comeback.

Stat could hear them now from the lifts down the corridor from his office. And only now, he allowed himself a slight smile. This was his life. This merry-go-round, this ego-trip tension, this eternal nonsensical banter...

'LADIES AND GENTLEMEN, I GIVE YOU,
REX TRENTON AND THE EDGE OF DARKNESS!'

'It's a fucking disgrace! Rural England. It's a fucking disgrace!' Alan Kent, the returned original drummer, waved a small brochure in front of his face. Yebut stared at him. Rex and Damon barely looked up from their ubiquitous slouch. Benny was asleep.

'Rural England,' Alan repeated for unnecessary emphasis, lobbing the Bedingford Opera programme at Yebut's head.

'Ought to be fucking paved over. The Rural England Bypass. Farleigh Wallop to Hadrian's Wall. The M-Incredibly-Necessary!'

Yebut, bass player of the last twenty-two wilderness years, stopped rubbing his forehead, his eyes wide in horror.

'What about the cows?' he gaped.

'What cows?'

'The cows. In the fields. In rural England.'

'Pave them over.'

'Yeah but—' Which, as always, elicited a full chorus of 'Yebut, Yebut, Yebut, Yebut!'

Yebut ignored it as usual. 'Yeah but, what about them, eh? They're good cows are. Yeah, good they are...'

'Fucking waste of space. All that standing around doing sod all. Mooing and chewing and staring. Yeah, just staring, what's that all about then?' Alan demanded, with a look as if he'd just grabbed Yebut's lapels.

When Alan was in the mood for a fight, Yebut was easy prey. So many bullies charmed and courted, carrying their tyranny like a concealed handgun. Alan was the other breed, who displayed his full weaponry in broad daylight and gave you fair warning before he blew your head off. Still, Yebut never seemed to get out of the way.

'What about beef then, eh?' Yebut offered triumphantly. 'What about beef burgers?'

Rex smiled at him. 'Or stew. I love stew.'

'With dumplings,' Damon added.

'Or Beef Wellington, now there's—'

'Beef Wellington? *Beef Wellington*?' Alan was outraged. 'Rural England-speak that is!'

'Anyway, who needs any of it? I, for one, could live on bacon.' Damon had clearly decided against the rare consensus with Rex. But it was not enough to dissuade Yebut from his original point.

'Yeah but, what about milk?'

'Ah milk, yeah, you've got something there...'

The room fell silent.

'There's always goats.' A plume of cigar smoke preceded Stat into the room. Accustomed to having the last word and sorting every argument, he said no more until he had crossed the room and lowered himself into his enormous leather chair. The outer edges of his egg-stained belly squeezed against the desk so that a roll of fat sandwiched the wood on either side. He lay down his cigar in the brimming ashtray and interlocked his hands across the desk.

'Alright boys, the deal is... well, there is no deal.' Stat pushed a crumpled flyer across the desk, confirming the official closure of The Lumpwood Club. Damon had gone back to his newspaper and barely raised his head. Alan just shrugged and Yebut was wiping something off his shoe with a licked finger, a mellow blankness resettling over his face that betrayed very little connection to reality. Rex alone seemed to be focusing. But still he said nothing.

'So, the rumours are true. The club is closing at the end of July. We have no gig.' Stat paused before delivering the final blow. 'We have no offers. We have no money. We don't really have any other options.'

It was brutal, but Stat knew he had to finally make them understand. The Edge of Darkness was broke. Not just short of a bit of cash flow for a few weeks, but down in the gutter, stony broke. The Lumpwood comeback gig, which was to kick start their recovery, was on a promise from an old friend and venue promoter. And now, with six weeks to go until the fabled phoenix return, the club was closing. The band still owing tens of thousands of pounds, Stat had no further favours to call in, nor any immediate sources of cash to fund any more notions of a comeback. No tour, no album. Not even a single and a one-off gig in someone's back garden.

'Yeah but, but, but...' Even for Yebut this was excessive. 'I just gave up me job in B&Q! Just walked out. You know I did. Said we were getting it back together. What am I supposed to do?'

Stat sighed. This was going to hit them all hard. Yebut had been working in the DIY store on the Holloway Road for seven years now. He played in a couple of function bands at the weekends and occasionally got asked to deputise for someone half reasonable. Alan had just about managed to avoid the real world, in B&Q or anywhere else, by juggling five bands, playing pubs, clubs, weddings and bar mitzvahs almost every day of the week. Re-forming the band, he had cleared his diary willingly and hopefully. But whether a DIY store or an empty suburban pub, it was work that neither of them could afford to have lost.

Benny had been sofa surfing in contented obscurity for the last twenty years, somehow making a few odd jobs and a modest inheritance from his great aunt stretch to gargantuan quantities of dope. Rex, and to some extent Damon, were in the paradoxical position of being too long out of the loop, yet too defined to easily slot in anywhere else. And frankly, at 65 and 66 respectively, just too old to start again. They had never been able to envisage a 'proper job'. This was all they could do. They looked at each other briefly, a tiny wisp of connection before it was lost. The only thing Rex and Damon ever really had in common was a colossal opinion of themselves.

Damon sat back in his seat, not wanting to look as if he cared. A solitary raised eyebrow, a bit of a sigh, another cigarette and back to the newspaper. Rex stretched, his hand fluttering over the pulse in his neck. He nodded, the focus direct. Stat understood what he was saying. He was clean; he was sober; he was out of rehab. This could not happen now.

They sat and looked at each other, as if the movie of these last forty-five years was playing across both their faces. And neither of them could stand for the final curtain.

6

MOTHER AND DAUGHTER AND A
WISE OLD LADY

Tony Bennett blared from the kitchen windowsill of 7 Trefusis Lane the next morning. Particularly worrisome given Marilyn's spectacular distaste for the man who, it was claimed, originally led Horace astray. Really, Shelley preferred her visits when her mother hated her father. It was so much less confusing.

'Good morning, Sheldon! There's coffee in the pot. Sorry I can't join you, I am rather busy with the last batch. Do you know you can make this suet pudding with absolutely anything to hand in the pantry?' Marilyn crooned, as if reading from some old Victorian cook book. 'This one's rhubarb compote.'

Marilyn helpfully turned down the stereo. Shelley settled herself at the table, contemplating the plate of jam roly-poly in front of her, her mother's mood and how much longer she could hold out before ruining it.

'Oh yes,' Marilyn continued. 'Weekend magazine today! Aren't we lucky? I'll just pop these in the oven and fetch it from the shop. That stupid paper boy has obviously bunked off again.'

'No need, Mum.' Shelley slowly drew the newspaper from behind her back.

'Oh, how thoughtful, darling! You can read it to me, won't that be fun?'

'*No*', was the obvious answer, but Shelley knew that, as usual, the job was better hers.

This morning *The Telegraph* journalist promised revelations more suited to one of the tabloids, so she skipped the introduction and began to read from the two-page magazine spread. All Horace's usual self-indulgent nonsense about the struggle to make it at the ENO when you came from such a modest background. Shelley marvelled at how much mileage her father could continue to get out of the journey from West Sussex to Covent Garden. Horsham was hardly the ghetto.

But suddenly, she tripped over her words.

'Why have you stopped, Sheldon?'

'Oh, well, it's a bit tedious, isn't it? It's just the same old stuff. Surely you've heard all this before.'

'Really, Sheldon, don't be so ridiculous. Of course I've heard it before. I was there for most of it. That's why I want to hear it again, naturally. And in *The Telegraph* as well! It's been an age. They must have sent that Simon chap over to America especially. Although if he had only waited a few weeks, ha, ha! Go on, carry on, it was getting good anyway, his plans for the future and all that.'

'Yes, well, I really don't think they actually *mean* that. I'll just put it away in the ottoman with all your other clippings, shall I?' Ashamed of her cowardice, Shelley rose halfway out of her chair.

'Don't be silly, you haven't even finished your coffee.'

'It's time I was going, anyway. I'm sure Matthew has a shed-load for me to do and—'

'Finish reading the article, Sheldon. I will not tell you again.' The steel that had been missing this morning had returned.

The phone rang. Marilyn wiped her flour-covered hands, gave her daughter one last warning look and strode out to the hall to answer it. Shelley could hear the clipped tones being transferred to someone else.

'Oh, Harriet, how *nice* of you to ring...'

Shelley leapt out of the kitchen and snatched the phone from her mother's hand. 'Hello, Harriet. Thank you for your concern. She'll call you back.' She threw the receiver back into its cradle, knowing that, however much she didn't want the job, her mother hearing from Harriet Pordage that her husband's 'plans for the future' were very unlikely to be making much use of Marilyn's hard-earned suet puddings, would be ten times worse. She led her back to the kitchen, sat down, took a deep breath and continued to read:

'Harper wears the earnest but excited expression he does so well, as he reveals that his unexpected performance at the first Bedingford Opera Festival in his home village in Hampshire on Saturday 24th June will also be his last. Both in opera and in Britain. He says, *"It's time for a new era in my life. For some time now, I have been enjoying performing in a different way. It's time to be honest about it and to formally announce that I am setting aside my career in opera. Now I have my soul and feet on a new mountain. Vegas is where my heart is now and the variety stage where my voice sings sweetest. England is no more than a memory to me. There's nothing there for me anymore"...'*

Shelley thought it would be OK to stop there. She lay the paper down on the table, slowly and deliberately, hesitating to look at her mother and what she knew would be her billboard-advertising hurt.

Marilyn sat down, clutching the side of the table.

'Did you know about this?' she demanded, without giving the slightest pause for denial. 'You did, didn't you? You must have done! Cohorting with those wretched Wolstenholmes, talking him into it. Is that it? Sell more tickets if it's going to be a last hurrah? It's a joke then... Yes, oh yes, it's a wheeze to sell tickets. Of course! Once he's here—'

'No, Mum,' Shelley ventured a hand over her mother's floury knuckles. Marilyn snatched them away.

'So you did know! Plotted it all, I expect!'

'How could you possibly think that?'

'Form Sheldon, form! What have you managed to get out of him this time?'

Shelley remained speechless, glued to her chair, until Marilyn eventually sunk into hers.

'Just leave, won't you?'

'But—'

'Get out of my sight!'

'Good heavens, child. Whatever is the matter?' Shelley had not heard that voice in almost two years, and her eyes and heart instinctively rose. Victoria Wolstenholme lowered herself onto the riverside bench beside her with no further invitation.

'Indulge me, dear,' Victoria boomed. 'I just could not spend one more minute in that disastrous house. Do you know that pumped up little brat from the orchestra company has just had the temerity to suggest we employ a rat catcher? Would you believe it? Am I to have no companionship at all?'

Shelley could not help a small smile breaking through her sadness.

'That's better,' Victoria winked. 'Right then, now you know things cannot possibly be so catastrophic as me losing my night time camaraderie, might you like to tell me what brings you to tears on the edge of this glorious river? Please do not attempt to impart the smallest notion that you were planning to throw yourself in it. That would be a very inconvenient prelude to my lunch hour.'

'Oh, it's nothing really, Victoria,' Shelley sighed, staring into the spearmint coolness of the River Yarn.

'Well, I doubt that very much, Shelley dear. Do not forget that I have known you for many more years than you have known yourself. Although one has to concede that for most persons that is by no means difficult, since they rarely achieve that knowledge in their entire lifetime.'

'I think you're right there.'

'Undoubtedly. And so?'

'So, I thought I would be OK, Victoria, really. I thought being away so long it would be alright this time to come back here for a while. I thought I had moved on a bit in the last couple of years in London. And now...' Shelley's words disappeared into nothing. Victoria's speciality.

'And now you have been reminded of your place,' she happily took over. 'And it is a place in which you do not fit. And neither are you expected to. You are only expected to understand. Understand a world that is beyond understanding.'

'I should be able to understand her by now, Victoria, shouldn't I? I thought I had, but it's just the same. We've just had the most awful row.'

'Marilyn, of course,' Victoria nodded. 'How did I know?'

'She can really say some things that woman, I'd almost forgotten. Or at least I thought I'd reached some kind of accommodation with it all.'

'Folly dear, of the highest degree. Why on earth should you? Have either of your parents ever made the smallest accommodation to understand *you*? No, indeed, I am making perfect sense.' Again, Shelley had to smile. 'Better. Do keep going. In an hour or so we shall be having high kicks to match the Folies Bergère!'

Victoria shifted in her seat, rummaged in her huge black bag, and drew out a cheese and pickle sandwich. She broke it in half and handed one piece to Shelley.

'Do you know, I have developed quite a taste for these things since Mrs Burlington introduced me to Lidl? Do you see those brown squares? Perfectly formed, are they not? I do not know how they do it. I have never seen a chutney like it in all my eighty-six years. The Bedingford Women's Wheelers have nothing on this Branston person, I can tell you. Eat up now, crying is so exhausting, you do need to replace the juice. Here...' Victoria drew out a small leather flask and unscrewed two silver shot glasses. 'This pickle thing can only be made better with a spot of amontillado.'

Victoria was right, of course. There was something both energising and soothing about the combination of pickle and sherry. But, Shelley remembered, she usually was right. She had never understood how this formidable woman could have attracted so much suspicion over the years. Not least from Marilyn, who willingly bought into the rumours around her marrying a Viscount on the eve of his father's death, and who was dead two years later himself. Despite the fact that Victoria worked for a living all her life, had absolutely nothing to gain from a dead husband and demotion to the widowed *Dowager* Countess, and had never so much as looked at another man in the sixty-odd years since, the suspicion remained, and Marilyn always discouraged any association with her. Shelley's frequent visits to the Manor throughout her childhood were just another evidence of her disrespect for her mother, as Marilyn saw it.

'I know she's suffered,' Shelley sighed.

'We all carry heavy burdens, Shelley dear. The only difference is the volume at which Marilyn carries hers.' Victoria passed another tot of sherry. 'You know, it is a strange quirk of human nature, although I concede by no means peculiar to yourself, that one can keep putting oneself back into a situation that is no less than toxic, for some misguided notion that one can *do it differently* or *make it better*. *Differently* we never manage – obviously – how can anything become different when we continue to do precisely the same thing? *Better* it never becomes either, because nine times out of ten it is not ours to make better, and a good deal worse we become for the trying.' Victoria fixed Shelley with her lively emerald eyes. 'Sometimes Shelley – and do not breathe a word I ever said this to anyone or I shall be forced to deny it – sometimes it is better to just give up. And much as it would pain me to see it, my advice would be to go back whence you came as soon as possible and, saving extreme calls of duty – and I think you know what I mean by that – stay away.'

'But where would I go now, Victoria? I've lost the flat in London and I don't have a job anymore.'

'Really? How so?'

'I resigned last week.'

'Mmm, hasty. Especially when the alternative seems to be a summer chez Marilyn. Could you not get another one next term, some other college that might appreciate your deep under-standing of the finer points of making a fucking great big noise? Or whatever it is that you Acoustics Professors do.'

'I teach Acoustics, Victoria, and am very unlikely now to get to a professorship! Besides, I'm really not sure more academia is where I want to go. Although I change my mind every day.'

'Another pitiful misunderstanding in the lives of the young, I fear. No idea what they want and almost always wrong when they think they do. In which case, it ought to be apparent that it really doesn't matter, Shelley dear. And once you understand that – and I mean really understand it – I guarantee that you absolutely know what you want. And more than that, will prob-ably find it is no more than a gnat's chuff away.'

Shelley snorted.

'You see? Better again. Now, tell me honestly, what really possessed you to abandon everything like that and come back here?'

'I had a letter from Horace. You know I was always going to help Matthew at the Festival where I could. But Dad asked me to come specifically to look after his sound. He's always been nervous about outdoor gigs, and he said if I look after him and make sure he sounded good, I could go back to the States with him afterwards.'

Victoria lay her hands in her lap on top of the remains of her second sandwich.

'Oh dear, I see. And may I surmise that this is an opportunity you have been wanting for some time and which finally gave you the nudge to resign?'

'Yes, Victoria. You know, I've never really wanted to be in libraries, lecture halls and classrooms. I've only ever really wanted to be in the midst of it all, hearing it all. I've only ever wanted to be behind a sound desk. It was like a thunderbolt reminding me, you know?'

'And our dear Horace has finally heard that wish, you think? Finally allowing you out of the prison of academic expectation and onto the real world stage, so to speak. Or behind it, I suppose.'

'Well, no Victoria, in front of it usually. The sound desk you see, it—'

'Don't mince fucking hairs, dear.'

'Well, yes then, he's got a new residency at the MGM for three years. If it goes well at the Festival, he says he will ensure his sound job is mine.'

'I see. And I would be foolish, would I not, to interpret that possibility as anything less than mightily exciting, judging by the dilation of your pupils?'

'Yes, but,' she winced. 'After this, Dad is never coming back to Britain, back to...'

'Ah. And I suppose you are at severe pains not to disclose either this revelation or your current employment status to your mother.'

'Well, she knows the first one now. It was in *The Telegraph* this morning.'

'Good grief, Marilyn's bible! She must be spitting feathers.'

'Yes, and in my direction, I'm afraid. She already thinks I am somehow behind it. If she finds out that I already knew and have jacked my job to be a part of it...'

'Well, you must do what you can to ensure that she does not. And if possible, do try to find somewhere else to pass the next couple of weeks. I fear this continuing onslaught is not good for your psyche. You are a trusting and sensitive soul, Shelley dear. I do not like to think of you suffering any more... *disappointment.* I rather wish we could offer you a room at the Manor, but I can't see how that will be possible at the moment. The East Wing was condemned eighteen months ago and the only remaining rooms not overtaken by wildlife are being used by the festival crew and equipment. But I will give it some thought.'

'Oh, that's alright, Victoria. I really should stay and at least try and help her deal with it.'

Shelley looked at her watch. From years of practice, she was timing her absence from the house quite precisely. Too short, and she would return whilst the artillery was still firing in her direction; too long, and she risked being too late to prevent the guns turning elsewhere. It was a lesson she had learned piecemeal throughout her teens but received the masterclass at 17 when she had come home from school late to find her mother in the bath, the water stone cold, a six-inch needle poking out of her thigh, overdosed on the insulin Horace kept for his diabetes, his very amateur moonshine and a packet of cocaine she had found in his coat pocket. Eighteen months of psychiatrists and counsellors and drugs, most of which seemed to make her worse. And her father, the great entertainer, came home once a month. *For One Night Only,* ironically, the name of the massive crossover variety hit that still kept them in the family house. And it was Shelley who barely survived.

'Your ears have always been remarkable, Shelley dear. Hear what I am saying.' Victoria pinned her with eyes of such unaccustomed compassion that Shelley almost burst into tears. 'Now I regret I must alight this fine bench. Since dear Matthew got caught by the bailiffs, *again*, I fear my absence for too long leaves the marvellous Fat Stat alone to curb his excessive attention to the tombola. And you, dear child, must do your best to bear the burden of the parental home for a short while longer, in the enduring hope that it will only be a couple of weeks and you will finally be free to choose your own path— Oh, my goodness!'

'Graham, what are you doing here? Again,' Shelley sighed as Graham Tweedle appeared from behind the pampas by the bench.

'Oh, Shelley, what a surprise. How lovely to see you again so soon. Lady Bedingford,' he added curtly. 'I am just taking some baseline readings along this stretch of the river.' Graham thrust his prize noise meter under Shelley's nose and just as quickly whipped it away again. 'Would you like to see what this one does? Perhaps you'd like to help me with—'

'No thank you, Graham. It's very kind, but Victoria has an appointment with a tombola. We were just leaving.' Both women rose from the bench and hurried away down the path.

'Nice work, Shelley dear. I almost broke his nose and I do so want to avoid a custodial sentence before this wretched festival sees me off altogether.'

Shelley kissed her cheek as they stopped by the footpath that would take them their separate ways, but Victoria clutched her arm.

'Now dear, Matthew will be so pleased to see you. I insist you come as soon as Marilyn is properly... *settled*, shall we say,' she winked. 'If such a state exists...'

Shelley was not sure if she was more relieved or worried that her mother was not home when she returned that afternoon. *The Telegraph Magazine* was ripped and scattered on the kitchen table. Out of habit, she checked every room, including both bathrooms. The empty house unnerved her a little. There had been so much noise lately, the place now rattled with silence and made its spotless order feel even more oppressive than usual. She trod carefully from empty room to empty room. The whole place was unfeasibly clean. All the walls looked freshly painted, the furniture measured in with a protractor, and the curtains standing to attention like guards on parade. In comparison, Shelley felt like an eBay delivery brought into the house by mistake.

She had always been wary of the show-home nature of Marilyn's decor. Too much care lavished on the place and not enough attention paid to the life that should be going on inside it. A blemish-free, steam-cleaned armchair with meticulously ironed antimacassar was poor compensation for the emptiness of the seat itself. At times Shelley felt her sadness as a pang of sympathy. But her mother never allowed that, and would turn it into guilt as swiftly as a conjuror pulls knotted handkerchiefs where a dove flew a moment ago.

She sat down in the kitchen to wait. Two hours later, a huge man in a T-shirt with 'Crew' on it arrived at the door with a brown envelope. Inside was a large iron key attached to a parcel tag by an old piece of rope and marked 'Robert Henry's Folly'. A brief handwritten note accompanied the old key:

You might have to climb your way in over all of Robert's frightful junk (have a car boot sale, we need the cash!) but at least for the moment, let this place be yours, if you need it. Use it well, my dear. Victoria.

7

MARILYN TURNS

Marilyn Harper was a broken woman. There would be no other reason for being in Winchester on a Saturday – Market Day, when all the riff-raff joined in. But she had had to get out, and to somewhere anonymous where there was less likelihood of having to speak to anyone she knew. She had left *The Telegraph* article open and torn on her kitchen table, and fled. She did not know how she had got from there to here, or how long it had taken, but at least she could no longer hear the unanswered phone ringing. It had not stopped all morning.

Marilyn thought it could not get any worse until she passed in front of The Guildhall noticeboard. There it was, plain as day.

Bedingford Opera Festival
24th June - 28th August
<u>Opening Concert</u>
FOR ONE NIGHT ONLY
Legendary tenor Horace Harper returns to the classical stage for
his LAST EVER opera performance...

Marilyn had not cried all morning, but the rest of the poster text was blurring now. The humiliation! Even Prontaprint knew before she did that her husband was finally gone.

Her nails dug deep into the paper and tore it from the notice board. A few people stopped to stare, one or two hesitating, wondering if this woman might need some help, but Marilyn just ripped it to pieces, scattered it to the ground and kept on walking.

With the continued blurry unreality of the day and her clouded eyes, Marilyn was not quite sure how or why she ended up in the library. She was not a frequent visitor and was not expecting to be the slightest bit moved by it. Indeed, she suspected that her current preoccupation would see off any real hope of peace and contentment for some time to come, if not forever. The thought of an eternity of these infernal skirmishes around the borders of her Horace-related consciousness only intensified the throbbing in her temples and the persistent compulsion that she could not go home. At least not until suitably defended.

The hushed shelves settled a quiet purpose over her. She went through Assisted Suicide to Cookery to Engineering and found something calming in all three.

'Marilyn, my dear friend, how nice to see you out and about. I was *so* worried about you this morning.' Marilyn looked up to see Harriet Pordage standing over her, with the library's entire supply of Bedingford Opera flyers in her hand. Harriet stuffed them into her handbag and sat down beside her. Half an hour later, they were both booked into a boutique hotel off the high street. Two Nurofen, a large brandy and a lobster linguine later still, Marilyn was feeling quite different. Her good friend Harriet would take her home tomorrow and she'd get back to where she was supposed to be. It was time to give up this charade. Time for her to accept the truth and to finally just deal with it.

8

THE DRUM PADLOCK

Pip had had the argument with himself a thousand times overnight. Keep trying in the village, or give up this daily torture? He was tired of the words in his head. He was tired of everything. Barely any sleep again, he was just bloody tired.

He reached for the copy of the *Mid-Hampshire Gazette* lying open on the workbench. Like tossing a coin that fell on heads only to reveal the necessity for it to be tails, he threw it across the shed. The paper ripped in mid-air, a scrappy corner remaining in his hand of half a situation vacant in Poundland.

Pip was well aware of the opportunities open to 'someone like him' in the real world now: shelf stacker, warehouseman, kitchen porter, some poor sod making minute adjustments to jam tarts on a production line. And a little more of him died every time he could bring himself to look at the advertisements. Picturing himself in silence in some concrete shell, waiting for someone to begrudgingly signal him a statutory 15-minute break for the minimum wage.

In comparison, despite her demanding eccentricity, Pip understood that Marilyn Harper had been gracious in her offer of employment so far. Continuing to turn up, acquiescent and on-time at the start of another week, was by far his best option right now. Besides, he had learned that if he ignored the back-firing, as she seemed to, loosened the grip of his muscles and leaned into the bone-shaking vibration of her lawnmower, there was something quite peaceful about mowing. Especially on vast lawns like hers where he could just go up and down, up and down. It had direction, a purpose, the kind of focused, monotonous task that seemed to anchor the otherwise storm-tossed boat of his thoughts, which persistently pulled him further and further into darker waters. And perhaps he was beginning to understand Marilyn's devotion to her lawn stripes, creating some kind of order to maintain a small sense of being in control of something.

He pulled himself up. He'd made up his mind. His body would just have to be forced to follow.

He stopped halfway up Trefusis Lane. Shelley was sitting on the grass in front of the Harper house. His thoughts immediately quickened, once again searching fruitlessly in his memory banks for something appropriate to say if she didn't shift before he got there. Accepting her small invitation into the kitchen last week, he recognised he was in some ways quite desperate for some normal conversation, but had since regretted the impulse as he had been reminded just how rubbish at it he was these days. Once upon a time, Ma and Bill would complain they could never shut him up. Every so often still, he would forget himself and just do or say something without thinking, without remembering, without crippling internal analysis of motive and method. And then find himself adrift with no real means of navigation back-wards or forwards. Times like that morning – and the one he felt sure he was about to have if he stepped any closer – when he could feel the silences pulsating with inadequacy. Or else he'd be halfway through a monologue before he realised the words in his head had been unleashed and were rattling out of his mouth. Every one of them nonsense, no doubt.

Ground to a halt on the pavement, Pip watched as Shelley put her hands over her ears. Only then did he spot the littered state of the garden, and Marilyn at the upstairs window. Shelley sat motionless on the grass as if she could not muster the energy for movement, staring ahead at the debris strewn across the lawn, clutching a reel of cables and a tool bag to her stomach. Pip ran up to the driveway as rain began to spit. The upstairs window opened again and a wooden board flew out. Shelley instinctively raised the cable reel above her head for protection, but Pip had already intercepted its descent and managed to catch it before it hit her. The edge caught his hand and cut through the skin. He raised it to his mouth as he looked up at the window.

'Hey! What the hell is going on here?'

Marilyn hesitated, a touch of shock and bewilderment in her eyes, before she straightened herself and slammed the window shut. Shelley still had not moved, gripping the tool bag as if it were ballast in this shipwreck of a morning.

Pip tentatively knelt down on the dampening grass beside her. 'Are you OK?'

Shelley looked down at his bleeding hand, which she reached out and touched. 'I'm sorry,' she said, still dazed. 'That must hurt.'

'It's nothing.' He pulled it away. 'But we better get you inside quick before all your stuff is ruined. I'll go and talk to her.'

'There's no point, really.'

'Well, you can't sit here all day. Is there anywhere else you can go? Just for a bit maybe, until she calms down?'

Pip watched as Shelley's focus changed, the daze dissipating, eyes fixed ahead of her with some determination.

'OK, if that's the way it's going to be.' She looked up to the window and shouted, 'Yes, I do have somewhere else to go!'

She turned back to Pip. 'Thank you for your help. Don't worry, you carry on. I'll pick all this up.'

'Don't be daft. Is it far?'

'Just across the road, actually.'

'The Manor?'

'Well, sort of.' Now there was a hint of a smile. 'And it's about bloody time.'

Shelley began to pick up her possessions scattered across the garden. 'I'll get the wheelbarrow,' Pip suggested, and she smiled again. So he did too...

Shelley's tools and belongings piled up in the barrow, Pip wheeled it across the road. She was striking a decent pace, and he wordlessly followed, as if she had some renewed purpose that was contagious. Three elderly gents were busy setting up deckchairs at the main gate and Pip instinctively looked behind him, checking for others joining them, hurriedly preparing to turn in. But Shelley kept going. 'East Gate,' she turned and called, and that was all.

The East Gate was about a quarter of a mile along the road and round to the left as the Manor wall curved northwards away from Trefusis Lane. Pip had never noticed it before. Not surprising perhaps, it was clearly unused, a lot smaller than the main gate, with a similarly crafted iron gate, but this one was completely overgrown and there didn't look much hope of getting in. Shelley trailed a hand along the ivy-smothered railing, pushing the vegetation aside to reveal a rusted keylock which didn't look too functional, and a large padlock hanging beside it. It was quite unlike any padlock Pip had ever seen. Victorian, he guessed, ornate tarnished brass and, instead of numbers, the four wheels on the barrel were letters.

Shelley ground them into position.

'Let's hope this hasn't changed,' she muttered. 'Bingo!' It was the first proper smile of the day, but Pip did not return it this time as he stared at the open padlock. The released letters spelled out D-R-U-M.

'What?' Shelley's smile faltered. Pip appeared to be caught in suspension, a look of fascination turning slowly to some kind of horror. 'Pip? What is it?'

'Nothing,' he dismissed. 'Wh... What does it mean?'

'D-R-U-M? It's a round thing you hit, Pip.'

He continued to stare between her and it. 'Why?'

'To make music?'

'On a padlock! Stop taking the piss!'

'Oh, OK...'

'No, look, I'm sorry, sorry... Forget it. Let's just go in, shall we?' He shoved the wheelbarrow through the gate and up the path ahead.

But the place was not getting any less surprising. Through the overgrown shrubs and thigh-high grass stood a castle. Much smaller even than Ma and Bill's tiny two-up-two-down, but a castle nonetheless. A single turret made of the same grey stone as the manor walls, two latticed windows at the front and back, and a heavy wooden door on the side. It stood entirely on its own, the Manor in the distance.

'This is Robert Henry's Folly,' Shelley said. 'Named after Matthew's elder brother who built it in the 1950s apparently, a few years before he died, I think.'

'What on earth for? That place not big enough for him or something?' Pip nodded towards the Manor without dropping the wheelbarrow.

'Apparently not,' she laughed. 'I don't really know much about it. Victoria told me once that he had very noisy habits, that's all. This was his place to go. Like the garden shed for normal blokes, I guess. Oh, sorry...'

Pip did not know what 'noisy habits' meant. Perhaps it was some posh people's euphemism that he ought not to query. Half the time he had no idea what people were talking about, so best not throw any more spotlight on his incomprehension by pursuing the matter. Or her apologetic reference to the garden shed. His present castle, he supposed.

The key that Shelley pulled from her pocket was quite the biggest he had ever seen outside of a museum. It was stiff in the lock, but gave a satisfying click as it opened.

He peered in behind her. 'Blimey!'

The circular room before them looked like it had been left in suspension for decades, but had obviously been well-loved. There was a mid-century sofa under the window, a small table and two upright chairs. At the end, there was a narrow doorway to an alcove with a tiny kitchen, toilet and bathroom. To the side of the alcove there was a stone spiral staircase with a locked door on the side of it.

'Well, this is nice!' Shelley grinned. 'It'll do fine.'

'Bit small,' Pip muttered. She raised her eyebrows, but decided against another reference to the shed.

'Come on, let's have a peek upstairs. I can't imagine what else there'd be!'

Honestly, Pip thought, she was like a kid in a sweet shop now. No-one would suspect she'd just been chucked out of her home and assaulted by her mother. But it was clearly infectious as his concentration broke again and he skipped up the stairs behind her.

He stopped dead at the top of the stairs. There, in the middle of this curious old place, was a drum kit. A magnificent vintage set in white and gold, with two bass drums emblazoned with a large L on one and B on the other. A pile of single drums in sparkling green was also stacked against the wall.

'There, you see? Noisy habits,' Shelley giggled as she drew her hand through a layer of dust over one of the cymbals. 'Surprised Matthew hasn't flogged this off by now, though.'

'I'm not,' Pip breathed, unable to stop staring, his eyes flicking between her and the drums as if they couldn't quite process which was the most noteworthy. Nothing quite so beautiful had been in his life for a very long time. 'That's Louis Bellson's 1955 Gretsch kit.'

'What?' Shelley laughed.

'I never thought I'd ever see something like that.'

'Ah, I see, so you haven't just had a seizure. You're a drum geek.'

'Drum geek?' His gaze intensified. He had that habit, she noticed, as if all his communication was having to go through some parallel internal dialogue. 'Yeah, I guess I am.' The intensity broke and he laughed, a surprisingly joyful, musical laugh, his bright blue eyes dancing. And again, it completely transformed him.

'Can you play?' Shelley asked, and it was immediately lost.

'Na,' he said, eyes dropping to the floor, his foot twitching. 'I better be going.' His hand was already on the stair rail, which he seemed to be gripping with unnecessary force.

'Do you have to get back to the madhouse or are you going on to another job now?'

'Don't think I will,' he said, his grip loosening as if he'd been rescued. 'Your mother could do with some time to calm down.'

'She's...' Shelley hesitated, 'not good on her own.'

'She should've thought about that before she chucked you out.'

Shelley felt the familiar prickle in her chest moving down to her stomach.

'I'll keep an eye on her,' Pip said, as if he could see it.

'Thank you. That's very kind.'

Despite his foot havering over the top step, he hadn't moved, looking at her as if he needed permission to leave.

'Well, I'm going up to the Manor. Would you like to come with me instead?' she said, finding that she wasn't particularly interested in giving it. 'Perhaps there might be a bit of work going with the festival preparations.'

'Really? How patronising.'

'Is it?' Shelley was genuinely shocked by the response. The man was a minefield.

'No, probably not, sorry.'

'Come on, then...'

It seemed very odd to Pip that he was being taken to this place this morning. Odder still that his body appeared to be allowing it to happen. Although the nearer they got to the Manor House and the people milling around the stables, the more it was beginning to rebel. He remembered the only time he had come to Bedingford Manor before, with his Gosport Primary School's urban exchange project when he was seven. Walking in crocodile, holding hands with Charlie, marching rhythmically behind the huge bottom of Miss Snowden whilst she constantly called out reminders of their expected conduct in this grand place. And he felt exactly like that today. Someone else was in charge, this place was something *other*, and conduct was expected that was not natural and that he was not capable of on his own. But today, there was no Charlie to giggle with and no wobbly bottom to giggle over to break the tension. It was a rather nice one, actually.

'I'm hardly dressed for this,' Pip muttered as he trotted to keep up with her and his eyes and mind off bottoms.

'What on earth are you talking about?' Shelley laughed. 'What do you think you're going into, Buckingham Palace?'

Pip shrugged, still feeling uneasy. It wasn't as if he really gave a toss that his host was a member of the aristocracy. It was just that class was a state of mind as much as a reality, and he had never quite been able to escape the venomous spittle of his father's mouth demanding that he 'stop getting ideas above his fucking station!'

'Well anyway, me neither,' Shelley smiled. And yes, she certainly was much less polished than her mother, or anyone else around here, in her tatty jeans and oversized jumper that just screamed out to be cuddled... Pip winced. He really was going to have to stop this. But she was taking it off now to accommodate the growing heat of the sun, casually pulling it over her head and dragging the T-shirt beneath up with it. Oh dear, yes, he was definitely going to have to stop. This confusing intrigue was mutating quite alarmingly now. Especially as she just grinned at him, retrieving her wayward T-shirt from halfway up her stomach and ruffling her tousled hair back into place. And that was alien to him as well. He hadn't felt *that* in a very long time.

Pip followed her up a roughly tarmacked drive, through trees and rhododendrons in full bloom in mauve and purple, pink and red. He gasped slightly, the scent smashing right through his memory banks. This was the bush he had hidden in at the end of that day. The bush where he had crouched, watching through a tiny gap as Miss Snowden finally gave up her peeved huffing and the school coach trundled away without him. The bush where Bill had found him an hour later and taken him home to Ma to wait for his father to collect him. Trevor had arrived a week later. Pip had to be dragged out screaming.

'I've always loved this place,' Shelley broke through his thoughts. 'It's only across the road, but it feels a million miles away.' She hardly needed to say it – as Pip watched her face, he could see the calm and lightness growing with each step along the drive. His memories faded back to the present, and he began to feel a little less like a trespasser himself.

'Did you come here a lot?'

'Oh,' she sighed. 'It was my second home, really. Spent quite a bit of my childhood here. Ed – Matthew's son – was my best friend and he, Matthew and Victoria became my family really, for a while anyway. Sorry, Matthew – Lord Bedingford – and Victoria, she's the widow of Matthew's brother Robert, the one who built the Folly? And the one who was supposed to still be the Earl.'

Pip knew all of this in some distant way. Ma and Bill had always been devoted fans of Lord and Lady Bedingford (at least this one, they never had any time for Katherine, Matthew's estranged wife). But he was enjoying the anonymity of ignorance, and it comforted him that he was still capable of being interested in something.

They were rounding a bend towards the house now though, relieving him of any urge to do anything about it.

Although there was plenty of activity towards the stables, the front of the house was deserted. The Manor was not large. Given the overture of the endless wall, the gates, the driveway, the grounds, the Folly 'castle' and other buildings dotted about, Pip was a little surprised. It had seemed a lot bigger when he was seven. It was not particularly grand either, with little symmetry and what looked like a whole piece missing, like a child's abandoned Lego construction.

'Yes, I know, awful isn't it?' A rich, plumy voice drifted from below as Pip stood transfixed by the steps.

'My great-great-great-great-grandfather built it in 1787. He was quite mad by then, you understand, always preferred horses to people. Hence not bothering to finish the house and making the stables twice the size and grandeur.'

Pip's mouth dropped. 'I think it is... wonderful.'

'Indeed,' a small, sad smile came to his lips. 'You are quite right about that, too... Shelley! How marvellous, at last. It's so good to see you!'

Matthew stood up from the steps, shoving another creditor's letter down the back of his trousers. Shelley wrapped her arms around him and he leaned into the embrace, holding on tightly for far longer than most people would think appropriate. Having grown up bowing to remote family members and saluting prefects, when Matthew had first encountered Shelley's spontaneous hugging, it had felt positively indecent. But it had unlocked something in him, and these days his body leapt into the most encompassing bear hug given the slightest provocation. It was probably another reason he no longer got invited to lunch.

'Oh Shelley, I've been an awful arse, you know,' he said, turning her towards the stables. Pip stepped away, his awkwardness returning amidst such obvious affection, and no longer being part of the communication.

But Shelley drew him back. 'Matthew, this is Pip Berry. Pip, this is Matthew, Lord Bedingford. Pip's doing some work in the village. I thought there might be something here for him too, with the festival preparations.'

Matthew stopped and hugged him as well. All this was rather surprising. Pip did not know quite what he had expected of a peer of the realm. Perhaps not a polished, stately figure dressed in ermine, hunting and shooting and being waited on hand and foot – or anything else that might have been in the Ladybird Book of the Aristocracy – but certainly not this lean, dishevelled, twinkly old boy in a crumpled white shirt and pink slacks, which looked like they'd come from a jumble sale, stuffed into a pair of grubby wellingtons, going around hugging people.

'Good, good...' Matthew released him far more quickly than he had Shelley, his attention still well and truly on her. 'Well, welcome and all that. I'll introduce you to Tree and Morris round the back. I'm sure they'll make use of you if they can.'

Morris was all gummy smiles now as Matthew needlessly pulled his Access All Areas lanyard out of his pocket at the stable gate. Morris was enormous. Pip stared up at him a good eight inches. But as he looked up even higher, introductions to Tree were not all that necessary.

'Right ho, must dash, we've got all sorts to discuss!' Matthew hurriedly turned Shelley back towards the house, but failed to avoid the advance of Stat, clearly on the warpath and heading their way.

'Ah, Lester, we bring fresh blood,' he made a futile attempt to divert him. 'Can we make use of another pair of hands? Pip here—'

'Oh yes, of course we fucking can! Another wage, no problem! Have you seen this? Apparently, the Council sent it to you four weeks ago.'

Matthew shifted onto his toes. The papers that had been slapped into his chest looked official, so the answer was *probably not*, but he did not like the look on Stat's face, so he adopted the air of ignorance he was so good at and remained silent. He'd had too much honesty this week already.

'They turned up this morning wanting to inspect the sound attenuation measures in their list of conditions for our licence.'

'What sound attenuation measures?'

'Precisely!' Stat flicked derisively through half a dozen pages. 'Apparently they gave you notice they were coming three days ago following, *I quote,* "a breach of conditions, with 72dB recorded at Yarnside Bridge, approximately 130 metres from the performance space, on Thursday 8 June at 12.25pm." Puts us on an official warning, apparently, God damn it!'

'Oh.'

'Oh? Is that all you can say? Where's the noise consultants' report? When are the sound boys coming to measure up?'

'Ah, I don't think they are, I... um, *lost* the Darwin.'

'You *what?* You haven't paid them? Did you not think that might be something I should know about? Preferably more than two weeks before opening night. Sod all I can do about it now! Or perhaps you have a few more Victorian heirlooms going spare that you haven't told me about.'

Matthew shuffled his feet. 'But it's alright surely,' he ventured hopefully. 'Last Thursday, the breach could only have been a power drill.'

'And that, apparently, makes no difference!' Stat waved the sheaf of Council conditions again. 'We were so nearly there, Matthew! We might just have been able to pull this off. James at the ticketing company tells me we're virtually sold out. It's bad enough the first weekend being a trial for the noise conditions, but now they can close us down before anyone's even bellowed a note!'

Matthew's hands hovered around his temples. 'What can we

do in a fortnight?'

'What, without a magic wand?' Stat clucked. Matthew was well aware that Stat had a good deal riding on this festival too, but he had directed his question to Shelley.

'Perhaps I can help?' She held out her hand to the Council letter crumpling in Stat's hand.

'I don't think so, dear,' he muttered, lighting a new cigar from the chewed remains of the current one.

'If I could just take a look at the letter?' she persisted. Matthew snatched it from Stat's hand and gave it to her anyway. She skimmed it with little surprise, as Stat continued his tirade.

'Shall we walk and talk?' Shelley suggested, heading towards the stage, and Matthew twitched a smile of cautious relief. 'Hmm, you haven't got much in the way of sound proofing, have you...?'

Pip was already there, sitting on the edge of the stage, as workmen banged and crashed behind him, moving his head from one angle to another before stopping still, staring intently towards the west wall.

'Bit near that wall, innit?' he said. 'That's your main issue, I would have thought.'

'Yes, absolutely,' Shelley agreed, a little surprised at the intervention.

'Especially with Tweedle-twat monitoring in Trefusis Lane and Yarnside Drive. Can you move this?' He turned to the two men and patted the stage.

'Oh yes, obviously! No problem,' Stat puffed. 'Let's just pick the whole thing up and put it in the middle of the woods, shall we?'

'Great idea,' Pip ignored him and returned to Shelley. 'Just a bit, I mean. If it could just be angled across another thirty degrees or something, it'd be a start.'

'Look, we absolutely cannot move the stage!' Stat continued to protest. 'Anyway, what... who...?'

'Yeah, yeah, alright then.'

Stat and Matthew were still staring at him, not his favourite thing right now, but Shelley seemed open to his participation, so he returned his attention to her. 'It's opera, yeah? So presumably no amplification? And the big lungs'll mostly be poncing about in that middle bit probably, with the orchestra down there in front?'

'That's usually about what happens,' she grinned.

'Seen that there?' Pip pointed towards the wall to a gap between a beech copse and a long row of poplar. 'Those trees on the right should do a lot of the job for you along Yarnside Drive.'

'Yes! So we just need to concentrate on that bit in the middle, really.' Shelley returned her attention to Stat and Matthew. 'Maybe all we need is something along that stretch. I could make some calls. There's a pretty good screening company in Southampton.'

'And how much is that going to cost?'

'A few thousand, I should think.' As soon as she said it, she knew it was hopeless, even without both Stat and Matthew slowly shaking their heads. 'Oh, sorry...'

'And anyway, how are we supposed to know how loud a fucking power drill is?' Stat demanded.

'What you looking at me for?' Pip retorted. 'She's the expert.'

'The Council recorded 72 decibels at roughly 130 metres, let's call it a divisible 128 to make it easier on ourselves...' Shelley waved for silence as she worked it out. 'So, that would be 114 decibels at one metre from the drill, let's say roughly the stage edge, here.'

'What?'

'Inverse Square Law. Never mind. The point is, at that volume, at that distance, we are in trouble.'

'Yeah, but that was a power drill, not a bunch of opera singers... Oh, for fuck's sake, they're that loud, aren't they?' Stat's shoulders slumped as he read the look on Shelley's face.

'Afraid so, and sadly my father holds the world record for the loudest note recorded on a stage. Thankfully, that was a long time ago, but it's pretty likely he'll hit above 100dB on a few occasions. Did your acoustic engineers not do this kind of modelling?' Matthew's mixed expression of cluelessness and guilt indicated that there was no way of telling whether they did or not. But since Darwin had been his only means of paying them before they walked out last week, they were never going to know now.

'What does it matter anyway?' Stat resigned. 'It's a bloody stone courtyard! It's not as if we can move it further away.'

'Oh dear, oh dear,' Matthew started to panic. 'Shelley, please, isn't there anything else we can do?'

'Yes!' she called, already striding to the side of the stage. 'Can we get hold of any more of that canvas? If it's just that bit between the trees, I might be able to come up with some rudimentary sound screening. I've been experimenting with an idea lately... How long have we got?'

'Ten days until the tech rehearsal.'

'Oh...'

Stat's phone cut through the heavy silence.

'For heaven's sake, Rex, what is it now...? What, Rex... calm down, where are you...? They want you to what...? Who...? Who's staring at you...?'

'Well, we can try, can't we?' Matthew ventured, as Stat turned away with his phone. He had called in so many favours to get this far, his instinctive distaste for it had long since been worn down. But it was altogether different with Shelley. She had provided more light in his life than he could already repay. 'Can't we?' he squeaked, looking between her and Pip.

Shelley was smiling again, but Pip suddenly looked very uneasy. 'Nothing to do with me,' he concluded and walked off.

She was on her own with this one.

9

REX MEETS HIMSELF

Rex Trenton stopped on the pavement of an unusually quiet backstreet in Islington, on the pretence of finishing his cigarette, but actually because the lack of what he might call a 'door' was beginning to unnerve him. He had been early for his appointment at the Christie Feathers Agency, but that had only sentenced him to pacing up and down the road in search of somewhere remotely inviting to spend his morning.

It was the waiting that was the torture. It had only been three days since the band's meeting in Stat's office, but every hour felt like it was ticking down with the heavy load of reality. Rex wondered if Stat had tried hard enough not to be so brutal. These were his dreams here, being crushed under the weight of it. Be patient, was all Stat could say. He was doing well in Hampshire, he said. If he could make a success of the opera, there'd be a little more to fund another venue for the band. Perhaps he had already found it – for next year.

Riddles and promises. Dangled like a fecking carrot. Next year? Another *year*? Rex could barely stand another minute. Forced to rely on Stat for 'pocket money' every week, it was beneath him. He needed more, *now*. He needed his life back.

So that is what he had demanded. And this is how Stat had responded. Calling him yesterday to say some people working for George Harrison's outfit wanted him for a film. A film! At last. Another way back, surely? A pretty good one, actually. Had he remembered to say thank you? Must have done...

Now all he had to do was find the bloody door and, bingo, walk through it and back out the other side to his old life.

So why was he sweating so much? Why was his fag packet empty? Why did he want the toilet again, even though he'd just been at the petrol station down the road? This was tiresome. And completely out of place.

Finally, Rex determined that this blue hunk of metal with the tiniest bit of signage reading 'CFA' must be it. He stood for a moment, searching in vain for a bell, or even a door handle. Eventually, he spotted a tiny intercom on the left, ridiculously placed at waist height. He bent over and pressed the only button on it.

'Yep?' The voice was distinctly unreassuring.

'Is this the Christie Feathers Agency?'

'Yep.'

'It's Rex Trenton.' Silence. 'I've come for the part.'

'Oh, *the* part, eh? And exactly what part would that be?'

'The part. In the film?'

'Ah, the *filum* is it? To be sure.' It was the smallest indication of Rex's Irish roots, but the receptionist leapt on it as a further source of mockery.

The unexpected challenge hit Rex hard. He was not used to this. Even in prison, he had rarely had to ask for anything. And it wasn't so much arrogance or obstinacy that dictated his next move, more that he was simply adrift.

'OK, byc,' he concluded and removed his finger from the intercom. The door buzzed and it clicked open. Rex paused for a moment, then remembered the parlous state of his bank balance, his life in general, and the fact that he'd get the wanker receptionist fired as soon as the credits rolled. He pushed open the door.

The hallway was no bigger than the brush mat on the floor, with a white-painted staircase immediately before him. It was ridiculously steep and narrow and if Stat had accompanied him, as he had offered to do, he would surely have found himself wedged at the bottom.

At the top of the stairs was an old fire door, sturdy cream wood and thick criss-crossed glass. Rex had a job to heft it open, and it reminded him of his old school; and the only hospital he had ever been in; and, come to think of it, the doors in the recreation centre at HMP Ford. This was an institutional door. The morning was not getting any better.

Rex surreptitiously sniffed his armpits. He continued to sweat and his stomach was still churning, and he realised that had very little to do with the steep stairs he had just climbed. These were feelings he used to medicate against. Many years ago, they told him that life was exciting and passionate and fast. Then they became monsters to knock out with weapons of drugs and alcohol. Until the uppers and the downers turned their armoury on each other. Now Rex did all he could to avoid feeling anything like it at all. This morning, for some reason, it was all rather more than he bargained for.

OK, how bad could it be? Rex shook his chestnut curls, his head held high. These people were going to put him in a film and he could always be relied upon to rise to any occasion. (One of the reasons his three wives left him). He leaned on the reception desk and opened his mouth to speak.

'Yeah, it's OK, I've found you,' the elaborately painted boy said, without looking up. 'You're down to try for Waymo Steel, the drug addled rock star, yeah?'

'Uh, I beg your pardon. *Try for...?*' Rex did not need to complete the sentence as his eyes roamed the room before him. It was a large space, still over-filled. A group of short-skirted young women in the far section, the same orange hue of foundation spread over their collective expectant faces. A smaller group of old granny types on the left. One of them was actually knitting. And in the middle, lacing the couches that ran from one end of the room to the other, were rows of...

Well, rows of *him*.

Some blond, some dark, some balding, some straight, some curly – but every hair long. Some wearing denim, some white jeans, some leathers – but all of them skintight. A little more variation on top – some open flared shirts, some skinny T-shirts, one bloke in the corner with no shirt at all. But basically, they were all Rex Trenton. Or, in Rex's mind anyway, laughably pale imitations of him.

But then, as Rex found the air suddenly cooling all around him, he knew that, to the smirking receptionist at least, so was he.

'D...do you have a quiet room?' Rex was extremely unhappy at the hesitation in his own voice. 'I'd like to make a private call.'

'Bit of an empty corner round there at the end of the young ladies,' the boy nodded across the room and watched as Rex appeared to stagger a little when he finally let go of the desk...

'They want me to...to...' Dispensing with any pleasantries, Rex spluttered into the phone, clearly finding the evil word 'audition' beyond his grasp.

'What Rex? Calm down. Where are you?'

'I'm at... at... Stat, they're all staring at me!' It wasn't untrue; although most of the 'Rex's' were attempting to be subtle about it, thirty-odd pairs of eyes had been focused in his direction from the moment he walked into the room.

'Who? Who's staring at you?'

'Everyone!'

'But you like that, Rex, remember?' Stat sighed. 'Now come on, what's happening and what's the matter?'

Rex curled his hand even further around the phone and drew

in to whisper. 'You said they wanted me for the part, Stat. You said I just had to come down here and meet them.'

'Yes, so?'

'They want me to audition, Stat!' There, he'd finally said it. 'Audition! Me!' And now most of the young women and grannies were looking at him as well. Rex lowered his voice again. 'I've never had to audition for anything in my life, Stat. People just give me things.'

Stat sighed. Sincerely, his heart went out to the man. The words were just pathetic. And delivered in the confused whine of a five-year-old who doesn't understand why he can't have another tube of smarties.

'Yes well, they will, Rex. I'm sure it's just a formality, the part's yours for sure. You're unique, lovey, you know that. There's only ever been one Rex Trenton.'

Rex blew out a heavy stream of air. 'You're not in this room, mate.'

It took another ten minutes of Stat's ubiquitous soothing to penetrate Rex's indignation enough to agree to stay. He lowered himself onto a tiny plastic chair at the end of the orange women.

'Ahem! Cooey!' the receptionist trilled across the room. 'In the right section please, Mr Trenton.' He nodded towards the other Rex's with another smirk and Rex had an overwhelming urge to punch his lights out. 'And while you're at it, you might want a copy of the script.'

Rex rose and picked up a thin wad of paper from the receptionist's outstretched hand, silently returning to the 'right' section.

He surveyed them all, 'his group', studying their own scripts in furrowed concentration, and a wave of sadness flowed over him. They all looked sad, pathetic, outdated. It was all he could do to stay in his seat; until his name was called. Thank God, he could soon escape this murky, cracked mirror being held up to himself this morning.

Rex walked into the audition room with the drawn-in swagger for which he was once famous, as if every door were not quite wide enough.

'It's OK, Rex. May I call you Rex? The audition hasn't started yet. Just relax and be yourself for a moment.'

Rex attempted to smile, but he was completely lost now. This was himself, wasn't it? And if it wasn't, why was he here with thirty other blokes being it too?

The two men and a woman sitting behind the desk in front of him were all staring at him. Questioning looks, he did not comprehend. Until he realised he was standing on one leg, his right leg cocked at the knee like a flamingo. He slowly lowered it, recalling with some surprise that he used to do that when he was a boy at school, standing in the corner of the room, facing the wall, or waiting outside the Headmaster's office. As far as he could remember, he had not done it since.

'Perhaps you'd like to give us the first scene on page two. You've probably noticed it's a few lines, probably the most syllables Waymo Steel strings together in the whole film, eh?'

Rex did not reciprocate the younger man's smile. He did not move or speak. The three of them were slipping out of focus and into slow motion. One of them seemed to be saying something. Rex could see his mouth opening and closing. And all were looking at him as if he were some pitiable wretch off the street.

Finally, the woman got up and crossed to the front of the desk. She put a hand on Rex's arm. 'Perhaps you better just go on home now, Mr Trenton.'

Rex was not quite sure where he had been for the preceding moments, but now the voice broke through. It was a tone and the gentlest of touches that he had not heard or felt for years.

And suddenly he ached for it.

.   .   .

It wasn't the first time Stat had been telephoned from a police station in the middle of the night on behalf of Reginald Alexander Trenton, but he had hoped he had seen the last. He'd spent the past twenty years watching helplessly as Rex slipped further and further into the dark world of nothingness that was fame without achievement. His behaviour getting worse and worse as his clips on the news and in the tabloid and music press became shorter and shorter. Arrested time after time for drunk and disorderly, lewd behaviour, or possession.

Now, after he had been clean, sober and at liberty for the last nine months, it seemed he had spectacularly managed to combine all three.

10

THE MYSTERY OF THE LAWNMOWER

Pip was still very much in two minds about turning up for work in Marilyn Harper's garden the next day. Especially as Graham Tweedle appeared to be back in force, with his equipment and a rotund young assistant, perhaps for reinforcements. But, for some reason, Marilyn seemed to be acting rather nicely towards the pair of them. Tweedle's appalling obstruction to her gardening plans last week, not to mention any distress at having thrown her daughter out the previous day, apparently quite forgotten.

'You know, Mr Tweedle, I really am most awfully sorry for the hoo-ha last week. I wasn't quite thinking straight, not really in full possession of the facts, so to speak. I'm sure you under-stand. Would you like a slice of suet bread pudding?'

'Oh, well, thank you very much, Mrs Harper. That's... *kind* of you. And please, call me Graham.'

'You're a professional, Mr Tweedle. I absolutely respect that. I just wanted you to know that, despite my little... *aberration* last week, if there is anything I can do to assist you with your work today, please do not hesitate to ask. And there's plenty more where that came from, if you and Stacey would like it.' Marilyn sniffed slightly as the lardy square remained resting in Graham's hand. 'Oh yes, plenty, plenty more.'

'Please don't encourage her, Mrs Harper. I never hear the end of it when she breaks her diet.'

'Oh and look, here's Pip now. I'm sure I can ask him to help if you need it. He's really proving terribly flexible. Aren't you, Pip dear?'

'Aren't I what?'

'Very flexible!'

Pip stared at her. 'If you say so.'

'I do, dear. Now step this way a moment, a word if you please.' Marilyn took his arm, a little too foxily for Pip's liking, and turned him away from Tweedle towards the back of the house.

'There's still something wrong with my mower, Pip.'

'Oh really, you think?'

'Yes, yes, don't think I haven't noticed those enormous things you've been wearing on your head. Do you know though, they might be quite fetching if they didn't flatten all that hair. Have you considered a bit of a trim at some point, by any chance?' Pip pulled his head away from Marilyn's hand, which seemed intent on demonstrating. 'So, what do you think is wrong with it?'

'Hasn't seen a barber for fifteen years?'

'Not the hair. As if you didn't know. The mower, dear.'

'Engine.'

'Really?'

'Sure of it.' He was not. But 'engine' was ludicrously encompassing and if a few more hours' work might be wangled on the pretence of trying to fix it, he wouldn't have to attempt to approach anybody else this week.

'Can you fix it?' Worked like a dream.

'Well, I can try. Might take some time. Shall I get started?'

'Absolutely not!' Marilyn screeched. 'Harriet's seen my lawn stripes and wants hers exactly the same. Just find out what is causing it. And, Harriet says, plenty of the neighbours will also need help with theirs,' she winked. It was beginning to make his toes twitch. 'Now, be a darling and get to the bottom of it for me, then we can be of some proper service to our community, can't we?!'

Pip wondered if she wasn't in the grip of some kind of hysteria, but at least he still had a job. He turned back to the lawnmower, trying to work out what exactly he was going to get to the bottom of.

'If you could do that today, please. Got to dash now, so much to do! Oh, and there's a box of steak and kidney puddings in the utility room. Please take as many as you would like home for your tea.' She swept away, concluding, 'Good afternoon to you, Mr Tweedle, please continue with your most valuable work!'

Pip doubted that the one ring Calor Gas stove in his shed could run to heating a steak and kidney pudding. But Ma had appreciated the treacle sponge that was Mrs Harper's last offering, and so he guessed they would all be eating well again tonight. Between Ma and Marilyn, he certainly wasn't going without food, whatever else his current circumstances lacked. Like a cat, getting fed everywhere he went. Perhaps he could take one to Shelley, maybe to—

'Is Shelley likely to be home today, do you know?' Graham Tweedle appeared by his side as if he could read his mind.

'Why?'

'She was interested in my equipment, that's all.' Graham straightened his shoulders, holding his precious noise meter behind his back.

'Think she'll be busy for a while,' Pip concluded and walked off. She'd be too busy for either of them, he was quite sure of that.

Pip wheeled the lawnmower back to the shed and stared at it for a bit, as if just by looking he might glean the inspiration to diagnose it, not to mention the requisite skills to fix it. In the end, he gave up and went to trim the box hedge. A couple more hours of avoidance and he knew his time was running out. He returned to the shed, picked up the petrol carton, kicked open the door, dragging the enormous beast behind him, and set off home, balancing eight steak and kidney puddings in the grass collector.

'Knocking off early again, son?' Bill said warily as Pip wheeled the lawnmower up the path towards him.

'I need a favour, Bill. I have to fix this thing before tomorrow and no idea how.'

'What's wrong with it?'

'It makes a hell of a racket, really rattles, you know? And backfires, a lot. I think that's the main thing.'

'Hmm,' Bill stroked his chin, but looked delighted none-theless. 'Well, you leave it with me, son, and I'll see what I can do.'

Pip was only ten minutes delivering the puddings to Ma, but Bill seemed to have it all sorted.

'Think that's your problem.' The old man looked a little disappointed at the paucity of the task as he sniffed the petrol carton. Then, to Pip's horror, he dipped his finger in and licked it. 'That's not petrol, son... it's vodka.'

11

THE VILLAGE TURNS

It had been another restless night, and Pip managed to avoid Mrs Harper for most of the next morning. It was a meagre job, but it was all he had and he felt sure that the disclosure that he'd been fuelling her lawnmower with vodka would end in his dismissal. And not just for the clear evidence of gardening incompetence; he suspected that a hefty stash of vodka in her garden shed was unlikely to be something that Marilyn Harper would want to be common knowledge.

But she seemed remarkably calm about it.

'Vodka? I see. But what on earth possessed you to put vodka in it?'

'The tank was dry, so I just filled it up from this carton marked *petrol*.' Pip held it up in mitigation. 'I really am sorry, but I didn't think to taste it, you know.'

'Well no, of course not. And I am sure I can't imagine how that got there.' Marilyn bristled, but instantly brightened. 'Anyway, you can't be blamed, Pip dear. The important thing is that you found out what it was. Or...' she paused and beamed. 'You knew already! Yes, yes, that must be it! Pip, darling, you are an absolute genius!'

'What?'

'Oh yes, indeed! And now I have the secret of its operation.'

'So... you *don't* want me to get it drained and filled properly?' Pip continued to gingerly feel his way through this conversation, convinced he could not be following it correctly, despite how hard he was trying to keep up with this woman.

'Absolutely not! We shall just claim it as an act of genius so typical of your gardening expertise. I discovered you first, they'll remember that!'

'Right,' Pip nodded, but was at a complete loss now.

'Although perhaps we won't go mentioning where you found quite that amount of vodka, shall we? Now, be a darling and make a start digging up the dahlias at the back, would you? And leave everything else to me!'

'But you've only just put them in,' he called after her.

'Irrelevant!' she sang. 'New plan!'

Pip had no idea what she was talking about, any more than he had known a dahlia from a dandelion two weeks ago, but he was learning fast, and a tiny bit of calm edged into his bones as Marilyn left him to get on with it. Every couple of minutes, he would look up to check that she, or anyone, was really not there. He'd got away with it, again, and the unexpected solitude amidst the greens and reds and yellows of this brimming garden was beginning to trade him a few moments of peace. Moments where he could stop and look and listen and smell something decent and sweet and pure. Cutting away. Clearing space. Planting anew. Moments where he could convince himself that, if he could just keep up with these people, this might be somewhere he could begin to shape another identity. His foot remained slow, and he breathed a little easier.

These were the moments he would hold on to...

It soon became clear that the whole of south Bedingford was convinced, too. Marilyn returned later to announce bookings for nine other gardens in the road in the next week, another half a dozen around the corner in Yarnside Drive, and a special commission from Harriet Pordage to begin tomorrow afternoon.

Pip was well aware that going from one to seventeen gardens in two days was a conspicuous victory that could completely transform his current prospects. He should be celebrating. But his foot was tapping already and the nerves rising like lava.

Too much? Too many people? Too much lying...?

He immediately went in search of another patch to tidy, and the volcano subsided. Less than eager to unleash it again with inactivity, he kept on working well into the evening, and it was eight o'clock by the time he finally packed away and returned the tools to the shed.

Still, he dawdled, pulling his jacket tightly around him as he made his way back out to the road. It was not cold, but he needed to feel something close to him. The evenings were always the worst. Nothing to do, nowhere to go. Sometimes he would steal himself to sit and watch TV with Ma and Bill, but the room was not much bigger than his shed and always dominated by the children's toys and minor violence.

Aimlessly, he ambled over Yarnside Bridge instead, to the village centre and towards The Huntsman's Arms. He hesitated on the threshold, but turned away. Too depressing sitting drinking on his own, he couldn't join in and seemed to have lost the skill to start a conversation himself.

'Alright, Pip?' Dr Page crossed the road in front of him, accompanied by Councillor Pennington, who nodded with a faint smile. That was odd, Pip thought, until he remembered that both of them were on the list of new customers Marilyn had presented this afternoon. He turned to see the pub door being held open for him. So he followed in.

The Huntsman's front door didn't go anywhere. Directly in front was a massive old chimney with solid doors to the left and right, which meant that visitors had to choose between the bars on either side with nothing that might help them make the choice. The locals just referred to it as 'which side of the fire?' and it had become a bit of a badge for those in the know. Which side of the fire you were spoke volumes in Bedingford.

The bar on the left was quieter and more ordered than the one on the right side. Visitors, newcomers, the more serious types, or anyone just wanting a bit of peace and quiet would usually be 'left-siders'. On the rare occasions Pip had set foot in the pub, he would always go in there. It was just easier, less effort, and more anonymous. Tonight, however, emboldened by these small hints of acceptance, he was going to do it differently.

The 'right-siders' were plentiful tonight, and the noise was thick and competitive. It had been so long since Pip had been in a crowd, it was an assault that unbalanced him. He fixed his eyes on the two men ahead and followed to the bar, leaning on it for stability, next to the incongruous three-foot high replica of the Statue of David. Just one of the pub's many little Renaissance touches that were the inevitable consequence of the landlord and landlady being called Mick and Angela.

'Oh, better add another pint for Pip here, Mick,' the Councillor sighed.

Pip was more than happy to accept a freebie from this man, who had never so much as given him the time of day before, but was slightly irritated by the lack of enthusiasm in the request. It was not as if he was asking. For anything, really.

'Thank you,' he muttered to his new friend, nonetheless.

'So Pip, well then...' Pennington continued to struggle. Pip watched his face fidget into various positions and let him get on with it. 'So, have you had a good day?' he finally plumped for.

'Alright thanks, Mr Pennington,' Pip shrugged over the rim of his pint glass.

'Councillor.'

'Eh?'

'*Councillor* Pennington.'

'Yeah, whatever.'

'What have you been up to today, then?' Dr Page took over as Councillor Pennington seemed to be ruffled out of all proportion to this exchange.

'Oh, you know,' Pip shrugged again. 'Bit of Tennyson this morning, checked on the horses, renewed me membership to the National Trust, that sort of thing.' Out of the corner of his eye, Pip noticed Shelley approaching the bar, trying to divert laughter as Councillor Pennington stared at her.

'Hi, Pip. How's it going?' she smiled, although he could not fail to detect a little wariness in it. No less than he expected. He had not behaved well the last time they had met, throwing his opinions around like that and then just waltzing off.

'Half of Thumper and Ros' usual concoction please, Mick,' she said.

'Sheldon, I didn't know you were back,' Dr Page interrupted. 'Your mother never mentioned it when she came in to the surgery this morning.'

'Is she OK?' Shelley's wary smile got a little warier.

'Just a social call.'

'No thanks to you if she wasn't,' Councillor Pennington sniffed. Pip stared at him. 'I don't suppose you're back because you've changed your mind since last time? Your poor mother was so disappointed.'

'Oh, Terence,' Dr Page rolled his eyes. ' Please could we give this a rest?'

'I would very much like to have that luxury, Malcolm, but it's the burden of public office that I have to care about my community.'

'She wanted me to lie, Councillor,' Shelley protested wearily. 'To make up some phoney environmental health case for potential damage to the growth of her dahlias from an outdoor orchestra.'

'It's not phoney, Sheldon, not in the least! Vera Swainsborough at Oak Farm said her pigs refused to eat the last time they had a concert at the Manor. So it's far from nonsense, there's serious damage to be had, and not one attempt made by those Wolstenholmes at appeasement!'

'Appeasement?' Shelley muttered. 'Some of these bloody locals need tranquillisation.'

Pip snorted, but quickly corrected himself. It wasn't helping.

'Well, nice to see you both,' Shelley lied. 'Join us next door if you like, Pip,' she nodded left-side before glancing back at the Councillor. 'It's a bit noisy in here.'

Pip hesitated, but as Councillor Pennington continued to bluster, he slipped off his stool and followed her.

'Thank you,' he said simply as they passed through the doors.

'Well, I can't imagine you'd be enjoying an evening with those two old windbags,' she smiled graciously.

As expected, the 'left side' was much quieter than the right, and Pip had to admit he was very glad of it. A couple were having dinner in silence and two old men were playing dominoes in the corner, but the rest of the room was empty. Even the lush velour wallpaper and soft furnishings quietened the place, and Pip's senses calmed.

'I'm just waiting for Rosamund Pordage,' Shelley said, as she set the two drinks down. 'She wants me to waitress one of her posh events in London tomorrow night – she's a high-class party planner. Funny how I'm still the one buying the drinks,' she grinned.

'Doesn't sound too appealing. Will you do it?'

'I'd really rather not, but I expect so. We used to do it together for holiday money when we were students. I was pleased to see the back of it, to be honest, but now it's her business organising the sodding things, I occasionally still get the call. Only when she's really desperate, thankfully.'

Pip nodded, couldn't think of anything else to say, so just sipped his pint.

'So how is my mother, really?' Shelley saved him again.

'Not sure I can say it in polite company.'

'Nothing polite about it,' Shelley returned his grin.

'Well, if you really want to know, now she thinks the excellence of her lawn stripes is caused by her mower being fuelled by vodka.' Now he'd said it, and to her, he felt an uncontrollable urge just to convulse with laughter. For a split second, this place, these people, his situation, was not some great big scary monster that racked his bones every day with its roar; it was just bloody funny.

'I can't begin to work that one out.' Shelley didn't seem to have the same dilemma and giggled heartily.

'Me neither. But the petrol can in your shed? Apparently it's vodka. I put it in by mistake. Told you I'm not a gardener, didn't I?' he smirked. 'Anyway, she's somehow connected the two, I think. News seems to have spread like wildfire. I've got seventeen jobs in the next two weeks now, including Pordage palace.'

'Oh well, that's good at least.'

'Guess so... So, the stash in the shed? I suppose it's the drink, is it, that makes her so... volatile?'

'She's teetotal,' Shelley said, her smile falling. 'It'll be Dad's.'

'Oh, really? Well, that's a bit of a relief, I suppose.'

'Is it? Well, don't be tempted to drink it, must have been there for years. Him and a few of the villagers used to have a potato-brewing moonshine operation in the cellar in the '80s. He'd hide the stuff everywhere.'

'Ha, really? Wish I could find it then. I could make a fortune at the moment, a lot cheaper than the Smirnoff at the village shop.'

'Yeah well, like I said, I wouldn't drink it if I were you.'

'Na, more of a cake man meself. That's my bit of addiction, you know,' Pip laughed and was gladdened by the return of hers, feeling a tiny bit more comfort seeping into his bones, his feet stilling and his words stacking up in his throat. 'So, how's it going at the Manor? Any developments with the acoustic screens? I am sorry about the other day, by the way. It was arrogant of me. Like I said, you're the expert.'

'It was pretty helpful, actually. For some reason, Stat – the promoter guy – seemed to take more notice of you.'

'Ah, yeah,' Pip raised his eyebrows. 'Difficult for someone with your particular disability, innit? Especially in the music business.'

'Disability?' Shelley played along.

'Born without the aid of a dick.'

'Well, goodness, we all need one of those from time to time!' Rosamund Pordage plonked herself down opposite, swinging several carrier bags onto the seat next to her. 'Thank you, Shelley, you're a star.' She took a hefty swig of gin, mango and passion fruit. 'And hello,' she smiled at Pip. 'Rosamund Pordage, pleased to meet you.' Pip gingerly shook the tips of her outstretched fingers. 'Discussing penises with village newbies, Shelley? Do tell all.'

'Sorry,' Shelley mouthed silently at Pip. 'Ros, this is Pip, our mothers' new gardener, even if he's not sure that's what he is. My money's on some kind of musician. Pretty deft understanding of the politics as well as the acoustics.' Shelley grinned, but it was quickly lost as Pip looked quite horrified. 'They're not all bad,' she attempted a joke. 'Sorry,' she repeated aloud this time, but it clearly was not working.

'Oh, not one of those ghastly opera singers, surely. No, clearly not.' Rosamund continued to look Pip up and down, managing to convey both disdain and approval at once.

'Well, I'm sure you've got lots to talk about. I better be going... Sorry.' Drinks spilled as Pip got up, knocking into the table and pushing past Rosamund's chair.

He stopped on the pavement, alarmed by the quickening of

his heartbeat, and the unstoppable urge to tap, tap, tap on the ground. Timothy Smollett waved from the pub garden. He ran. Again.

And, as he counted his pounding footsteps on the silent paths and pavements, Pip was reminded once more that, if normality was what he was seeking, clearly he had a long way to go yet.

12

A BALL, A LAWYER AND A
DANGEROUS CIGAR

Shelley had been up half the night sketching diagrams, trying to ignore the futility of attempting to sound-screen an opera with a few off-cuts of tarpaulin. The prospect of another late night dodging drunken lawyers at Rosamund's city ball was even less appealing than it had been yesterday. But she had some more promising errands to run in London tomorrow, so she steeled herself and hoped that Rosamund's 'pocket money', as she called it, would stretch to a few buckets of coffee.

Pip was sitting on the low wall of the Smollett's house at the top of Trefusis Lane as she made her way to the station. He was staring at his feet, which were relentlessly moving, as she had noticed they had a habit of doing. There was a closed distance about him, as if no world existed past a foot or two around him. He did not look up as she approached, even as she said his name, appearing totally lost to something.

'Pip?' She was right beside him now.

'Oh... hello,' he said with the bemused startle of someone having their barricades unexpectedly invaded.

'Hi, you alright?'

'Yeah,' he replied, unconvincingly. 'You? How's the Folly?'

Shelley could almost see the blanket being hauled.

'Oh, it's great. Crazy atmospheric,' she laughed, sitting down on the wall beside him. It seemed to startle him even more and a touch of fright came to his eyes, which made her want to double the apologies. That or just give him an enormous hug and spirit him away to some place of refuge. *Where did that come from?*

'Glad I've caught you, actually. I didn't fancy sneaking round to Mum's to apologise,' she said instead. 'I'm really sorry about last night. We both clearly offended you and—'

'Oh no, no, of course not,' Pip quickly protested, as if coming out of water and gulping as much air as possible to reverse the deprivation. But there was nothing more.

'OK, look, I just wanted to say that.' Still nothing. 'If you're sure you're OK,' she persisted.

Pip sighed. 'Yes, yes, of course... I'm sorry, it's just that— Oh, you don't want to know.'

'Try me.'

A similar fright returned immediately to his eyes. Shelley contemplated yet another apology, but as the silence pulsed on, decided he might just be inviting her to mind her own business.

She saved him the trouble, unzipping her rucksack. 'I've got a train to catch so I'll be off, but I also wanted to say that I'm staying in London, so why don't you have the Folly for a couple of nights?' She held out the big iron key, but Pip did not move or speak, his eyebrows knitting.

'How about that?' she prompted.

'Why?' He was looking at her as if she had two heads or something. Christ, he was hard work.

'Well, it can't be easy living in a shed, can it?' she laughed. 'Thought you might like an ordinary roof over your head for a couple of days. Well, it's not that ordinary, and it's hardly the Ritz, but it is technically indoors.'

'But who knows what I might do?' He was looking at her with that direction again; his incredulity seemed entirely sincere. It did nothing but strengthen Shelley's resolve.

'So lay off the heavy cake then, eh?' she smiled. 'Look, just take the key. You remember the padlock code? I'll be back Friday morning.' And giving him no further opportunity to resist, she left.

'OK,' he whispered after her. 'Thank you...'

'I am surprised to see you here, Shelley. I expect my sister strong-armed you, but not really your style, is it?'

Russell Pordage had surpassed himself this evening. It wasn't just the formal black-tie suit, the Great Hall at Lincoln's Inn was teeming with them tonight. Russell's suit, however, had the subtlest shimmer of midnight blue. It was so elusive that it was only when it caught the light of a chandelier that you could be sure it was there at all. His tie glistened, like catching the wing of a magpie in the sun. Shelley realised she was staring at Russell's throat and feared he had noticed, as he smiled, that easy smile. She also feared she might be flushing. There were a hundred of these penguins in this grand hall this evening, how come it was Russell Pordage who managed, in the most discreet kind of way, to stand out?

'Well no, I... hypocritical, I know.'

The break in her voice was only the most recent of the day's annoyances. That she was wasting so much of the time she desperately needed for the opera preparations serving drinks, dressed in a pornographically short, off-the-shoulder cocktail dress to this bunch of city tossers, had already been compounded by finding that the ball was in aid of the campaign to re-legalise fox hunting. Shelley had a long-held distaste for the 'country sports' that were so popular around the village as she was growing up. She had been grounded for a month for joining a feeble anti-hunt protest one year. Despite it being the occasion when Russell was first blooded, it was he who persuaded Marilyn to let her out on bonfire night.

And that was another disturbing thing: Russell had so far been the only man in the room who had taken a champagne flute from her tray without glancing down her cleavage. He smiled again as he took the glass with a polite sip and it was Shelley who found herself saying 'thank you'.

Russell looked as if he was about to say more, but at that moment was joined by the most elegant woman in the room. Expensively cut and highlighted poker-straight blonde hair, in a sea of expensively cut and highlighted poker-straight blonde hair, she walked one stilettoed foot deftly crossing in front of the other in the telltale manner of the professionally trained.

'There you are, Russell. Sir Neville has been waiting at his table for over ten minutes. You know we really shouldn't keep him.' She smiled down (a full six inches) to Shelley, with the mouth-turning acrobatics that broadcast breeding and politeness, along with the utmost contempt.

'Yes, of course, Isobel darling,' Russell turned obediently as the woman stamped her property by linking his arm. 'I understand,' he concluded, but he was looking at Shelley.

The evening was interminably long and Shelley vowed she would never, *ever*, do this again, however much Rosamund pleaded. Russell was on his second brandy as he contemplated taking a luxury Cuban cigar from Shelley's after dinner tray.

'Should I, Sheldon, or should I not?' Again that smile, the slight lilt to her name ensuring she was in no doubt that it was delivered tongue in cheek. It had puzzled her from childhood how Russell was the only person who could ever make it sound OK. She never knew how that was, but when he did use her full name, he always managed to do so whilst still acknowledging her well-known distaste. It had an affection to it.

'I know, I think I will, but could you please see if there are any of the Louixs?' He leaned in a little. 'I never like the smoking veranda, perhaps you could bring it out to the terrace.'

Of course, Shelley could have asked any of the other waiting staff to do the job for her, but she was tired and fed up with this evening and felt like a break. Besides, there was something kind in the invitation, and Shelley needed a little kindness.

'You're in luck,' she said as she carried the silver tray outside holding one single, gossamer-thin wrapped cigar. 'Rolled it on the thighs of a couple of virgins in the kitchen myself.'

'Ha! I expect no less from you. You always went the extra mile. Surprised you could find any, though.' Shelley pretended to tut, but Russell was offering her the cigar. 'Come on, we'll share it. I heard you hadn't quite managed to kick the habit. And believe me, these babies are as smooth as silk.' Shelley hesitated. 'Come on, the night's nearly over. Your repulsive duty must surely be almost done now. I'll vouch for you if anyone questions this tiny absence, OK? For old time's sake?'

The words transported her back to the very first cheap cigarette they had shared, behind his sixth form common room when she was thirteen. He had just led six other prefects out of it, lining them up between her and Robin Dibble's gang. They never bothered her again.

What the hell, Shelley thought. There was an emptiness in her chest that might just as well be filled by something ludicrously expensive. *Breathing* was probably the much better option. Horace had always drummed that into her. As a singer for whom it was a tool of the trade, Horace had made breathing a way of life. That he was still doing it at all after all the years with Marilyn was a blessed mystery.

The cigar was smooth as silk; the inhalation curled around Shelley's throat and into her lungs like mist over a hilltop. She was calmed, delighted and alarmed all at once. The last thing she needed was more encouragement and another bad habit. Especially one that would normally cost her the whole evening's wages for two or three puffs. The momentary relief was winning though, and she stole another draw before passing it back like an illicit joint.

Russell hardly took any for himself before returning it.

'Don't encourage me,' she laughed.

'But I think encouragement is exactly what you need, Shelley. And deserve.'

Shelley lost a little of her schoolgirl playfulness at that. The silky smoke-filled air on this terrace seemed to have sparked with the hint of danger. That, too, Russell seemed aware.

'Oh, I know,' he sighed. 'It's all very well for me to say.' He turned to rest on the stone pillar overlooking the lawn, his softly spoken words seeming to merge with the wizard beard light of the cigar smoke. 'But I do know how difficult it can be growing up in a household where the expectation might as well be papered on the walls.'

'Yes, I suppose so,' Shelley hesitated, wondering how the conversation had deepened so seamlessly.

'Well, perhaps now you're back home, there might be more opportunity for us to talk. It's been so many years.' Russell turned it equally seamlessly back. 'You're helping with the opera, I believe?'

'Mmm.'

'You don't sound too sure.'

'Oh, I am.' She held out the cigar, annoying herself that she was watching it go. 'It's just something's come up and it's proving a little difficult to solve.'

'How so?' Russell took another couple of cursory puffs and passed the cigar back to her.

'I promised Matthew that I could help him with some acoustic screening, to lessen the sound leaving the Manor grounds into the village. You should see some of the Council's conditions! Really, Russell, I wish someone like you could have been batting for Matthew when all this was drawn up. I think it's been like shitting an elephant for the poor love. It's no wonder he hasn't had his finger on every button. Anyway, the bottom line is that I have to do ten thousand pounds' worth of sound proofing for a bunch of petunias and a tangerine at Christmas.' Shelley drew too heavily on the cigar at that and felt a little lightheaded.

'I'm sure you'll work it out, Shelley. You always were so imaginative with these things. And tenacious,' he added. 'Do you remember when you hung my mother's velvet curtains from the goal posts in our garden and played Metallica on your little CD player, to see how much difference the curtains made to the volume?'

'Ah yes,' Shelley giggled, finally. 'Well, I just need something similar to that now, but bigger. A lot fucking bigger! With any luck, I think I might have figured out the metaphorical velvet curtains, but the goal posts?' She shook her head at the hopelessness of the quest.

'What might you have in mind?'

'Yacht masts?' she laughed. 'I don't know, really. I'm hoping some inspiration will strike me before too long. Preferably something that's vaguely achievable.'

'Well, I have every confidence in you. And when this is all over and you are the toast of Bedingford, I hope I will have the opportunity to celebrate with you as well.'

'Oh, I'm not staying. If this is a success, I'm going back with Dad to Las Vegas.'

It was the first time Shelley had said this without feeling relief and excitement; suddenly a touch of fright rippled in her chest, her hand flew to her earlobe and she pulled it.

'You still do that,' Russell smiled, swirling a final smoky exhalation into the cool night air. He gently touched her arm. 'Like I always say, Shelley – don't worry. Don't *ever* worry.'

Russell Pordage had staminous lungs that could bark a courtroom into rapt silence, but turned down a few notches it had quite a different dynamic. Shelley was blessed and cursed to be finely attuned to such changes in dynamics. And tonight it was even more soothing than the supremely high-ticket cigar.

13

THE CALL OF THE DRUMS

Pip finally made it to the first door on his mowing list after Shelley left him. Marilyn had suggested he spend the first day introducing himself to his new customers, assessing the size of their gardens, the condition of their mowers and how much vodka they would need for the tanks. But, he was ashamed to realise, even that was creating a debilitating level of anxiety. Shelley's surprising intervention seemed to have provided just enough distraction to propel him up Mrs Geddes' drive.

The day that followed turned out to be far more manageable than he feared. Everyone welcomed him, vodka bottles at the ready, or wallets open for him to make a trip to the village shop. Except for Timothy Smollett at Number 5, who got quite angry when Pip pointed out he had an *electric* mower. Pip tried to delicately suggest that he could 'probably' do a good job of his lawn anyway, but Mr Smollett sent him packing. He relented by the end of the day, gleefully presenting Pip with a ropey old petrol strimmer he'd unearthed at the back of his garage.

Pip's embarrassment at the nonsense of this whole thing had not really wavered by the end of the road but, alert to the continuing undercurrent of condescension at almost every house, he slipped into the role of snake oil salesman and just took the money. It was a good job he didn't have a drink problem though, the amount of vodka that was changing hands in Bedingford that day. The village shop ran out by 4pm and Mrs Page had to resort to gin.

Surprisingly, Harriet Pordage alone treated him with some intelligence, subtly suggesting that Marilyn was delusional and that she was quite sure he was skilled enough to mow lawns perfectly well without the aid of alcohol. But to show willing, and not to upset her old friend, 'her man' Donald could do with a little help in the garden anyway.

The Pordage lawn was so vast it was mowed with a diesel tractor, so she was probably right.

'Of course it's all the most frightful mess,' Harriet sniffed. It wasn't. 'I am not sure that Donald can really cope any more. I mean, he's only 72. You'd think there was plenty of mileage left, wouldn't you?'

Pip shrugged. Really, he was not sure he could take much more of these people. But, he reminded himself, his situation had significantly improved since he had been doing.

Harriet was the last of the calls he was going to make today. He had coped reasonably well, he thought, and was beginning to feel a little calmer. But now, as he approached the corner of the estate wall, it all returned. He crossed the road towards the drum lock gate, and back again, ten or more times that late afternoon. It would be so nice to sleep in a proper bed for a bit, make his own toast, have somewhere to sit in the evening...

But he knew what would happen there.

He walked on and went home.

Two hours later, he succumbed to the inevitable and returned, with a small pack of clothes and provisions. Checking left and right at the gate, and again at the Folly door, he stood for a moment and tried to be rational. He had a key, for God's sake! How long was it going to be before he stopped feeling like the guilty party? As if he was perpetually waiting to be found out.

He slipped the huge key into the lock. It did not move. He tried to force it, but still it would not budge. So would this be it? After all that turmoil? Relief and disappointment traded insults in his mind. He leaned on the door handle. It clicked open, and he fell in. Of course, he had never conceived that it might have been left unlocked. He had not long come from a place where you locked up your toilet roll in case someone nicked it. It had only been a couple of weeks since he had stopped hiding his toothbrush in the shed.

The circular room looked quite different to how it had done only three days before. The light was warmer, the bulb changed, the table moved out a little, the sofa with a soft blanket thrown over it, candles on the windowsill, and wildflowers in a beaker on the table. He slipped off his backpack and went to make himself a cup of tea. It seemed completely the right thing to do; the thing he would do every time he came home to a place like this. Obviously then you'd sit down with a ginger biscuit (or six) flick through the post, stretch your gardening legs, and contemplate your dinner...

But it had to come. It was up there. He was down here.

He took his bag and stepped up the stairs.

For a while, he just sat on the floor and looked at the old drum kit, his feet paddling air, his drumsticks turning over and over in his hand. Then he got up and sat on the stool. For a while longer, he sat and stared. Shimmering gold shells, pristine white heads, the mirror rims sparkling up into his eyes. The stories they were telling him. Tracing a hand around the edge and across the head of the snare drum, and then all the tom-toms, slowly, one by one, he closed his eyes. He turned his head towards the drums as if they were speaking to him.

'You're beautiful,' he spoke back. 'You sound beautiful.'

He picked up the sticks. The nausea spiralled. Hovering

above the drums, they felt odd in his hands. Were they too heavy, or too light? How could he tell? His hands were shaking, his palms clammy. He had no tape for his fingers. What if he could not hold them? What if they just flew out of his hands as soon as he raised them in the air? Abandoning him again, as they had before, and all else eventually did.

He lay the sticks down on the rim of the snare. His eyes fell, head dropped, he breathed for a moment. The stick lifted, it tapped against the snare rim. So lightly. He stared at it, as if it had done it by itself. He drew the stick around the edge of the head. It made a different sound.

'Of course you can't!'

The old soundtrack played over and over in his head, the volume rising.

'Who do you think you are?'

'Stop getting ideas above your fucking station...'

The words prodded at his chest, first a tap, then a fist, then a knife through his heart.

'Of...course...you...CAN'T!'

And then he hit it. Crisp and resonant, it sent something new to his fingers. Raising the stick in his left hand, he brought it down square in the middle.

'I can!' The right hand followed, bang! 'I *can!* You can't hear me now! I CAN!'

Pip could not be sure if he'd screamed the words aloud, but the stick had hit the snare with such force the sound was still travelling up his arm. And it was being followed by another, and another, and another. Slowly at first like a marching cadet band, then rolling one after another until, sticks flailing, he was blasting round the kit with the full-blown artillery.

Within seconds he was lost to it, oblivious to every feeling but the motion of vibrations down his arms into the sticks, through his feet into the kick pedals, firing back from the drumheads and resounding through his whole body. The loss, the anger, fear and frustration rendered into sound. Until all else, even thought itself, became drowned out by it.

The evening darkened unseen, the rising moon's reflection off the crash cymbal startled him. He stopped, breathless and sweating, and somewhere else entirely.

Pip sank to the floor, cradling the snare drum in his arms, the tears falling.

The dam had broken.

14

THE HOPE OF YACHT MASTS
AND CAKE

'What is the meaning of this?' Marilyn threw open the kitchen window as a flatbed lorry reversed up her drive. It was carrying what looked like half a ship. The driver got out and handed Pip an envelope. Marilyn bustled down the path with an indignant wave and snatched it from Pip's hand.

'Oh, naturally... Excuse me!' The driver was already leaving, alarmingly on foot. 'I have no idea what this is all about, but my daughter no longer lives here, so kindly take whatever all this nonsense is away, right now!'

'No can do, missus, got a train to catch, another truck to pick up in Brighton at midday.'

'Not my problem, I'm afraid. Take this away immediately or I will call the police!'

The driver sighed, looking to Pip in the hope of assistance. None was offered.

'Well, have you got a forwarding address then?'

'No, I do not.' The driver shrugged and turned to leave. 'Take the registration number please, Pip, while I phone Sergeant Riordan.' Marilyn turned back towards the house, tearing the envelope in two and dropping it into Pip's compost bag.

The driver sloped back to his cab, fiddling with his phone.

Pip hesitated. He had felt an immediate frisson, knowing instinctively what the cargo might be and where it should be headed. But it did not feel safe to go back to that place. Something had been allowed to happen there, and he knew, like the addict that he was, it would not be possible to settle for just a little bit – it was all or nothing. He had already decided that it had to be nothing.

But at this moment, the customary terror in his stomach appeared to be something else. Was it *excitement?* He could not tell, and the lorry driver was not hanging around long enough for him to debate it any further.

He grabbed the torn paper and banged on the cab door. 'I know where this has to go. It's not far and you could still catch your train...'

The protest group at the main gate was half the size of last week, and twice the arthritis; the truck had rumbled through the gate before any of them could even get to their feet. Pip directed the driver, not to the Folly or even the Manor itself, but left from the gate along a gravel path parallel to the west wall, stopping behind the deserted stable courtyard, between the beech trees and the row of poplars.

The driver dropped the keys into Pip's hand and jumped out. 'But what about the lorry?'

The driver pointed at the envelope. 'It's all in there, I think...'

Shelley was kneeling on the grass behind the Folly, rolling out a sheet of padded material next to an assortment of other bits and pieces of various shapes, sizes, colours and conditions, her eyes fixed in concentration. She looked up as Pip ran across the grounds and her smile was immediate and genuine, in some unspoken enthusiasm for something. As if everything could be an opportunity, she seemed to pass seamlessly from one to the other. It reminded him of himself in better days.

'Hi, Pip!'

Now he was here, it seemed he had forgotten how to speak, and why he had run all the way to do so. He searched the ground for something else to unlock his voice.

'You got some material then, that's good.'

'Is it?' she laughed. 'This bit from my old college, the rest begged from everyone else in my contacts book.'

'But it looks great! The lacing down the middle, for the wind, yeah?'

'Yeah...' her smile was curious, experimental. He knew he was surprising her and, strangely, it gave him confidence.

'Genius! You might want to do that with a couple more pieces though, do you think? Might provide a bit of additional flexibility? Wind's often south westerly in these parts in the evenings. Think it's all the hot air from the old farts in Yarnside Drive.'

'Yeah, I was thinking that,' she smiled, much more securely now. 'Although Christ knows what happens then. Don't suppose you've had any bright ideas about the small matter of hanging it?'

'Yeah,' he replied boldly. 'Come this way, madam.'

It was Shelley's turn to be speechless as they approached the lorry. Pip handed her the keys and the torn envelope. She opened it and held the pieces together.

I was incredibly successful in getting this shipyard in Southampton off a fraud charge last year. Funnily enough, I still have one or two documents in my safe at Chambers. It really wasn't that hard to persuade them they could spare a few bits. You can borrow the lorry as well for the duration. Hope it might help? Russell.

Shelley sat down on the grass and puffed out a steady stream of air. 'Oh my God, it's perfect!'

'Yeah? Well, can I help?'

It seemed he could not stop himself...

'I brought this,' Pip said at the door of the Folly the following afternoon, sheepishly holding out a heavy fruit cake, as if it was not conceivable that just bringing himself was enough. 'From your mother.'

'You are joking, of course.' Shelley couldn't avoid the lilt of hopefulness in her voice.

'Well, let's just say she didn't object when I suggested it.'

'Oh well, thank you, I suppose. Cup of tea then, before we start?'

'Sounds good,' Pip replied with a nervous smile as he followed her into the Folly.

'My mother has always thought everything can be cured by cake.'

'Yeah, I have been treated to quite a few over the last couple of weeks, as it happens.' He tentatively sat down at the table. 'It might be the only thing I agree with her, though. Not sure I've ever found anything that wasn't made at least a little better by a bit of cake.'

Shelley naturally thought he was joking, so laughed, which clearly embarrassed him, so she stopped.

'Obviously, I'm not saying it's a terribly sophisticated therapeutic method,' he shrugged with a slightly easier, self-deprecating smile.

'Well then, better tuck in.' Shelley cut two generous slices of the lardy cake. She had always been a bit sneery of this habit of her mother's as just another illustration of her lack of emotional sophistication, but it had to be said that the Worzel Gummidge approach to life's problems did often prove soothing. Shelley felt a pang of affection for her mother then. Perhaps this was all she could offer. But then she remembered she had had these pangs constantly over the years, like a taut rubber band pinging her back to hope and renewed attempts to connect. She knew she really needed to give these up.

'Not sure why she has to put suet in *everything* though,' Pip clucked, ungluing his tongue from the roof of his mouth. 'But at least the crates of it have gone from the drive now. Says she won't be needing them anymore.'

Shelley nodded distantly. 'My father's favourite.'

'I know it must be hard. I can see you care a lot about her.'

Shelley snorted.

'You do, it's obvious. And maybe she doesn't deserve it. Mr Smollett says she's always been a nightmare.' The levity seemed intended at loosening them both. 'Maybe she just has a lot of difficulty admitting when she's wrong. Don't we all?'

'True,' Shelley replied. 'Trouble is, this time she isn't. I can't give her what she wants this time.' Feeling a touch of rising nausea, Shelley thought this was a good enough opportunity to test his theory and took a hefty bite of cake. 'Oh well, less harmful than whisky or heroin I suppose— I'm so sorry, that was tactless.'

Pip looked at her without a hint of comprehension, and then he seemed to get it and disappointment flooded his face. Shelley opened her mouth for another apology, but he stopped her.

'No, it's OK,' he said softly. 'Do you know...?' He shook his head. 'Oh look, sorry, you really don't want to.'

'Try me,' Shelley said, again. And for a moment, it looked like he might this time. But just like before, he turned it away.

'Better get started, I think,' he said and strode outside.

And so the pattern was set for the next two days. Whenever he had any time between jobs and at the end of each afternoon, Pip arrived at the Folly. Most of the time he would sit quietly helping Shelley cutting and lacing canvas on the ground outside, or experimenting with ways to attach it to the masts. There were moments when he would smile and gabble enthusiastically, usually something pretty helpful to the many challenges of sound-screening an opera with college offcuts and a collection of yacht masts. But most of the time, he worked intently and wordlessly. Sometimes she would speak to him and he would be so engrossed in his task there would be no response at all. But Shelley was finding his silent help unexpectedly calming, as well as useful. It seemed completely obvious to him what she was trying to do, and he seemed genuinely interested in her work. It gave her confidence. Although he was never still – looking around him constantly, his feet or fingers tapping out rhythms – his company was relaxing; the urgency of the task forgotten, time did not seem important to him. She had never seen him check a watch or a phone, wasn't sure he even had one. He was just there, focused on the now, the task in hand and, when she spoke, on her.

But, like a forest deer, so quick to startle and bolt at the slightest crack of a twig.

'You've done this before?' he asked as she studied her drawings. 'When you've been engineering other events?'

'Only in my head,' she shrugged, and hesitated. 'I've never really engineered another event.'

He put down the rope he was holding and his head cocked. It was all he needed to do to remind her that he was totally focused on her response.

And her breath caught a little.

'I'll get cake?' he smiled.

And she told him then, the hopes and dreams and plans that were never allowed out of her mouth. The silent fantasy that had grown ever since she had watched her father record *For One Night Only* when she was nine, and the brief whirlwind of 'popular' recording and appearances that followed. Marilyn had been horrified at her husband's new direction. As far as she was concerned, it was like Thomas Hardy writing sketch shows. She had allowed Shelley to accompany Horace to the studio and the variety performances that followed, only because she was convinced her young daughter would make a nuisance of herself and be one more disruption to Horace's plebeian leanings. But he, all the musicians and crew, had been astounded at how little trouble she was. Sitting quietly at the back, captivated by the man at the mixing desk, watching him turning all those coloured knobs back and forth, pushing and pulling sliders up and down, punching buttons and grasping headphones. It seemed to Shelley, her ears trained to each of the musicians behind the glass or on the stages, that each movement, big or small, was at exactly the right point every time.

She begged her father to let her leave school and take her with him when he got his first American tour and his Las Vegas residency shortly after. He wouldn't, and never had, unusually siding with her mother. The music business was no place for someone like *her*, they said. For the first time in years, her parents agreed on something. And Shelley really wanted to be a thing they agreed on. Taking her remarkable hearing and sharp brain into academia seemed a reasonable compromise.

But, like all compromise made entirely from someone else's will, it never was reasonable.

'I'm sorry about that,' Pip said simply.

Shelley shrugged, embarrassed by what she perceived as the paucity of her suffering. 'I'm lucky I get to do it now. Even if we are making it up.'

His lips twitched, slowly repeating, '*we*?' It seemed to confuse him. Then he shook his head. 'You speak for yourself.' And the twinkly grin secured her a little more.

It was only when she tried to turn the conversation towards him that some invisible line was crossed. He would go so far and then become agitated. His feet would twitch and tap, the rest of him closed up, he'd look away, go back to his task, or just leave. Sometimes, his eyes would flick to the upstairs window of the Folly, as if it wasn't her and this task that was keeping him here at all. Occasionally, he would disappear inside for a few minutes and Shelley knew he was upstairs; she could just see his shadow through the tall arched window, sitting with the drums. Each time, he would come back less agitated. Each time, she would gently suggest he play them. Each time, he would decline.

Shelley could not begin to fathom why he was so clearly fascinated by Robert's old drum kit whilst maintaining such a stubborn refusal to play it. It was obvious enough he must be able to, wanted to. And, as far as she was concerned, there was nothing stopping him. But her attempts to loosen his resistance were met with the full range of responses, from polite decline, to vehement refusal, to silent ignoring.

'Why don't you go and play?' she persisted the next day. 'It's OK.' She had been at the wall when he'd arrived a few minutes earlier and he was clearly embarrassed to be found coming down the stairs when she returned.

'It isn't,' he replied, almost pushing past her.

'Why not?'

'You ask a lot of questions.'

'It's how I communicate. How do you do it?'

'I listen.'

Shelley left it, but the agitation persisted all morning, his endlessly tapping feet hitting the side of the screens and rucking the canvas. She sighed, putting down the rope she was lacing.

'I'm going up to the Manor in a bit,' she said. 'Stat wants me to help stage-manage the orchestra. He seems to have revised his opinion of my dicklessness since I fielded those calls from the District Council.'

Still, Pip refused to join her smile. No words even, just intently watching her face, as he always did, as if waiting for something more to come. She had got used to it by now, but today the intensity in his eyes seemed to be saying his agitation was her fault.

Then it just melted into regret. 'Oh sorry, yes of course, you want me to go.'

'No,' she protested as he made to get up. 'I only meant that I may be a while.' She glanced up to the Folly window. 'So why don't you...?'

He was staring at her again, but his voice was low. 'No.'

'It's just that—'

'I said no.'

Pip returned to nailing canvas to one of the masts with even more gusto than before.

'Alright,' she conceded. 'I'll be off then. You stay if you want to...'

She got halfway to the path.

'Wait!' he called, sheepishly pulling a torch from his back pocket. 'Take this.'

'Why?'

'Please. Would you—?' he screwed up his face, as if pushing the words through quarantine. 'Could you, maybe, shine it up at the window when you're on your way back? Say, when you get to the shrubbery at the end of the lawn?'

'Why?' she repeated, but then just nodded. Shelley was a past master at having to read between the lines of someone needing something. She took the torch and left.

Perhaps this was progress enough.

Stat was stomping around again in front of the Manor, cigar hanging from his mouth, phone permanently glued to his ear. He beckoned Shelley whilst trying to wrap up another babysitting conversation.

'Look, lovey, I can't do anything about this one now... I know, Rex, I know, it's a travesty... You *what?* Oh, for fuck's sake, it's only a bit of dog shit! You know how lucky you are to only get community service this time. No, I can't... No! Now please, this once, just *do it,* Rex!' Stat thrust the phone back into the lining of his shorts, pulling another from his back pocket. 'I'll call you back... Jesus,' he sighed. 'Do you want another job?'

'I think there's enough to do here, don't you?' she smiled. 'Edge of Darkness again? What is it this time?' Now that Stat had warmed to her, she rather enjoyed his rants and showbiz tales.

'LSD.'

'Oh God, really?'

'Yeah, Lead Singer's Disease. It's a terrible affliction, causes all sorts of delusions. When they've got it, they don't really think they exist unless they're reading about themselves somewhere every week. Although, apparently, a little photo in the *Daily Mirror* doing community service in Regent's Park doesn't count. Rex has downed his pooper scooper.' Stat lit another cigar with the remains of the old one and blew out smoke in a long-suffering sigh. 'A few days ago, he decided his ego was so deflated it needed tequila to resuscitate it. After six months dry, he was on the floor after a couple of shots and fell asleep in Piccadilly Circus with his trousers around his ankles. At least that's what he says. The Lord Speaker's wife, who apparently fell over him, is considering charges for assault. For fuck's sake, what am I going to do with him then? So far he's got away with a few days community service for drunk and disorderly and he's still staging rebellion! Damon's threatening to go back to his bar in Spain unless they re-open the Lumpwood Club especially for him, Yebut's homeless as of next weekend, and Alan's joining a Ceilidh band in Essex because the fiddle player has an empty caravan in Brentwood for a few weeks. Trying to keep control of this lot is like stirring a box of Maltesers.'

The smaller of Stat's phones buzzed again, a loud fart ringtone which he had assigned only to band texts. It was a picture of a bar top in Soho, lined up with six double shots and a jug of grapefruit juice. Rex had written simply, 'You don't take me seriously.'

Stat left for London within minutes. Shelley considered that his opinion of her had risen far too high if he expected her to take charge of the opera company's stage management recce this afternoon, especially as Matthew and Victoria were nowhere to be seen.

'But I don't know what I'm doing!' she called after him.

Stat turned, paused, then said one of the hardest things a man of his age can say to a young woman.

'Yes, you do.'

As it turned out, the Musical Director was cock-a-hoop to be met by Horace Harper's own daughter and he left far happier than he had arrived, with Shelley's 'confident' assurances that everything would be in place for the technical rehearsal on Thursday. Including her father.

Shelley could only hope that would be true. She had not heard from Horace since his letter last month, despite regular messages left on his phone and at his hotel home in Las Vegas, apart from one email forwarding a flight number, arriving on Thursday morning, with the make and model of a car. Presumably the one he expected to be picked up in.

It was a curious juxtaposition, she thought as she walked back to the Folly – her shoulders dropping and her smile securing with every blooming rhododendron – between the settling calm of this place she loved so much and the chaos of her absent father, with whom she had very little connection anymore.

And she would be leaving one for the other...

Approaching the shrubbery at the end of the lawn, she fumbled in her bag for Pip's torch and flashed it at the Folly in the distance. Pip was at the window immediately. He smiled and waved. By the time she got to the door, he was downstairs and swinging his backpack over his shoulder. No words but looking at her directly, as he always did, there was a calm about him she had not seen before.

'See you tomorrow?' she said, there didn't seem a need for any more. He nodded. 'Stat's put me in charge of the technical rehearsal preparations as well. If I'm not here when you arrive, you just make yourself at home. How about that?'

Pip smiled again and walked to the door. He stopped and turned a final time.

'Thank you...'

15

THE PROBLEM OF AN AUDIENCE

Pip was very much in demand now, making his way up and down
Trefusis Lane and Yarnside Drive converting lawnmowers to
vodka. Every one of his new customers insisted it improved the
cut of their lawn. Mrs Page even claimed superior results for her
gin. And the demand was growing as more and more residents
wanted it too. All of them were the same: he'd drain the tank, fill
it with vodka and mow the lawn; then they'd say, that'll do, thank
you, come back in a month. It was both a relief and a disappointment. Obviously he needed the work, the busyness was distracting, and he had come to appreciate mowing, with its small easy
victories. But he couldn't blame them – it was such a racket that
they all slammed their doors and windows shut as soon as he
started the engine.

Besides, he had somewhere else to go now.

Three times in two days Shelley had left him at the Folly to
play the drums on his own. He hugged the confidence to himself
and let the relief wash through him. It was OK. He could still do
it. That night in Belgium, when the fear had first reared out of
nowhere and smashed over him like a tidal wave, had left him

torn, tattered and drowning ever since. But now he knew that his passion for the drums had remained completely watertight.

Of course, it was obvious now. It wasn't the drums that had failed him. It was *the audience*. All of them. At first with their lack of expectation, eventually with their excess of it. So, surely, all he needed to do was to keep it a secret. Just for himself. If he only made his noise for himself and remained silent to the world, then perhaps the world would *finally* become silent to him.

It appeared, however, that Pip's appearances at the Manor had not gone unnoticed. Rosamund cornered him in the Pordage garden.

'Shelley's moved back into the Manor, hasn't she?'

Pip was climbing onto the Pordage's mowing tractor, but she stood right in front of him.

'Sort of,' he replied. Rosamund stared at the top of his head. He removed his ear defenders.

'That is not progress,' she said, looking crossly at him, as if whatever problem she had with Shelley's whereabouts was his fault. 'And you've been making yourself at home there too, it seems.'

'Helping her with the festival preparations, that's all,' he muttered. He had no idea how she would know. Especially as her mother had not been protesting at the gate for days now. In fact, the demonstrators had dwindled to old Mrs Beresford and her sciatic dachshund, and Marilyn said that she was only there because her telly was on the blink.

'Yes, Russell told me about her pioneering sound screens. Really, my brother is ridiculous sometimes. I mean, yacht masts? Whatever will he think of next?'

'They're pretty helpful, actually,' Pip said.

'Yes, he's that too. And whatever it is Russell is supposed to be doing, Shelley always wins. Do you get what I'm saying?'

'Not really, no...'

Marilyn bustled up the drive then.

'Mmm, very good, Pip,' she sniffed, surveying the Pordage front garden.

'Yeah,' he replied, finding himself unexpectedly undisturbed by her presence and even a little relieved by her familiarity. 'Especially that bit in the corner over there, look.' He pointed to an untidy tuft of weeds with a wonky stripe mown through the middle of it.

Marilyn's eyes shone. 'Ah yes, very good indeed!'

Marilyn had made him promise that, whatever jobs he was given, she would always be his priority. Pip knew from the look on her face that he had chosen exactly the right way to show it. And the smile they shared then felt a bit like... *trust?* He examined the feeling, remembering a time when the notion came quite naturally to him. A time when the world was a benign sort of place and he had an unerring belief of his place in it. When people were pleased to see and hear him, and he was rewarded with their applause and expectation; not crucified by it. It was an odd feeling to glimpse something like that again, however fleeting. It felt... *nice*.

'Mind if I get on now? I'm running a bit late,' Pip diverted the memory from where it was inevitably heading, his foot beginning to tap.

Marilyn turned to Rosamund as he left them. 'Oh, my dear, what a find he is!'

'Mmm, a bit shifty though, don't you think? Very direct when you talk to him, never takes his eyes off you. It's rather disturbing.'

'Well, he spends most of the time ignoring me, I know, but when he doesn't, he really is remarkably attentive! Don't think I don't know why you really wear those things on your head, Pip dear!' Marilyn called after him, not expecting a response. Inevitably, he didn't turn from his protected mowing. 'But we all need to shut the world out from time to time, don't we? There's no harm in that.'

'Yes,' Rosamund concluded with a languorous stretch of her neck. 'He might just have to be a bit careful whose world he's getting himself into...'

Pip was accosted by Mrs Beresford's rolled up newspaper as he attempted to get Marilyn's 'borrowed' ladder through the Manor gate that afternoon. He tried his best to run past without hitting her with it, or treading on her yapping dog.

'What exactly *is* their problem?' Pip lay down the ladder to help Shelley assemble the homemade screens to take to the Manor wall. 'I know this place is completely anal about quiet, but a bit of singing for a few nights?'

'I know,' she smiled. 'It's caused a lot of problems in the past. The odd concert Matthew's tried – even charity ones to support the village – certain people have been very vocal in their opposition. Apparently, it spoils their enjoyment of their own properties and is an invasion of their human rights. Or something.'

'Some people just don't know when they're well off.'

'I suppose everybody has their limits. Even snowflakes can be a noise nuisance to something, did you know that?'

'Well, of course I didn't know that!' Pip snorted, but there was no derision in it; he was captivated.

'A snowflake can add thirty decibels to underwater noise levels. Never going to bother us of course, but easily enough to annoy a porpoise.'

As he laughed, sitting in the middle of this beautiful place, Pip had a sudden, improbable feeling that they were the only people who had ever been here. He raised his eyes to her again as she resumed her task. Hers were crossed slightly, her head turned in the way it always did when she was trying to tune into something. He had done that for years and, in that moment, it felt completely right that he was sitting here with her. He hadn't felt 'right' anywhere with anyone for such a long time, he had a very real desire, in that same moment, that *he* was the something she was listening for.

His foot twitched.

'I saw Rosamund earlier,' he dowsed the urge to run with an attempt to turn the conversation again. 'She seemed interested in what you were doing *back* at the Manor, as she said. Didn't seem all that pleased about it.'

'No, she's never liked me coming here.'

'Why not?'

'Oh, it's a stupid old story. Her family and Matthew's have bad blood going back centuries, that's all. Apparently, an ancestral Pordage lost the estate in a card game about three hundred years ago. Matthew and Victoria are completely uninterested in any of it, but Ros and Russell's family could never let it go. Ros, in particular, is very influenced by her mother, and Harriet is a very accomplished flag-bearer for the woes of the past.'

'Yeah, that does sound stupid. I'm not sure about her, you know, she has an untrustworthy mouth.'

Shelley laughed at him, but was reminded that she had not yet been paid for last week's waitressing, and Rosamund had promised no cocktail dresses. The latest in a long line of her old friend saying one thing but meaning something completely different if it served her purpose.

'So, you've managed to escape all the old village ghosts and stories?' Encouraged that Pip was speaking at length, Shelley felt it safe to return the enquiry, and hoped it wasn't too contrived. He did seem to be relaxing over the last couple of days, since giving her the torch. There were even glimpses of what she might call *'conversation'*.

'How long have you lived here?'

'Oh, well, difficult to say really,' Pip replied, not entirely freely. 'I first came here when I was seven, but it was on and off for a long while.'

'That's fostering, I guess?' she gently fished.

Pip shrugged. 'I was here pretty much permanently since my 15th birthday. In the end, Ma and Bill refused to send me back. Things got... well, things changed for me, and my father could never really handle it.'

Pip signalled his withdrawal from the conversation at that point by getting to his feet.

'That doesn't sound all that good, Pip. I'm sorry.'

He shrugged again. He didn't have many memories of his father that he hadn't obliterated and was not keen on handing them out to others as if they meant something. But his foot was tapping again, his eyes drawn unstoppably to the upstairs Folly window. 'Do you want some more coffee, or are you going up to the Manor again soon?'

'Yeah, soon,' Shelley replied, sensing that might be all the co-operation for the day. She knew a veiled request when she heard it. But her knowing smile seemed to disarm him and he sat back down. Encouraged, she continued. 'I don't remember seeing you at St Bride's.'

'No, I went to the Cathedral School... Yeah, I know, it's always a surprise.'

'I'm sorry...' Shelley did not think her eyebrows had raised that much.

'Don't worry about it. I'm used to it. People can't help what they see and hear. Anyway, Bill and Ma never paid, of course. I used to be good at something, that's all.'

'Not percussion, is it, by any chance?' she laughed. 'Why don't you go and play? It's OK.'

'It isn't,' he repeated firmly and immediately, both fear and warning in his direct eyes.

'Unless I leave.'

And so she did.

16

LOOKING AT THE SAME MOON

Horace Harper was too big for England. He knew that now more than ever as he sat on the enormous bed in his suite at the MGM Las Vegas, looking out over the luxurious pad that had become his home. He had had the same room for four years, give or take a few appearances elsewhere. Of course, it was a remarkable room by British standards, wide enough for a decent pitch and putt. When Horace had first arrived and seen the size of the bed, he had been quite perplexed. What on earth were you supposed to do with it all? But now it seemed completely normal. On the occasions he had to travel to LA – or worst of all, New York, where hotel rooms were rabbit hutches in comparison – a nightly claustrophobia nagged him into wakefulness. He would sleep for a day whenever he returned to Vegas.

Horace stared forlornly at the bed. Going back to England would be ten times worse. *Everything* was just so... *small*. His New York claustrophobia tugged at his breathing. He could feel it already, niggling away, before he had even set foot on the plane.

And these brown-nosed twits on the screen in front of him weren't helping. He closed the lid of his laptop on the last of the hangers-on. That had been his third, and mercifully last, Zoom rehearsal with the Wessex Operatic Society. *Really, could Matthew not have done better than that?* But actually, he hated to admit, they were *quite* good. They'd been rehearsing for weeks with a stand-in for him (*ludicrously inadequate*) and had sent a recording of their performances, which they had copied step by step, eyebrow movement by eyebrow movement, from his last productions. Horace remembered every note of the assortment of popular arias he would be singing, of course, though barely any of the staging and movements. That was the point of sending him the video, he supposed, but he had not yet got through it without falling asleep. Then he remembered that it didn't really matter and gave up watching it all together. When *he* was on the stage, *they* would just have to move. That's all.

Through the last three Zooms he'd hummed along, interspersing 'helpful' notes to the cast. He was pretty sure that they'd got most of it, so there wouldn't be a problem with the performance. The only problem was the outdoors. Horace did not like performing outdoors, he liked walls. The air was unpredictable outdoors. Still, Shelley would be sorting that out for him. That was the point of her being there. Well, one of them.

A pang of conscience for his daughter arrived unbidden then. Horace always tried to avoid those. After all, Shelley had grown up alright. She was bright, attractive, attentive, not too pushy (he hated that in a woman) and certainly not stiff as a broom handle like her mother. He rather enjoyed her company actually, sometimes, as far as he could remember. Not nearly enough to settle for England though; he would be coming back to Vegas as soon as possible. Of course, he always came back to Vegas, but this time he would not have to lie about it. This time everyone would know that's what he was doing. And where he was staying.

The truth was that Horace Harper had left his family twenty-five years ago. This century it was time they understood it. He'd paid his dues, he deserved his freedom. His reward must surely now to be honest about it.

The conclusion calmed him and persuaded him he needed a little more reward. He texted Shelley:

> Sorry, I'll have to miss the tech rehearsal. I'm sure everyone knows it as much as I do and you have it all together. I'll be there for the dress on Friday…

When Shelley reached the Manor that afternoon, the final piece of the grandstand seating had been placed in the centre of the courtyard and Matthew was inspecting it, strolling up and down the aisles with his hands behind his back, like King Charles at a guards' parade. She could tell by the look on his face that he didn't have a clue what he was looking for.

It had been Stat's idea to squeeze in another four rows and sell the additional tickets on a special allocation at an inflated price. There was nothing special about them, but word of mouth about the unique setting of this endeavour had gathered so much momentum in the specialist press and social media, another ninety-six people immediately fell for it. Shelley suspected Matthew was just passing some time, distracting himself with another reassurance of the late arrival of his good fortune.

She set to work directing the skeletal crew to assemble the hay bales that they had begged, borrowed, and occasionally stolen from neighbouring farms, to help dampen the sound escaping to the wall. Everyone knew she was intent on giving this as much of a chance as she could and, in an unspoken response to her obvious commitment and gentle encouragement, they worked like Trojans in the remaining hours of the day to get it done.

Shelley only managed to check her phone as she was returning to the Folly. Since his text to say he would not be there for tomorrow's technical rehearsal, Horace had drip-fed her inbox with eighteen more emails over the last six hours, each with some punctilious request or question. Her eyelids fell, wondering how she could ever have complained about Horace's radio silence over the last few weeks. Compiling yet another list in her head, she walked, her phone to her ear, first to the chauffeur company – for the fourth time, they reminded her – then to the tool hire depot in Winchester to check her booking for the mobile crane to get the screens up on the wall tomorrow. As they had confirmed this morning, they politely reiterated, they would be there at midday. Then she, mentally at least, started on the rest.

Her head crammed full of cranes, planes and automobiles, the muted sound of drumming breaking through her consciousness was a little disorientating. She scanned around and behind her, the shrubbery at the end of the lawn long past. She stopped, patted her pockets and checked her tool belt. No torch. She briefly considered going back to the Manor, but it was surely too late now. Besides, as the sound became more distinct, she didn't want to.

Nevertheless, she tried to mitigate her forgetfulness by making as much noise as possible on her entrance to the Folly, banging the door and stomping around downstairs to announce her arrival. Nothing penetrated the relentless drumming. She gave up and sat down at the table to listen.

Eventually it stopped, and before Shelley could contemplate running out of the door and pretending to come back in again, Pip came dancing down the stairs. Still holding his drumsticks, rapidly tapping and rolling against the walls and banisters, as if they were just extensions to his arms, shimmying across each step in perfect rhythm and fluid movement, completely in his body and lost in a world of his own, his silent lips popping to the beat. Shelley could not help a delighted grin spreading across her face, and a warmth flowing through her body to... oh, all sorts of places.

He stopped dead at the bottom of the stairs, just staring, the disturbing hint of fright, which had gradually been replaced by something much warmer over the last few days, instantly returning to his eyes.

'Jesus Christ, Pip! That was fucking incredible!'

He didn't move. Shelley's excited smile dwindled.

'I...I'm sorry, I forgot the torch.' She didn't like the break in her voice; it seemed to match the fear on his face. Something had completely changed.

'Really.' His eyes were a little scary now. 'Wasn't it obvious enough to you or something? I don't want to be heard!'

'That's a pity,' she ventured. 'Because I like to listen.' It was brave, she could feel that.

'I can't be heard...' His voice was quieter now, the fire in his eyes dimming. It gave her courage.

'But I don't get it, Pip. Why ever not? What a gift!'

'Gift?' he snapped back. 'Yeah, handed to me on a plate.'

'Pip, I—'

'Forget it.' He waved her away and walked out.

'Damn,' she breathed, kicking herself that this surely spelled the end of his visits this time. But as she looked out of the window, he was kneeling on the grass with one of her sketched diagrams in his hand, manically unlacing one of the panels and refastening it in a different way.

She emerged outside, the remainder of Marilyn's cake in hand. 'Peace offering.'

'It's crap. The coconut is completely inappropriate.'

She laughed. His nose twitched, as if he couldn't quite work out how not to join her when he was that annoyed.

'I'm very sorry, Pip,' she said, kneeling tentatively on the grass beside him. 'I should have known how important it was to you.'

He stared at her. 'Why on earth should you? I shouldn't have snapped at you like that. *I'm* sorry.'

'So why is it like that, Pip?' she ventured. 'You're very impressive, you know. Don't you know that?'

'I don't want your sympathy!'

'Who said anything about sympathy?'

Pip fidgeted, pulling up a handful of grass. 'Sorry. Of course not. I did it again. Sorry.'

'Stop apologising, it's OK, really. I am just very, very nosey.'

Pip sighed. 'I wish you could understand,' he implored her with his eyes. 'I have to do it for me now, not anyone else. It's mine. There's very little that is now, but that is. It has to be just... *mine*.'

'OK,' she nodded, even if she could not entirely grasp it. 'So how about we say no more about it then? They're there,' she pointed up to the top window. 'You just come and go as you please, whenever you want to. I promise not to listen, always carry a torch and I won't mention it again.'

He was still staring at her. 'I... I can't... now.'

'Why not?'

'You—' His shoulders slumped. 'You're very kind,' he concluded, with difficulty, looking at her as if she was some kind of Mensa puzzle.

'Nothing to do with it,' she grinned. 'It's only so I can ensure your continued labour. It's the tech rehearsal tomorrow, the Council will be monitoring and I really need to have the screens up by then. The crane's due at midday.'

Finally, he cautiously smiled. 'OK...'

The crane arrived. The wrong one. Half an hour of phone calls and Shelley was forced to accept that they could not send the right one until tomorrow morning. Another half an hour to the Council failing to postpone the noise monitoring until tomorrow's dress rehearsal, then Stat phoned to say that the orchestra was having difficulty fitting into the pit area. The opera company was complaining that the hay bales would interfere with their ability to get on and off the stage. The company delivering the plush seating for the kitted-out stables around the courtyard (the *really* expensive seats) was late and due to arrive in the middle of the technical rehearsal. Horace's stand-in had a sore throat. And it was raining.

It was going to be a very long day.

By 7pm and the end of the tech, Shelley thought she could crawl into bed and sleep for a week. But she had to wait. The Council letter was hand delivered at 8.30pm. The Music Noise Level had been recorded in Trefusis Lane exceeding permitted conditions by 7dB for a period of longer than fifteen minutes. A further breach had therefore occurred and if this happened once more, a stop notice would be issued closing down the rest of the summer season.

Matthew started panicking. Nothing seemed to penetrate, until Victoria slapped him.

Stat was pink and the air was blue with where he was going to shove their poxy seven decibels. But he calmed down enough to conclude, 'The screens will manage that tomorrow though, won't they?' It didn't sound much like a question. Shelley nodded. They ought to, and more, she was confident of that. There was no point sharing her remaining worry that Horace's vocal capacity *may* just be a *teensy* bit more powerful than his stand-in.

She fell into bed that night. She and Pip had worked tirelessly to help achieve this. Now she just had to get enough sleep to see it through. She looked out of the Folly window. The moon was three quarters full and bounced off the crash cymbal, sending tentacles of light across the room.

She wondered if he could see it, from the shed across the village...

17

THE DRESS REHEARSAL

'I've taken the day off. I'm all yours.' Pip was at the Folly by 9am the next morning. It was not entirely true, he only had one small job to do that day. All his customers were vodka'd up, the village had returned to its normal hushed routine, and he to a much reduced level of occupation. A kind of focused equanimity had even descended over Marilyn in the last couple of days.

But more than that, he had been feeling the rising trepidation in Shelley's voice whenever today's monitored rehearsal was mentioned. He had woken this morning with an unfamiliar and all-encompassing urge to be the one to do something about it. He glanced at her now, a lump appearing in his throat. She'd be gone in a matter of days. *If* this was a success. It was an uncomfortable tension, therefore, to feel so deeply that he wanted to help her make it so.

Shelley was growing more nervous as the morning ticked on. She talked when she was nervous. Pip could barely keep up with half of it, whilst trying to follow her repeated 'suggestions' to check and re-check the screens. But there was a closeness about knowing these things about her: her hopes and dreams and passions, as well as her fears, spoken and unspoken. He wished he could tell his own stories sometimes, but something happened to his body when he tried, and the chaos descended. Watching Shelley's nervous energy somehow calmed him. He could hear her stories better, then. He could barely tell his own to himself.

The right crane arrived. Followed immediately by Horace's car. Mrs Beresford didn't stand a chance. Pip watched Shelley's head swivel between them, as the crane forked up the gravel towards the west wall and Horace's car sped towards the Manor front door. He touched her arm. 'You go. I'll sort the crane out.'

He could read the mixture of relief and caution on her face. Her design involved the acoustic screens being suspended on the yacht masts using their own winch mechanism for raising, lowering or angling. The screens were also laced in a very particular way, ensuring adequate overlaps to strengthen the acoustic properties. Strong winds could open the gaps unless the lacing was done precisely according to her design.

'I know,' he said. 'I know...'

Shelley didn't recognise her father at first. He had certainly put on weight since she had last seen him five years ago. There was a distinct tone of shoe polish to his remaining hair too, and an unmistakable layer of foundation. But for all that, his eyes seemed brighter, a sharper hue of green, more like her own.

Horace strode towards her without a hint of awkwardness and held out his hand. The hesitation was all hers, as his hand hung straight and confident. Was she really being invited to shake hands with her father? She wanted to hug him. Or rather, she wanted to want to. Shelley had had to imagine love for so long she considered herself rather good at it. But her imagination at this moment only confused her, merely hinting at what she *ought* to be feeling and giving very little clue to what she actually was.

Then she remembered how Matthew had greeted her.

'You're late,' she said.

'And?'

It was going to be another long day.

Shelley thought she would at least attempt feather-smoothing by first showing Horace around the beautiful court-yard setting. It looked like the tiny crew had worked through the night on the finishing touches. Morris and Tree were still there, stringing fairytale lighting from the highest of the stable lintels. The covered stables and the grandstand seating were dressed with velvet drapes and cushions; the stage fully adorned, the hay bales adjusted and disguised; the Palladian arch providing the most spectacular entrance for the audience. All with the backdrop of the Manor which would be uplit from the early evening. The surrounding grounds were a magical mystery tour of stalls, tables, chairs and picnic blankets in every nook and cranny. Horace was sure to be impressed.

He wasn't. He was expecting a 'proper pavilion'. Shelley suspected that Matthew hadn't done much to disavow him of that notion, but diverted her father from going up to the Manor to have a go at him by reciting the sales figures and feeding him the remains of Marilyn's suet fruit cake. Horace decided he would share it – as well as his opinions – with the Musical Director, and Shelley breathed a sigh of relief to have a few moments to check on her screens.

Pip waved from on top of the wall and she was surprised and delighted to see that all the screening was up, the crane operator was checking the winches and Pip was lacing the canvas overlaps. She felt an unexpected tickle behind her eyes and had to pinch her nose to blink it back. Relief, she supposed, that something was going OK. Someone was just quietly doing the right thing.

Pip jumped down from the wall, brushing his hands on his trousers. 'I think that's it!'

Shelley silently and gratefully scanned the screens.

'I think it is...'

. . .

Crane gone, winches checked and angled for the prevailing wind, one of the choristers arrived to tell her that Horace was not happy about the height of the back of the grandstand. Shelley glanced up at her screens for a final time, raised her eyebrows to Pip and, after days of her father's incessant demands, found she couldn't give a toss all of a sudden.

'Did he say the *height* of the grandstand?' Pip sniggered. 'What's he on?'

'He's a bit nervous of outdoor performances,' she replied. Horace always had been, since famously being unheard at an open air gala when she was 12-years old. Shelley had run to the front of house crew and reeled off a list of suggestions for improvement which saved the second half. He had been delighted. Ever since then, Shelley had associated the precision of her hearing with her father's approval. And she always enjoyed her father's approval as it drowned out the noise of him and her mother screaming at each other.

'I expect he thinks there'll be sound dropout up there some-where. I'll be spending most of the rehearsal chair-hopping to find out, and orienting him if there is.'

'Oh, really?' Pip looked improbably excited by that prospect. 'Can I help with anything?'

'Thought you'd never ask,' she grinned. 'You've obviously got a great sense for these things. I'd appreciate your opinions.'

'OK! You go back, I'll tidy up here and come over before it starts.'

'You know, I don't think I could have done this without you, Pip. Thank you.' She looked at him, wondering if her focus was as direct as his had a tendency to be, and sensed that it wasn't just his expertise that she was thanking him for. The direction of his clear blue eyes, the mischievous lilt of his smile (when it happened), the crease around his eyes when he laughed (increas-ingly), the growing ease and warmth of their conversation, had lifted her and given her confidence that she was doing something valuable. And that, together, they might just be able to pull this off.

'I owe you one,' he said.

'Do you?'

He glanced towards the Folly, unseen in the distance, and shrugged.

'Dream team, you and me,' she laughed.

Pip stared straight back at her. 'I'd like to think so.'

Shelley blinked, and could feel herself doing so. The chorister appeared with another note:

And have you got any more of that cake?

She looked to the sky, sighed indicatively, and ran away...

Horace was singing exercises alone on the stage when Pip arrived. Shelley was nowhere to be seen in the courtyard, so he leaned against the stage beneath Horace with his hands on the wood, transfixed. Close up, it was the most magnificent human instrument. The sound coming out of him was incredible. Pip could feel some of those notes in his rib cage.

Horace stopped to take out a notebook, giving Pip a perfunctory glance as he did so. He scribbled something, tore the paper off and held it up. The young chorister scurried onto the stage and took it from him, and Horace resumed his exercises.

'You've acquired a taste for opera, then?' Shelley appeared beside him.

'Sorry, what?' Pip said, finally taking his eyes off Horace.

'Yes, you are standing quite close,' she raised her voice and leaned towards his ear. 'I wouldn't recommend that.'

Horace's newly appointed messenger boy handed her the note. She sighed again. 'I did ask if he could perhaps take it down a notch or two. He hasn't spoken to me since. But these incessant notes are getting ridiculous! This is going to be impossible. I better go and *apologise.*' She accompanied the last word with finger inverted commas. 'I don't know what I'm thinking going away with him to America,' she laughed.

'*THEN DON'T!*' echoed unbidden around Pip's head, louder than any of Horace's notes. He had to check himself for reassurance that he had not shouted it.

'But I suppose he is a lot easier to manage indoors,' she concluded, and he breathed again...

Her 'apology' accepted, Shelley spent the dress rehearsal unencumbered by further notes, as she passed around the court-yard intently assessing the quality of the sound from every space in the arena. Well, half the spaces. Soon into the first Act, she paused to watch Pip quietly move from the left of one row, to the middle of another, to the right of a third. He'd taken off his shoes, as he often did. Each time he sat with his hands on the seat in front, with the most intense focus, his eyes scanning every-thing around him in each space, near and far, as he listened. He seemed to pay as much attention to the perspex ceiling above and the space around him as to the stage. They had a code, one finger to five, to signal where they thought the sound travelled best and where less so. Anything scoring only one or two was particularly noted and both of them would return to check it again. Anything still scoring low, Shelley marked on a seating plan. It comforted her that they always agreed, even when one of them had first highlighted something the other had missed. And, engaged in this game of musical chairs, she noticed she felt the calmest she had all week.

Remarkably, the dress rehearsal went with no further inter-ruptions from the stage. Shelley had to concede that, whatever his other shortcomings, her father knew his craft and his plat-form and as soon as the metaphorical curtain rose, he was utterly present, precise and autonomous. And, to their credit, the unfamiliar opera company fitted around him with the utmost grace, accuracy and faithfulness.

It seemed to relax Horace, too. He made straight for her when they had finished.

'Shelley love, I'm sorry. It was a long flight, I was a bit bothered by quite how *outdoors* this stage is and, as you know, I will not be contained by bureaucrats. But you have clearly worked very hard for me. Now, Victoria is kindly organising a brandy and some dinner for my room, so I'll retire and see you in the morning. I know you will do a great job for me tomorrow. Thank you.'

Shelley thought she must be nearer the edge than she had conceived, as tears pricked her eyes again at that. But, as she watched him go, she spotted Victoria hauling Lidl carrier bags up the Manor steps, and Matthew on his knees at the door of one of the stable 'box seats', attempting to sew a torn seat cushion cover. And she knew with no further doubt who she was really doing it for...

It was an inevitably anxious wait for word from the Council that evening until Stat, phone to his ear at the door of his makeshift stable office, raised his arm with a tight, closed fist. A cheer went up through the remaining orchestra, singers and crew. Shelley watched the whoops and smiles ripple across the courtyard and had a fleeting, improbable feeling that she wanted to tell her mother. All her hard work had paid off, they'd made it, this might just work now. And what an arse Horace had been all day. Perhaps they would laugh about that. She dimly recalled that they did occasionally, from time to time...

But Stat appeared by her side, high-fiving and patting her on the back. Victoria joined in from an upstairs window, waving a pair of bloomers, and Matthew tripped over a seating barrier as he rushed to enclose her in the most encompassing hug.

Over Matthew's shoulder, she could see Pip standing a little way away, hands in pockets, head lowered but eyes lifted to her. His smile was like a sunrise, his mouth rising on one side first until it gently bathed his face.

He held his thumbs up, waved, and walked away.

18

SHOWTIME

Matthew had been confined to the library for the last hour. He was a nuisance, apparently. Stat and Victoria had tired of his pacing and constant offers to 'help' and packed him off with a copy of *Classic Rock Magazine* and a Terry's chocolate orange.

Matthew had always loved this library, a small oasis at the back of the Manor that he had so far managed to keep from the seedy crumbling of the other rooms. But today there was so much happening on the other side of the door, he needed not to be in it.

He stuck his nose out into the hall. The performance day buzz was palpable. The rooms full of people, pumped with activity. Players preparing, crew members running, event organisers counting and recounting. A faint hum of practised scales floated down the stairs, voices murmuring, sometimes laughing. Sung scales competed with guttural vocal exercises, which sounded like the singers were giving birth or on a fairground ride. Life. All of it a mushy blur in Matthew's failing ears, but it was life, the like of which the Manor had not heard in years. Matthew slipped out to be amongst it, to get nearer to individual sounds, sharpen the mush, and silence his own clamorous nerves.

It was a gratifyingly warm late June day, but not too hot for the early birds to spend their pre-performance hours lazing on the unshaded grass, and spending their cash in the criminally overpriced concession trailers that laced the lawns. It had been a stroke of genius on Stat's part to not allow the guests to bring their own food and to price the tickets according to the size and quality of the hampers included. Of course there were some that opted for the 'ticket only' package, but that was the point of the hog roast and the fresh bread oven. Forty-five minutes of sniffing that in the air, they didn't stand a chance.

Matthew moved hastily past the rotating dead pig and into the cream tea tent. His smile dwindled. The Bedingford Women's Wheelers had lobbied so hard to have a fundraising opportunity at this event. And here was Ma Godfrey, perhaps their least enthusiastic member, alone in the Wheelers' tent; a solitary tupperware box of homemade scones and a stack of paper cups in front of her.

'Well, where is everybody, Margaret?'

'Oh, I just don't know my Lord, no-one's turned up! No sight nor sound of any of the ladies since I arrived this morning. Bill's gone to have a scout round the village now.'

Matthew patted her arm. 'There, there, Margaret dear, I'm sure there's a perfectly good explanation for it. Delay in the kitchens or some such thing.'

'Do you really think so?' Ma sniffed. The prospect of spending her afternoon here alone seemed to be causing an unusual amount of upset.

'Absolutely sure of it, my good woman!' He was not, but then again, he was not in the least bit bothered. He'd be glad of the absence of the lot of them from what was turning out to be this glorious day.

Suitably soothed by some perceived authority, which was completely fictional but comforting nonetheless, Ma returned to the trestle tables to rearrange the paper cups and try not to worry, whilst Matthew moved on to the beer tent. Now this really *was* something and, unlike next door, alive with activity. Garlands of hops and vines, interspersed with fairy lights, uniformed young men and women preparing the tables, a small trestle on one side for a few barrels of local real ale and cider, the rest of the tent devoted to a huge variety of champagne, wines, exotic juices, and a Gin Palace. Damn, this could really be an event for the annual social calendar! Ascot, Henley, Wimbledon, Glastonbury... *Bedingford*. Matthew's imagination willingly took flight once again, from debt and despair, to his happy place on the sunny shores of solvency and salvation. And music.

It bothered him only slightly, as he continued his passageway through the grounds, that the Scouts and Guides burger barbecue was also missing, along with the Rotary Club tombola and the Parish Council produce stall. Odd.

But then again, quietly pleasing!

'Bit of a gap here, Matthew.' Shelley appeared at his side. 'Should we send out for word or something?'

'Not sure I can be arsed, my dear,' Matthew winked. 'It's not as if the village has given us an easy ride with this thing, is it? Practically ransomed us to get their snouts in the trough as it is.'

'True. Perhaps they have decided to back off after all. They've certainly left us in peace at the gate for the last few days.'

'Just leave it then, Shelley, I think. Perhaps we could let the apple juice and the hog roast people spread out a bit. If the buggers turn up after all, we'll say it's too late. Not in their conditions, ha ha!'

'Oh, and isn't that Victoria?' Shelley pointed towards Morris, driving a golf buggy across the lawn towards the Cream Tea Tent, Victoria in the passenger seat and a trailer full of Lidl bags being pulled behind. 'I think she's on it, don't you...?'

· · ·

Shelley walked back towards the stables. Out front it was the calm before the storm, but here everyone was running. She breathed deeply and resolved to keep walking slowly. Her anticipation was already building to uncomfortable levels.

Stat was in his office in the end stable, directing procedures like air traffic control, a walkie-talkie in one hand, a phone in another, a second and third phone in the pockets of his shorts. Horace had been busy all day doing press and radio in one of the stable galleries next door. Shelley cautiously looked in on him. It was fine. Horace looked absolutely delighted chatting on the phone to the bloke from Radio 2. He'd had Radio 3 this morning and was not half so interested.

Stat beckoned through the stable window. Scarcely missing a beat on any of the three conversations he was holding down, he waved a scrappy note and an envelope at her. 'For you. Tree picked them up at the gate earlier.'

The crumpled note was scrawled:

Thanks for the pass! Harriet Pordage's got me doing emergency maintenance, might be a bit late, but I'll be there by the screens don't worry! Good luck, Pip :)

Shelley recognised Russell's handwriting on the other envelope. Inside were two tiny bracelet charms, one of a treble clef, the other of a yacht. She opened the note to read:

I've the utmost faith in you, Shelley. Hope everything goes well for you afterwards and hope to see you then, Russell.

Hands behind back, 'Access all Areas' laminate hung around his neck, Matthew strode towards the backstage. Grey metal gates barred the way, another imposing security man standing between them. With both Morris and Tree deployed in Stat's 'area most likely' – by the beer and champagne tent – the backstage gate was being taken care of by another shaved head and bushy goatee, with the ubiquitous legs akimbo and hands crossed in front of his privates. Matthew gleefully waved his pass like a child with a gold medal. The man carelessly nodded and allowed him to step through the small gap between the temporary fencing.

Men and women jostled and passed, carrying instruments, shielding them from impact, plucking a string or two, polishing a bit of brass, puckering and unpuckering lips, rotating necks and shrugging shoulders. A sea of black and white movement, one way and another; they all seemed to know what they were doing and where they were going, even if it was in entirely different directions. Matthew winced as a crew man scraped a last-minute sound board across the corner of a Georgian baluster to avoid him. He squeezed past a tuba and, finally, agreed with Stat and Victoria – he was in the way. He shuffled out again, needlessly checking and plumping the seat cushions as he passed through the courtyard and back out to the lawns.

The sun was dimming now, casting a pleasing coppery glow over the proceedings. The air was still warm, with just one or two blankets appearing over knees instead of under bottoms. The lawns were heaving with people, the champagne, wine and gin kicking in and the murmuring chatter crescendoing to a mellow babble of laughter and conversation. Matthew felt his own swell of pride and expectation rising with it. Or it could just be nausea.

A bell rang, and the crowd began to shuffle. Twenty minutes to the performance start. Matthew gulped, fingering the paper bag in his trouser pocket and praying he would not need it. Picnickers rose and stretched and shook their blankets; queues at the luxury portaloos began to grow and fidget; barked orders at the wine tent became more urgent. The anticipatory buzz mounted as swathes of people funnelled towards the courtyard entrance arch.

Matthew picked up his pace to find his own seat. At the end and slightly in front of the first row were placed two tatty red velvet dining chairs. He lowered himself into the one nearest the string section, turning to watch the rows behind fill with people, creaking and scraping and banging on wood rising above the chatter. Shelley was pacing up the aisles, a phone to her ear. Matthew breathed in deeply, and momentarily felt as if he, too, could leap to his feet, raise his arms and launch into a conducting frenzy.

The five-minute bell rang. From his vantage point at the very side of the stage, Matthew could just see the heavy black curtain swaying, and could sense the maelstrom beyond. He could almost taste the adrenaline and hear the rattle of bottles of beta blockers.

Five minutes rolled into ten. The audience did not seem too bothered as they continued to chat, but Matthew was feeling very hot now, his breathing shallow and his heart beating a little too fast for the comfort of a 74-year-old. He looked to the empty seat beside him with some concern. But then Victoria emerged, in her wedding dress, with a feather boa and an ostrich plume hat.

'I brought us both a brandy, Matthew dear. It looked as if you were hyperventilating out here.' Victoria slowly lowered herself into the seat beside him.

'Oh Victoria, at last, haven't seen you for hours. How is it back there? I didn't dare look.' Matthew took the crystal tumbler and gratefully sipped at the brandy.

'Small crisis, I'm afraid. Second oboe fainted clean out. Poor blighter, can't be more than 19. They say it's his first big engagement.'

'Oh lord, oh dear, oh dear—'

'It's alright, Matthew. For heaven's sake pull yourself together. I gave him a shake, a tot from the hip flask and a slice of lemon drizzle. He's fine.'

A hush settled around the audience behind them. The lights

over the terraces slowly dimmed in sequence with the glow emerging over the stage. There was nothing more he could do now. The violinists were leading the procession into the orchestra pit. Matthew's mouth clunked open. He tipped the remainder of the brandy into it in a desperate attempt to activate his sleeping saliva glands. His tongue was like sandpaper, his head shrivelling and his heart rattling his ribcage so much that he thought he too might faint. He had never envisaged quite such a level of performance anxiety; he was not even on the stage and it seemed to be pulsing through his veins. The conductor strode into the pit and the audience's spontaneous clapping felt like a herd of elephants thundering over Matthew's head. Oh dear, oh dear, this was not pleasant at all. How on earth did these performers cope?

The conductor raised his arms, a practised disdain on his face as if he were chewing a toffee. The last vestiges of applause died to absolute silence. Instruments were raised to mouth and shoulder. Everyone hung over the precipice of one impending note. The violinists drew their bows, thirty-four arms gliding over a swell of strings, rolling out over the terraces. Wind players gurned in anticipation of receiving their instruments. Sticks were raised above the timpani. The second oboist licked cake crumbs from his lips and closed them over his reed. The collective inhalation echoed by the spellbound audience, the curtain raised, and there stood Horace Harper in all his foundation-smothered glory, his rib cage expanding like a hot air balloon, mouth opened, the first great notes effortlessly emanating from his large frame and—

BOOM!

An explosion ripped the air. Super-charged already, Matthew's bottom actually left the chair. The grandstand behind also rocked slightly as the audience collectively jumped, looking skyward, a hint of horror on many a quizzical face, searching fruitlessly for the source of such a frightful interruption.

But there was nothing.

Horace and the orchestra only skipped a beat and resumed

immediately, despite the faces of the players matching the unease of the audience. In the moments that followed, the musicians began to regain confidence, even if many in the audience did not yet manage it, continuing to fidget and look around, expecting some kind of explanation or follow up.

And then it came. In the distance, a throaty roar of an unknown engine, and one that had clearly seen better days. It futted and snarled into life. So faint in the face of the far closer proximity of the sixty-six-piece orchestra before them, but like an irritating gnat, it continued to buzz around the edges of the audience's consciousness.

Then it was joined by another. And another, and another, each back-firing alarmingly as it roared into being. Car alarms activated. A siren in the distance. A growing growl of machinery, equipment, appliances – whatever they were – crescendoed in from beyond the west wall, the bass line to the rattle and percussion of back-firing engines, thundering closer and closer, louder and louder.

Matthew and the audience turned towards the frightful noise. Shelley was already running to the wall. Someone was on top of it. The sound screens were unlaced and gaping in the breeze.

The conductor waved his arms with even more gusto, as if this was all a competition. But the audience was restless now, the dissonance of their growing mutterings rising to meet the onslaught from beyond the Manor walls. It had reached the car park now, setting off more and more alarms. The struggling orchestra's dwindling contribution to the melee was soon no match at all. Horace continued to employ his considerable lung capacity to just sing louder and louder, but he, too, was now failing to compete with the audience's discontent. Even Matthew's poor ears could hear distinct complaints being shouted between them. He and Victoria exchanged horror-stricken looks, watching helplessly as the audience, one by one, began to rise. Muttering criticisms, those with the benefit of the most flutes of champagne over the course of the afternoon shouting their displeasure. A few even began hurling the remains of their picnics at the stage.

The conductor turned, his arms falling, Horace finally stopping mid-note and the orchestra dying to an untidy thread of hapless squeaks. The conductor was looking at Matthew. And then, so it seemed, was the whole orchestra and opera company. Those in the remaining audience who noticed the direction of their discontent turned their gaze on him too. The rest were leaving noisily, grumbling and shouting, shielding their ears from the ongoing onslaught and shuffling in unison across the seats, flooding back through the arch and onto the lawns towards the exits.

A seriously malfunctioning diesel tractor circled the screaming car park before heading back to the Manor gate. The audience sweeping to their cars, every one of them found a flyer under the windscreen wiper: 'Horace Harper has a tiny penis', followed by a bank account and the telephone number of the Inland Revenue...

Shelley stood shaking and tearful by the west wall. The orchestra and cast finally retired from the stage, Stat flailing around trying to manage their bewildered disgruntlement, leaving Matthew and Victoria alone in their chairs. Horace fled from the stage to his own car for his emergency whisky in the glove compartment, only to find it showered with suet.

Matthew opened his mouth, but nothing came out. He just sat there, dumbstruck. And watched them all leave.

PART II

A SILENT SCREAM

0dB
...but it depends who's listening

19

FALLOUT & DESPAIR

Shelley, Stat and Victoria were up half the night, roaming the grounds, searching the village, desperately seeking clues; talking, talking, talking; batting incredulity between them. As if by not stopping, they would somehow find the answer to the havoc that had been wrought that evening.

But after the initial traffic chaos from the departing audience, the village was deserted by 10pm. Silent as the night descending, doors closed, curtains were drawn, not a person, or a lawnmower, in sight. Even the Manor seemed frozen in motion. The orchestra and opera company swiftly dispersed. The bewildered crew and concessions staff downed tools as the reality of future revenue began to dawn. Only Horace was left and he had fled to his room with his whisky, claiming 'emotional exhaustion'.

The only sound that remained by midnight was the flapping of Shelley's acoustic curtains in the stiff south westerly wind, unfastened from top to bottom...

As the night wore on and the three of them swooped and dived on a rollercoaster of adrenaline and despair, Matthew alone showed no emotion. Electing to stay at the Manor as everything fell apart around him, he offered no exclamations and no lamentations, displayed no highs or lows, as if he was wandering around in his own mental Norfolk. Finally shuffling to his beloved 'throne' chair in the drawing room, he closed the door on it all.

When they all got up the next morning, he was still there, sitting silently, eyes open, but not really present.

Victoria stayed with him whilst Shelley set off around the village again. A Sunday morning in Bedingford, just like any other. A few people going to church or pub, more washing cars or tending their gardens. All in quiet, contented activity, not a piece of machinery between them. Not one of them had anything to say to her. No-one knew what she was talking about. The traditional village hush had wrapped itself around the place once more, and it was as pristine as ever. All the litter had been removed, the remaining flyers gathered up and speared in a pile on the middle railing of the Manor gate. Like a musical box that had completed its turn, the village had closed around the incidents of last night and not a word more would be spoken about it.

Stat retreated to the closet of his makeshift office to manage the fallout. Throughout the day, the crew lined up for payment, phone demands escalated, ticket agency updates became frantic as more and more people requested refunds. Social media pinged and buzzed with one terrible review after another. The kindest of them acknowledging that it was a noble ambition in a beautiful setting with a promising programme, but what was the point if it was so clearly over-ambitious and under-managed that they could not even secure the co-operation of the community and a quiet enough environment to actually hear it?

It might have been the kindest response, but the words 'under-managed' were a dagger in Stat's heart. He could feel it twinge and pulse. He had *managed* in every way possible over the years. Since cutting his teeth in the business in the early '70s, when he did most of it from the pub or the bath, to the bewildering array of devices and networks available to him now, usually all at once. Minutely, ruthlessly, micro-, even over-, but never, ever *under* managed.

Stat stumbled out to the courtyard. The stage set suspended in its last place, the company and crew gone, he had written his final cheque. There was no more for the rest that was inevitably waiting in the wings, and he knew Matthew had no money to pay him back for all that had gone out of his own pocket already. It was over, in so many ways, for all of them.

Over-ambitious and under-managed...

He stared out at this beautiful Manor. No wonder Matthew tried so hard. Locating Shelley standing staring up towards the west wall, her magnificent acoustic screens still open in the wind, he knew that's why they all had. But for once in his life, Stat wondered if he had the stomach for any more. Sending word back to the band in London with more reassurances and promises was all he could do. But the promises were as hollow as the event coffers. He could not see how the season could continue now. Even if the Council (miraculously) allowed it. Even if the reviews did not see off any future potential audiences. There was simply *no* money left.

The deserted stage sang out to him with some long-forgotten glory as he watched his own curtain call, the one he had played in his mind so many times over the last couple of years. The Edge of Darkness' triumphant return, his last gift to them before gracefully bowing out on top. The empty terraces roared with the imagined adulation of the crowd, gradually rolling away to nothing now. And finally, he saw the stage as it was, silent and empty.

And Rex in a B&Q apron with Yebut.

He'd rather die.

Turning towards Shelley in the distance, her head cocked, listening for something still, trying to figure it all out, as she always did, Stat attempted to make as much noise as possible.

Willing her to hear *him* as he fell to the floor, clutching his chest whilst simultaneously trying to locate one of his phones in his breast pocket.

Shelley got to him first, snatching the phone from his hand, as his eyes closed.

20

A SNAKE IN THE GRASS

Shelley lay awake in Edward's old bed, Sunday night having long passed into Monday morning. She had not wanted to be alone at the Folly, and Stat would not be needing the room now.

She hadn't left the hospital for six hours. Stat was sitting up by then, demanding they give him his phone back. It was clear the nurses were tiring of him already, but for Shelley, it was the most glorious sound of the weekend.

The consultant delivered his cautionary conclusion that Stat had suffered only a minor heart attack, but changes would need to be made, starting with a period of complete rest. Stat responded to the news by spending an hour on the phone to the local police, securing Inspector Foster's cautious agreement to 'look into' the 'possibility' of a criminal offence having been committed on Saturday night. He then made Shelley promise to go down to the Council Offices in the morning whilst he followed up with the police. Finally she left, with a letter marked 'Private and Confidential' addressed to Rex, and a copy for his solicitor.

Well, it was something else to do whilst she struggled to make sense of anything that had happened this weekend. And it was good to have a focus other than Matthew's gaunt, shadowy presence in his throne chair downstairs, which flickered behind her eyelids every time she closed them.

Matthew had barely twitched when she returned from the hospital and broke the news of Stat's heart attack. He had not spoken a word since Saturday night; she suspected he had not even heard any. Sandwiches curled and endless cups of tea went cold at his side. A mound of crumbs remained whenever Victoria left the room, proving only that her vigilance was providing another field day for Beryl, or the rat family. Shelley was glad only that Matthew had some company through the night. Funny how she didn't have such fears for her 'emotionally exhausted' father down the corridor.

But at least Horace was still here. His evidence would surely be crucial for both police and Council. Her new twin missions for the morning.

Shelley heard the floorboards creak downstairs. Punctured by wakefulness, she got up and crept down, hoping that Matthew might finally have moved to his bed.

Matthew was still there, motionless, last night's cocoa on the floor, a thick skin covering it and a telltale rat trail from the remains of the accompanying supper. Beryl raised her eyes and gave a cursory wag, but Matthew did not move, even as she whispered his name. Not a flicker of movement or comprehension. He had his eyes closed and she hoped he was sleeping, but doubted it. She fetched two blankets and lay one over him. He must have got up at some point – a photo of Edward lay under his hands in his lap.

Shelley took the other blanket and sat down on the window seat. Horace, suitcase in hand, was creeping down the front steps. She jumped up again.

'Hey!' she whispered, pulling the front door to a quiet close behind her. Her father was already bustling across the gravel towards his replacement car. 'Where are you going?'

Horace dropped his suitcase but recovered quickly.

'Sorry Shel, can't stay in this madhouse a moment longer.' He picked up the case and kept walking. 'Got a plane to catch.'

'But... but what about the festival? What about Matthew? What about... *me*?' Horace stopped still again, as if caught in the headlights with the swag and desperately trying to think of an alibi. 'What about the job?'

Eventually he turned, smiled and touched her arm. 'We have to be strong, Sheldon, you know that. Of course I'd love to have you with me, but your mother needs you more. She will need you here.' Horace drew himself up to his full five feet six inches. 'I will just have to manage on my own.'

'You what?'

'I know, it's so hard on us both. It always has been. But we just have to put our feelings last.'

'You are joking, of course.' Shelley could feel a volcanic heat rising in her chest. The kind she had dowsed for years, but the seismic vibration was cracking the fault lines now. She watched as Horace's poor-me calm turned to alarm and realised she was shaking.

'You bastard!' The lava finally erupted. 'It's never about you, is it? With your eccentric, hysterical wife and naïve, *sensitive* daughter! Poor Horace, all he's ever done is provide for his family, but he's artistic, you know, can't be dealing with that kind of thing.'

'Shelley! What's come over you? Sarcasm doesn't befit you. Now come on, you know I'm right... I've got you something,' he concluded with inappropriate cheeriness, reaching into the car. 'A gardenia.' He held out a single bloom and an envelope.

The first thing he had ever bought her, the first time she had saved him, as he stumbled out of The Huntsman's, the first to hear the car coming round the corner at such speed. She could hear his voice still as he had tucked a single white flower behind her left ear. *'Now everyone will know about your beautiful ears.'*

He had tickled her lobe as she giggled. *'And you see, wearing one of these behind this ear, you'll always be my girl.'*

For years afterwards, Horace had sent her a gardenia on her birthday – a real one, a picture, a perfume, an ornament, something from all over the globe, with the message that she was the most important thing in his world and, even though he was not there, she would always be *'my* girl'. She never really liked the scent, she always gave the products and perfumes to Rosamund, who loved it. In amongst her mad to-do list before the rehearsals this week, Shelley had had to go to Ros and borrow some back. Because it didn't matter what she liked or didn't like. Horace did; *that's* what mattered.

She snatched the flower and ripped it to shreds, throwing the petals in his face. 'Fuck you!'

She slammed the front door and stood with her back to it.

The letterbox opened. 'Sheldon... love... there's a letter too, for your mother. Be a darling and give it to her, will you? Shel...?'

Shelley ground the letter into the doormat with her heel and went back to Matthew. She took her blanket and sat down on the floor, her back to his chair. Her eyes pinned open, she stared mindlessly at a furious chaffinch, equally mindlessly head-butting the window in the early morning light, fighting some imagined foe in the glass, bashing into it time and time again and apparently not getting the message that he would not get through.

She slapped a cushion over her head, too raw to bear the metaphor.

'I'm sorry,' she said, taking Matthew's hand and closing her eyes to stop the tears. 'I'm sorry...'

Victoria strode into the drawing room with the paper and the first of the morning's food aid to find Shelley sitting on the floor at Matthew's knee next to Beryl, leaning back on his chair, a blanket over her but very much awake.

'Good grief, child! Don't tell me you've been here all night as well. Anyone would think we have no other rooms in the house.' Victoria set down her tray, fruitlessly holding a cup of coffee in front of Matthew's face. She sighed at the usual lack of response. 'Right, I am calling Dr Page. This has gone on quite long enough.' Matthew twitched, slowly raised his eyes, took the cup and drank it down in one. 'Careful dear, it's hot!' But Victoria suspected he would not have noticed if it had been sulphuric acid. Matthew glanced at Shelley sitting by his side, blinked slowly, as if capturing something with an old Brownie camera, and returned to his silent vigil.

'Well, it's progress, I suppose,' Victoria sighed. 'Alright, no interventions just yet. Now, breakfast, Shelley. I refuse to eat alone.' Victoria lowered herself onto the poof by the window, the only other piece of furniture in the room, and placed the tray on an upturned packing crate. She was gratified that no-one had come to collect the few bits the crew had donated for the opera company to eat their sandwiches.

She glanced out of the window with a heavy heart. It all looked so desolate and pointless now.

'Do you think we should draw the curtains?' Shelley said. 'Seeing it all like this might upset him even more.'

'I don't think he's even noticed...'

To see Matthew such a pale shadow of himself shook her. His silence sitting hushed and burning deep within him, drawing the life out of his face as a fire sucks oxygen from around itself. To be honest, her brother-in-law looked a little like a corpse. They had pinned so many hopes, spent so much of the last months in planning and negotiation – two of the things for which Matthew was least equipped – Victoria could only surmise that the sudden vacuum left by the apparent demise of the festival had literally sucked the life out of him.

'But I'll be buggered if it's taking you down too, Shelley dear. I am only glad that you didn't have to give up your job for nothing. When will you be leaving for America?'

'I'm not.'

'Come now, Shelley. I know you care deeply about Matthew and I, and it gladdens my soul every day, but I will not have you putting your life on hold a moment longer. Not for us.'

'I'm not going, Victoria.'

'Shelley—'

'Horace has left.'

'*What*?'

'I'm so sorry, Victoria. I know he said he'd help you salvage something, do another performance or something, but he's gone. Crept out this morning, the fucking snake!'

'Indeed! But never mind about the opera, what about you? What about the job, Las Vegas "and all that jazz"?'

'He's not taking me. My mother needs me more, he says. She *always* does, he *always* says. I honestly think he was never going to take me.'

'Oh dear, oh dear. I wondered what this was. Found it on the mat, addressed to Marilyn, with a bloody great boot mark on it. I assume that's yours, and that's his writing?'

Shelley took the envelope and turned it in her hands. 'Oh well,' she sighed, ripping it open and peering inside.

No letter, not even a note. Just the divorce petition.

She handed it to Victoria without a word.

'Oh dear, dear me. The cowardly chicken! I should have known. A leopard and his spots and all that. Goodness me, he's a whole fucking menagerie!'

'Yeah, and it's me that *should have known*. It's obvious, isn't it? I am so stupid. I am always so, so stupid!'

'Now, we'll have none of that.'

'But I am! Always thinking things will change just because I want them to. I've always been the same. And what happens? Fuck all!'

Victoria was not sure she had ever seen her placid Shelley so angry. 'It's very disappointing, Shelley, indeed. I regret that you have been disappointed all your life. And I have no doubt your current emotion is nothing to do with a potential divorce.'

'Oh, I couldn't care less about a divorce. God knows it's been long enough coming. Who bloody well cares whether they stay, go, or kill each other? It's just me, isn't it? Standing in the middle, relaying the destruction and managing the fallout. Every bloody time! This is going to crucify her, and he damn well knows it. So, he's made sure I'm here to pick up the pieces, hasn't he? *Again*!'

'It would seem so.'

'Oh God, oh God, oh God! I am so fucking naïve!'

'Shelley, stop.' Victoria put a hand on her arm and watched her chest inflate like a bursting balloon.

'I'll be alright,' she muttered. 'It's nothing.'

'I doubt that.'

'It's nothing compared to your loss. I'm so sorry, I'm being stupid.'

Victoria had seen that look so many times over the years. The one that screamed and then smiled, like a rainbow after a hurricane. She opened her mouth to argue, but Shelley was off again.

'I better get going.'

'Where?'

'The Council Offices. If Stat can get somewhere with the police, I have to at least find out what they've got.'

The front door slammed before Victoria could stop her embarking on the next crusade.

And she wondered just how much longer the armour would hold.

21

RIORDAN ON THE CASE

Sergeant Riordan was distinctly peeved at this assignment. He was already in a foul mood at the way the weekend had turned out. It wasn't as if he had wanted the massive disruption of a summer of public concerts on his patch in the first place, but he had taken a certain satisfaction in knowing that his small contribution over the last six months was finally coming to fruition. Lining up all the public order pins, so to speak. Of course, they had never seen anything like this in Mid Hampshire and the research and preparation from a public safety, law and order point of view had been pleasingly significant. Riordan might actually say, engrossing. A breath of fresh air to a man approaching his twilight years in the force that he had joined thirty-four years ago. And the Inspector had said, if he pulled it off without a hitch, there might even be a promotion in it for him. About time too!

But of course there was a hitch. Nine hundred of the bloody things, as a disgruntled audience had taken out their frustration over the drowned-out concert to make a damn fine mess of Trefusis Lane and right the way through the village, chucking the remains of their snooty picnics and Horace Harper's penis flyers everywhere. Not to mention the traffic chaos on the B598 and halfway up the A31 as the lot of them descended at once, three hours before they were supposed to and whilst the Highways Agency was seeing to a crash on the M3.

Inspector Foster had not been pleased. As if it was Riordan's fault. And it was surely not a police matter anyway – you can't go around prosecuting nine hundred people for littering. Besides, the village had cleared it up in nanoseconds. Councillor Pennington was claiming the Bedingford Estate had breached its licence conditions, but that was entirely a matter for the local authority, wasn't it?

But the event organisers had lodged a complaint, insisting that the events of Saturday night were the direct result of sabotage – clearly then a violation of the law. The fat chap had bent Inspector Foster's ear for nearly an hour yesterday, insisting their sound screens had been tampered with and suggesting a whole host of public order offences, trespass and criminal damage. And he was on the phone again this morning.

Well, perhaps at least Riordan could get his teeth into a little investigative police work. He didn't get the opportunity for much of that anymore. Sniffing out a criminal, questioning witnesses, bringing them in... Alright, public disorder by the misuse of a posse of lawnmowers was perhaps not the crime of the century, but it was *his* case.

But this sleepy Monday morning, even that was being knocked out of Riordan's hands. As he and PC Hatter passed from door to door, the Bedingford villagers were unanimously horrified at any suggestion that they had been doing anything more than legitimately tending their gardens on a balmy summer's evening. Was it any crime if they happened to want to mow their lawns all at the same time? Yes, of course, they were all a *bit* noisy – they were sorry about that – but that Berry lad, who they had all so graciously given a little work on his recent release from prison, had put vodka in all the engines instead of petrol.

High concentration of ethanol (or something like that, how should they know?) disturbs the fuel mix, causes it to backfire and make a terrible noise, apparently. Come to think of it, no, they hadn't had sight nor sound of Pip Berry since he ran away down Trefusis Lane on Saturday night...

It was hardly a case for Miss Marple, therefore. A short visit to Bill and Ma Godfrey at the old Orchard Cottages located their ex-foster boy living in the allotment shed at the bottom of their garden. A total investigative marathon from station door to shed door of eighty-two minutes...

As far as Pip was concerned, he was on the run again. Holed up in this shed, just like the last time. He could sense the presence at his door even before he lifted his eyes over the window frame.

Pip had not been out of the shed for two days. It had been his usual knee jerk reaction to run on Saturday night – that immediate, familiar feeling of deep dread flooding over him, which could only be met by escape. He still didn't really understand what had happened that night, or what it had to do with him, but he had known that it did the moment he'd seen them all amassing from the top of the wall.

As soon as he had arrived at the Manor on Saturday evening he had run as fast as he could through the grounds, his heart pounding at the gap blowing wider and wider in the unlaced screens. Shinning up the wall, he'd barely grabbed the ties before he saw Harriet Pordage on the other side, standing on Yarnside Bridge, smiling at him with her thumbs up. Marilyn and everyone else down the street grinning and waving at him, poised in their front gardens about to ignite their lawnmowers, and pretty much anything else with an engine that could be found throughout the village. Just before Timothy Smollett's petrol strimmer exploded.

Identikit. Just like last time. His fault, not his fault. Who would know? Who would tell them?

And now, it was as if he could smell it, the scent of the law, coming up the garden path. He glanced at the window behind him. His reflex response was to run again, but his legs were shaking and his feet paddling air, as the memory of that dark and evil place he had left only three months before ripped through him again. And it felt like the march of commandants on the gravel coming towards him...

When they opened the shed door, Sergeant Riordan and PC Hatter found Pip sitting on a shelf in the corner of the shed, knees drawn up to his chest, his arms around them in a tight lock. He looked like a cornered animal, and Riordan was a little taken aback. He was no stranger to that kind of look of defiance, but the clear hint of terror in Pip's unusually direct eyes almost knocked him from his script to offer the lad a blanket and a thermos of tea. It all seemed somewhat out of proportion to the matters of the day.

'I ain't done nothing,' Pip offered immediately.

'Well then, Mr Berry, that's nice and appropriate isn't it, because nobody said you had, did they?'

'Do they teach cheerful sarcasm at Police College or some-thing?' Pip muttered, but the defiance still did not feel real.

'Look, Pip – can I call you Pip?'

'Philip, wiv an F, if you don't mind.'

'Alright, *Philip*, have it your own way,' Riordan sighed. 'Where were you the night before last, around eight o'clock?' This really was going to be the shortest investigation in the history of policing. And it was spectacularly pointless.

Pip, nevertheless, seemed intent on prolonging the matter. 'I don't have to say anything.'

'Oh, don't be ridiculous, Philip!'

'What? I know my rights, I don't.'

Riordan sighed again. 'Have you been out of this shed in the last two days, Mr Berry?'

'Might not have,' Pip mumbled. 'So?' The mock defiance was back. 'What if I haven't? And what if it was three days, eh?'

'Well, what if it wasn't? What if, say, *two* days ago, on the evening of Saturday 24th June at – ooh, shall we take a very rough estimate – 8.11pm – you were in Trefusis Lane conducting an orchestrated noise nuisance sufficient to constitute a breach of the peace—'

'Breach of the peace?' Pip spluttered. 'It was only a bunch of fucking lawnmowers!' His eyes fell. 'Oh, bollocks...'

Riordan smirked and continued cheerily. 'And so shall we surmise, Philip, that you *have,* in fact, been out of this shed in the last three days? But perhaps not the last two. Because if you had, young man, you would probably have worked out by now that you have achieved, in the space of about a minute and a half, what most of this village has been attempting for the last eighteen months. I doubt there is an officer in Mid Hampshire who would dare have you arrested. The public order consequences of that would be far more significant.'

Pip stared at him, as if he had no comprehension at all. Ma and Bill were at the shed window, silently mouthing encouragement.

'The festival is very unlikely to survive this. At least that's what Councillor Pennington has been at pains to assure everybody, and he should know. But that's hardly a police matter; none of this is— What are they doing?' Riordan's eyes had been moving back and forth between Pip in front of him and Ma and Bill at the window. Pip waved his arm in an attempt to shoo them away. 'So, if you wouldn't mind, *Philip,* just accompanying me down to the station for half an hour or so, having a bit of a chat about it, perhaps even getting a smidgen of a telling off for being somewhere you shouldn't and being a bit noisy about it, we can all be home and happy by teatime, OK?'

Bill shuffled round to the path as Pip followed them out of the shed. 'Do you want me to come with you, son? Help you out this time, you know?' he said, wiggling his eyebrows in a less than subtle manner. Pip's shoulders sank even further. The old man really wasn't helping.

'No, thank you, Bill. It'll be fine, really...'

Pip stopped on the steps of the police station. His legs did not seem to want to make the short climb. He had been in a very similar place only a few months before and had ended up in prison for three months. The slightest thought he was anywhere near that again was the fastest finger on his panic button.

'It's OK, Philip, nothing to worry about. We're just going to have an informal chat. Clear a few things up.' The Sergeant gave him a cheerful nod and Pip determined to try to hang onto the reality that this was all something and nothing, if he could just keep it together.

He was led to a room that didn't look much scarier than a business meeting room. PC Hatter even made him a nice cup of tea, and Pip attempted to persuade himself that this wasn't bad. Especially when a couple of ginger nuts appeared by the side of his cup, with a shy, encouraging smile from the young police officer. Inspector Foster, whose wife had been one of his more reasonable vodka-conversion customers, even waved at him through the glass-panelled door.

'Alright then, just a few questions. I still have to caution you, Philip, and you are entitled to a solicitor present – them's the rules – but you are not under arrest and you are free to leave at any time. Is that understood?' Pip nodded, but the caution was already re-igniting the memories and his legs started to bounce. He was beginning to feel quite displaced, as if his body belonged to someone else. It certainly seemed to be behaving badly, and without very much direction from an extremely muzzy mind.

'It's fine,' he said, for his own benefit mostly, and fixed his attention on the Sergeant's face in an attempt to stop it wondering any further into La La Land. 'And *Pip* is OK.'

'Excellent. So Pip, just for the record can you tell us where you *really* were between eight and eight-thirty on Saturday night?'

'At Bedingford Manor for the opera concert.'

'Opera is your thing, is it?'

'No, but—'

'Specifically, between eight and eight-thirty, were you in the Manor grounds?'

'Yes.'

'You didn't leave the Manor grounds?'

'Well, yes, I did, sort of.'

'Why?'

'I noticed a gap in the acoustic screening. The concert was about to start and I went to see if I could fix it.'

'So, you climbed up on to the Manor wall?'

'Yes.'

'Did you fix it?'

'No.'

'Why not?'

'I got distracted.'

'By what?'

'The people. All the people in Trefusis Lane, and round into Yarnside Drive, on the road and out in their gardens with all their garden machinery.'

'Like lawnmowers?'

'Yes, a lot of lawnmowers.'

'What happened then?'

'Then the noise started. I... think... I'm pretty sure it started then. I saw them all start the engines at once. Timothy Smollett's petrol strimmer exploded. I am sure of that.'

'The petrol strimmer and lawnmowers that the villagers say you had modified with vodka.'

'Yes, all of them at once. No wonder the opera had to be stopped. The noise must have been fearful.'

'Must have been?'

'Was.'

'Are you alright, Pip?'

'I... I...' Pip knew then that he was getting it wrong. 'I think I want to leave now.'

Pip could see Riordan's eyes narrow, but he was fading out of focus. *Please stop this happening...*

'OK, but just give me a few minutes, would you?'

Left alone, Pip tried hard to breathe. He had been taught relaxation visualisation during his short stay in prison and attempted to conjure up a little 'mental movie' now, in which he finished his tea, had another brief chat with Riordan, before signing a release form and walking out into the bright summer sunshine... Back to his luxury pad in... Pip got no further than the teacup and the room was closing in on him. Keys turning in locks, metal doors slamming, his head to the cold stone walls.

He screwed his eyes shut and shook his head, as if physically trying to dispel the images. He'd never been able to master this visualisation thing. Or else his imagination was just too finely tuned, and far too willing to run riot. When he was young, it would run off into bright pastures, conjuring escapes and rescues and music. In recent times, it only had legs to travel down, into dark places of judgment, confinement and silence. No amount of reasoning, Buddha bells, or crap positive thinking could make him feel safe there.

This monumental battle, between dark imagination and the fading conviction that he had done nothing wrong, only deepened with the prolonged absence of Sergeant Riordan. The same conviction had done him no good last time, and there was no longer anyone here to tell him otherwise. The 'few minutes' ticked into an hour. Pip looked again at the huge clock on the wall, as he had done every minute since he'd been left in here. He remembered all the interview rooms he had been in before and they, too, had a clock of similar proportions. Was it a joke? Time. Must they remind everyone who comes in here how *time* is the feature of their current predicament? Where were you at such-and-such a *time*? How *long* can they hold you? How much *time* will you serve?

Yet still he compulsively watched the passage of time, kept rhythmic company by his endlessly moving feet. He slapped his hands onto his thighs in a desperate effort to keep them still, but the thumping continued to reverberate around his whole body. He had always had a problem keeping his legs still, even before the panic attacks started. Ma used to say that was why he played the drums – it was the only instrument that gave him something to do with the bloody things.

Other than run.

The door was still unlocked.

22

RUSSELL STEPS IN

Shelley sat on the verge in front of the Manor, stealing herself to go back through the gates; for the second time today, an unwelcome letter turning in her hands. After a fruitless morning at the Council offices, she had succeeded only in coming away with formal confirmation that the noise conditions had been breached and no further performances would be permitted. Graham Tweedle had been nauseatingly sympathetic to her insistence that the village disturbance had caused it, but 'sadly' his monitoring proved that, in the momentary quiet after the first explosion, Horace had achieved a consistent peak of 11dB above permitted levels in Trefusis Lane. Shelley had failed to persuade him that, even if that were so, it could only have been recorded at that level because someone had tampered with the sound screens. Not a matter for the local authority, he said, and advised her to consult the police.

She held the Council letter over the drain on the kerb, teasing it up and down between the metal guards. Matthew was in a very precarious state already and, for once, she appreciated the merits of his traditional filing system.

'Hey! They've let you out then?' Rosamund loomed over

her. Shelley did not answer. 'Come on, joke? What's nicked your biscuit?'

'Nothing. I'm fine.'

'Of course you're not. Suppose it's the festival fiasco. Sorry to hear. After all your hard work and all that.' Rosamund plonked herself down on the grass beside her and lit a cigarette. 'It's a bit inconvenient all round, I expect,' she added, as Shelley still did not speak. What would be the point? *Inconvenient?* Where would she start?

'Let's be honest, it was never going to work, was it?' Rosamund continued, regardless. 'I know the villagers wouldn't really mean any harm, but what with your gardener friend upping the ante and all that—'

'What?' Shelley finally looked up. 'Pip? What's he got to do with it?'

'You didn't know? Arrested him a couple of hours ago, apparently.'

'What the hell for?'

'Oh, Russell did say, but—'

'How on earth does Russell know?'

'How does Russell know half the things he does, Shelley? Probably why he's so incredibly successful. Hey, come on, don't look like that. I always knew the bloke was shifty. The way his eyes always follow you, far too intrusive. The Maters love it, don't they? But I think it's very unnerving.'

'I always thought it was... nice.'

'Typical. Anyway, who cares about him? He's obviously got form. It's no surprise to me.'

'Form?'

'Only released in March, apparently.'

'Yes, yes, I know, but— No!' Shelley scrambled to her feet. 'I refuse to believe it. This has nothing to do with Pip! When's Russell back today?'

'He's working at home this morning, but he— Hey, wait for me...!'

Russell's home office was a wing of the Pordage house, separated by a heavy oak door from the main dining room, which the family knew better than to open uninvited. His expression was therefore far from pleased when Shelley barged in. But his brow relaxed immediately.

'Russell, I'm so sorry to disturb you, but I need—' She stopped, unsure of what she needed.

'You know *you* never require an appointment, Shelley. It's been far too long, and now twice in one month, I am honoured. Come in. Tea?'

'No, it's fine, thank you. I just needed to ask what you know about Pip Berry. Ros said you'd heard he'd been arrested?'

'Oh yes, the new gardener chappy, with the interesting way with machinery? Not charged yet, I doubt, but definitely being questioned for the opera disturbance.'

'But why? What are the charges?'

'Breach of the peace, for a start. But more troublingly, trespass and criminal damage, I believe. People are insisting on it.'

'What people? I don't understand.'

'Matthew, I should think. Awful business to get so out of hand.'

'Matthew hasn't moved from his chair in two days.'

'Well, I don't know then, Shelley, I'm sorry, must be the festival organisers. Something to do with the insurance, I expect. Not that they have much hope there, I wouldn't have thought. Pity,' Russell added pointedly.

'Well, yes, of course Stat has reported it to the police. The opera was disrupted deliberately, it's obvious. And the screens were tampered with, Russell, to make it worse. We're sure of it. But what's all that got to do with Pip? He's not responsible!'

'Why not, Shelley? Is there something you're not telling me?'

'Well, for a start, he can't be *trespassing* because he had a full pass. I gave it to him.'

Russell raised an eyebrow. 'Really? Well, that might have some bearing—'

'I'm going to the police station.'

'Shelley, wait,' he touched her arm. 'You look a bit pale. Why don't you stay here with Rosamund for a bit, don't trouble yourself, I'll phone them.'

'Oh please, Russell, could you help? Find out something?'

Russell looked at his watch and picked up the phone. 'I'll do what I can.'

Shelley could only hear one side of the conversation, but she pitied the poor officer on the other end of the line. He didn't stand a chance...

Sergeant Riordan was having a cup of tea and a chat about the next inter-station pub quiz when the call came in. He had concluded that Pip Berry was unlikely to be any real bother to anyone, but it wouldn't do the lad any harm to stew for a few minutes more. After all, he had just learned that he'd been in trouble before and there was rarely any smoke without fire. He was doing him a favour, leaving him a bit longer, lessen the likelihood of finding himself in here again. Perhaps he would send the rudderless young man off with a police recruitment pack when he finally left here, get him thinking about a decent career. He sensed Philip Berry was not without intelligence, even if that didn't always translate into eloquence. And PC Hatter seemed to have taken a bit of a shine to him.

She was on the front desk this afternoon and took the call.

'Sergeant, man on the line says he's got information about the Bedingford Manor case. Says he'll only talk to you.'

'Really?' he replied, raising his eyebrows at his assistant. 'What nonsense.'

This had never happened to Riordan before, and he was secretly rather pleased about it. Important, though, to give the opposite impression on both counts. He sighed, clattered down his teacup and strode through to the telephones.

'Sergeant Riordan speaking,' he intoned as if he were in some ancient Agatha Christie novel, winking incongruously at PC Hatter and so utterly failing to disguise his delight at the way this afternoon was turning out.

The caller was rather surprising but, even though he wouldn't dream of admitting that either, Riordan was quite relieved at Russell Pordage's intervention. He had to give it to him, it was a most eloquent recitation of the flimsy foundation for holding Pip Berry, or indeed anyone at all, in connection with Saturday night. Personally he'd trust Riordan's 'exceptional judgment', Pordage said (he'd quote him on that) but he doubted the CPS would be that impressed delivering this to them, and did he think that 'Inspector Foster might like him to make any further examination?'

Really, the bloke was such class...

'Right then, Elaine, I think it's time we put all this to bed, don't you?' Riordan concluded as he put the phone down. 'I'll just check in with the Inspector and then perhaps you would like to do the honours of cautioning Mr Berry and letting him go?'

PC Hatter beamed...

'Between you and me, Shelley, I don't think they're going to charge him,' Russell said as he hung up. 'But I'll keep in touch, shall I, and let you know later?'

'Thank you, Russell, you're a... rock.' As she said it, she realised the room was swimming a little. Russell was sat very still and straight in his chair. She found herself willing her own spine to lengthen, as Victoria used to teach her, and instantly feeling a little better.

'You will help him, won't you?'

'Of course, if that's what you want. But I don't think it will come to that. In the meantime, don't worry, Shelley... Don't *ever* worry.' They said the last bit together, and both laughed.

Shelley didn't know if she was worried or not. She didn't really know what or where she was. Everything seemed topsy-turvy at the moment. She still felt a little dizzy and then remembered she hadn't eaten all day. Rosamund, unusually, seemed to have noticed that too and insisted she stay for dinner.

'I need to get back to see how Matthew is. Give Victoria a break. I've been out all day.'

'Oh for goodness' sake, Sheldon, stop playing the Good Samaritan! It's a wonder this village hasn't run out of lame causes for you to rescue. How on earth have we survived whilst you've been away?'

'That's nice, Ros. Bye.' Shelley stiffened, but it was a little too close to her own truth spot for comfort...

'Ah Riordan, good timing, take a look at this.' Inspector Foster tapped his computer screen as the Sergeant approached the desk. 'Email from that annoying festival promoter again, says he was sent this photo anonymously.'

Riordan's heart sank a little. There on the screen was a clear photo of a bloke standing on top of the Bedingford Manor wall, fiddling with the acoustic screening. It looked a lot like Pip Berry.

'Mr Berkeley-Staten is still claiming sabotage and insisting we pursue charges,' the Inspector continued. 'And then, look, there's this one from Vera Swainsborough. Said she took it when she was walking back from one of their community protests at the Bedingford Manor gate.'

Riordan peered in closer. This one was most definitely Pip,

very much looking like he was 'breaking in' through a hidden door on the east wall that neither they nor Mrs Swainsborough had ever noticed before.

'This is tiresome, Bob,' the Inspector concluded. 'But we are going to have to investigate. Especially as Mr Berry is still on licence.'

'Is he?'

'Two more weeks, it seems. Get on to his Probation Officer, would you? And see what you and Elaine can find out about these photos?'

'He's still here voluntarily.'

'Well, I don't expect he will be in a minute, so you better arrest him. Besides, apparently he did a runner and skipped bail last time. In which case you better make sure he's still in the building...'

It was with pitiful relief that Pip raised his eyes to Sergeant Riordan and his assistant when they appeared at the door, a hopeful twitch of a smile on his lips. Despite his innate sarcasm, the officer had been kind and reassuring about his prospects today. The police usually were nice, in Pip's experience. Not like those TV cop shows, always shouting and needling and aggressively insinuating.

At first, anyway. Until you buggered it up.

Riordan hesitated at the door, closing it slowly and precisely. Pip's hopeful smile fell and his legs started up again.

'I'm sorry to keep you waiting, Philip,' Riordan began, and Pip just thought he was going to scream now. He could not do this again. Just *could not*. He even doubted whether he could stand another minute in this room.

'There's been a few phone calls.' Once again, the sergeant appeared unprofessionally open about the matter. 'I'm afraid I'm not going to be able to let you go quite yet.' Riordan drew himself up to his full height and inhaled deeply, as if he had never done this before. 'So... Philip Berry, I am arresting you on suspicion of breach of the peace, trespass and causing criminal damage at Bedingford Manor on Saturday 24th June—'

'*What...?*' Pip could hardly breathe now, for souping up a few lawnmowers could surely not have come to this. 'No, this isn't happening. Look, I never thought that—'

Sergeant Riordan stopped him with his eyes and completed the familiar spiel.

Pip stared at the door. Running or sitting here, both were impossible now.

He was booked in and searched. His possessions, which amounted to a leather bracelet, a padlock, the drum kit charm around his neck, three pretty deep green stones and £5.22, were bagged up and signed for. And if it hadn't been for the kindness of Sergeant Riordan, who still seemed to think it was OK to put a calming hand on his shaking arm, Pip felt sure he could not survive this.

The duty officer led him away.

'Another call from Mr Pordage, Sarge,' PC Hatter shouted from the front desk whilst convulsing at the apparent hilarity of the rhyme. Riordan noticed she'd put some make-up on her eyes as well. This day was getting more and more flummoxing. He was beginning to feel like a pinball, ricocheting between the bells and whistles of this ridiculous game.

He had to agree with Pordage, though. It did seem a little harsh to leave the lad in the cells overnight. On the other hand, he had form, not to mention the fact that he had done a runner the last time he was offered bail. It was all looking a bit more of a conundrum than Riordan would have liked before he knocked off for the day.

PC Hatter returned then, turning something small in her

hand, followed by Inspector Foster's secretary. She opened her palm to reveal the three deep green stones that had been emptied from Pip's pockets.

'Dave showed these to Natalie on her way out and she said they looked just like the stones in her engagement ring.'

'Emeralds,' Natalie crowed, thrusting her hand under Riordan's nose, despite the fact that he, and the rest of the station, had seen the ring a million times already.

'A passing resemblance maybe...' Riordan sniffed, reluctant to contemplate having to change his mind again.

'I'm pretty sure. I must have looked at hundreds before Tony *decided* to buy this one. I've already texted the Inspector.' Now she looked positively triumphant, and Riordan balked at the obvious snub. This was *his* case. He had better take control and stamp his authority right now.

'Well, don't let us keep you,' he concluded and strode off to the custody suite, with a clearly disappointed PC Hatter and the 'emeralds' trotting behind.

Riordan opened the door with confident authority, but was not at all happy at the thought that he might, after all, have been taken for a ride. Was this man who seemed so out of place here, in fact, just where he should be? Certainly, Riordan was long enough in the tooth to know something of the ways of the criminal mind, and one should never really take anything on face value – most of them were hiding something. But then again, Riordan had achieved substantial success in taking everything he possibly could on face value. It had rarely let him down. In this case, he had seldom seen such genuine fright in a chap before, especially when he was merely being questioned for pootling around somewhere he shouldn't have been. This meant one of two things as far as Riordan was concerned: Pip Berry was either completely out of his depth in anything to do with the law, or he was concealing something very much more serious than fiddling about with some lawnmowers.

But he wasn't going to get any more clues now. Pip refused to speak another word. He would not answer any questions and barely even looked at him. So Riordan found himself at the end of his shift, having to leave the frightened young man in the holding cell overnight after all.

Because they almost certainly would have to charge him now.

23

INSIDE OR OUT

Victoria was delighted. Matthew ate some dinner! It was a master stroke on Shelley's part – the village shop's venison moussaka, his absolute favourite, resistance was futile.

But any glimmer of light was quickly snuffed out as Shelley quietly handed him the Council's formal closure notice. Her hand remained on his arm as a single tear rolled down Matthew's cheek.

Victoria remained with him for the evening, but was equally watchful of Shelley, who did not seem able to settle. Like an actor compelled to read their poor notices, she continued to trawl the social media fallout and ticket agency updates. And, much as Victoria loathed his family, it was a relief when Russell Pordage phoned to provide something else to stop her.

'Russell? More news?'

'They're keeping him in overnight, I'm afraid. The police have got hold of some photos, apparently showing our man up to no good.'

'What photos?'

'Just trying to find out now... Ah!'

'Russell, how do you do these things?'

'Don't ask, Shelley. I have my ways, if I have to. And you asked me, so I have to... Shelley...?'

'I'm OK,' she sniffed. For some reason her eyes were a little watery, must be the antique dust in here.

'Your organiser chappy certainly seems intent on proving there's a criminal case to answer. Seems he's got hold of a photo clearly showing our Mr Berry on top of the Manor wall tampering with the screens, as he has implied.'

'When was this photo taken?'

'I'm sorry?'

'The photo of Pip on the wall – can you find out when it was taken?'

'Well, let's see, shall we?'

'You've got it? How do you—?'

'Don't ask, Shelley, like I said,' Russell cut her off, but she could tell he was smiling. 'Just texting to you now... Is it possible to find out in the file details or something? I don't know about these technical things, I'm afraid. I'm just a lowly lawyer.'

'No need.' Shelley pinched wide the photo. 'See the light on that ivy? I'd say that was taken about midday. Probably on one of the days Pip was *helping* me get this fucking thing sorted!'

'And this one? From one of the villagers.'

Shelley flicked down to Pip 'breaking in' through the hidden gate.

'What the hell is going on here? It's a padlock. He has the combination to avoid getting abused at the main gate every time he – freely, because I invited him – came and went to the bloody Folly!'

'I can hear you're angry, Shelley. Quite understandable. Leave it with me. I'll put an end to this once and for all. We'll talk tomorrow. Meet me at The Huntsman's, eight-thirty...?'

. . .

With no more of the small comforts he had been provided since his arrest – the tea, the ginger nuts, the subtle encouraging smiles and words – Pip lay awake all night in this small white enclosure. Sometimes his chest would heave with the effort of drawing enough air to serve his wired body. Increasingly convinced he would not be able to stop from hurling himself at the door and pleading for help. He had suffered this throughout his early weeks in prison, a spiralling vortex whipping through his body, which only served to confirm the artillery of his thoughts, that he was going to die, or go mad here.

He tried to count the cold white tiles, the same from floor to ceiling, but never got past a couple of rows before he had to start again. Over and over, until he was exhausted. He always knew the experience of prison would stay with him for a very long time. The only thing that ever comforted him was the thought that he would *never* put himself in such a position again. He would *never* have to deal with these feelings again.

But here he was. On top of everything else, so full of self-loathing that he had allowed it to happen. Even if, back in the midst of this farcical village, he still did not quite know how. He knew he had to be strong. He'd had that battered into him in there, literally – they must not see you cry. But tonight, he just could not keep it up anymore. And he just could not keep warm, his body shaking through the night in a heady mix of panic and cold.

And nobody knew who he was here. Nobody knew what he needed.

Then he remembered – he'd made it that way.

'Mr Stent is on his way,' PC Hatter attempted a lightness of tone, although nothing very much seemed to penetrate the glazed and battered man before her. He looked even more worn than he had the day before. Dark circles beneath his eyes, the slightly unpredictable hair even more unruly now, and a deep sadness about his whole being. It was difficult for Hatter not to feel sorry for him, even though her training warned against it. Most disturbingly, he didn't seem to be following what anyone was saying today, almost as if he wasn't there at all. Even when it had been clearly explained that he would most likely be facing charges of burglary and theft of property now, as well as breach of the peace, trespass and criminal damage, he seemed to have no will to respond. His gaze, previously so direct, had turned inward, or lost somewhere else, staring to the corners of the room or the middle distance. Right now, his attention was firmly directed to his hands on the desk, and he wasn't responding to anything.

Sergeant Riordan returned and silently raised an eyebrow. She shook her head.

'Not co-operating, Philip?' No response. 'Come on now,' Riordan cajoled. 'You must understand that you are in some trouble now and it would be much better for you if you communicated with us.' Nothing. Riordan sighed and flicked Pip's chin upwards to look at him. This removed focus was beginning to feel a bit wilful. 'Do you understand?' Pip's attention remained on Riordan's face. He said nothing, but something changed, and sadly Riordan had to conclude that he did. 'Well,' he sighed. 'Perhaps Mr Stent will have better luck.'

When it finally came, Pip's voice was a delicate, strangled thing. 'Please, could you get me someone else? I... um...' The words did not seem able to pass through his throat. Not surprising, as they'd never got as far as his lips before. 'I... might need some help.'

'I don't think that will be necessary.' A very different quality of voice boomed through the open door at that moment. 'A word please, Sergeant, and then some time with *my client* if you don't mind...'

· · ·

'Right then, first things first, are you OK?' Pip glanced past Russell Pordage, but he had returned to the room alone and PC Hatter was on her way out. 'Not very communicative? I understand it hasn't been helping very much. It didn't help you very much last time either, did it?' Now Russell had his attention. 'Yes, I've got your file. No need to dwell on that, but it doesn't look as if you were terribly well represented by Basingstoke's finest, Frederick Stent. That isn't going to happen now, alright?'

Pip's eyebrows knitted, but Russell's direction seemed to demand an answer. He nodded vacantly.

'Now, I have left the Sergeant in no doubt that any evidence in their possession suggesting charges against you, of trespass or criminal damage on Saturday night, is so incapable of standing up to scrutiny that you would wish to save the police the embarrassment of any further investigation.'

'Evidence?'

'This was all explained to you last night, surely, before they banged you up for the night? If not, this is all going to be even easier for me to dispense with.'

'Yes, yes, of course,' Pip replied, a little too quickly.

Russell eyed him coolly. 'Alright. Of course, if the police choose to pursue a charge of breach of the peace, I can't legitimately claim the same, given that it *was* in fact your *modifications* to the garden machinery involved that caused the most disturbance.'

'Yes, but—'

'I wouldn't bother, Pip. I won't be wasting any of our time on that either. However, the small matter of the emeralds found in your possession, less easy to deal with.'

'What emeralds?'

'In your pocket?' Pip patted his trousers. 'Not now, obviously,' Russell tutted. 'You're really not very good at this, are you?'

'The little green stones?'

'The emeralds, yes. The police have sent them for analysis,

but they assure me they have an expert identifier in-house already, so they are pretty sure of the outcome. I suppose one shouldn't blame them for assuming that they don't belong to you?'

'No, they don't, but—'

'Or for extrapolating from your record that they might be linked to further drug supply?'

'*What*?'

'Where did they come from?'

'Off a snare drum, but—'

'*Off* a snare drum. Oh, this just gets better, doesn't it? Like the snare drum that the drugs just happened to be found *inside* last time?'

'Oh, for fuck's sake...'

'Look, Pip, like I said, we don't have to go there. But you must know how bad this looks. Even with the most cursory of examinations, it's going to lead to a charge, at the very least. Yes, it's *very* distressing, I can see that in your face, and you do seem to be getting a little confused and tongue-tied. And I'm on your side. Imagine how much worse it's going to be in a minute when they interview you again...' Russell sat back in his seat. 'Until, of course, they learn the stones were a loan from my mother that you were merely conveying to Marilyn Harper. A *fact* to which both women will gladly testify.'

'Why would they do that?'

'Well, we just have to square a circle, Pip, tie up the loose ends of the weekend past. My mother and all the other villagers were most distressed to learn that their *legitimate gardening activities* might be the cause of any kind of criminal proceedings. So, all you have to do is admit to causing the disturbance, and I can ensure that no charges are brought – for any of it. Then everyone's happy and can all move on.'

'I don't suppose anyone at the Manor thinks that.'

'Pip, the Council recorded a noise breach in Trefusis Lane *from* the stage. *That* is why the festival has been shut down. Of course the lawnmowers recorded decibels way over that, but the point is *they* weren't prohibited! You'd be serving nobody by being moral about it and refusing to co-operate. It's not good for you, Pip. You're still on probation, I understand. One whiff of trouble and it's straight back inside, isn't it?'

'Don't you think I know that?'

'Well, you take responsibility for this small matter and I can ensure that none of it gets taken any further, which, as we both know, will only end one way... Look, of course it's bad for the Wolstenholmes, but there's no reason anybody else should be affected by this any more than they have to, is there? Including Shelley. *Especially* Shelley.'

'What's Shelley got to do with it?'

'Absolutely nothing, Pip. But she thinks she has. She blames herself; thinks she could have prevented the Council's injunction if her screens had been better.'

'They would have been just fine if they hadn't been tampered with.' For the first time, Pip's eyes matched the confident authority of Russell's own.

'That may be so, I have no idea about these things, but the police have you down for that, too. As you know, the photographs—'

'What photographs?'

'What's the matter with you? Am I really wasting my time here? This was all explained to you last night, surely.' Russell leaned forward as if he was disciplining a recalcitrant child. 'Look, whatever happened, Shelley has no fault in it. I have no doubt of that. But it would be far better for her to believe it as well, don't you think?' The question was clearly rhetorical. 'Well, actually, whilst I am here to help *you*, I don't care what you think. Shelley is not strong like you and me, Pip, and I will defend her to the day I die. Am I making myself understood?'

'Not really, no.' *Not strong?* She was the most powerful person he had ever met.

'I defend, Pip, that's what I do. And you'd be well to remember that. You could be facing a whole lot of trouble, and this is a very small thing for you to do to avoid it. And, as an added bonus, you'd have *me* on your side as well as all the others.'

'How soon would I be able to leave here?'

'Oh, I'd say about twenty minutes?'

'OK...'

24

CASE CLOSED

The Huntsman's was full and buzzing. Pip knew he should be waiting next door amongst it – Russell Pordage would surely be the right-sider to top all right-siders – but he couldn't handle the competing noises today. The immediacy of the day's fears had retreated since his release from the police station, but his whole radar seemed off. The tuning fork of his body still reverberating with all sorts of unwelcome vibrations, he did not think he could manage any more. But the lawyer, who had so unexpectedly sprung him from custody this morning, was late. Eight o'clock he said, and it was ten past now.

Pip twirled an empty glass on the table, round and round and round. He had returned to his shed from the police station this morning feeling like he'd never listen to anyone or anything ever again. He certainly did not fancy his chances of making it to the bar, and the focus on the hypnotic rotation of the glass at least shut out the rest of the place.

He was free. But he'd bought it.

Ten minutes with 'his lawyer' in that custody suite and Pip was in no doubt that Russell Pordage would wipe the floor with anyone on the other side. It was equally clear that he had better ensure he wasn't the one *on* 'the other side'. So, he had made the statement. He said, as clearly as he could, that he had orchestrated the 'breach of the peace' that they still insisted it was called. He refused to admit to the 'criminal damage' of tampering with the acoustic screens at the Manor. Pordage had been a bit peeved at that, but confident enough they could do without it, since he'd pretty much debunked the photographic evidence already.

But at least someone was trying to help him. Nobody managed that last time. He should be grateful. And he was. Sort of. Except he still had no idea why. That was really the only reason he was here tonight, that he might find out. He briefly entertained the fantasy that Shelley had arranged the help. But since the other part of the bargain was that he wasn't to say anything about it to her, or indeed say *anything at all* to her *ever again*, it seemed unlikely.

Job done. The thunderstorm of fear had receded to its usual casual rumble. But Pip had never known such emptiness in his life.

Eight-twenty. Too long. He could not stay a moment longer. But he better at least check in the right side before running away again.

People smiled at him. As he made his way to the bar, almost everyone nodded or waved a cheery greeting. Others whispered in corners. Of course, he couldn't hear what they were saying, but he knew they were talking about him by the lowered gaze, different mouth shapes and the break in their inanity. He only had to look. He had learned that years ago.

He stood at the end of the bar, holding onto it for stability. He didn't want a drink. The last two days had wrung him so thin the boundaries of himself seemed to be dissolving into the noise and energy around him. A couple of pints and he feared he might lose himself altogether.

Nobody had directly approached him so far, but Timothy

Smollett looked as if he was preparing to. Pip picked up another abandoned glass and headed back to the left side. Russell Pordage would just have to be bothered to look as well. He'd give him ten more minutes.

He stopped, alarm rising to his throat. Shelley was sitting down at a tiny table by the unlit fire. He didn't know what to do. Just walk past her? Leave? Sit down immediately and beg her to listen to him, as she had been trying to do for weeks? But that was not allowed, now.

She looked up and saved him the trouble. For a moment, she just stared at him, and then she beckoned. Still, he did not move.

'Pip,' she said. 'Sit down.'

'I don't think—'

'I would like you to sit down.' The measured, clipped edges of her speech were so unfamiliar his heart pitched and his foot began to tap again.

'Tell me you had nothing to do with all this, Pip.' He did not reply. 'I want to believe that. Everyone says otherwise. But if you look at me and tell me, I will believe you.'

'I... I can't.' Pip spoke too quietly, his eyes darting to the opening door.

'What?'

'I can't,' he repeated.

'You, more than anyone, knew what was at stake.' She was looking at him so directly, as if she was seeking the answer in his eyes. It made it very difficult to return his usual direction. 'There's something going on here, Pip. I want to believe that you didn't know anything about it.'

'You have to forget about it, excuse me...' He turned to leave, feeling the imperative to run in his hyperactive feet. They twitched and kicked like a bull preparing to charge, and banged straight into Russell Pordage.

'Shelley, I'm so sorry to keep you waiting. What can I get you?' He glanced at Pip. 'What are you doing here?'

'What do you mean? You—'

'Is my client bothering you, Shelley?'

'Yes,' she replied, still looking steadily at Pip. 'He is bothering me a great deal.'

'Well, we can't have that, can we? Off you go.' The whole pub was watching now and Russell looked completely at home taking this stage.

'Now hang on a minute—' Pip began to protest, but Timothy Smollett's hand appeared on his arm. He looked down at it in complete bewilderment.

'I think you might have been about to say something you were going to regret, Mr Berry.' Pip glanced between the command in Russell's eyes, the warning in Timothy Smollett's and the hurt in Shelley's and felt very inconvenient emotion prick his own. 'We wouldn't want that now would we, not now that the village has your best interests at heart.'

'Oh, do they?' Pip snorted. 'Is that so?'

'Do you think then, Mr Berry, that you might have something to say on the matter?' Russell was in front of him now and Pip was instantly transported back to the dock, feeling the power that this man no doubt wielded in court every day.

He glanced at Shelley. 'I... I'm not sure...' But that was to be the most that Pip was going to have to say on any matter. Russell simply laughed, and for a moment Pip did not quite know where to put himself. He was never any good at confrontation anyway. Russell turned as if he was just casually going to the bar, but then in true court room style, swept back to face him.

'Now, look here,' he breathed with a steel that the entire room, not least Pip, found quite alarming. 'I have absolutely no idea what game you think you are playing, but let me assure you it stops right now. Is that understood?'

'*What*?' This really was quite beyond Pip now and his mouth gaped. 'I haven't—'

'That's quite enough!' The barrister was ready to bring the case to a close. 'It is a balmy Tuesday evening and I am enjoying a rare hour in my local hostelry, and when I am lying in my bed tonight savouring this small oasis in my otherwise interminably busy and important life, I should hate to have to recall that I wasted more than a minute and a half talking to a grubby little shit like you. Do I make myself clear?'

Pip's foot finally disobeyed, kicking out at the table leg, his borrowed pint spilling over Shelley's jeans. But this time, his feet kept going. He looked back at her. 'I'm sorry,' he croaked and stumbled out of the pub.

Nobody stopped him.

And so it would seem that, despite the wind change in some of the villagers, Pip would forever remain a left-sider.

Shelley was annoyed to find herself close to tears by the time Russell returned, with a large glass of wine and a bar cloth. She swallowed the tears for a smile and a hefty glug of the wine.

'Do you always talk to your clients like that?'

'Reserved only for special cases,' Russell sat down, with a far more genuine smile.

'But is he your client now? I don't think I quite understand.' Shelley was fairly sure she didn't *quite understand* very much at all at the moment.

'Yes, I fear so. And I also fear it's true, everything everybody said about him.'

'I'm not sure I can believe it.'

'Do you not, Shelley? I'm sorry then, because he's admitted it. The noise, the screens, the lot.'

'Seriously?'

'Well, it would be serious, but I pretty swiftly saw off all that. Especially since you said you let him in to the grounds, that helped enormously. Got him off with a caution.' Russell took a large mouthful of his own wine. 'There are... *other matters*, though, that weren't quite so easy.'

'Other matters?' Shelley was completely at sea now. 'What other matters?'

'Client confidentiality, Shelley.'

'Oh, I see.'

'Your distress is hard for me to bear, Shelley,' Russell sighed. 'Look, I will tell you this much, just for your own protection, you understand. After the opera night, the police found a valuable amount of emeralds in his possession. Highly unlikely to be his. My money's on them belonging to our friend the Earl of Bedingford, which makes it burglary. Unless you're saying you let him in there as well,' Russell laughed. 'Oh... you did, didn't you?'

'I... I...'

'Ah well, just theft then, bad enough. Oh, Shelley, I am so sorry!' Tears welled in her eyes and Russell shifted to the seat beside her to put a gentle arm around her shoulders; so gentle she barely felt it. 'I'd tell you more if I could, you know that. Especially as it seems you might have befriended the man?' Shelley didn't respond. Is that what she had done? That made him sound more like a dog. 'Such a blow when we're found so mistaken about someone, isn't it? But at least I've seen to it that there will be no case to answer, and everyone can put it all behind them.'

'But, but... why would you do all this?'

'Because you asked me to, Shelley,' Russell snorted.

'No! I mean yes, I suppose I did. But no, not now! Oh, what the hell am I going to tell Matthew and Victoria? This whole thing has ruined them!'

'Well, probably best not to tell them anything, isn't it? Seeing as it was you who let him in.'

'Oh, God...'

'Anyway, they don't know him, do they?'

'Matthew's met him, but I don't think Victoria has.'

'Oh well, nobody's likely to say anything, are they? I'll see to it the jewels are returned and nobody's any the wiser, are they? Especially as the Council has shut down the festival anyway. Given his precarious mental health, perhaps it's better if no more was said about any of it and poor Matthew can just move on. Perhaps he could sell the emeralds. I daresay he could do with the money now.' Russell touched her arm. 'You don't need to feel guilty, Shelley, because you've nothing to feel guilty about. None of this is your fault, you must believe that.'

But she couldn't...

'Good Lord, Shelley, whatever is the matter?' Victoria bustled to the front door where Shelley stood, flattened against it, gulping air as if she was drowning. She could not remember the last time she had really cried, but it was coming thick and fast now, in urgent, breathless gasps that willed her just to scream. The intensity frightened her. Not just the breaking wave of betrayal by someone she was beginning to think was a friend, but the whole tide of loss and disappointment she had dammed up before. Stuck fast to the door as if it could be a replacement for her own flood defences, they crumbled now.

'Please, Shelley, tell me what is it?' Victoria put a hand on her arm, drawing her towards her.

'It's over, isn't it?' She sank to the floor. Victoria attempted to kneel beside her. 'Look at all this.' Shelley waved a hand across the Manor, before scraping her sleeve across her sodden eyes. 'And you. And Matthew! It's all my fault! My delusional mother, my lying father, my foolish dreams and rubbish work, and some secretive low-life I invited into your home.'

'Sheldon, what are you talking about? None of this is your fault.'

'He had kind eyes, Victoria. I knew there was something

hidden about him, but he helped me. He looked at me so directly, as if it all mattered, you know?'

'I'm sorry, Shelley, I do not. Who are we talking about?'

'He had a kind face. I thought— Well, I don't think too well, obviously.' She fumbled for her ringing phone. 'And it's going to stop right now!'

'Who is it now?' Victoria sighed.

'Russell.'

'Russell Pordage?'

'Yes. I can always rely on Russell,' she concluded quietly, taking the phone upstairs, as if she'd never really realised it before.

25

THE PROBLEM OF PROTECTION

The secateurs clicked like cicadas; the cars hummed past at twenty miles an hour; the postman rode his bike over the bridge. It was a typical Bedingford morning, for everyone except him.

Pip was looking a bit white. Marilyn's answer was, as usual, cake. And so he found himself, for the second time, crossing the rubicon of the utility room into the Harper kitchen. He was not sure the honour was making him feel any better, but he wasn't averse to the tiny remaining hope that cake *might*. Ridiculous as he knew it was, people the world over attempted the same short-term relief with many a worse substance than a Victoria sponge. It struck him as particularly ironic, however, that despite liking the odd pint of real ale, he had never been interested in any of the substances freely available during his time on the road – which only made it even more ridiculous that for the second time in a matter of months, he had been the one on the receiving end of criminal charges. If he didn't feel quite so much despair about it, it would almost be funny. Here he was, the cake champion of the rock world, surrounded by excess all over the place, and he was the one twice in the clink.

'I understand Harriet has offered you a permanent job,'

Marilyn beamed over a hefty slice of bread pudding. It wasn't one of his favourites, but beggars can't be choosers. 'How wonderful!'

'Not sure I want to take it.'

'Oh really, Pip, of course you must! It's awful all this business, and completely right that Russell and Harriet have lent their considerable weight to your case. It's absolutely atrocious all those people saying you ruined the festival like that. How some people exaggerate! We were only trying to keep our lawns tidy. What's wrong with all of us doing that at once? And who could have known Timothy Smollett's strimmer would explode like that? Nobody can *really* blame you for that.' Marilyn blinked and began cutting her slice into perfectly formed squares. 'For the best that you've accepted it, though. We want to protect you, Pip, you must know that.'

'Oh, you as well, eh? Really?'

'Yes, of course! With your record and all that. A caution for a bit of a disturbance is far better than another prison sentence, obviously.'

'Obviously. And you know all about that now, do you?'

'Well, we know how easily young people can be led astray these days. We don't blame you for the... *substances*. I'm sure you just meant to relax a bit.'

'Relax a bit? With that lot? I'd have been on the ceiling till Christmas.'

'Well, not for me to say.' Marilyn blinked again, her cake squares now being cut into tiny triangles. 'Oh look, here she is. Morning, Harriet!'

Harriet Pordage let herself in through the kitchen door. Marilyn's face twitched. 'Oh, you've brought cake, how... *lovely*. From the village shop. Pity Pip already has some. *Homemade*. Would you like some more, Pip darling? I'm sure it's returning a little colour to your cheeks.'

Pip very much doubted that, but Harriet saved him the

trouble of declining. 'Come along then, young man. I brought the Bentley.'

'For 200 yards?'

'In case you had... *equipment*,' Harriet sniffed, looking very ambivalent about this whole thing. 'Anyway, we need to be quick about it. Russell wants to see you and he has a meeting in town with the Secretary of State for the Environment at two, so chop, chop!'

'Look, I don't believe Russell wants to see me at all. And it's very kind and all that – possibly – but I really don't think I want to—' He stopped. Bill was at the window, his thumbs up, beaming.

'Ma said to bring some stuff, Pip son.' Bill had his hands on his wheelbarrow, full of his special compost, trays of seedlings, and even one or two of his favourite tools. 'Pleased as punch she is on your promotion!'

'There you are then,' Harriet concluded, and within seconds, Bill was loading Pip's meagre dowry into the boot of her Bentley...

Russell was preparing to leave when they arrived back at Glebe House, but ushered Pip into his office.

'First things first, Pip,' he wasted no time. 'I need to apologise for my performance last night in The Huntsman's. I have certain things to protect, you understand. But I hope you also understand by now that one of them is *you*. And Shelley, of course.'

'You said you wanted to keep Shelley out of this.'

'I did, Pip, and I will. Believe me, that is high on my priorities. I think I have persuaded her that none of this was her fault, but it would be considerably easier for her to accept if she could blame someone else. And someone who was *not* her mother. Marilyn suffers too. She is grieving, Pip, however much it might seem like something else. To have her daughter turn against her any more would not be kind.'

'And *your* mother? What does she get out of all this?'

Russell's face clouded and Pip could not tell if the look was anger, obstinacy, or disappointment – a bit of all these things was coming out of his silence. But it probably wasn't worth working it out. In his experience barristers, like actors, could illuminate or obscure at will, and take you wherever they wanted.

'Never mind my mother. Protecting her is my job too. You can just reap the benefits of her patronage. Believe me, she does it rather well, so I'd just enjoy it if I were you. Shelley, on the other hand, you will steer well clear, as we have already discussed. Although that won't be hard, since this place is so toxic for her, and her father has betrayed her *again*, I am arranging for her to get away from here, in peace.'

Pip nodded silently, a gaping hole opening up in his gut.

'Look, we both made promises, Pip, only you seem a little unsure about yours.' Russell came round to the other side of his desk and sat on the corner, leaning towards him. 'Are you?'

'No,' Pip sighed. 'I suppose not.'

'Good.' Russell rose again, continuing to pack his briefcase. 'Then we will get along just fine.' He strode to the door, indicating this 'interview' was over. 'You've had some bad luck, that's all, but you've come a long way in a couple of days, Pip. Try to remember that. It can only get better from now on...'

It had been some time since Shelley had been down this end of the village, yet she knew it all so well. She stopped by the stream that trickled from the River Yarn alongside the path here. A moorhen was struggling to build a nest at the water's edge, battling to shove twigs against the metal grid that held back vegetation and other debris. Shelley had seen her in the same spot in previous years, when the nest had been repeatedly swept away by flooding. She wondered why on earth she would keep returning to such an unsafe place? Habit, Shelley supposed. She knew about that.

Perhaps Russell and Victoria were right – she needed to move on, not backwards in this place. Perhaps she really could do nothing for her mother; perhaps she never could. Perhaps she could do nothing for Matthew. After all, she had failed him so totally, been so naïve and deceived. But she could not go without looking one more time for the truth to persuade her otherwise. To look directly into those eyes that had always been so direct with her. Eyes that she never imagined could hold so many lies behind them.

She didn't quite know the way in, or the allotment visiting rules, but she could see Bill sitting on a bench at the side, drinking tea from a thermos, unwrapping a pork pie from kitchen paper like a precious jewel. As soon as he saw her, he waved, immediately shifting up the bench to make room for her. Well, she couldn't back out now.

'Oh, Miss Harper, what a lovely surprise! Please come in, come in.'

Shelley hung at the gate. 'Don't get up, Bill, it's fine. I don't want to disturb you.'

'Nonsense, my girl. Come in, sit down. No disturbing, just having me tea. What brings you all the way down here, then? Is it Pip you're after? Not here so much anymore, I'm afraid...' A wave of relief broke over her and slapped back against a shore of disappointment. 'Well, I'm not afraid at all!' Bill beamed. 'Got a promotion he has! Everybody's being so kind. You too.'

'I haven't done anything, Bill.'

'Giving him the chance to play the drums again? That aren't nothing, my girl, that a precious gift.'

'I heard him play once, Bill. Did you know how good he is?'

'Of course we do.'

'Why does he hide it?'

'Pip's always been good at hiding things,' Bill muttered, and her disappointment rose to her throat again. 'And it's a terrible thing he's gone and done now.' Bill was comically tutting, but there was genuine anguish in his eyes. 'The Earl and his family always been so good to us. Why would he want to go and ruin it all for them like that? I don't know what's up with him, I really don't. Couldn't believe the last time, but— Oi, you! Where do you think you're going?' Bill shuffled to the edge of the bench, spilling tea and spraying pie crumbs, wagging a finger at the figure approaching the shed. 'This is private property, you know!'

Shelley put a hand on his arm. 'It's just Pip, Bill. Put your glasses on.'

'They're for reading, and don't take me for a fool! What's going on here?'

'Nothing, look, it's just Pip.' Pip was staring at her too and she was really doubting the wisdom of coming here now. Perhaps they were both a good deal stranger than she had ever thought.

'Well, that's a relief,' Pip stopped staring and his lips flirted with the tiniest self-conscious smile. 'I haven't had a peep of recognition all bloody afternoon. For goodness' sake, it's not that different, is it?' Bill was still gaping. 'Is it?' The question was so searching, Shelley was confused to find herself amused and concerned at the same time.

It seemed an age since she'd seen that direct focus, the one she thought she had come here to find. Now there was quite a lot more to see. His hair was still long enough to cover his ears and curl over the neck of a smart new designer T-shirt, but the face was quite transformed.

'I've been shopping with your mother and Harriet.' Pip's eyes flicked to the ground and back to her. 'They insisted on smartening me up a bit, the haircut and... everything.' He looked really uncomfortable now, and without the beard, it did seem as if another layer had been peeled back. 'Well, like I say, not my idea, you know,' he mumbled, fumbling for his padlock in the unfamiliar pocket of an expensive-looking pair of jeans.

Shelley flushed with relief at the release from his scrutiny, even if she could not entirely stop hers. She had always thought the beard suited him. She liked it. This *was* different. She liked it too. Her heart sank as she realised that, with or without, she liked... *it all*.

'Oh well, then!' Bill beamed, cutting through her turmoil. 'They cleaning you up then, Mrs Harper and Mrs Pordage? It'll all be alright now, Pip son. Landed on his feet, he has there,' he turned back to Shelley. 'Proper job up at the big house, and your mother in *The Gazette* this morning too.'

'What?'

'Lovely letter to the editor. You haven't read it? I got it here somewhere.' Bill scrambled for the paper and thrust it at her.

Shelley sighed, so tired of reading about her parents' Machiavellian intentions in the newspapers. Whether it be *The Telegraph* or the *Mid Hampshire Gazette*, she had finally had enough of it. Alarmed to find her eyes misting again, she read Marilyn's 'official apology' that the legitimate gardening intentions of her neighbours had disrupted the concert in Bedingford at the weekend. Her gardener, it read, had taken full responsibility for the level of noise getting out of hand. But she did not wish the wider community to judge him harshly; the village had taken him to their hearts. Besides, she had it on good authority that the Council recorded a breach of the noise conditions the other way round, so the festival would have been closed down anyway. Which they all thought was '*very unfortunate...*'

Slapped back into reality, it was the last straw for Shelley. She got up, fished in her pocket and thrust Horace's divorce petition into Pip's hands.

'Give her this. She's your problem now – and vice versa, it seems. You deserve each other!'

26

REX MAKES A STAND

When Shelley arrived back at the hospital, Stat was on the phone again. He nodded as she peevishly mouthed, 'Rex?'

'He's really quite contrite,' Stat responded to her protective annoyance as he hung up. 'He's trying to hire a car to come and take me home.' The phone rang again. 'No, Rex, I haven't got your driving licence... Well, where did you last see it, lovey...? And you didn't get it back when you came out of The Priory...? Well, I think it might be out of date now anyway... That might be quite difficult... Swansea... Yes, you can get a train to Swansea, but—'

Shelley grabbed the phone. 'Rex? This is Shelley Harper. I'm taking Stat back to Bedingford Manor and I'll bring him home tomorrow if you can't get here. Now get off the phone, go and find your own bloody driving licence, and get some shopping in for his return. And don't you dare phone from Tesco asking how to use a fucking trolley!'

Stat smirked as she hung up.

'How old is that man?'

'But you can't take me back to the Manor, Shelley.'

'Why not? Victoria was quite adamant. She might as well have two invalids as one, she said.'

'That woman's a marvel.'

'Settled then. Now, is there anything you need in the meantime...?'

That afternoon Shelley cleaned Stat's car and filled it with petrol, plus the shopping she feared Rex would not manage. She needed to be doing something. She could not bear to listen to her own thoughts, or sit in silence with Matthew another minute. He was eating and moving about a little at night, but always returning to his motionless vigil, staring into the middle distance, as if watching some old silent movie of his life. And Victoria was tiring of her persistent questions about how to help him. She had told her quite bluntly this morning that she was going to tip him out of that chair and put it on the compost heap if he hadn't moved by the weekend, and Shelley needed to fuck off and do something else with her life before she desiccates in pity.

All the signals were pointing in the same direction. Somewhere out of here.

Victoria replaced her bag on the coat hook and looked in on Matthew. They'd be on their own again after today. Perhaps they could begin to get back to normal. Whatever that was now.

'Tea?' she offered, as usual, not expecting a reply.

'Oh, how jolly nice,' an affected voice spat from the open front door. Victoria barely had time to turn before the stranger strode into the drawing room.

'Rex Trenton,' he said. 'The singer.'

'*The* singer?' Victoria squinted.

'D'you want an autograph?'

'Don't be ridiculous.'

'And you must be Lord La-di-da,' Rex turned on Matthew, sitting silently in his chair. 'This is where you spend all your time, is it? On your bony privileged arse, being served tea by old ladies, whilst everyone else kills themselves working.'

'Excuse me, young man!' Victoria marched over, tugging at his leathered sleeve. At 65 last birthday, Rex had not been called 'young man' for a very long time indeed. He was delighted, which only powdered his gunshot.

'Fuck off, tea lady. I came to say some things, and that's what I am going to do. I'm collecting Stat. He needs to rest, which obviously means no income for a while, so I want to know what *he* is going to do about it! I've made a list of our costed requirements. I'll just leave that with you, shall I?' Rex thrust a folded piece of foolscap into Matthew's lap, before Victoria slapped him and pushed him out of the door.

'Get out of here, right now!'

'And you'll organise for my band to have a fully supported weekend gig here at your expense!' Rex threw back, ridiculously given the circumstances, but he was on a roll. 'Nationally promoted, all proceeds—'

Stat stood before him in the hallway. 'Rex, for God's sake! What on earth do you think you're doing? I'm so sorry Matthew, he's been under a lot of pressure—'

'Too bloody right I have! And it's all his fault. Look at you, Stat. Taking the piss, the lot of them!'

'And *who* do you think he was doing it all for?' Shelley jumped down the stairs, firing. 'Why don't you wake up, you selfish, deluded bastard!'

'Oi, Florence Nightingale, who do you think you are? Fuck off!'

'Stop!' Everybody turned to Matthew, rising slowly from his chair, at last. 'I will not have this in my house! I'm sorry,' he turned to Stat. 'I will do what I can. Now you must go home to rest.'

'I'll take you,' Shelley confirmed, looking darkly at Rex. 'I don't suppose he's located his fabled driving licence?'

'No, came on the train, but so what? Who's to know?'

'I'll get my bag,' Stat sighed. 'Thank you, Shelley. *We* would be very grateful...'

Shelley touched Matthew's arm. 'Russell says I can stay in his flat for a while, but I'll come back and—'

'No, Shelley, please do not.'

'But—'

'I would like it, please, if you would just go now and get on with your life. If Russell can help you settle until you find out what that is, I would be most grateful. There is nothing for you here.'

'But Matthew, I want to help you, I—'

'Look, see? I can move, and if I promise to stay upright, do you promise you will give yourself some time for a change? I don't want you putting your life on hold a moment longer on my account. I shall look forward to hearing how you get on, and the odd visit from time to time would be... lovely. Now please, go. All of you...'

Victoria stood on the steps and watched them all leave. Matthew sat back down in his chair, his hand slowly reaching for Rex's list, like Frankenstein's hand from a fairground box, snatching it from his lap to disappear down the side of the chair cushion...

An old woman took a photo as the car swept out of the gate. Rex thrust his head out of the rear window, puckered his lips into an exaggerated kiss and gave her the V-sign. She took another two shots. Shelley wound down her window. 'For God's sake, it's over, OK? Have you not had enough?'

The woman scuttled off, her dog limping behind.

27

BRIGHT LIGHTS, BIG CITY

Damon, Yebut, Benny and Alan sat waiting in Stat's flat when Shelley delivered him home. There were a few things on the kitchen table – eggs, butter, white bread, mayonnaise, a bottle of Jack Daniels, and a bumper bar of Dairy Milk. Stat looked quite overwhelmed at the 'kindness'.

Rex leaned against the kitchen cupboards with his leg tucked behind him, as if he needed the support, despite the resolutely cock-sure look on his face. He had not spoken a word for the entire journey back to London.

'I think I'll just have a lie down,' Stat said. 'Be right as rain in a couple of days, Rex. No need to worry.' Rex's flamingo leg wavered a little, but not enough for any forward propulsion. Shelley moved to help Stat into the adjoining bedroom. 'I'll be fine,' he waved her away with a weak smile, and tottered off on his own.

'Yeah, and so will we,' Rex sniffed. 'You can go now, we can manage...'

. . .

Mistakenly stepping onto the eastbound Circle Line only echoed Shelley's clouded panic at not having any real destination, or any particular purpose to serve anymore, after her dismissal from Stat's flat. But as the tube rattled out of yet another tunnel, she stayed where she was, spending the next two hours riding round the Circle without leaving a station; gradually calmed by the anonymity, the regular beat of the train on the tracks and the feeling of going somewhere. Even if the somewheres were completely irrelevant.

She finally got off at High Street Kensington. At least Russell had offered her another direction. One more wave of guilt washed over her as she turned the key in the lock of his Georgian terrace basement flat. She had to take a moment on the doorstep to process the disappointment. She so wanted to leave the guilt behind and rebuild her resilience back in the city, not just add another strain of it.

She stepped into Russell's lavish flat, marvelling at the careful taste and homely luxury of each of the rooms, but still feeling as though she was taking something that wasn't hers. It was freely given, she had to remind herself, as Russell's gestures throughout the years tended to be. To her mind, she had never given him very much in return. Apart from making him laugh.

Her name was written on a piece of court notepaper on the door of one of the two bedrooms. Flowers sat in a vase on the bedside table with a note:

Shelley, so glad you decided to come. This is your room, I hope it will do! Let it be yours for as long as you need it. I may see you later in the week, but if it's a long day in Chambers, don't feel you need to wait up...

She didn't see him for three days, although he had clearly been there two of those nights, leaving her notes in the kitchen and something new and inviting in the fridge. And, although never really losing the longing for some real human contact, she determined to enjoy what she could. Perhaps the solitude would do her good for a bit, whilst she steeled herself to accept her fate and search a little harder for a new academic job.

Her heart was not in it. Where it really was, she was trying hard not to acknowledge.

Until *The Daily Mirror* did the job for her.

It had been a very long time since the British tabloids had shown any consistent interest in Rex Trenton. Thirty-odd years ago, when he was in and out of notorious nightclubs, rehab centres, and Government Minister's daughter's knickers, he was rarely far from their pages. Three decades later, his 'assault' on the Lord Speaker's wife last month had been something of a reincarnation, in all the wrong ways. The Lady had decided not to press charges. Rumours were circulating that she'd quite enjoyed it anyway and she didn't want to give any more oxygen to the flame of publicity. For Rex, it wasn't quite that simple. The flame had been lit and was being tended nicely by lazy journalists, who saw an easy opportunity to fill a few more column inches dragging up all the old stuff about him and the Minister's daughter which had sparked the demise of them both. Sir Heston Wraysbury was reported to be furious. Again.

The current regurgitation of all these old stories beginning to run its course, and the tabloids unable to get any meaningful comment from the horses' mouths, *The Daily Mirror* had taken to running a tongue-in-cheek 'Where's Wally' feature on Rex over the last couple of weeks. Readers sent in pictures of grizzled old rockers, in chip shops, betting booths, and Asda. Today's *Daily Mirror*, however, claimed to have cracked it. Whoever Mrs Imelda Beresford of Winchester was, her camera shaken snap of 'Rex Trenton' being driven out of the gate of the Hampshire stately home of the Earl of Bedingford had earned her the prize –

a bottle of Irish whiskey and an Edge of Darkness bargain bin 'greatest hits' CD.

Shelley stared at the picture, barely registering the incongruity, a lump appearing in her throat merely at the sight of the Manor gates. It was still there that evening, and her third glass of Russell's champagne was doing very little to shift it. Russell had been adamant they 'celebrate' when he returned home earlier than usual, carrying three bottles and a Harrods hamper. Almost an hour later and Shelley still had no idea what they were celebrating. The image of the Manor gates imprinted behind her eyes, like blinking into the sun, she downed another glass in an attempt to see something else.

It still felt like commiserating...

'I'm not sure you know how long I've been waiting for this to happen, Shelley.' Russell's voice broke through the early morning champagne-fuelled muzz, combining with a deep musky aftershave and cigar smoke into a confusing cocktail for the senses. For a moment, Shelley was not sure what was sound, what was smell and what was feel.

Oh. She could feel *that*. She sprung upright, a delicate glass tumbling to the floor from the bedside table and the duvet slipping down to her navel. She grabbed it back.

'And I know you perhaps didn't plan it to. Not just yet, anyway. Here, let me get that.' Russell leaned over and pulled the duvet back up to her chin. She wasn't looking, but she could tell he was smiling. She saw that protective smile a lot in her mind over the years. He turned her chin towards him. 'Everything at your call from now on, Shelley. Absolutely your call. Whatever my other shortcomings, I have an enormous capacity to wait. Especially for things worth waiting for.' His gaze drilled right through her, displaying an enormous capacity to convey that she was making that completely impossible.

'How about some breakfast?' Russell leapt out of bed and padded to the dressing gown on the back of the door.

Oh dear. That was impressive as well.

He called her from the kitchen a little later. 'All done, come and get it!' Shelley paused, but had so far failed to navigate the maze of surprise, horror, anxiety, warmth and thrill she was currently experiencing and couldn't stay here pinned to the headboard all day, so she got up, taking the second dressing gown from the back of the door.

Russell gave her no further opportunity for embarrassment or uncertainty as he chatted away about pretty much everything else, before announcing he was late for Chambers and hoped he'd see her this evening. Ten minutes later he was back, dressed in his exquisite suit, leaving her with the tiniest of brotherly pecks on the cheek. At the same time a look in his eye that was about as far from brotherly as you could get without criminal charges.

'I think I still need to go back to Bedingford, Russell,' she caught him at the door.

He turned, frowned, and despite his lateness, sat down again, closing yesterday's *Daily Mirror*, which she seemed so intent on studying.

'But it's not good for you, Shelley. We talked about it. We agreed, didn't we?'

'Yes, but—'

'It pains me to see how much that place hurts you, Shelley. I think I've come to an accommodation with it over the years. I've always wanted to belong there, but never really felt it. Perhaps we both have to accept that it's not for us and we just belong somewhere else.'

'I... I don't know.'

'Well, why not stay for the rest of the week anyway, have a twirl around the city while you're footloose and fancy free, eh? Take a little time for yourself.'

'That's what Victoria says.'

'Well, the batty old dear gets some things right. Settled then, yes? And I'll come back with you at the weekend and we can see how it is...'

Shelley stood for a moment, watching the closed door. She contemplated ringing Stat, see how *he* was. But clearly, he wasn't her problem. She'd ring the Manor again then, check on Matthew. But he had been at pains to show her that he didn't need her either. It was confusing. For so many years, Shelley had presented herself as a blank canvas for people to paint whatever they wanted. This had gone on so long and ran so deep that, now she was finally risking finding out what she really wanted for herself, the disentanglement was proving painful.

Russell offered her a little tranquilliser, that's all.

28

MATTHEW ON THE EDGE

Pip stared at his reflection in the shed window in the early dawn light; something he was not at all accustomed to, despite the careful attention he had learned to pay to other people's faces. The five o'clock shadow was more like a solar eclipse. Shaving was not something he had missed at all.

And who was this person, anyway?

Did he look good? He'd had to look good in other ways for two weeks, and he'd done it, played the game, gone along with every suggestion. But he hadn't really been there. Moving along as if on a travelator, with no real volition. So many things going round in his head, but the loudest soundtrack remained the unfamiliar gritted clip to *her* voice that night in The Huntsman's. Her words, her bewilderment, her reaching out to him? To believe? And he could do nothing to respond to any of them. He was not allowed. It had seemed like no choice; a no-brainer compared to even five more minutes in a cell. But it had turned out to be torture.

His final meeting with his Probation Officer yesterday and he was, officially, free. But what did freedom mean, now? Safety? He had run from prison to this village for a second time, the only place of safety he remembered. But the constant churning in his stomach and the heaviness of his heart shouted loud and clear that it was not safe. He had felt moments of safety in that Folly with... *her*. Moments in that Folly when he had glimpsed possibility – that he might make it, he might have something after all, if he could only have *this*. When he became the drums, as he always did, when he was *just* a drummer. And when he looked out of the window to the woman sprawled out on the grass below, creating something, investing in something. Investing in... *him?*

If he'd only had the courage to be honest.

He felt it like a punch in the stomach then. He had lost far more than even he had feared. Without her, he had lost the opportunity to play again, to play for himself. But more than that, he had lost someone who, in however small a way, had seen his reality. And the bereavement of that was far worse than any of the panic he had felt at the prospect of losing his liberty again. His liberty had been in that mad, silly castle, amidst that mad, silly circus, with this mad, silly... *love?*

He'd traded his real liberty for just more silence.

It was four o'clock in the morning. And he had to go...

Pip stopped at the drum padlock gate. One more look before he left for good? It was early, no-one would know. Perhaps he could just touch that beautiful drum kit one more time. Perhaps she would be there, too. In some metaphorical way, he knew she had gone. He deserved the added torture of that. To be certain of all he had lost.

The padlock did not open on D.R.U.M. Of course. Locked out of that as well, it was obvious. Pip sank down to the grass verge and, finally, cried.

The warmth of the waxing sun tightened his heavy head. It was time for him to go. He got as far as the Main Gate. He glanced through the railings, even though he knew the Folly could not be seen from here, only the long drive up to the Manor in the distance.

And the Earl of Bedingford on the roof.

Matthew was sitting on the parapet between two chimneys, his hands on the rafters, his legs apart, dangling over the edge, and his head looking down between them. There was no movement, but Pip knew immediately why he was there. Even at this distance, he could see it and feel it.

And he knew it was wrong.

It wasn't easy getting up and over the gates, but drummer's arms proved useful, and before he could stop to argue with himself, he was on the other side and running towards the Manor.

Victoria rushed out in her nightgown, followed by Beryl. 'Matthew! Please stop this nonsense. Come away from the edge now, please!' She turned towards Pip panting up the steps. 'Who the fuck are you?'

'How long's he been up there?'

'I...I don't know,' Victoria gulped, it was obvious that didn't happen very much and it frightened her. 'A falling roof slate crashed into my window a few minutes ago. I got up to see what it was, and there were his legs dangling up there above me. Oh no, oh my goodness!'

'How would he get up there?'

'The attic, I suppose, but I can't get to it.'

'Have you phoned the police?'

'N...no, good idea.'

'And show me the attic.'

Despite her stature, Victoria was slower up the stairs than Pip felt like, but he followed her to the attic hatch. The ladder was down and he scaled it in seconds. In similar seconds, he was back.

'He's locked the roof window behind him. Is there anyone else around?' Victoria shook her head slowly, as if she had never felt it so keenly. 'Phone the police,' he repeated. 'Fire brigade, whatever, I don't know...'

When Victoria returned outside a few minutes later, Pip was two-thirds of the way up the side of the building. Her jaw dropped. The fire escape was only partial, and the wisteria was proving an unreliable substitute. She gasped as a rusty step disappeared beneath his foot and Pip was left clinging to an upstairs windowsill. She had no idea how he managed to pull himself up, but gave silent thanks that her 'burglar', or whatever he was, came equipped with such arms.

Powered by adrenaline and years of constant drumming, Pip finally pulled himself up over the rafters at the side of the house. He paused for a moment, a bit alarmed at what he had done, the flat gravelled roof swimming beneath his jelly legs.

The wind was getting up. Matthew was gently swaying.

'Lord Bedingford,' Pip said quietly, not wanting to startle him. 'Matthew...' But Matthew did not move or show any acknowledgment of his presence. Pip hesitated to approach from behind, but since the alternative was a fifty-foot drop, had very little choice. He came slowly forward, repeating Matthew's name. Still no response, until he just sat down beside him.

Pip could see Victoria's hand fly to her mouth as Matthew pitched forward then, but he had already tucked his hand into his trouser belt. Both men's legs dangling over the precipice, Matthew's initial startle mutated into a direct stare. No real fright at this near stranger appearing from nowhere, just a silent, confused direction. And Pip knew with no doubt, as he had immediately sensed at the Manor Gate, this man didn't want to do this. He *knew* it. Glancing down at his own wrist, a faint purple line only just visible, the knife had been too blunt to even break the skin. He hadn't either.

'Pip,' he said, holding out his free hand. 'You probably don't remember.'

Matthew did not take his hand. It would have been too much

of a gift if he had. Pip knew that with both hands he could pretty quickly bundle the Earl out of harm's way. But there was something so confused and desperate in Matthew's eyes that he wanted a gentler approach anyway.

'What's all this about, then?'

Matthew did not answer, but his hand tightened around Victoria's hip flask as he crumpled the piece of paper he was holding in the other.

'Have you written a note?' Pip nodded down at it. Matthew peered at Pip as if he was speaking French and he was trying to remember his O'level. He tentatively shook his head.

'Oh. How is she supposed to know what you're doing, then?' Pip cocked his head towards Victoria, still rooted to the ground, staring up at them.

'She's not,' Matthew no more than mouthed, but it sounded like a question.

'Well, she bloody well will in a minute.'

The two men's eyes locked then and Pip let it be for a moment.

'What would you write if you did?' he continued matter-of-factly. 'I'll tell you what, let's go down and write it now, eh? I know, we could both do it, and then we'll both come back tomorrow and jump together. How about that?' Matthew's mouth twitched. It was enough to keep Pip going. 'I don't mind. Plenty of ammunition for mine. I've got a list as long as your arm, you know. I'll tell you about it. You first though.'

As Matthew continued to stare at him and another gust of wind blew through his hair, Pip raised his voice a little. 'So, what's so bad about being the Earl of Bedingford, then?' Pip knew that, now more than ever, but he could feel Matthew's trouser belt straining at his fingers and just wanted to keep him talking. Or at least listening.

Another rush of wind smacked their faces. Matthew

continued to stare silently at him. Pip's eyes widened in recognition.

'You can't really hear me, can you?'

Matthew twitched again. Pip touched his free hand to Matthew's face. 'One?' he asked, gently turning his head one way. 'Or both?' He turned it the other way. And Matthew held it there. Pip nodded. 'Better in the left, eh? Sorry then, I sat down on the wrong side.'

Matthew continued to stare at him whilst keeping his head turned. Pip's chest tightened. But as he breathed into it, he had never felt so certain in his life. Something he had, something he was, that another person needed.

'How long's that been going on then?' he continued breezily into Matthew's better ear, as if nothing of the remotest significance had crossed his consciousness.

'Started to go about two years ago.'

'And you've never told anyone.' Matthew's direction increased as he stared at Pip. He didn't need to answer.

'I woke up one day last week and this one seemed hardly there at all.' Matthew's hand raised vaguely to his right ear. Pip nodded and waited for more. Matthew's eyes, so far dry, started to fill. 'You see?' he demanded. 'It *was* the last time I'd hear it, after all. I've lost all this.' He waved across the Manor grounds but couldn't seem to look at it any more. 'And it *was* my last chance, after all.' He could have been talking about any number of things, but it was becoming clear what was uppermost in his mind. 'The *music...*'

Pip stared straight back at him and nodded. 'I expect there's been a lot of music over the years. Up here,' he tapped Matthew's head. 'In here,' he put his hand over his heart. Matthew seemed transfixed by him, and Pip was not letting go. 'Opera is it then? What you like?'

'Not really, I just did it for the money,' Matthew retorted with self-directed venom. 'The last chance to hear music performed in my home and I wasted it on bloody opera! Much rather listen to Progressive Rock.'

'Ah well, that is a tragedy. I can see your point now.'

A hint of a smile battled to break through and Matthew's trouser belt loosened around Pip's fingers.

'How old are you, then?'

'74,' Matthew muttered, turning away. 'Whatever difference that makes.' The spell seemed broken suddenly, as if Matthew had glimpsed something but had been reminded how futile it was.

'There you go, your ears have had a good innings, as they say. Stupidly probably. But there is something lovely about that.'

Matthew's head still turned away, he muttered something else. Pip bristled at the faintest sound of sirens screaming up the driveway directly below, but touched Matthew's face and gently turned it back towards him.

'I'm afraid you're going to have to look at me if we're going to carry on this conversation. It looks like the cavalry have arrived, it's windy up here, and I've been deaf since I was 15.'

29

THE HERO OF THE HOUR

Nobody knew how Pip talked Matthew down. Victoria had watched helplessly from below as he just stared at the younger man holding his face in his hands and speaking to him. It all happened so quickly then, Matthew bursting into tears, falling into the stranger's arms, and together they had shuffled from the edge before Sergeant Riordan even had his loudhailer out. By the time the fire brigade got to the attic, Pip had unlocked the roof window and was leading the Earl back down the steps.

Sat in his throne chair with a blanket around him, Matthew was having his vitals assessed and Pip a couple of bleeding gashes to his arms and leg dressed but, satisfied that no major injuries had been sustained and no further misdemeanour had taken place, the firefighters, police and paramedics left. The medics handed Matthew a leaflet about support services; the fire officer gave him a cautionary warning about the state of his fire escape and a best practice advice note. Both disappeared down the side of his chair cushion.

Sergeant Riordan put a hand on Pip's shoulder before following them out. He looked relieved.

An hour later and Pip had not been allowed to leave, sitting opposite on the threadbare window seat whilst Victoria plied them both with sweet tea. Matthew was silent again, but he was drinking the tea and nibbling at a slice of ginger cake. He continued to stare at Pip. Victoria looked on, her chest heaving a little still, but hiding her emotion at Matthew's salvation by proceeding to give Pip elocution lessons.

'Are you sure that cut on your hand is alright, young man?' she persisted as she brought more tea.

'They said so, didn't they? It's nothing.'

'*Nuffin?* What is nuffin? Is it a new sport?'

Pip had initially been tempted to tell her to *fuck off*. In one of the few enduring certainties of his life, he knew that his speech remained extremely good. He'd heard it clearly for fifteen years, remembered it well, and most of it was muscle memory anyway. He'd been born and lived in a hearing world, and constant practice, paying close attention to his voice, had been one of the main ways he had kept his deafness hidden for years. But it soon became clear that Victoria's problem was the words he chose, in the remnants of the South London accent he was born into, not the manner in which he delivered them. She seemed completely oblivious to any potential offence. In fact, for her, the use of 'ain't' where 'is not' should be employed was the far greater wound. But, while he was paying attention to what she was saying, he noticed his heart rate lower and the knowledge that he was completely the wrong person to feel welcome in this place was momentarily forgotten.

And Victoria's voice was astounding. Partly it was the low register of the eloquent boom, but he had never come across anyone who was less effort to understand. It fascinated him immediately and gave him an unusual sense of fair play.

'Yeah, I'm sure.'

'*Yes*, Pip, if you please.'

'Don't you ever let up?' But there was a twinkle in his eye and something passed between them then that he didn't quite understand.

'Never. Be under no illusion about that.'

'Would you excuse me for a minute, if that's allowed?' Pip got up and crossed the room without waiting for an answer. 'I promise not to leave without your permission.' He almost felt like smiling; this unexpected warmth was a very peculiar turn of events this morning.

'Resorting to insult, dear boy, is no guarantee of my continued good nature!'

Pip did not turn and a flicker of surprise crossed Victoria's face.

'He's not ignoring you, Victoria,' Matthew finally spoke. 'He's deaf.'

'*Really?* Great heavens, that passed me by.' She looked a little annoyed at this unaccustomed state of affairs. 'You'd never know, would you? How deaf?'

'Much more than me,' Matthew replied, fixing her steadily with his eyes.

'Thank you, Matthew, for finally trusting me enough to tell me. I do know, you know.'

Matthew nodded slowly. Nothing would surprise him now. 'It was the last straw, I think,' he said, finally allowing the trust to grow. 'I rang The Samaritans this morning. The man spoke so gently I couldn't make out what he was saying.'

When Pip returned to the room, Matthew was crying again and Victoria appeared completely unmoved.

'Well, why on earth all the secrecy?' She was looking at both of them. 'So, you can't hear very well. Why is it so necessary to hide it?'

'I don't,' Pip replied defiantly, casting a disappointed look at Matthew at the loss of the confidence between them. 'I've just had plenty of opportunity to learn that it's mostly unhelpful to volunteer the information.'

'Really?'

'I'm not ashamed of it, if that's what you're thinking.'

'Of course not. Why on earth should you be?'

'Practice? I've had an enormous amount of very diligent teachers.'

'Your sarcasm is most illuminating.'

'Goodo.'

'One can have too much of it, however. But, I must say, this conversation is proving somewhat circular. If we are going to continue like this, I do hope your lip reading skills are up to scratch.'

'Reckon I can cope.'

'If *you* are going to continue like this, that's the least of his worries,' Matthew hiccuped in the first hint of humour since the opera night.

'I'm guessing you have no problem hearing her, do you?' Pip grinned and Matthew almost returned it.

What he really wanted to say was that he didn't either. Victoria's voice and face, her whole demeanour, fascinated him. He could sit and listen to it, work it out, for hours. He didn't yet have the confidence, or the inclination, to tell her that, though. He was not at all sure what was going on here.

Victoria pretended to sigh. 'Alright, as we are at a fairly natal stage of our relationship, I will concede the point until I uncover the full truth. Most disabilities are hidden, I suppose.'

Pip rolled his eyes. 'I've long since given up regarding it as a disability.'

'Indeed, my apologies. I rather fell into that one. I will not allow it to happen again. The disabling factor in most cases is other people's expectations, is that not it?'

Pip felt suddenly hot, impaled on the sharp nail of insight. From the first of so many people to suggest in his teens that 'of course he would have to give up his music', to the violent mocking of his criminally disappointed father, to the terrifying bullying in prison, *other people's expectations* had become the defining feature of his life. At first defying them and, eventually, avoiding them at all costs.

'It appears, however, that you do have some disability with your legs,' Victoria nodded to the floor. 'They seem to have a life of their own.' Pip slapped his hands on his thighs in a determined effort to still them. But she was right, they did, and this conversation was pumping it full of oxygen.

As a teenager, when Pip knew that he could do nothing else with his life except be a musician, he began to experience a hot terror of people finding out about his increasing deafness. At the same time becoming exceptionally skilled in other forms of 'hearing'. He gradually came to realise that he could tune his body to augment his remaining hearing and, with complete dedication and determination, had over the years achieved a completely different relationship with sound. A relationship he wouldn't trade back now for anything. But over the same years, he had become so expert at hiding it that even the mention of other people's expectations of him (rather different and considerably lower) flicked the switch of that same terror, bypassing his brain straight to his highly sensitised body.

'Look, I think I'll go now...' Pip attempted to head for the door, but Matthew rose from his chair to embrace him so quickly and genuinely, it stopped him in his tracks.

Matthew took both his hands in his. 'You were absolutely right. Of course I didn't want to do it. Thank you.'

This seemed to be the last straw for Victoria. 'Then how the bloody fuck could you, Matthew? How *could* you? After... *everything*. Or did you think that I'd had so much practice with Robert, I'd just *get on with it?* This week of all weeks as well.'

'I know, I know. I am so, so sorry. I didn't really want to. I don't know what came over me.'

'Then promise me you will never, ever, even think of doing that again!'

'I promise.'

'Then you will excuse me for a moment.' Victoria's eloquent boom wavered for the first time. 'I am going upstairs for a short while. When I return, there will not be one more word about it. *Ever.*'

A moment later, Victoria reappeared at the door.

'Your rucksack is still in the hall, Pip. By its size, it looks as if you were planning to go somewhere somewhat permanently. I do hope that is not the case. I rather think we should like to get to know you better. Isn't that right, Matthew?'

'Oh, yes!'

'There will be a dinner Friday night – pension day for both of us – we will expect you at 8pm sharp. Are both things understood?' She turned at the door. 'No need for dress.'

'But you're not going anywhere, are you?' Matthew said, as she disappeared. 'Because you already said you're going to show me other ways to hear music.'

'Am I?'

'You promised!'

'Ah...'

As Pip walked down the Manor steps a few minutes later, a stuffed dog toy landed at his feet. He turned to look up at the open window, where Victoria stood holding up four fingers on each hand and a knitting needle.

'Eight sharp,' she mouthed.

Pip had no idea why he would be in the slightest inclined to obey her. But he was.

30

THE ELOQUENCE OF INSIGHT

Pip did not know what he expected of his first ever dinner at a stately home, but it probably wasn't boil in the bag liver and an arctic roll.

'I do apologise, Pip dear, Matthew has already made a start on the Campari.' Victoria shooed him into the dining room. 'He's been reasonably good of late, what with sitting mute in his chair for the last two weeks, I am allowing him this small relaxation in inhibition.'

Matthew was sitting at the head of a huge but desolate old dining table, laid out with three places at one end, staring into a glass of lurid orange liquid and counting his fingers from behind it. His smile was immediate and broad, if a little crooked. He rose unsteadily to his feet and immediately embraced him.

'I am so relieved you came, Pip! Victoria was sure you would, but I thought I knew better. I should know by now,' he giggled. 'Come, come, sit down!' Matthew swept a hand over the table. Pip drew another big breath, instinctively looking back to the door. That old habit he still couldn't shake from prison – always check your escape route is clear.

Victoria touched his arm. 'It is most important that you are comfortable, Pip. Benignly giggly as he is now, Matthew may not be here if it hadn't been for you. You do know, don't you? You haven't just saved his life, you have given him hope... Am I making myself understood?'

Pip nodded, gingerly taking hold of the chair she held out for him. Matthew muttered something over his glass. Pip checked the door again.

Victoria clearly registered his unease, even if she misinterpreted the cause. 'Matthew! You are making it quite impossible for our guest. Sit up straight and stop mumbling this instant!'

Matthew responded with a lopsided grin and an exaggeratedly mouthed 'sorry.'

'It's OK,' Pip was quick to reassure, uncomfortable and unaccustomed to drawing any attention to his deafness. 'I'm not used to this kind of thing, that's all. It's good to know it's just because he's pissed.'

'Well, we'll see, won't we?' Victoria sat down opposite. 'Now, I have seated myself directly in front of you, with perhaps a little more light than would normally be polite for a dinner party with an 86-year-old, since it will inevitably be me to whom you need to pay the most attention, and I should like to be assured that we will get on absolutely fine.' She paused, looking closely at him. 'I am using that sentence as a control.'

Pip burst out laughing. No-one had ever offered him so many words at once as Victoria did. Not anyone who knew he was deaf, anyway. It was fascinating. It gave him context and flow and rhythm, and a relaxing amount of time to home in on certain key words, without them all being strictly essential. And the tone of her mellifluent boom was gorgeous, her face expressive, her lip shapes clear and eloquent. Victoria fired her perfectly rounded vowels from the slow, precise rolls of the mouth of a Dickensian orator. Her tone, facial expression and gesture were fascinatingly animated, whilst her head, neck and posture remained fluidly upright.

'Too much?' she said, as his silent contemplation continued.

'No! No, please go on.' He was hooked.

'How much of it did you get?'

'Um, I don't know. Maybe half? But yes, thank you, sitting in front of me is very helpful, the extra light is good, and you're looking pretty fine for 86.'

'Goodness me, I bless the day you strolled into our life, Pip! A man with the presence of mind to flirt with a wizened old harridan such as myself, or even so much as possess the merest inkling that she may still own the relevant inclination, is entirely and utterly compelling in its extraordinary rarity! You are a fine and heartening example of remaining humanity.'

Pip bit his lower lip, the anxiety giving way to a suppressed giggle. 'Maybe a *teeny bit* too much.'

'Marvellous! You see? I am learning to understand *you*. We *are* getting on absolutely fine. Now, excuse me...' Victoria rose from the table, but stopped by his side. 'And please do not hesitate to say, Pip. It is a good deal easier for me to repeat myself than for you to do what you are doing.'

Pip watched her go. He was fairly sure nobody had ever said anything like that to him before either, putting the onus on themselves, acknowledging the effort he was making already.

With no other competing noise, Pip could hear a sense of a person's voice – the tone, rhythm and modulation – but rarely the individual words. For that, he relied entirely on lip reading, or as he preferred to call it, *people reading*. The lips were the major clue to the puzzle, but the rest of the face offered more. Gestures, breathing, pauses, even silences, provided further pieces. Memory, imagination and guesswork filled in the rest. Like a painter brushing attention across the different parts of the canvas to build up a more complete picture of sound, he was good at it by now. He knew that. How else would he have been able to keep it to himself all these years? He was full of dodges, tricks and manoeuvres – a conversational trapeze artist. Most often he landed on his feet, sometimes in a pre-erected safety net, occasionally flat on his face.

But *touch* was where his real skill lay. Pip's true ear was his whole body. If he could touch people as they spoke, he'd have to work half as hard. Except he'd probably be arrested. But *music* was different. Music was touch. Music was feeling. Music was real conversation.

Pip looked at Matthew, stroking his glass and drumming his fingers, and a sudden warmth filled his heart. Matthew would be alright. Matthew was a toucher.

Victoria returned with a bottle of vodka and a large bowl of Twiglets. Pip declined the vodka. He didn't think he could face that ever again, so was presented with the dusty old bottle of Campari by Matthew's side instead. He sipped at the unaccustomed drink, unusually eager to hear more. There was a strange, unfamiliar calm creeping over him as Matthew ploughed through his glass and Victoria chatted away as if they had known each other for years. Her complete lack of what he had come to know as 'normal' reactions to his deafness – avoidance, awkwardness, annoyance, or just plain shouting – was astonishingly refreshing. He leaned in a little, unconsciously touching his ear and steering well clear of the kind of mouthfuls Matthew was taking of this weird fluorescent stuff. Victoria's voice and delivery continued to fascinate, and educate him, and the more familiar he became with the type of sound she produced, and the meaning of her accompanying gestures, the quicker his expectations complemented the lip reading, so that by the time she wheeled in dinner on a hostess trolley, he was even beginning to match her. Her ubiquitous preference for twenty words where five would normally do was even a challenge that Pip was starting to enjoy.

The speed at which Victoria passed over any further curiosity about his deafness shocked him. That was what telling people did to you – it took away your ability to see yourself in any other terms than someone who couldn't hear. He had resigned himself to a lifetime of the rest of himself being invisible, unless he kept quiet about it. And this stranger, this militantly eloquent woman, had sought to educate herself enough to communicate with him and then waved it away with no more significance than the colour of his shoes.

It soon became clear, however, that Victoria had plenty of other challenges for him, especially since learning he was living in a shed and getting most of his patronage from Harriet Pordage these days.

'How come this pair of most unfortunate circumstances?' she continued to quiz. 'By which I mean the latter having far more detriment to body and mind.'

'It's a long story.'

'Excellent.' Victoria wiggled further into her chair. 'My favourite. I do hope you like liver. It's not for everyone, I concede, but I find those people tend to lack moral fibre.'

'It's fine, thank you.'

'I thought as much. Proceed.'

He did his best, leaving out most of it, which, of course, made the rest of it completely nonsensical. Matthew just listened, with a beatific smile on his face throughout. It seemed the more he drank, the more he heard, and he obviously enjoyed the experience so much he kept ploughing through the Campari until he fell off his chair and Victoria had to ask Pip to help her get him upstairs and into bed.

'Well, at least he's back sleeping in his own room. Another very worthy tick in your goody box, Pip.'

'Perhaps I should go now,' he ventured on their return downstairs.

'I do hope you will not. We have yet to experience Lidl's finest dessert and I rather think you have much more on which to educate me.'

Victoria shepherded him back into the dining room and

presented the arctic roll, giving him no further opportunity for argument.

'Now then, young man, we will pass over the indiscretion of your short spell in prison, to which you alluded in distressingly inadequate detail, to pursue a rather more significant one.' Victoria generously sliced the arctic roll and handed it to him with a distinctly prompting raise of her eyebrows. 'I shall not be indelicate enough as to enquire for what reason you found yourself in such an establishment. Should it be that you are prone to violent attacks on helpless old ladies, then I am somewhat passed the point of doing very much about it, since we are in the middle of the Hampshire countryside with not a conscious soul within screaming distance, and I have an antique emerald necklace around my neck, am wearing a platinum Rolex, and am carrying a Faberge vanity case in my handbag. The entirety of my wordly goods. My nursing home insurance policy, if you like.'

'Then you are even barmier than you sound.'

'Perhaps. Yet not a flicker of the slightest trepidation is about my person.'

'That is entirely justified. Oh fuck, I'm sounding like you now!'

'Indeed so! I am an exceptionally good judge of character, Pip. So if you will permit me another summation, I am rather good at them. You have found yourself coming of age in a society where the free market is king, luck favours the rich and most mouthy, and the rest are left to scrabble around with whatever is left. You have clearly lost a little confidence, and you have a criminal record. Not a happy set of circumstances.'

'Yep, you are good at it.'

'Thank you. And all of this appears considerably deteriorated by a complete inability to have acquired any particular skills or happened upon anything that you enjoy doing.'

'Well, I wouldn't say that.'

'I fully considered that you would not. That is entirely my reason for suggesting it.'

'Eh?'

'Am I to surmise from that short relapse into vulgarity that you require clarification of my last remark?'

'Yes, please.'

'Well, what *can* you do? What do you *enjoy* doing?'

'Oh. Right. Well... I suppose that... music... really is... my bag... you know?' Pip belly-flopped towards any further disclosure. Suddenly the ease had been broken and, despite the ice cream, it felt very hot in here. He might have to put a stop to this conversation pretty soon and found that strangely disappointing.

'I do not.' Victoria replied. 'Ah, I concede, a distant memory of John Lennon has surfaced to my consciousness. Your "bag" then, if we really must descend to this level. Do you play a musical instrument?'

'Yes. No.'

Victoria rolled her eyes. '*What* instrument? Please excuse my exclamation, Pip, but you are testing my patience.'

'I'm sorry about that.' Pip sighed. It had to end somewhere. 'The drums.'

Victoria flinched and was, finally, silenced.

But it never lasted. 'I see.' Her eyes narrowed. 'And, lest this is not entirely palpable, with any degree of enthusiasm?'

'I love them.' That came out without filter. Victoria seemed to appreciate it.

'May I say, Pip, that your immediacy is exceedingly welcome. I am almost overcome with relief that we are finally getting somewhere.'

'Are we?'

'Clearly. And if it is the drums that serve the purpose of my quest, I shall possibly have to go and have a lie down from the most marvellous kismet! And so, may I next enquire, is the apparent adoration of this particular instrument accompanied by any degree of... *accomplishment*?' She rolled the word around her mouth like a delicious fruit.

'Depends what you mean...'

'I mean, Pip, and really you continue to force me into the most unfamiliar directness – are you any good?'

'Oh. Well. Difficult to say, innit?'

'Is it? I rather doubt that. You will have gathered by the level of my observance and judgment thus far, Pip, that I have arrived at some considerable understanding of humankind in my 86 years. And this, amongst a great many other things, allows me to conclude with utter conviction that the expediency and volume of a man's enunciation of his abilities is almost always directly inverse to their quality and quantity.'

'Do you know, I have noticed that as well?'

'All credit to you.'

'It's just about sex, you know.'

'Indeed, and would you care to tell me what isn't? No, please do not answer that question. We have but moments remaining of this delightful evening. May we reserve the discussion about sex for another time?'

'Be glad to.'

'Good. And so, since you have not immediately offered the notion that you are the next Buddy Rich, John Bonham or Dave Grohl—'

'Bloody hell, Victoria!'

'My right-on-ness continues to astound. So, I am left to conclude that either you really are not very good at all, or you are under the illusion that I should interpret expression of the contrary as arrogance or conceit? I am, I should educate you, somewhat exaggeratedly fond of modesty in a man. As one rightly should cherish such a rare and precious jewel.'

'Ha! Don't like us much, do you?'

'An unfortunate misconception, Pip. It is just that one is so frequently disappointed. And please, I urge you to disregard my fondness for masculine humility in this particular instance, and do me the courtesy of honestly admitting whether you are, or are not, any good at all at the seat of your beloved percussion. I will, of course, accept the limitations of self-judgment, but please do try.'

'Oh, alright then. Yes.'

'Yes what? Yes you will try, or yes you are?'

'You're not making this easy, are you? Yes to both. Yes, I am trying, because I don't find this very easy. And... OK... Yes, I am.'

'Mmm. I find my instinctive pleasure at such a conclusion somewhat muted by your evident discomfort. But it is not a complete surprise from what I have gathered of your character. How good?'

'Bloody good!'

'Mmm again. I surmise from the alarmingly expeditious rise in both your temperature and volume that I have hit a nerve. Which is wholly welcome! It is difficult, I am to assume, for you to admit that you are good at something?'

'No. Well, perhaps. But it's much more than that... Oh shit, I don't think I want to get into this. It's very personal, you know. I don't talk about it. Let's just say, I haven't got a kit and I don't play anymore.'

'I see, then I must reserve judgment for some time later,' she fixed him steadily, an unreadable smile inching up her face. 'When you do.' She glanced at the clock on the wall. 'Fifteen hours to go, Robert. Isn't this something?'

Pip squinted to comprehend, but his body was restless and his eyelids were dropping.

'I see I have exhausted you,' Victoria finally conceded. 'And I am sorry. I must congratulate you, Pip. I know Matthew has been glazing over when I speak for years. Your attention is quite remarkable. Everyone should learn it.' She gathered up the pudding plates. 'So, I would like you to return tomorrow morning and I shall say what remains to be said without words. Please deliver your agreement on that to me now.'

Pip held her eye and let out a long breath. It was as if he had no real volition in the matter. Reason screamed that this would be impossible. Whatever was happening here, it could not continue.

But his heart soared for something else.

He nodded.

'Good. And now, embrace me please, Pip, and be on your way...'

31

THE TRUTH ABOUT THE FOLLY

A small stone hit Pip in the back on his way up the Pordage front lawn the next day.

'Come here, please!' Victoria barked from the pavement. 'You didn't say you were working this morning. This is incredibly tiresome, not least because I am forced to the curtilage of a Pordage.' Pip hardly liked to look at her words but shuffled from the shrubbery towards the wall. 'Speed if you please, lest I be caught loitering and they have me shot.'

'Pordages not your friends then?'

'Do not evade the point, Philip! That is far too long a story and I know you would rather hear me tell it than look at me directly to know my sincere disappointment.'

'I'm sorry.'

'Meaningless.'

'Look, I can't come.'

'Oh, yes you can. And you absolutely should. I surmise that last night's *insights*, shall we say, frightened you. Clearly you have decided not to test that fear. But, this is part of my point, Pip, you need the practice.'

'I've had quite enough practice facing fear, thank you very much!'

'And you'd really rather avoid any more of it. Hit a nerve again, excellent! Well, there's still time. No later than 1pm, if you please. That is most important. So whenever you can break from your... *ahem*... work.' Victoria turned away, but retraced her steps, looking at him so directly Pip could not fail to see the change of tone. 'I do understand, Pip, but please do try.'

'Morning, Countess!' Russell waved as he unlocked his car in the drive, managing to say the title as if it were something you'd win at a cheap raffle. Victoria raised her hand in a distinctly ambivalent gesture and continued walking. Russell smirked. 'Can I have a word, Pip?'

Pip met him halfway. He had not yet fully worked out Russell's sound and always tried to get as close as possible before he began speaking. Perversely, Russell seemed to like that.

'Compliant as always, Pip. You're better than a dog with a treat in my pocket.' He was not close enough to catch that either, or any intention behind it. But he'd already had enough opportunity to conclude that Russell was one of the more challenging people to understand. Pip could only guess that, after so many years of practising courtroom inscrutability, the muscles that tighten and the lines that appear in response to emotion had become so under-employed on Russell's face that it was difficult to detect any at all.

'Must say I'm a bit surprised to see you talking to her, Pip. I assume she and the Earl don't know about your part in recent events?'

'No.'

'And I expect you'd like to keep it that way, wouldn't you?'

'Look, keep them out of it, OK? I'm not having anything to do with them. Let's just leave it at that, shall we?'

'Spirited, Pip. Well, of course it's not for me to say. I'm on your side, remember? I'm only concerned you don't get into any further *situations*, and returning to the Manor might make it a bit difficult for you to keep things to yourself, don't you think?'

'It had crossed my mind, yes.'

'Although I am becoming aware that you are extremely good at keeping things to yourself, isn't that right?' Pip was not sure if he imagined it, but Russell's lip movements seemed to be slower and more exaggerated with that last comment. He did not answer.

'Well, there's no need for me to tell them, is there? And whilst you keep your end of our bargain, then I have no reason to get in the way, have I? I expect Shelley would be disappointed though, and that is a concern to me.'

'What's Shelley got to do with it?'

'She wouldn't like to see them hurt any more than they are already. She's very close to Matthew, you know.'

'Not close enough,' Pip muttered.

'And what's that supposed to mean?'

'Nothing.'

'No, come on, I would like to know what you meant by that.'

'Really, nothing... just that perhaps he might need her now, and she's not here, is she? Wherever she's gone.'

'Well, I can help you there. She's with me, back in London. Speaking of which, so should I be. I have a lovely weekend planned for her... Anything else you need?' Pip was still standing there, and his foot had burrowed a hole in a patch of gravel.

'No, no, of course not.'

'Good, just let me know if there is...'

Well, he wasn't going to, but with *'she's with me'* looping relentlessly through his head for the next hour, at his lunch break Pip's gravel-burrowing feet took him straight across the road, through the deserted open gate and up to the Manor.

'Faith restored, excellent!' Victoria met him on the steps with a broad smile. 'I commend you on finding a little courage.'

'I just wanted to come, that's all.'

Pip was beginning to surprise himself with his own honesty. It seemed to come out of nowhere when she was around. Although Victoria had exhausted him last night, he had not really wanted to leave. He marvelled at the comprehension and trade in wit; more had passed his lips in that one evening than had done in the last twelve months. There were moments when he even heard glimpses of his old self. It was confusing; he was not sure who that was anymore. But he was still here, in the village; he hadn't run away. And, he suspected, that was not because he had suddenly secured a decent job and the acceptance and appreciation of a silent village, but because of a loud, foul-mouthed, aristocratic old lady who mined for truth, paid no attention to his hearing loss, and saw way past his barriers. An electricity rippled through his chest then, and it wasn't panic. In the end, perhaps this place still had more to keep him than he had to run from.

'Even better. Now, a little stroll? I have something to show you, as I indicated last night...'

Pip followed Victoria across the grounds, constantly checking her face to ensure that the unusual silence was real, but feeling renewed twists of discomfort as they approached the Folly, which only intensified as she unlocked the door.

It felt cold, as if frozen in time. The wild flowers had wilted in a dried up mug on the table and the sill was damp where the window had been left open. One of Shelley's jumpers remained slung over the back of a chair. Pip glanced up the stairs, but Victoria was heading to the big oak door at the back of the kitchen. Unlocking it, she stepped gingerly down a set of stone steps. He followed.

'I do hope there is still some workable electricity down here.' Victoria patted the dark stone wall at the entrance to a basement cellar. 'Ah yes, illumination! In every sense,' she added, noting Pip's wide-eyed shock as the flickering light revealed a huge space... stacked full of percussion.

Before them in the main part of the room were three full drum kits, towers of single drums, cymbals piled up against the walls, timpani, xylophones, glockenspiel, a vibraphone and, there in the corner, a full-size marimba. The furniture was minimal, the walls bare and the edges sharp and clean. But the end in which they were standing was a smaller quarter, covered floor-to-ceiling with Middle Eastern rugs and deep red velvet curtains, thick spongy armchairs and a sofa, dotted between shelves and displays of small percussion instruments, as if the owner could never decide where to sit, or what he might like to pick up next. The air here was thick with resonance, but Pip could barely breathe it. This was a place to hear *people*; the other end to hear *music*. If ever someone were to design a room just for him, this was it. His eyes began to fill.

'Indeed!' Victoria was reading him now. 'And so my motivation for the pleasure of your company this morning is entirely and delightfully exonerated,' her voice boomed even more than usual in this magnificent resonating chamber. But Pip was finding it difficult to focus on what she was saying, except to realise that she was unfathomably pleased about something. If he didn't know her better by now, he would have described the look on her face as 'smug'. But she was giving him no further opportunity for analysis; Victoria was settling herself in for the long haul.

'Now then, I have never been able to bring myself to part with Robert's collection, however bad our circumstances have become. It's all been kept locked down here exactly as he left it, lest Matthew be tempted by another disastrous day at the races. And now perhaps I know why,' she said, leading him through the treasure trove of instruments. 'As you may not know, my late husband had somewhat of an obsession with percussion. Despite the fact he had absolutely no skill! His father allowed him to convert this Folly to play, mercifully far enough away from the Manor for the old man not to hear him, but he placed strict limitations on its development. Building this basement, I suspect, was Robert's little way of getting one up on him. Although why on earth anyone would actually want to play anything down here, I do not know.'

But Pip did. The air was cool but dense, he could almost hear the walls, the acoustics in here would feel incredible. He wanted to touch everything.

'And now, you will take your choice of drum kit, Pip, and any other accoutrement that may assist your passage back into musical consummation. Although decidedly not, please, the marimba. It cost a small fortune in 1957, I have high hopes for its resale value at some point, and you are not yet ascended *that* far in my good books... Please do close your mouth, Philip. I have let it pass thus far, but it really is most unbecoming.'

Pip clamped it shut.

'You are also, I see, having great difficulty maintaining your focus on my face. This is quite delightful! Now then, which will you choose? The red, the silver, or the blue one?' Victoria pointed expansively. 'I fear I know very little else about any of them to help you make your choice. But no doubt you might. Perhaps you can even help me value one or two pieces which may have some advantage to sell. I think the time is finally approaching.' A sadness flickered across her face for a moment, but she twitched it away.

'No, I... I can't,' Pip spluttered.

'No, you can't what? Help me? Or choose? I rather hoped I would not have to make the one conditional upon the other. You have done enough for us already.'

'No, I haven't.'

'Please do not argue with me, Pip. It never works. If you haven't realised that yet, I am heartily disappointed. Now, if it were me, I would take the red one. It's just so pretty! And I believe it to have some provenance, a gift to dear Robert from John Paul Getty shortly after he moved to Guildford, and with a dedication from its original owner, Buddy Rich. Or was that the green one, can't remember. Whatever happened to that...?' Her eyes roamed the room, but there was no fourth drum kit. 'Robert had a particular obsession with Buddy Rich and Louis Bellson. Sadly, none of it translated into one iota of talent. But, as my insights have uncovered, I rather think that may not be the case with you. So it would have a fitting home.'

'I can't take that!'

'Philip! Please be in no doubt that I shall lock you inside this basement until you have rendered me with so plausible an expla-nation of your resistance that I shall be forced to concede defeat in this particular exchange. And let me tell you now, that will not happen!' Pip was too distracted to get any of that and just gaped silently at her.

'*Which?*' she abbreviated, helpfully, pointing again at each of the three kits settling on the red one and sighing as the silence continued. 'Your acquiescence now please, young man!'

'Well, if you're really sure... could I perhaps choose the Louis Bellson kit upstairs, instead? Would that be possible... at all?' Pip's voice was little more than a squeak now, looking directly at her once more, searching. But the truth was, those drums had *chosen him*.

'Upstairs? You have been to the Folly before? Ah yes, stupid of me, you know the lovely Shelley, of course?'

'Yes. No.'

'Oh, here we go again... Has she heard you play by any chance?'

'Once.'

'Hmm. And may I enquire with what words she described such an experience?'

'Fucking incredible.'

'Quite so! You see, I am never wrong. She has the best ears in the business— Oh, my goodness! You mean a performance on Robert's *treasure drums* was what she was referring to as "fucking incredible"? Bugger me, this is even better than I imagined!'

'Is it?' Pip gulped.

'Robert adored these things, Pip. And I adored him. And have never such since. That kit was his favourite, for some unknown reason. He was completely unskilled and lacked any form of co-ordination and it was the loudest and biggest of the lot, outrageously unsuited to a person with his vertical limitations. Somewhat like yourself.'

'You telling me I'm short?'

'And this is a revelation, clearly. Robert just liked to look at it. Sometimes he would even sleep up there with it. And the thought that he might, one day, be able to play it was the only thing that kept him from killing himself sooner, I think. Although everyone thought it was me, I regret that I was not enough.'

'Oh Jesus, no. He... *killed himself?*'

'Indeed. July 1964. The 15th Pip. At about 1.30pm. I mark it with something extraordinarily life-affirming every year.'

'What? No...'

'And I have truly excelled myself in 2023. Robert would have been so proud of me. He always was.'

'Oh, shit... Here, have this.'

'I have no need of a tissue, thank you, Pip. I have managed thus far without.'

'Mind if I have it, then?'

'In my day, it was not permitted for a man to cry. These days it is a little different, but not enough, I fear. It never stopped Robert, and that is all I need to say on the matter to assure you of my heartfelt warmth at the anticipation of your apparent emotion.'

'Soppy twat, yeah?'

'Mmm, I detect your irony as always, Pip. And it is most welcome, as it remains one of my greatest pleasures.'

'But... Robert, he... God, I'm sorry. What a bloody waste. I can see now why you might be even more upset about Matthew's... uh... *mistake* the other night.'

'Indeed, living with the Wolstenholmes can be a precarious business. They don't always have the tightest grip on the sanctity of life and liberty. But I am lucky, Pip, for I have known love, and that is worth the grief.'

'D'you reckon?'

'We survive, Pip, for that is what we are born to do. Another thing that you and I share. We battle on the best we can, with a little good luck here and there. In which case, I know – good thinking, Victoria – you will also need somewhere to play. So you must have the Folly, too. I will give you the key, now that Shelley has sadly gone.'

'But... I can't.'

'Can you not? I know it's a bit of a butthole of a place these days, but surely must be better than your tiny old shed. Plus, my satisfaction at your presence continues to bewilder me.'

'Me too, to be honest.'

'Well, I am gaining some enlightenment on that front. Robert would be so delighted. I insist.'

'Uh... OK?'

'Excellent. You see, Pip? You can hear what needs to be heard perfectly well! Eventually.'

32

A TOUCH OF MUSIC

The thrill of letting himself into the Folly later that evening was so very different from the first time, when he had felt so much like a trespasser. Now it was *his,* apparently, and Pip could not help the excitement. He closed the window and picked up Shelley's discarded jumper, holding it to him for a moment before throwing it aside. The eternal battle, shut out the unwanted vibrations. Instead, he took the stairs two and three at a time, gratefully sinking behind the kit and laying into the drums. The thought that they might actually be *his* drums now, as well, energising him into new heights of connection.

But he heard the words 'fucking incredible' and saw her face again, and had to stop...

That first night, it railed against every instinct in his body to stay here. He did not deserve it, and he lay awake half the night. But he spent the lighter hours looking around him at this baffling place, in a calmer acceptance. He lay on the soft plump bed, making star shapes with his arms and legs, staring at the high white ceiling above and stone walls around him. For three months he had woken to dark, rattling wood, cold air, and the thunder of his own thoughts through his shivering muscles. This morning, he woke to bright light flooding floor-to-ceiling windows, a musty warmth in the air, and the quiet, heavy stillness of his limbs. He padded across the stone floor, the coolness seeping into his toes, and stretched at the window, gazing out at the meadow and the lake beyond. As if he had never really seen the estate before, it almost took his breath away.

Until he glimpsed the dismantled grandstand leaving on the back of a lorry, and knew it was, *supposedly*, all his fault...

Matthew appeared at the door of the Folly that evening with two bottles of home brew and another packet of Twiglets. He wasted no time getting to the point.

'How do you do it? *How* do you hear music?'

'How do *you* hear music?'

'Um... through my ears? I think.'

'Yes, but *how?*'

'I don't know.'

'Well then, neither do I.'

Matthew frowned.

'All I mean is sound is just vibration, isn't it? Of the air, or some other thing, like this drum,' Pip ran his fingers over the tatty green tom-tom he was cleaning up on the table. 'Or a violin string. I think that comes through my ears too, but I also hear it in my hands, my arms, my chest, my feet, my head. You get the picture?'

'Not really.'

'Shall I... Shall I show you?' Pip offered, as if holding his hand towards boiling water. But he could no longer withdraw it as Matthew lit up.

'Oh, yes please!'

As he led Matthew down into the basement, Pip knew that his body was brimming with a drama that was completely unnecessary. After all, he was just showing a harmless old gentleman something, wasn't he? Sharing some knowledge, gifting a tiny piece of the enormous understanding of sound that he had accumulated over the years to someone who needed to receive it. 'This is *not* a performance,' he repeated to himself over and over as they descended the stairs. By the time he switched on the light, he almost believed it.

'Where shall I sit?' Matthew beamed. He was in Pip's hands now and enjoying the prospect enormously.

Pip had never done this with anyone else before, except his old music teacher at the Cathedral School, but he knew exactly where to start. As they had done all those years ago in the school hall. The marimba. The salvation at first to a confused teenage boy rapidly losing his normal hearing and, with it, everyone's expectations of him as a budding musician. He had taken to spending any spare hour of every day learning how that marimba felt. Every beat, every touch, every stroke, every interval between each note. It was the school marimba that first taught him it was possible. He had begun to hope and, like oxygen through a bush fire, he burned through every piece of percussion he could find in his remaining school years. Spending the rest of the time at home in the shed, hearing and feeling and understanding every inch of his own drums. By the time his hearing loss became severe, he was addicted to the alternative possibilities. And even, occasionally, beginning not to care.

'Right here.' Pip cleared a space on the floor under the marimba. 'It's big enough. You could even lie down. That'd be good.' Matthew did as he was told, if a little slowly. 'I can't tell you how lucky we are to have this here. It's practically furniture, something your whole body can hear. And maybe if you start to feel this now, as it gets worse, you will compensate. More than that, perhaps. I wouldn't go back now for anything.'

Matthew swivelled round. 'You're not serious?'

'Yes, I think so. I can't really remember what it's like not to hear like this, *only* to hear through my ears.' Pip smiled at

Matthew's obvious scepticism, the tiny distant voice of certainty and confidence, which had become the most silent to him, trickling back into his tightened muscles. 'You're scared right now. Of course you are. I completely get it. But for me, whether it's terrible or desirable to be deaf is irrelevant. It's become so assimilated over the years that it's just part of my existence, like the use of this hand.' He waved a drumstick. 'If my hearing was restored – or my deafness lost, if you like – it would be like having that hand cut off... I'd get used to it, I suppose,' he grinned. 'I have before. But anyway, never mind that, just have a go, see what happens for you.'

Pip picked up a range of beaters from Robert's extensive shelves as Matthew wriggled into place under the marimba.

'Close your eyes, don't try to do anything. Just keep your body as open as possible and pay attention to what you feel...'

Half an hour in and Matthew was hooked. Pip could barely persuade him to leave at midnight. And every day from then on, Matthew insisted on visiting for a 'lesson'. And every day he shuffled in hunched and walked out taller. Pip's mantra repeating through his head at all times of the day: 'We can all *feel* sound. All we have to do is pay attention. That's all.'

'*Pay attention...*'

33

THE GIFT OF TRUST

Shelley had lived in London for six years but had never done the tourist thing. And Russell knew how to do it with style – the weekend turned out to be a sightseeing bonanza. He had popped back to Bedingford to collect some papers, *he said*, didn't want her worrying, she needed time to herself. Harriet had seen Victoria shopping in Winchester and heard that Matthew was planning a new venture, *he said*. All seemed to be well, but they could go back together next week if she still wanted to, *he said*. He now had the rest of the weekend undisturbed and Shelley deserved some fun for a change, *he said*... And queuing for the Tower of London with the biggest ice creams she'd ever seen, speeding past Big Ben on an open top red bus, gazing up the Mall at Buckingham Palace, looking out over London imagining her future from the London Eye, and both of them getting crapped on by pigeons in Trafalgar Square – Shelley had to admit, she had not had so much fun in years.

On Monday morning, Russell thought she might like to join him at The Ivy for lunch. On Tuesday, he had tickets for The Lion King. On Wednesday, he wondered if she had ever been inside the Old Bailey and would she like a tour...?

It was all *very* distracting.

'I think we should go back tomorrow,' *she said*. Every day. 'I'm *definitely* going back tomorrow,' she said the following Friday.

'OK,' Russell replied...

Shelley was up early the next morning. Even so, Russell got there first, whisking eggs in the kitchen. Her phone pinged an email. She sat down, her brow immediately furrowing.

'What is it?' he asked.

'The Vice Chancellor of Cambridge University,' she replied, bemused. 'Could I come in for a meeting on Monday morning? He wants to discuss the possibility of me heading up some new research linked to my study on sound transmission at outdoor events... *What?* How on earth did they know about that?'

'Wow, Shelley, that's a result!'

'Yes, but—'

'The answer you've been looking for! Right in your lap, too. Congratulations, you absolute star! Come on, let's go up for the weekend. I can do a couple of meetings online, show you round all my old student haunts.'

'Well, yes, but—'

'I miss the old place sometimes, you know. I've been thinking lately...'

Cambridge was lovely. It had been another full day of top-notch sightseeing. Their aparthotel overlooking the river was sumptuously comfortable and *another* gastronomically enlightening evening beckoned at *another* of Russell's favourite restaurants. But thunder was rumbling and the mother of all storms was forecast overnight, so he proposed a cosy indoor alternative.

When he returned with supplies, Shelley was frantically packing. Today's *Daily Mirror* open on the bed.

In the only further Rex Trenton-related story the tabloids

could get, since being snapped outside Bedingford Manor, the paper reported that the Earl of Bedingford had tried to kill himself last week, according to 'uncorroborated reports' from the early morning bin men, which also suggested that Rex Trenton's drummer had heroically saved him from throwing himself off the roof. Clearly unable to get any further comment or picture from Rex, the snippet included an old photo of him scowling over a pooper scooper in Regent's Park, an awful and ancient picture of Matthew on a very rare attendance at a society garden party, and a very startled snap of Edge of Darkness drummer Alan Kent in his underpants at the door of his mate's caravan in Brentwood.

'I've got to go. I've got to go back to the Manor! *Now!*'

Russell put a hand on her arm. It was shaking and her eyes unfocused, boring into the half-packed case.

'I've got to go. I should have known. I should have seen how unhappy he was.'

'Come now, Shelley. How could you think you have any guilt here? Nothing that man ever does is your fault.'

She didn't seem to be hearing him. 'I've got to go.'

'It's late Shelley, there's a fearful storm brewing and you're in no state to travel. Just try to calm down. We'll sort this out and I will come back with you first thing in the morning. OK?'

Shelley sank onto the bed and stared ahead of her, sniffing back the tears. She nodded, giving up to his reassurance and direction again. But she picked in silence at the supper he had brought, fidgeting and switching arms to rest on every minute, her eyes roaming back to the newspaper. Until Russell put it in the bin when she wasn't looking. On her third glass of wine, she began to feel sick and he suggested she went to bed and try to sleep. Alone.

'Victoria, I am so sorry!' Tears trapped in Shelley's eyes, but her words spilled out. 'How are you? Where's Matthew?' She glanced through the drawing room door towards his empty chair. 'Is he alright? What happened? Why? I mean, I know why, of course. I'm so sorry, I should have known. I should have been here...'

'Thank goodness, a small pause,' Victoria smiled far more heartily than Shelley was expecting, or thought appropriate. 'Matthew is at the Folly with our new friend. Goodness knows what they do in there. I daren't ask. I am treading a little carefully, Shelley, I suspect you understand. I fear I pushed him a little too quickly and look what happened. I am not the metaphysical kind, as you know, but I think Robert has sent us this gift so I can atone for my neglect of them both. So I'm letting them get on with it. Suffice to say, Matthew returns from his visits with a little light in his eyes, and that is quite enough for me.'

It obviously wasn't enough for Shelley and she was off running before Victoria could ease herself properly out of her chair...

When she burst through the door to the Folly, Shelley could hear faint deep rich tones from the open door in the kitchen. She crept up on it. The door had always been locked and she'd never seen, or heard, behind it before. She cautiously stepped down the cellar steps.

Matthew was lying underneath Robert's old marimba with his palms flat on the floor, his eyes wide with wonder. Pip stood with his back to her, carefully striking the keys with a yarn wrapped mallet. And her heart skipped. Just a little. She was appalled.

'Bottom of my neck!' Matthew declared. 'Definitely felt that one there. Oooh, that's a new one!' His eyes fell on her then and his enthusiastic smile broadened even further. 'Shelley! My dearest, what are you doing back? This is wonderful! *This* is wonderful!' Matthew stroked his hand across the base of the marimba, ending with it offered towards Pip, who seemed to be taking an inordinate amount of time to turn around.

'What is he doing here?'

'Well, my dear, I have to say, educating me in the most wonderful way! I had a moment there where I nearly felt myself again. I'd almost forgotten what it was like. Good heavens, Pip, Victoria is right, you really are sent from the Gods!'

'But...' Shelley could barely begin to recite her whole list of buts. 'Don't you know who he is?'

'Well, of course I do, my dear, you introduced us. For which my sincere thanks, without it I may not be here today.' Matthew's hearty smile dwindled then. 'Ah, I see. This may be why you're here. Bloody tabloids. I am so terribly sorry about that, wasted journey, I feel excessively foolish about it now. It rather gives me the creeps thinking about it, actually. Do you mind awfully if we do not?'

'What? No. You... He... *Rex Trenton's drummer?*'

'Oh, that nonsense, of course he isn't! Those rags never let facts get in the way of a good story, do they?' Matthew tutted, but gave her no chance for further interrogation, shuffling along the floor and patting the wooden boards by his side. 'Come and join me, Shelley, please do. It is absolutely enlightening!'

Shelley did not move. Her eyes turned to Pip and stayed there. 'I have no idea what this is all about,' she said steadily. 'But don't trust him, Matthew. Please, do not—'

'I think I'm going to go now,' Pip finally spoke and, like so many times before, did not wait for a response.

'Pip, wait!' Matthew called after him. 'Oh darn, that's useless.' Trying to wriggle his way out from beneath the marimba, he cursed his old bones. 'Run after him, Shelley, would you? Victoria'll have my guts for garters if I come back for dinner without him.'

'No chance,' Shelley retorted. 'What on earth is going on here, Matthew?'

Matthew scrabbled to his feet and up the stairs to the door, where he took off his shoe and lobbed it out after Pip. 'Goodness, I need to learn sign or semaphore or something.'

'Try a torch, he likes those,' Shelley scorned.

'Ah, is that how you communicated? Marvellous, isn't it?' Matthew picked up a pair of Pip's drumsticks from the windowsill. 'It's given me so much hope. What a talent! Quite remarkable, isn't it, when he can barely hear a bloody thing!'

'*What?*' Shelley's stomach hit the floor. 'What do you mean?'

'Ah yes, understood. Darn it, you didn't know. Oh dear, he will be awfully cross with me, letting the cat out of the bag... again! Probably why he's buggered off.'

'Are you saying he's... *deaf?*'

'As a post, as they say. Ridiculously inaccurately for anybody, as it turns out! Strictly speaking, he's not got much below about sixty decibels in one ear and ninety in the other. Qualifies as severe to profound, I am told. But his audiogram is a bit of a ski slope; he's not as bad with low frequencies. I'm getting to be a bit of an expert, actually!' Matthew beamed. 'My hearing loss is barely *moderate* at the moment!'

'You... you too?'

'Oh yes, but it's fine now. Pip says I might have years and there's so many other ways to "hear". I've experienced a bit of it now and am extremely confused to say that I am almost looking forward to it. He is just so enlightening! I can have hearing aids too, you know, although Pip doesn't like to use them much, and never for music. Besides, Pip says Victoria and I are loud enough for him without! Ha! Pip says she's got the most phenomenal dynamics and low register in her voice, barely needs to concentrate. I don't believe that for one moment, the woman's a walking Thesaurus, but now I've noticed it too! Pip says he'll come with me to the audiologist anyway...'

Pip says, Pip says, Pip says... Shelley felt quite dizzy with it all.

'Can we go back to the Manor please, Matthew? I think we need to talk...'

'Absolute poppycock!' Victoria was having none of Shelley's explanations as to why their new friend should never be allowed in this place. 'Stay here with Matthew please, and keep him out of that chair. He has that look in his eyes again. Pull yourself together, Matthew! It's all nonsense, and I shall be back shortly to prove it...'

Pip was sitting on the wall outside Marilyn Harper's house, twirling his drumsticks through his fingers in an effort to calm himself and find the courage to tell her he was, at last, about to leave. How different this was to the many times, only a few weeks back, when he would be doing very much the same trying to find the courage to stay. Staring at the pavement, kicking his feet against the wall until they hurt, he did not notice Victoria crossing the road until she was right in front of him.

'Yes, and well you might look like that,' she launched in, long before Pip had any hope of hiding his rising nausea. 'So it appears that, despite my considerable efforts, you have been withholding some very vital information from me. Information which, to any normal person, would render our relationship quite impossible. Is that not so?'

'Wh...what information?'

'Oh, don't be so ridiculous as to prolong this matter any further than it needs to! I am too tired for more cat-and-mouse today. It was you, apparently. The culprit, the imp, the arch mastermind behind a community protest so far in excess of reason that it ruined our hopes of resurrection, hastened our final bankruptcy, and sent Matthew to the roof and the edge of madness. Is that not so?'

'Mmmbbb...' It was all Pip could manage, an acquiescence of

sorts, but his lips now clamped tight, his lungs imploding, the impending loss sweeping through him like a hurricane.

'Well, of course it isn't!' Victoria bellowed. 'This is quite ridiculous. What on earth is going on here that such a nonsense has been allowed to gain any ground at all? How has this come to be?'

'B...because it's true?'

Victoria sighed. 'Oh, very well, if we must play this game. What was your motive?'

'Eh?'

'*Pardon*, Pip, if you please. What was your motive?' The silence pulsed on as Pip studied the pavement. Victoria flicked his chin up to face her again. 'Has no-one asked this before? Goodness, what a surprise! No motive. So, let's move on to evidence, shall we? Exhibit A for the defence.' Victoria snatched the drumsticks from his hand. 'You're a drummer!'

'So?' The tiny bemused twitch in his lips was the first hint of a smile he had managed, but it was quickly lost. This was killing him.

'So, if you wanted to make a fucking noise!'

'Victoria,' he sighed. 'Your logic is impeccable, as always, and I really am grateful. Seriously, I... You'll never know how much. But it's done now. I'm sorry, really sorry, you'll never know how much for that too. I can't say any more than that and I'm leaving now, of course.'

'Absolutely not! This has gone quite far enough. Come with me.' Victoria tugged his hand from his side, pulled him to his feet and down the road, dropping it only when his arm loosened enough for her to be confident he would follow on his own accord. She said nothing until they reached the bench by the bridge, in full view of the top of Trefusis Lane and half of Yarnside Drive. She rummaged in her bag, drew out a chocolate brownie, broke it in half and handed it to him, launching into a conversation about early twentieth century Prime Ministers and the state of the Unions. After ten minutes, his unwillingness to laugh long gone, she led him back through the Manor gates.

'That will be billboard enough, I think,' she concluded.

Out of view, she stopped and turned him to face her. 'I shall pursue this no further, Pip. For the moment, anyway. I trust that, for whatever reason you have allowed this charade to perpetuate, it has some benefit to you. But Matthew and I will have no truck with it. And Shelley too, when I tell her the truth.'

'You're very sure of this, aren't you? I don't know why.'

'Yes, I am. And if you don't know why by now, then I am heartily disappointed. You are not the only one who observes, Pip. I have watched you closely since we first met and I cannot see it. It is, therefore, not there.'

'Victoria, you are incredible.'

'Quite so. As I knew you would say. Because – and I will permit myself a telling analogy – half this village detests me, and they are arseholes. The other half patronises me to get to Matthew, and they are not very far distant from that same anal cavity. You, on the other hand, have done me the service of doing neither and are, therefore, *not* an arsehole. Not to mention – yet again – what you have done for Matthew. What you are *doing* for Matthew, which we should very much like you to continue. A little trust, therefore, is my reciprocal gift to you.' Victoria paused and fixed him with another soul-reading stare. 'Besides, one of the benefits of my vast age and wisdom is that I have long since learned that some secrets need keeping, and some lies save lives. Either your own, or those you love.'

Pip could do nothing now but stare back at her, wanting to see more words, pull more truth from her. But immediately that fleeting notion began to strangle his breathing. His heart rate quickened and his foot involuntarily kicked out at the grass verge.

Victoria's eyes loosened, and she smiled. 'Alright now, off you go, play your drums, release this madness.' She gave him an indicative shove towards the Folly. 'We are expecting you still for dinner at eight. Of course, I shall have to make it stretch to four now. How splendid!'

'Victoria, wait! I can't come now.'

'Why so?'

'Shelley, she—'

'You leave Shelley to me. She sees things as they are too, Pip. She has just not yet developed the confidence to trust herself, as I have. Please do not do anything else to disappoint her, however. She's been let down far too much already.'

'I... I'll try.'

34

THE LIQUID LEASH

The Lamb and Flag on the Mile End Road was fuller than Rex was expecting for a Tuesday night. People were staring at him. Some nodded and smiled, most turned away and whispered with their mates. There was a copy of last Saturday's *Daily Mirror* still in the magazine rack on the wall. Rex thought it was deliberate.

A five-piece band struggled to wedge themselves and their equipment into a tiny corner. Yebut was clearing glasses to make room for the PA on a bar table. Surprised to see Rex there, he returned his small smile with a much bigger one and went on helping his band mates set up. All in their fifties and sixties, but not looking anywhere near as good as he did, Rex knew nothing of this particular outfit, although he was pretty sure the keyboard player used to be in that band who had that massive hit about hats in 1984.

Rex leaned on the bar, eyeing the optics greedily. He ordered a diet coke and turned back to the crowd, willing the band to start, to drown out the choir in his head in full chorus of the usual anthems:

'It's been such a hard day/week/month/year/life (delete as appropriate) *you just need a little reward...'*

'One night won't hurt, you can start again tomorrow...'

And top of Rex's personal hit parade: *'You're so talented and misunderstood, you deserve it.'*

The liquid leash...

The band was good. Rex wasn't really surprised. Despite the relentless teasing, Yebut was a master of the four strings and he didn't play for any old rubbish. Unless there was money in it, and it didn't look as if there would be much of that here. Rex watched as the band hoisted the PA to the floor so they could squeeze around the table to drink their feeble rider, shaking hands, thanking people for their endless repetitions of the usual, 'What are you doing in a place like this?' and 'You could have been someone.'

'Survival,' the guitarist replied gracefully. They'd all heard it a million times before, from people who never seemed to realise that it was their unwillingness to pay a musician for their music that kept them 'in a place like this' and ensured that they weren't 'someone'.

It was depressing, and Rex had not come here tonight to be depressed...

Stat was half asleep when Yebut's text pinged:

AT LAMB & FLAG. REX DRINKING.

Stat stumbled out of bed, into his vest and shorts, and out to the landing. He stopped at the top of the stairs. The pain was astonishing. His foot missed the step and he ricocheted down the stairs.

He was killed instantly.

35

SPEAKER TO SOUL

All trace of crew and equipment gone, Shelley now had full custody of Edward's suite of dusty old rooms on the top floor of the Manor. But for the fourth night in a row, she snuck into Matthew's bedroom to watch him sleeping, still not able to forgive herself for not hearing his pain. She who heard so much had missed the point so comprehensively. Trying to curry favour with Horace and make money to save the Manor, when it was really about Matthew's very identity, and the realisation of his life's dream – to make a music venue of his own home, before it was too late for him to hear it.

As the sun rose, her eyelids dropping, a faint warmth of security growing with the rhythm of Matthew's peaceful snoring, she slipped back to her room. Resolving that she could not let any more harm come to him, her customary passion for the task battled with the certainty that she was less equipped for it than ever.

When she rejoined him in the kitchen later that morning, Matthew was at the table opening a letter.

'I know,' he said, reading her shock, his hand twitching over the flap of the envelope as if it contained a death sentence. 'You look tired, Shelley. Is everything alright?' He lay the envelope down, clearly using her presence to commute it.

She nodded, unconvincingly.

'Come with me to the Folly this morning, my love. Please do.' He had been trying to get her to accompany him to his lesson for days. Every morning, she refused. 'You're troubled by Pip, I know. I understand why you're finding it difficult, but if it helps, I trust him with my life. I did on the roof and I do now. But if I'd brought him into our home and Victoria had said "no", I would have believed her. Because that trust is greater. Because she knows, she is always right about these things, and I do best when I listen to her... I'm trying to listen better now.' He slowly unfolded the letter. 'She promised me a bottle of wine with dinner if I opened this.' He scanned it and pushed it over the table towards her. 'The Council's formal Enforcement Notice for the closure of the festival.'

'They've taken their time,' Shelley sniffed, another tide of emotion proving unbearable, so turning it to scorn.

'Look at the date, Shelley. I've had it over a fortnight. Victoria found it in the dog basket.' He poked at the wodge of paper without reading a further word. 'How on earth can anybody take twenty pages just to say "no"?'

Shelley took it from him. 'I'll read it later.'

Matthew's eyes lit up. 'Well, that calls for a reward for both of us then! Come along, I can't possibly be expected to bear two "nos" in one morning...'

As he opened the Folly door, Pip's immediate smile froze. It reminded Shelley of the startled deer of their earlier meetings, which had been gradually taming itself to approach with an open heart and a trusting hand. She nodded. He nodded back. Matthew was already halfway down the stairs. Oblivious to the unease that continued to pulsate between them, he kicked off his shoes and lowered himself under the marimba.

'Do come and join me, Shelley,' he repeated. 'We always start and finish here. It's wonderful.'

She shook her head, sitting down on the sofa to watch.

'What did I say about any more "nos"? Five minutes, that's all, and if you don't like it, I promise Pip and I will do without you. Won't we, Pip?'

'Sorry...' Pip twitched with incomprehension. 'What?'

'You're lying in the dark, Matthew,' Shelley pointed out. 'Look, I'm making things difficult.' She got to her feet, addressing Pip deliberately directly. It seemed so odd having to suddenly think about what and how she was speaking to him. She wanted to release them both from the awkwardness, but did not know how. She hesitated, casting a glance back to the marimba and the array of instruments in the room.

And Pip's focus changed, as if he was processing her hesitance. She remembered that, too. 'It's OK,' he said, although it sounded like a question. 'It's OK...'

Matthew shuffled under the marimba to make room for Shelley beside him, their heads into the room and their feet touching the wall. Pip picked up two yarn mallets. He always began and ended with a few moments of gentle sweeps over the marimba blocks. It visibly relaxed Matthew, helping him become more receptive at the beginning of 'the lesson' and calmer to face his day at the end. Shelley felt herself immediately sinking into the floor as the sweeps sent ripples and pulses, then waves, through every part of her. Her eyes prickled. She pushed her palms into the floorboards, holding back the flood. She did not want to relax.

She was relieved by the focus of the first exercise. Pip struck the notes of the marimba individually – high and low, hard and soft – and Matthew tried to identify where he was feeling each and call it out. Matthew jabbered away, finding delight in every new discovery. Or none. He didn't mind when he could not feel any change, the implication that Pip *could* seemed to excite him just as much. Shelley's captivation remained unspoken, tuning more and more into each note, increasingly fascinated by the B-Road journey of her attention through her body to locate the sound, rather than the customary superhighway of her ears.

After the marimba, Matthew shuffled across the floor to lean against a large guitar amplifier at the side, awaiting the next daily ritual and making no effort to disguise his delight at this one as well. Pip picked up the old record that Matthew had brought from his collection. 'Don't tell me,' he sighed. 'Pink Floyd.' Despite being encouraged to bring something a little more percussive, it had been a Pink Floyd LP every day. But Matthew knew and loved the music so well, Pip conceded it was probably the better learning tool. Matthew hardly needed it to flow through his ears to know exactly what was coming next, helping him to focus on what he was feeling everywhere else.

They leaned back into the speaker, palms placed on the wall behind. Shelley wordlessly followed suit, the music tickling and thumping through her back and shoulders and up through her hands and arms.

This was the music of the happier space of her childhood. Whenever she visited the Manor it had been on. She and Edward used to laugh and moan about it, swap the vinyls in their sleeves, smother the covers in stickers. But now, as she heard it through her whole body, it took her instantly to that place, speaker to soul with no wiring in between.

She closed her eyes as tears threatened again. And the sound changed. She'd never noticed that before...

The ancient needle crackled to the centre of Side One.

'So, what do we know now?' Pip sang.

'Being deaf doesn't mean I can't hear,' Matthew replied obediently. 'Only that there is something wrong with my ears.'

'Bingo!'

They sat back-to-back on the amplifier through Side Two. Then they tapped wood blocks; they held snare drums on their laps; they gathered around timpani with their hands splayed out over the skin, like they were holding a seance. And when the end came and Matthew shuffled back to the floor under the marimba, Shelley felt strangely disappointed.

The mallet strokes over the marimba encased her within seconds, the remaining knots in her muscles untying. She closed her eyes, and within seconds more fell into the sleep she had denied herself for days.

Matthew and Pip crept out of the basement and left her to it, returning a moment later to lay a blanket over her and a pillow under her head.

36

THE BURDEN OF SECRETS

Pip lay down his drumsticks and checked the time. He had free access to a percussion orchestra downstairs in the basement, but he played *his* drums upstairs in the Folly every morning before leaving for work. And even if he was doing the *wrong* thing all day, he had done the *right* thing already, and his days began to settle and make more sense. His gift was locked now in this small safe space. He didn't care about the gardening, whether he was good at it or not. That was the cloak he wore for the world. Whatever he gave to it, gave out for inspection and judgment, there would always be this reality to fall back on. This little secret. The secret that he was born on that drum stool and nobody was ever going to take that away from him again.

With a few minutes to spare, he skipped down to the basement. He had spent most of last week going through almost every piece in the room, touching, feeling, playing all that he could, cleaning up and ordering them on the floor, walls and display shelves. Wanting to know where every piece was and where he might find the sound he most wanted to feel that day. For Matthew's lesson today, he decided he wanted something big. Ducking under a line of gongs suspended from a department store clothes rail, he pulled the largest timpani out from the corner towards the openness of the room. In the space behind, a blanket lay over a green jazz bass drum. It stood alone but clearly matched the emerald snare and toms upstairs. There were no jewels added to this one but, unlike the others, it was pristine. There was a note stuck to the kick pedal:

V. A kit to match your emerald eyes. If I don't finish it and you have to sell, please get someone who knows to do it. R.

Victoria told him once that Robert had left these notes every-where in the weeks before he died. It was the closest she came to hating him, she said. But it didn't last and she kept them all. And a thought struck Pip then, as loudly as if he had head-butted the gong that hung above him. He could be that 'someone'. He would finish restoring those drums and complete Buddy Rich's emerald kit for Victoria, to keep or to sell if she wanted to. This was something he could give back, for the trust and acceptance she had shown to him.

Cutting Timothy Smollett's hedge that morning was a good opportunity to think about it some more. It was also a good opportunity to watch for curtain movement next door. Marilyn lived a small, quiet life now, punctuated by re-ordering her spice jars, shining her garden tools with Silvo and all the other tiny routines that preserved her safety and sanity. Whether her version of sanity was one that anyone else recognised remained irrelevant. But Pip understood the little rituals that seemed to exist to keep her safely away from her emotions. He understood why emotion might be terrifying for her – it had been terrorising him for long enough. And he wondered if he had also been attempting to exert control over his life in such seemingly pointless ways. He had recently come to realise that he may have done.

But lately, he had become more watchful of her. Marilyn's world, her rituals, did not seem to be working, and her days were becoming unpredictable. There were fair days and bad days and worse days, and the curtains could usually be relied upon to advertise which were which. Occasionally, since the opera, Pip would see her walking to the village shop, or even getting into her car, making a cake (or five) and insisting she read to him the most pertinent articles from the day's *Telegraph*. These Pip identified as 'fair days'. Most mornings, however, he would find her with curtains half open, sitting in dark glasses in the kitchen. She allowed him to make coffee, clear up a bit of debris, and join her over a full plate of Sussex biscuits (shop bought), which she devoured with transient zeal before complaining of stomach ache and going for a lie down. She would usually emerge a couple of hours later, pull the curtains wide open and potter about the garden, albeit slowly. If he was passing again in the early evening, which he had developed a habit of doing, she would be gathering her things together, going through some ritual of putting it all away, awaiting the watershed when she would set up the groundhog day of the one before. This was a 'bad day'.

The last time the curtains remained closed at midday, he had found her on the sofa in the lounge with a black eye and a twisted ankle. She didn't know how she had come about either, but hobbled out later to press a twenty-pound note into his hand, on the understanding that it would go no further than the two of them. He had kept the bargain so far, although slipped the note back into her handbag when she wasn't looking. This was a 'worse day'.

Today the curtains were still closed at 12.30.

Marilyn's kitchen door was unlocked and he checked round the house. From a visual point of view, the place remained disturbingly quiet. Her bed had not been slept in, all the upstairs curtains were open. It was only when he returned to the back garden that he noticed the shed door moving in intermittent bursts. He opened it to find Marilyn on the floor, a tumbled stool by her side and the contents of the upper shelves strewn around her, including four empty petrol/vodka cartons which had long since been exhausted powering her lawn maintenance.

Marilyn's clenched fist dropped to the floor. 'Oh... marvellous,' she drawled. 'I've been calling you for hours... possibly. I am not sure I can move my legs.'

A cursory examination, and a bit of discreet manipulation, and Pip was content that they had only gone to sleep under the weight of one of the fallen shelves. Her elbow, however, was bent at quite an unusual angle.

'I don't think I'm really cut out for this,' she winced as he sat her upright.

'No, I don't think so either,' he tried to smile. 'And I think we might have to let someone else take a look at that this time.'

She argued. He won. He wanted to call Shelley from the hospital. She won that one.

'Please,' she said so deploringly that he had to obey. 'I don't want her to see me like this.'

And so he carried another secret. He was getting very tired of them...

'Hello, Russell. Have you heard anything from the police about the emeralds yet, please?' Pip appeared at the door of Russell's home office later that afternoon. He had decided that at least there was one secret he could do something useful with now.

'When you knock, Pip, you are supposed to wait to be invited to "come in".'

'I'm sorry, if you're busy. But I would like to get them back to the Manor as soon as possible.'

'I must say, when you're not in custody, you do have a particular knack for getting to the point. The police gave them back to my mother last week, seeing it was she to whom you told them they belonged, remember? She's rather pleased about it actually, green is her favourite colour. She's thinking of having a bracelet made.'

'But that's not fair! You can't let Matthew and Victoria lose any more out of this than they have already.'

'Yes, I agree with you.'

'You *agree* with me?' he checked.

'Yes, of course. I shall ensure they are returned as soon as possible. Discreetly with no comeback on anyone, including you. We have a bargain, remember Pip? Returning them yourself might make it difficult for you to keep your side of it, don't you think?'

'Look, I don't need to lie anymore. Matthew and Victoria know I had nothing to do with the opera disturbance. But it's done now and I won't expose Marilyn.'

'Admirable. Leave it with me. Perhaps I could give them to Shelley to return, whilst she's spending *a few days* back there.'

'So you'll tell her all about it, then?' Pip asked hopefully.

'Be in no doubt, Pip, I've always told Shelley everything she needs to know...'

Pip was re-examining Buddy Rich's emerald bass drum when Matthew arrived for his lesson that evening, followed by Shelley. This time she looked at him, albeit briefly.

'I hope you don't mind,' she said. He shook his head, although he thought he probably did. Matthew's daily enthusiasm had settled him into this new role, and he had even begun to look forward to these lessons. They took him right back to his earliest self-experiments as a teenager and that blissful term when the young locum music teacher had been fascinated by his quest and enthusiastically helped him develop. Now he was disappointed to feel the old rattle of apprehension through his muscles at the prospect of further audience.

'I thought we might try and make you worse today,' he

attempted a joke instead, holding out a packet of earplugs. Matthew passed a pair to Shelley with an accepting smile, and held out his hand for another one. Pip looked at her; she shrugged. It seemed to be an indication of the submission of the both of them.

Pip watched them laughing together, trying to arrange themselves under the marimba, and his nerves steadied. Did this need to be about *performing* at all? What if it was just something he could give back to her, too? Might that begin to heal the damaged trust between them, without him having to say anything? In the way that he now realised he had always healed himself – not through words, but through his drums and through the feeling of sound.

'OK,' Pip paused after their few minutes warm up. 'Put the earplugs in and close your eyes. Try and feel the space, the resonance around you. Pay attention to your body, see what you can locate now when I strike the notes, without your ears. Shout it out if you like, but no-one'll hear you...'

'Alright,' he said sometime later, kicking their legs and gesturing to take out an ear plug. 'Now keep your eyes open when you put the plugs back in. Look at the instrument, look around you, see the space we are in. How does that affect what you are hearing? When I strike this note... And that one...? And this one...?'

And so the lesson continued, Shelley joining Matthew, following everything Pip said, so they were all really listening, feeling, watching. Patiently painting sound in that room...

An hour later they were standing in front of Pink Floyd at full blast, holding balloons to their stomach, ears still stuffed with the plugs, relying on the balloon to convey the vibrations more directly.

'It's too ticklish!' Matthew complained, unable to stop giggling. It was utterly infectious and suddenly they were all doing it until they were breathless.

'It's so lovely to see you laugh again, Shelley,' Matthew concluded, getting a grip on himself.

'You too!'

'Well, you young people must excuse me, my turn to cook dinner tonight.'

'What? You never cook, Matthew!'

'I know, but Victoria said I should try to improve. She won't be around forever, she says. Although I think it's the only thing she's wrong about!' Matthew giggled his way out and Shelley was still laughing as the door closed behind him.

'This is great!'

'Yeah, I can't wait to see what he comes up with,' Pip smiled, but it was much more hesitant now that Matthew had left. It seemed an age since there had been just the two of them. And everything was different then.

'No – Matthew,' she said, oblivious. 'His mood, his lightness. *Thank you.*' The sincerity was so loud, both lost their smile then, and a still silence wrapped around them for a moment.

'It's nothing,' he concluded, unwilling to hear either of them.

'It isn't. I can see you're making such a difference to him.'

'All this stuff here!' Pip lit up again. 'How can you not use it?'

'Not just that, it's the way you are, what you can do. You've given him so much hope, it's obvious.'

'He'll learn. Not hearing can have its advantages, you know. There's so much crap all around every minute these days. A lot of the time I am just blessed with a gentle purr. It can be quite relaxing. It's only when you introduce other people's expectations it can become a problem.' Despite the laughter, his awkwardness was never far from the surface. 'So I'm sorry if it changes things.'

'Of course it doesn't.'

'That's rarely true.'

'I have been wanting to say *I'm* sorry, actually,' she said. 'You know, I never realised.' Pip could feel the territory of this conversation shifting. He didn't want that either and didn't reply. 'You hide it very well,' she concluded instead.

'I don't hide it,' he sparked back immediately. 'It's who I am. I just don't advertise it, that's all. I've come to find that... *unhelpful*. At best, I might as well be wearing a T-shirt with "please shout at me" on it. At worst, well... let's just say some people can be very creative when it comes to lacking human decency.'

'I'm sorry, I didn't mean to—'

'Anyway, you learn pretty quickly if you can't hear to pretend that you can, otherwise people really don't want you around. There's something threatening about not being able to make themselves understood, I get it. Regardless of the fact that a lot of it's bollocks anyway. And of course, I can understand much more than they think.'

Shelley had seen that look so many times before, the one that burrowed straight through her. And now she understood it: he was waiting to see what she would say. He wanted to hear her.

'I think you do,' she concluded quietly, aware now, more than ever before, that nothing of very much consequence depended on volume. 'And you obviously understand what Matthew's going through in a way that I never could,' she added, a sadness creeping back over her face.

'I doubt it. But this,' he waved his hand over the collection of instruments in the room, unable to stay with the shift in gear for long. 'This I do understand. So really, I should be thanking you, shouldn't I?'

'For what?'

'For introducing me to it, letting me in, you know.'

Yes, she had, as Russell had pointed out. But right now, she couldn't find any of the unease about that which she had done.

'Will you play the drums now?' she asked, and the room instantly cooled again.

'Na, I don't think so.' Pip turned to inexplicably re-order a pile of beaters in the corner.

And Shelley had seen this so many times before too. Only now she realised what it was all about as well. He turned around, looked away. It was how he disengaged, closed down a conversation. He could not see it. It would become no more than that 'gentle purr', and she would no longer be there.

So she decided it was time she was not.

But she turned at the door and waited for his eyes to, almost imperceptibly, raise again.

'In that case,' she concluded, taking a small torch from her back pocket and waving it like a pendulum. 'Perhaps we could just carry on as before and I'll leave you to tell me what you need and when I get it wrong...'

37

THE SILENCE OF STILLNESS

Shelley put her fingers in her ears and stared at the copper bell above the bedroom door. She had been putting her fingers in her ears quite a lot in the last few days. Making herself not hear things. In an idle summer years ago, Matthew had reverse-engineered the ancient servant calling system so that Victoria could rouse him from wherever he was in the house. He had been using it to call Shelley from her room when he was about to leave for the Folly. This morning she was actively willing the bell to move. As she was becoming more aware than ever, sound was movement, and she needed to hear her call.

The bell refused to budge.

Trying to ignore the email tab on her laptop, she opened YouTube instead. Clicking on a random video, she turned the volume up to max and lay the laptop on her thighs. She leaned her back into the wall, pushed her fingers further into her ears and closed her eyes, tuning in to the muted conversation. A steady ebb and flow; she picked out different tones and rhythms, but very little sense, and hardly an actual word. She withdrew her fingers from her ears and looked away. She was being ridiculous. How could she *not* hear things? How could she conceive of not being able to? Her own hearing had always been so effortlessly good all her life. More than good, it was in demand.

Her hand hovered over the email from Cambridge University. Again. It had been hovering between there and her ears since she'd received the message two hours ago. They were keen to know if her 'family troubles' were any better and would she like to reschedule her interview for this Thursday afternoon? Nowhere amongst her own cacophony of questions and demands on herself could Shelley hear the response to give.

She jumped off the bed and headed out. She needed to listen to something else…

Pip sat by the lake in the meadow beside the Folly and stared at his feet. They were still. He could hear the real silence of stillness right through his body. He checked his ankles, up his legs, through his hips and torso, chest and arms. Still. Not a lot of noise in his head either, for a change.

'When *she* got it wrong'. The notion had bewildered him all night. He'd been the 'wrong' one for so long – defective, disabled, incapable. How embattled he had felt all his life, armoured and defended and under siege. How convinced that had made him that great things – impossible things – were expected of him, and it was up to him to accomplish them alone and unaided. If someone had ever said, 'Can I help you?' 'What do you need?' Perhaps they had. Perhaps he had just not heard them. Not because he was deaf but, for that, he did not allow himself to listen.

Now he *had* heard it. And it had quietened all the rest. But still, he did not know how to answer.

He heard the breeze tickle his ears and blow through his hair. Looking up and around, he heard the flapping of the wings of the swifts high above in the air; the burble of the lake as the fish glided through; the swoosh of the insects rowing on top of the water. Sometimes he had to remind himself that nobody could ever hope to hear these things. But they were moving, so he could. What was real and what was memory or imagination no longer had much significance.

He felt a change in the air through the tall grasses behind him, and turned.

'I'm sorry,' Shelley hesitated. 'I was just thinking I should circle round so as not to startle you. You beat me to it.' Her small smile seemed to be experimenting. 'I don't know how you do it.'

'That,' he pointed. 'What is that?'

'The miscanthus?'

'It moves a lot. Very noisy. Probably.'

'Probably.' She smiled a little more securely and sat down.

'Those,' he said, pointing at the row of beech trees crackling in the breeze in the distance. 'They're the noisiest.'

'Yes, copper beech, they always are.'

'See? I couldn't give a toss about trees and plants before I was deaf. Now look at me, expert!'

She tried to laugh, but was clearly somewhere else. Pip found himself with the loudest thought that he would like to be there too.

'Are you OK?'

'Yeah,' she breezed, whilst the rest of her said something else entirely. 'No Matthew? I've just been walking the grounds, thought I'd meet him here. I hope you don't mind me gate-crashing his lesson again. I... I've been kind of looking forward to it.'

'Sure. No problem.' Pip examined his feet. Still quiet. *Strange...*

He checked her periodically to make sure she wasn't speaking. Her lips weren't moving, but the rest of her was never still. He had always found her hugely expressive; her face, her body was a whole narrative. Like Victoria – and her mother actually, now he came to think about it – Shelley left much less to guesswork. In hindsight, he recognised that was one of the reasons he had felt an inch of settlement the moment they had met.

'What will you do now?' he decided to draw her out. 'Now that Las Vegas is out.'

'I don't know. I—' she hesitated, tracing her leg with her finger as if the gentle pressure might unlock her uncertainty. 'I've got an interview. A really good job. Cambridge University, a Research Fellowship to continue the work I've been doing at the college.'

'Blimey, that's a result.'

'Yes...'

'But you wouldn't be happy there?'

'Where?'

'I don't know. Cambridge, another university, a lab, or lecture theatre? One or all of them.'

'Is it obvious?'

'S'pose. If you're looking.'

Shelley nodded, but looked slightly annoyed about that. Despite her unease since her return, it was not an expression he had ever seen in her much.

Then her face softened, as if she had been given a reprieve. Pip followed the turn of her head to see Matthew calling as he trotted across the grass behind them.

'So sorry, late,' he puffed. 'But, oh dear, awfully sorry to ask, Pip – either of you – you wouldn't have any cash on you, would you?' He leaned over his knees to recover his breath. 'Terribly embarrassing, a group of Belgians has just turned up for the concert scheduled tonight. Seems none of the notifications about the season cancellation crossed the Channel. To be honest, I'm surprised we've got away with it so far. Victoria's giving them tea and cake and they're being awfully good about it, but I think we need to give them their money back at least, and we've only been able to scrape together £12.50. You wouldn't have anything you could lend us, would you? Crushing to have to ask—'

'You can have whatever I've got in my jar,' Pip interrupted. He'd only needed about five words out of Matthew's whole monologue. He returned within seconds, emptying his money jar into Matthew's hands. 'Marilyn and the Pordages pay by bank transfer these days, but everyone else...' he shrugged, trousering a tenner from Matthew's hand and closing his fingers over the rest. 'There should be three or four hundred there. Hope that'll do.'

'Oh dear, I don't know how to—'

'Call it rent, OK?'

Shelley smiled at him so much more warmly and securely than she had managed since her return, he considered four hundred quid cheap.

'I'll take it, Matthew,' she offered. 'Why don't you go ahead and have your lesson? I'll see if Victoria needs any help and maybe join you later.' She touched his wavering arm. 'Go and lie under the marimba, Matthew. It'll be alright...'

Shelley never made it back to the Folly that day. The Belgians were charmingly accepting of the lack of entertainment on offer tonight, but their interest in the Manor and its grounds was only surpassed by their interest in Horace. Shelley had been happy to vicariously entertain them with tales, but was glad when they finally left, lest she be in danger of telling the truth.

Something she felt in desperate need of herself...

'Of course it's lovely to see you, Shelley,' Russell pushed aside his papers as she sat down in his home office. 'But I confess to a little disappointment if it means you've decided to stay in Bedingford any longer. I was hoping we might get away from here again this week.'

'I'm still thinking, Russell. I don't want to leave Matthew again, at least not so soon.'

'But what about Cambridge? Surely you wouldn't pass that up?'

'They still want me to come for interview – this Thursday actually – but I haven't accepted yet. I'm not sure I'll go.'

'Not really a good way to get a job, Shelley.'

'I know, but—'

'Tell you what, I've had enough of today. Let's play hooky and go to the pub for dinner. Plan your sparkling new future in style, whatever it should be!'

Shelley had no idea 'whatever it should be'. She'd got so much wrong lately, she had very little faith left in her own judgment. But over dinner at The Huntsman's, she could be in little doubt about Russell's judgment – so enthusiastic about her prospects, and his. She would be a professor before long and he would have his own chambers, and he rather liked the new riverside development by The Cam that they had looked at in the estate agent's window. Must get the brochure...

It wasn't just the second bottle of wine he insisted on adding to their meal that was all rather intoxicating.

But, in a moment's break between plans and plates, she did need to ask. 'Russell, why did Pip Berry take the fall for the opera night disturbance?'

Russell paused, taking another sip of wine.

'He admitted it, Shelley, you know that.'

'Yes, but *why?* Victoria and Matthew are adamant he had nothing to do with it, and if they can believe that, it seems odd not to.'

'Does it? Have you asked him?'

'Well, no, not as such. Victoria says not to. She's quite keen on showing some trust. We show trust to him and he'll show trust to us, or something like that.'

'What, like a stray cat?'

Shelley frowned.

'Oh, come on, Shelley, you pick up too many waifs and strays as it is. Metaphorically speaking.'

'He's not... Oh, I don't know, it's hard to explain.'

'Is it?' Russell's nostrils flared a little. 'Look, I'm so sorry you are still being upset by all this, Shelley. That was one of the things I was seeking to avoid. I really didn't want to involve you, but I can see that you need something. The reason he "took the fall", as you put it, was simply because he accepted a bargain. My mother, and yours, were most distraught to hear the police were investigating criminal charges. Of course, the village protest was just a bit of nonsense. Got out of hand, that's all. I wanted to protect them from their *quite unforeseen* consequences. Mr Berry was on pretty dodgy ground. He needed a little *protection* as well. He was excessively shaken up by the whole thing, you know. We were really doing him a favour, given his past conviction. Another thing I didn't really want to tell you about, as I know how strongly you feel about such things, but he has a very serious record dealing Class A drugs.'

'You are joking!'

'I fear not. That was the reason he accepted the bargain. I can only surmise, and clearly so did the police, that he may have stolen the emeralds I told you about to fund a continuing drug habit – or worse, trade. Oh, Shelley, I am so sorry! Terrible memories for you, I know, with Horace's history, and Marilyn and all that.'

Shelley waved away the concern, but didn't have much of a voice left to clutch at straws. 'He doesn't look like a drug addict to me.'

'What does a drug addict look like these days, Shelley? Half the Inns of Court are off their tits on something most of the time... That's better, I hoped to see you smile. Now, please don't blame yourself. I expect he's become rather good at fooling people. It's not the first time.'

'What do you mean?' Shelley had contained her inconveniently pressing tears so far, but really thought she could take no more surprises now.

'Well, that was what he was done for last time. Dealing

heroin, apparently. I don't know the details, but we do know he went to prison so it must have been fairly serious. Of course, that wouldn't make it terribly easy to defend him, and he knew that. But at present, I have ensured that there is no case to answer, and I will do my utmost to prove there isn't, if it ever comes to it. If that's what you want.'

'What *I* want?'

'Yes, of course, that is what you asked of me, isn't it? And so as long as you're sure, it's all safe with me. Are you sure, Shelley?'

'I... I don't know...'

'Oh, Shelley, what can I do to help you? Look, I have the emeralds back from the police now. What if I give them to you and if you find out they are missing from the Manor, then you'll know I'm right, won't you?'

'Victoria's got an emerald necklace, her wedding present, but she never takes it off and I'm pretty sure she doesn't have anything else like that left anymore.'

'Well, if not jewellery, I'd look out for something to do with drums as well, if that helps?'

Shelley's heart sank even further.

'Here,' he dropped a small pouch into her hand. 'It's good news, Shelley. Perhaps they can sell them, help out a bit. Then perhaps we can all forget about it and move on... Anyway, that is quite enough about him. Or anyone else in the world, actually! Another glass?'

She nodded vaguely.

'And you'll think about going for the interview?'

'Yes, I suppose I will...'

38

WHAT DOES TRUST LOOK LIKE?

Pip was not at all sure about this daily growth of his audience; Victoria joined Matthew and Shelley in the Folly basement the next morning.

'It's alright, I won't intrude,' Victoria said, as if his unease was written all over his face. 'I just came to ask if you had finished cleaning up the emerald drum kit. We could really do with getting it to Winchester to be valued this afternoon. We need to find some money and—'

'Did you say *emerald*?' Shelley swung round. Victoria eyed her suspiciously; interruption was not something that happened to her all that often.

'Yes indeed, that one,' she pointed to a complete tower of drums neatly stacked in the corner. 'And real ones on some of them at that, would you believe? Mrs Burlington has just told me there's an antique and valuable musical instrument auction at Fortescues in Winchester next week, and jewels and jewellery the following week. I've just phoned them and if we hurry we can get it valued and into whichever catalogue they advise. Pip discovered it. He has kindly located all the parts and cleaned up the shells, so we can find out if the kit is worth more together with the jewels or separately with the emeralds taken off—'

'And what about the ones already taken off the snare, there?' Shelley pointed out, her eyes burying into him like a fish hook. Things had been pleasingly loosening lately, but something had changed in the last minute and it didn't look like she was letting him off to the downstream.

'Uh, yes,' Pip mumbled. 'The snare was upstairs with some of the other drums. A few of the stones had fallen off.'

'And where are they now?' Victoria demanded.

'I'm hoping Russell Pordage has them. I was waiting to get them back...' Pip looked to Shelley for reprieve, but none came. 'Look, the stones were in my pocket when the police arrested me. It was them that told me they were emeralds. I—' He stopped. Shelley had produced a pouch from her bag. She dropped the three jewels into Victoria's hand and stared at him.

'Yes, Russell had them.'

Pip searched for more, but her mouth moved no further. His brief swell of relief dissolved.

Pip had learned years ago that 'lip reading' was a ridiculously inadequate description. Lips just made shapes of words, it was the face that made sense of the pieces. The lips could be reciting the prayers of the Dalai Lama whilst the face screamed blue murder. Even without words, he knew how to hear disgust and disappointment when he saw it. And he knew she was leaving before she even turned.

The door slamming might have been a mere scratch to him, but it was a symphony for them all.

'You were saying?' Victoria turned back to him. 'They were in your pocket, why?'

Pip sighed. He'd lost her again and he couldn't even remember who he was supposed to be protecting and what script he was supposed to be reciting any more. God, he was so fed up with all this. Amongst these people – these good people. Still lies and fudges and sidesteps and pretence.

In the end, his truth was all he could be sure of anymore.

'I found the snare upstairs, before the opera. It was all beaten and broken. I thought it was beautiful, so I took it to my shed to fix up. That's all.' Despite the defiance in his tone, his breathing quickened and his feet twitched. He trod on the left one with his right and compulsively fingered a drumstick. 'The stones were still in my pocket when I was arrested. I'd forgotten about them, to be honest. I just thought they were paste, of course. I was actually planning to go into Howard's Hardware in town to ask whether epoxy or polyurethane adhesive would be better... I know, I'd bore meself if I had any choice. But I just wanted to make it right. Just make *something* right...' His shoulders dropped. 'That's all.'

'I see.' Victoria looked unexpectedly pleased with herself. Matthew was evidently not so sure. 'Oh, do stop whimpering, Matthew. If he'd meant to steal anything, would the rest of this lot still be here?'

Matthew's brow immediately uncreased and an enlightened smile returned to his face.

'I know I said I would not press you, Pip,' she continued. 'But we now have so many bits of the most obvious information, I really must seek resolution of all this. Shelley had the emeralds and she was evidently not pleased to find out their backstory. Or some of it at least, which is usually all you seem to manage. Please tell me how that might be.'

Pip sighed, finally giving up. 'Russell Pordage said he was going to return them to you. He... helped me at the police station. He said he would give them to Shelley to do it.'

'Well, that was very generous of him. He could have kept them for himself. No-one would have been any the wiser, would they? Since certain people seem preternaturally addicted to secrecy. You see what a little trust looks like, Pip?'

Pip squirmed. 'I'm sorry I—'

'And since you have been at the Manor for some considerable time, do you not think this was something worthy of exposure?'

'I wanted to. There are... issues.'

Victoria looked to the ceiling. 'Of course there are... But, since I have had a little time to attain some enlightenment, might I surmise that this was the rather blunt instrument which Russell Pordage has held over you in exchange for your silence regarding the opera night?'

'It's not his fault. I was in a mess. He was just trying to help me. And Shelley.'

'Hmm, I concede, he has always looked out for Shelley. You, on the other hand, I sincerely doubt. You, I suspect, are merely collateral damage.'

'Nice.'

'So, there we are. Makes perfect sense. How very Pordage. Sir Henry's father offered a most similar transaction to Robert back in the fifties, when he was dealing marijuana in the jazz clubs. They are jolly good at it and they always have something worth-while to trade. I cannot therefore judge you too harshly.'

'But I've ballsed up again. You told me not to disappoint Shelley any further, and I have done. I keep doing it.'

'I'll talk to her,' Victoria offered, again.

'No,' Pip determined. 'I'll do it this time. I've had enough of keeping quiet.'

'Splendid, at last!' Victoria beamed. 'My work here is done...'

39

PRESENCE

The return train from Waterloo out to Winchester was a lot more crowded than the Cambridge into London had been. The carriage buzzed with talk and activity. Shelley sat on her hands, feeling the vibration of the seat. She pushed herself into the corner to feel more from the wall and window. She put in her headphone buds without turning on her music, tuning instead into the muted conversations around her. Just like the YouTube video, it was no more than a senseless mush, obscured even further by the background noise of the train on the tracks. She opened the miniature bottle of Chardonnay she'd bought at the station. A couple of inches down and it was getting marginally easier. A few more words became audible as her tightened muscles loosened and stopped getting in her way quite so much.

Intrigued and emboldened by the wine, she raised her eyes to her travelling companions, and began to 'hear' a little more on their lips. The teenage girls opposite talking about music. She tried to guess the band name. An alarmingly engrossed couple that kept saying *elephant shoes*, or *olive juice*, to each other. The two women talking about a *brass band* or *marzipan*, and so it went on. Glimpsing how many words looked the same on the lips, or didn't look like anything at all, so much depended on context and guesswork, she marvelled at the skill that Pip must have developed. And the effort he had always been making, unknown to her.

She'd forgotten to be discreet. One of the women returned her obvious attention with an icy glare. She switched to the man in the seat opposite, talking on his phone about someone having *talent*, or *salad*. She giggled. She'd dispatched the mini bottle too quickly and was tempted to hop out at Woking and get another one. The man winked at her and cocked his head as he rose from his seat. Clearly he'd also noticed her attention and seemed to be angling to buy it for her if she felt like getting off the train with him. She sat back in her seat, gestured a polite decline and pretended she could not hear any further advances over 'the music' in her ears.

She finally lowered her eyes and returned to hearing the rise and fall of senseless conversations, punctuated by her own internal monologue. The response of the passengers to her focus reminded her again of Pip. The ambiguous intensity of his direct eye contact, which could feel both intrusive and vulnerable at the same time. She recalled how he would always lower his eyes periodically before lifting them again. An awkward shyness she had felt, but she knew now he was probably just giving her a break. Now she knew the truth about a lot of things. But Pip had obscured the truth from her in so many ways since they first met.

She leaned her head on the window and tried to hear a different monologue to the beat of the tracks.

Cambridge...Russell...Russell is my rock...Russell always tells me the truth...

She recalled Pip also once saying something about reality and imagination, and sometimes not knowing the difference anymore. And for a second she wondered what she could hear outside of herself and what was the voice within. She looked out of the window to the activity in the roads and gardens and shops passing by the tracks, and she heard his voice again. The warm, mischievous tones of his South London childhood, tempered by a Hampshire delicacy, the rare odd word that missed his internal ear, or had been forgotten in the non-hearing years, which came out as if he was from some obscure foreign country. 'When my eyes see something, there is always sound happening,' he had said in one of Matthew's lessons. 'I imagine the rustling of the trees, the rumble of cars on the road, the gush of a river. But who is to say how different people hear sound? Maybe half of it is always imagination...'

Imagination...Unpredictability...Secrecy...Uncertainty...
Cambridge...Russell...Reality...Direction...Certainty...

She closed her eyes and sank into the percussive vibration of the train on the tracks to the rhythm of her words, through her whole body...

'I DON'T WANT IT!'

Her eyes pinged open. It was a shock. The mush of everyone else's voices remained in her covered ears, but she'd never heard her own speak so loudly before.

Perhaps it was time she started listening for it again.

Shelley welcomed the long walk from the station to the village, wondering how she was going to translate one certainty into another enough to hear what she should do now. Turning into Trefusis Lane, she glanced up at her mother's house. An empty deckchair sat on the front lawn. She wondered whether, if it had been occupied, she would have approached. That fleeting feeling she sometimes had that she wanted to talk to her mother. Before she remembered it was not *her* mother she wanted to talk to, but some other version of one.

Bill was sitting on the bench by the Manor wall, elbows over his knees, looking in the same direction.

'Oh, Miss Harper, how lovely to see you again.'

'Don't get up, Bill. It's fine, I won't disturb you.'

'Nonsense, my girl. Have a seat. You look like you could do with one. It's peaceful here, in't it? I come and watch Pip sometimes, there in your mother's garden,' he nodded up the road, as Marilyn hobbled across the lawn, holding onto Pip's arm, her own arm in a sling. 'Make sure he's alright, you know, but far enough away not to be noticed. I don't want to interrupt him, not when he's working,' Bill added gravely.

Shelley watched as Pip lowered Marilyn into the deckchair, crouching beside her and handing her a mug and a magazine. 'But I wave from here sometimes,' Bill continued. 'Not much point in shouting, is there? Oh, hark at me, watch my mouth!'

'It's alright, Bill. I know about Pip's hearing.'

'Do you? Oh, right, OK...' Bill's puzzlement quickly turned to delight. 'Gosh, that's good! Ma'll be pleased as punch. Real progress that is if he's talking about it again. It's his anniversary on Sunday, you know? Seventeen years. We like to joke about that, or we used to. His "coming out".'

'Did he used to be open about it, Bill? Talk about... *stuff*, you know?'

'Are you kidding me? Talk, Pip? We could never shut the boy up! Except for them first couple of days every time he came back to us, quiet as a mouse he was then. Just used to spend hours on the phone listening to the speaking clock. It was the repetition, I think. The pips seemed to calm him down. Then he'd ramp up like a Duracell bunny. That's how we started to shorten his name to Pip. It seemed to fit. Rhythmic too, you know, what with the drums and all, cos he was pretty good at those by the time he was seven. Incredible combination, noisiest kid we ever had, I'm telling you! That's why we remember it like it were yesterday – his 15th birthday – the final time he came to us, see. Never went back to his father after that...'

'We hadn't seen him for a while and he turns up on his 15th birthday saying he didn't think he could hear,' Bill rattled on, as if a tiny key of truth had unlocked a floodgate of enforced silence. 'We knew something had been going on for a while. Poor mite, he must have been struggling for ages. *They* just said he was "slow". Pip weren't slow. There in't a mind that works faster that I know of. It's just that he had to learn things in a different way. And he certainly weren't slow at that! They saw it in the end, at that Cathedral School. Nobody seemed to know why it had got so bad, but his father's beatings won't have helped, that's for sure. When he came back he says it's bad in both ears but he thinks he can't hear at all in his right. Trevor was left-handed, see. We never let him go back after that... Oh, but he was so good, you know? Once he'd worked out he could still play the drums, play better even, play anything! The hearing didn't seem to matter. He's just got ears on the inside, like. It was only when he couldn't get any bands to take him he stopped talking about it. Now...' Bill shook his head in weary disappointment. 'Now, he barely talk about anything. I don't know what happened in that place, but it killed him, that's for sure.'

'Prison?' Shelley ventured, tentatively.

'Oh, this is brilliant!' Bill incongruously beamed across the road, thumbs in the air, even though Pip was no longer there. 'He's told you about that as well? Good lad, that's real progress!'

'No, well—'

'A terrible thing, of course it was. Me and Ma couldn't believe it! We never did really, but they sent him down, didn't they? Must be something in it, mustn't there?' Despite Bill's imploring eyes, he did not stop for answers. 'I just don't get it, though. I don't know much about them drugs, but it's all about going somewhere else, in't it? Now Pip see, he never been a boy who was anywhere else than where he was.'

'Well, yes Bill, I think you're right. He is always... very... *present*. Excuse me, I've got to go!' Shelley jumped up and kissed him. 'Thank you, Bill!'

. . .

This time Shelley was skirting round nobody. She threw down her bag beside him. Pip looked up instantly from the grass beside the lake.

'I've been talking to myself and listening to stuff, Pip,' she launched in immediately, with no doubt that he would understand what she meant. 'I'm hearing some things louder and clearer than I ever have. But I need to get better at knowing what's truth and what's lies.'

Pip nodded. 'I understand.'

'Russell told me about the bargain at the police station and I get why you might have accepted his help. For God's sake, I wanted you to! But if you stole those emeralds to fund a drug habit, I am pretty sure I'd eat my hat. But then, I have had to do a fair bit of hat-gorging recently. Do you understand what I am saying?'

Pip nodded again.

'If I listen to myself, the one who's *supposed* to hear things so fucking clearly, I don't believe you had anything to do with any of it. But I realise I am an unreliable microphone. If I listen to reason, you've kept things from me since we met, very important things, who you are. I was wrong about those and I don't know if I'm wrong now. Unless you tell me.'

'OK,' he said, slowly.

'Drugs, Pip, I have... *issues* with. My Dad's early career was fuelled by them. He emerged relatively unscathed. Mum, on the other hand, is made of different stuff. I don't need to say anymore, but this is my bit of honesty – they frighten me, Pip. Not very "modern" I know, I don't give a shit about that. But I do give a shit about the destruction they wreak.'

'Yes,' Pip agreed.

'Yes,' Shelley repeated. 'It doesn't fit, does it? With how you are, what you can do. And then Bill said something.'

'Bill? You've been talking to Bill about this?'

'No. Well, not really. I didn't do much of the talking. But he was so confused, Pip. You could tell he didn't believe any of it, the drugs, your conviction. You've always been so present, he said.'

'*Present*?' Pip checked. 'Doesn't sound like Bill.'

'Oh, well, something like that. But that's it, isn't it? You're just too present... What?' Her brow furrowed, because he was staring at her in bewilderment, the slightest quizzical smile twitching at his lips. 'I'm babbling, aren't I? Am I babbling? Did you get any of it?'

'Yes,' he nodded immediately. 'Thank you. Really. Thank you...'

For someone who was struggling with her own judgment, it seemed to Pip that she was demonstrating an astonishing act of faith. He looked out over the lake and swallowed hard. He so wanted to give it back.

'It's all nonsense, you know,' he finally said, so tentatively. None of this had ever come out of his mouth before and it would not come easily. 'The last time I was arrested – for possession of heroin – it turned out to be a ground up dog biscuit...'

And there he stalled.

Shelley sat down. 'What happened? Can you tell me?'

He wasn't at all sure that he could. 'I... um... fucked up,' he began, looking at her silently for a moment, perhaps to check she was really prepared to hear it. Or more so, that *he* was. He looked up to catch the swifts, but all he could hear was the heavy goods train of loss, doubt and pain thundering back over his tracks.

He tried to derail it. 'It's like Victoria says, too much secrecy, too much hiding. The way I have dealt with my deafness has made me far too used to hiding things. I don't like it, and I want it to stop!'

There was no more as he sat clutching and twisting the grass beside him. The time that had passed had worn the story to a sharp knife point. He wasn't sure he was capable of plunging it in.

But, for the first time, he wanted to try.

'Can I...?' He squinted, as if the words were just out of reach. 'Can I tell you about it? What it was like? What it *is* like?'

'Yes, please.' He watched her face. It didn't move any further and in this tiny act of openness, he felt his silence coming undone.

Pip Berry had been listening for years. He was finally ready to talk...

40

STRIKING A NEW CHORD

'You know, playing the drums was all I ever wanted,' Pip began his story as if hanging onto that was the only way he could. 'I worked so hard when I lost my hearing – really hard – until I knew I could do it. But always on my own. When I started to try and join bands, they wouldn't have it. Never got past the deaf thing. I kept trying, finished school, got really good at the lip reading, spent hours a day on it, practising with the telly or Ma and Bill. They were the best practice, of course, they never shut up.' He tried a smile. It quickly died.

'That's what Bill said about you,' Shelley grinned in an effort to resuscitate it.

'Yeah,' he shrugged, 'can you believe that?'

'All habits die without practice. So go on, why don't you practise on me?'

Pip stared at her as if her offerings were completely alien to him.

'Ma was worried...' He finally gave up to it, his foot tapping out each word, as if that too, through rhythm, was the only way he could tell this story. 'She didn't want me disappointed. But Bill always encouraged me to keep trying. So I went to audition after audition, same thing always happened. As soon as they found out I was deaf, no thanks. Until the day I turned up to one and just didn't tell them. And that was that from then on. I'd found the answer – just don't tell anyone. And I burned through any band I could find then. If they were halfway decent, after a couple of sessions I'd let them know – it's almost impossible to keep up in a band and usually they'd get twitchy about things I missed, or where I'd ask to place myself. You know, the drummer's supposed to be at the back, aren't they? I always wanted to be somewhere I could see them all... But usually by then they wanted me in, so they wanted to make it work. I left about six bands before much happened. I needed better musicians and most of them, to be honest, just talk a lot. But it was fabulous practice, really helped me believe I could do it. *If* I just kept quiet about the hearing. At least at first. So I guess I developed this habit of secrecy. And it seemed to work in the outside world as well. I think...' He hesitated. He'd never talked about it before and was trying to work out what he thought as he went along. 'When people find out, it's like I lose the power that I have, that I developed. I just become deficient or disabled, something to avoid, or pity. Things change. For them and for me...'

'Then I was in a pretty decent band at a gig in London and was approached by the manager of Surface Tension...' He noted Shelley's surprise. 'Yeah, I know, but Tommy Wilson was in hospital with throat cancer and they had tours booked. Anyway, I love all that '70s and '80s classic rock stuff – I started playing along to my Dad's old records when I was six or seven – so I jumped at it... Of course they were shocked when I told them about my hearing, but really curious, and they worked with me from the outset. It was great! Until it wasn't. The more recognition I got, the more difficult it was to hide it. More and more people knew, couldn't avoid it really. Then the awkwardness started, the avoidance. Or the questions, the freak show curiosity. Any media we got, the interviewers would go on about it. The other guys got a bit jealous, I think. Pissed off that I was getting all the attention. Crazy, eh? Let's be jealous of the musician who can't hear.'

'Not really. I've heard what you can do.'

'Well, they weren't jealous for long. They soon cottoned on that it was something they could use for publicity, so they encouraged it. Then came the dropped comments, like they were the old stalwarts giving the young disabled guy his chance, you know? Oh God, I hated it. I didn't know what to say! I just wanted to play the music, but all anyone wanted to talk about was how I did it. I have no fucking idea how I hear, *do you...?* Sorry,' he added, embarrassed by the outburst, his fingers drumming his thighs and deliberately slowing to a calmer tempo. 'Anyway, in the end I just stopped, refused to talk, refused the interviews, which just pissed them off even more. I guess I became more and more isolated all round, really. I hardly ever went to the parties anyway, found them all a bit much, to be honest. Too much noise. But the more I withdrew, the more annoyed they got about it. We were headlining an '80s retrospective tour around Europe with loads of old bands last summer, but something had changed, and one night I just felt this wave of panic come from nowhere before going on stage. That'd never happened before, and I don't know how I got through that night. I can't even remember it. But then I started to feel frightened going on stage every night. The nerves were catastrophic, interfered with what I could hear. I started to make mistakes. Actually, I don't know what came first to be honest, the fear, or the not being able to feel the sounds like I used to, but I guess they just fed off each other...'

'At first, the band tried to help. They gave me a supply of weed, thought it might calm me down. That was the first arrest. Not a great combination – deaf guy after his first smoke with far too much in it, let loose on the streets of Dublin. They had a devil of a job to catch me, and then I apparently laughed in the police officer's face and kissed him! Then, nothing. They took me to the station and I just stared at them, silently gaping for hours. I was overnight in a cell for that one. They let me go with a caution in the morning. The band just thought it was funny, very rock 'n' roll. It was their party piece for a while, told absolutely anyone. Especially as I had a reputation for being a bit of a softy when it came to all that. Can't really handle it, to be honest. As you know, cake's my thing...' Every now and then, the moment became too deep for Pip and he had to swiftly sprint back to the shallow end.

'But I was all over the place the next night on stage, and from that night, the panics got worse and worse, as the distance became greater and greater. It was always difficult on stage. I knew I could play, I knew what I could do, but playing with other people, all the other noise and input, you have to rely on the trust of your band mates, being able to read them, knowing what they were going to do all the time. If that goes, it's near on impossible. I kept it going from pure muscle memory, I think, but the fear just became too much in the end. I can't listen to others if I can't hear myself first. Then it started to spill out into every day. I woke up with it sometimes. I just wanted to stop, get off the bus, go home. Wherever that was... Then someone did the job for me, hiding ground up dog biscuit in my snare drum. The van got searched at Dover. And that started a whole new story...'

Pip had held most of his emotion under wraps throughout this tale, keeping himself very much to himself. Shelley could feel his containment, as if he were placing himself in a small box, talking to the walls, only occasionally popping the lid to peek out.

'Can you tell it?' she gently asked.

'I don't know,' he said. 'I've never really heard it before. I don't really know what happened. Still. All sorts of stories go through my head... Even when the tests came back, they were pretty convinced there was more to it than feeding my dog. It must be an additive or something, and the rest, the real stuff, I was hiding somewhere else. Plus, the little bag of hash they found in my coat pocket didn't help. I was so mucked up by then and desperate to get home, I'd forgotten it was even there, to be honest.'

'Where did the dog biscuit come from? The band?'

'I don't know. They said not. But there'd always been practical jokes, and I get it, I can walk into some fairly amusing situations sometimes. But that one just... *wasn't.*'

'So, it wasn't yours? And there wasn't anything else?'

'No! That's the whole point! I can't do drugs, not even the soft ones, messes with my senses. Sorry,' he repeated, agitated by his spark of anger as much as the tale itself. He attempted another smile in its place. 'Bit like this fucking panic. Maybe I should try again and start, eh?'

'D'you fancy a drink instead?'

'Yeah, yeah, that would be nice...'

'Go on Pip, if you can, I really want to hear what happened.'

Pip took a sip of the wine she had brought from the petrol station on the main road, served in the ancient whisky tumblers that were the only thing available in the Folly, as he read her words. And the something else that was in her face, without the words – a quiet receptivity, an invitation. Victoria had tried, he understood that now, with words and wisdom, she'd opened him up to the possibility of truth. All this had lived unspoken in his head like an unwanted lodger for so long it would not be evicted easily. But so much more had passed his lips this evening already than ever had before. And it occurred to Pip how much of a man's thoughts can remain silent until the right person is there to amplify them.

'We all got hauled in,' he continued. 'Everybody in the band said it wasn't theirs. I said it wasn't mine. It was in my drums, you work it out. They let them go, kept me in. I didn't tell them I was deaf. Same old, same old. I know now that was stupid, but I didn't know any other way to be. I was proud, I was naïve, I was scared. But I was terribly panicked and I couldn't hear, couldn't read the voices well. To be honest, I can't really remember all of it, but I think it clouded the way the investigation went after that. When they finally found out I was deaf, I got help, but it was a bit too late, and it was all the wrong sort – they got me a sign language interpreter. I mean, I have no idea about sign, might as well have been translating into Chinese! But they didn't know how to help me and I didn't know how to ask... I got by for a bit. The police interviews, solicitors and that, fairly easy, they always sit in front of you, in bright lights and ask direct questions. Besides, my answer to pretty much everything was "No". *"No, it's not mine..." "No, I don't know where it came from..." "No, I don't know what it's for..."* Maybe I got it wrong sometimes. The panic was escalating, I was understanding less and less of what people were saying to me. I don't know what came first, just like the stage fright. I know I was giving some answers that were clearly not the right ones, but by the time I finally admitted I needed help, it was a bit too late...'

'I don't really know if it would have made any difference, to be honest. In the end, it was my stupidity. If I'd just waited. If I hadn't been so frightened, maybe none of it would have happened. If I'd been calm enough to wait. I came back here to Bedingford when I should have stayed in London. I thought I'd feel safe here. I needed to feel safe. But, of course, not my "home address". They said I skipped bail and put me straight on remand. In Belmarsh – my local prison, lucky me. They never found any other evidence, but they weren't particularly speedy at coming to that conclusion, either. In the end, I was convicted of possession of a Class B drug – the bit of weed in my pocket. They dropped the "intent to supply Class A" and sentenced me to three months as a second offence after Dublin. I'd already served it. I'd been in Belmarsh for 13 weeks, 4 days, 7 hours and 23 minutes...' He paused, gritting his teeth, the words becoming smaller and smaller. 'And that's about it. I don't think I can say any more. Some people are just evil, I think. I really had no conception of that before. I lost many things before I went in there, but I'd lost everything by the time I came out... I'm sorry, would you excuse me...?'

When Pip returned to the lake from the Folly, his footsteps were calculated, rhythmic. Shelley had topped up his glass and offered it to him in wordless invitation.

'The truth is,' he said, finally, his chest rising with deliberate breath. 'I haven't really got my balance back. It's the panics, you see. They upset everything. Everything vibrates. They put new noises everywhere, in my head, in my body. It distorts the resonating chambers. I can't hear myself, so I can't hear, full stop. When the panics started, for the first time in my life, I was *really* deaf. And that made me really scared. So I've spent a long time on my own, hoping for it to come back, by distracting myself, trying so hard to do other things, the gardening and that. And it worked, a little bit, sometimes. But then in the Folly, making the sound screens, you letting me play the drums again – that was the turning point, really. When I realised I could still do it, I still had that. I didn't have to perform; I could still have that. But when I got hauled in after the opera, it all just went. I couldn't control it again. I'd have probably agreed to anything to get out of there. So, I'm sorry. I am really, really sorry. I had nothing to do with any of it, but please know that I am truly sorry for all the lies... I don't want them anymore.'

Pip looked up to see tears in her eyes. 'Oh God, please don't... I'm so sorry, I didn't mean to upset you any more than I have already.'

'I asked Russell to help you.' Shelley swallowed her instinctive emotion. 'I had no idea there was so much to it.'

'Of course you didn't, I never tell anyone anything, do I?'

'But when he told me you'd admitted it all, the screens and everything—'

'Oh, I never admitted tampering with the screens! I refused that much. They dropped that one. I don't know how Russell did it. They had incriminating photos and everything.'

'Well, I think I do,' Shelley muttered.

'I'm sorry,' he concluded, as if it needed saying again and again. 'Please believe me.'

'I do.'

'Thank you.' Pip's shoulders dropped at last. 'I don't want to hide anymore. I get to live here – thanks to you – I can be how I am. Maybe that has not proved possible out there, but I can live with that. Out there I'd rather be the thick, malleable gardener. It doesn't matter, because it does not take my heart and soul. I can keep that safe, to myself, here. I don't need anything else. I just need the quiet and to play. Being here, playing, helping Matthew feel sounds, I'm beginning to hear it all again. I'm happy. Performance I can't do, that's OK, maybe I don't need it anymore. It was always a real struggle being on stage anyway. Even a normal level of performance anxiety put me right out of sorts. I have to be completely silent in my body to hear what I'm playing... So, I suppose what I'm saying is that I would like to stay here. But if you remain unhappy about it, then I will go. No question.'

'I'm not unhappy about it,' Shelley gently smiled. 'I would like you to stay...'

In the moments that followed, Pip's heart took on a steady rhythm, his lungs stretched and fell back without his will, his thoughts quietened to a distant whisper, and the sound of the world dropped to that gentle purr.

And a new chord was struck. Pip listened to it with his usual attention, but he did not expect it to amplify.

41

LISTENING TO YOURSELF

Pip was early. He stood in the hallway, feeling the silence of the house. The dining room was locked, so he sat down in the drawing room to wait, looking out at this kind of ancient wonderland and feeling himself, like Alice, growing smaller and smaller in Matthew's beloved high-backed chair, wondering again what he was doing in the midst of this grandeur and checking the door in case someone was coming to order him out. Beginning to hear whispers in his head that this was all just some other elaborate hoax – of course a peer of the realm and the two most beautiful women he had ever met would not be welcoming him into their home and throwing him a birthday dinner. He needed to hear something else. He needed movement.

Downstairs in the basement, Victoria stood in the kitchen in front of an open fridge, a puddle of food and smashed crockery on the floor. She did not see him, bent over, her hand on her hip, her face a cloud of pain. She straightened slowly, looking out of the window, seeming to go through some narrative in her head until she was upright again, repeating silently until her face uncreased and she could move on to the cupboard to fetch a dustpan and brush.

Pip retreated from the door, knowing instinctively that she would not want him to have seen. He waited for a moment before heralding his appearance with loud footsteps.

'Goodness me,' she said. 'I thought we'd been visited by the Grenadier Guards. Are your feet deaf, as well? Yes, I know, I've had a little accident.'

'Here, let me.' Pip took the dustpan and brush and made light work of it.

'Thank you, Pip. Sadly, conjuring a replacement dinner for your birthday may be a little more difficult. My comeuppance for attempting to disguise a Lidl casserole as a homemade Coq au Vin, I suppose. At least I didn't drop the red wine,' she sighed, turning to put the precious bottle safely back in the cupboard. 'Oh dear, I am sorry. I so wanted it to be nice.'

Pip had not heard the tone in her voice so weary before.

'Couldn't help noticing, Victoria, but you have got a really nice looking trout in the fridge, and those shelves are full of all sorts of old stuff.'

'Philip, really! Is it your habit to be carousing through the cupboards of your hosts the moment their back is turned?'

'Na, but... sorry, I just thought—'

'Well, do not. That rather splendid creature is a gift from Mrs Burlington's grandson who manages the water courses at Itchen Park, and who visited briefly on Saturday. I have not the slightest inclination, or the requisite skill – I do so hate such admissions – to do anything with the poor blighter. And thus it sits there still, staring up at me with those glazed eyes every time I resign to make a cup of tea, until the moment I shall reluctantly consign it to the waste bin. I suppose we could have a whip round, phone for a takeaway.'

'Let me make sure I read this right – you'd rather have a takeaway than that gorgeous looking thing in your fridge? Is that what you're saying?'

'I am not saying anything of the kind, Pip! I am somewhat

exaggeratedly fond of fine food. I have just never been arsed to learn how to cook it.'

'Oh right, with you now. No problem. Wheel yourself up to the chair by the Rayburn then and I'll get to work, OK? You can keep talking while I concoct, yeah?'

'Pip, am I to deduce from this excessively promising drivel that you are offering to cook supper?'

'Well, if my "drivel" is so "excessively promising"?' he guessed, and was quite pleased with himself that she didn't disagree. 'I think you might just let me, yeah?'

'Mmm, I concede this is entirely true, and more than a little welcome. I am heartened by your apparent, if unfamiliar, confidence, in anticipation that you might produce something edible, at the very least.'

'At the very least.'

'It's been over five years since we had to let Marie, our housekeeper, go and I do so miss her.' Victoria lowered herself more slowly than usual into the warm chair. She winced again and then got some smoke from the burned edges of the casserole in her eye. Pip did not feel inclined to point out that there wasn't any and the dish was already in the bin.

'Not that I am suggesting my predicament has the slightest significance compared to the deprivation of the masses, but I am 86 and – I hesitate to admit it – have lost a great deal of my alacrity in the business of movement. Not terribly useful in helping to maintain a place like this. And even Beryl and the rats turn their noses up at anything Matthew tries to cook.'

'Ah well, Shelley's back for a while, isn't she? And you got me now,' he hesitated. 'If that's what you want.'

'It appears to be.'

'That's settled then. We'll take it in turns to cook. How about that?'

'I am speechless, Pip. Twice in one evening! Please do not allow it to happen again.'

'You haven't got any dill, have you?' He searched the ancient racks. 'Or I could do something with chervil...'

'Some ten yards from the back door, you will find a small herb garden. Please avail yourself of anything you need.'

'Result!'

'Excuse me?'

'Just an expression. You don't have to learn that one. Back in a mo...'

Shelley sat by the lake, staring down at the email open on her phone. Even though it had only been a couple of days and a hundred odd miles, the letter from Cambridge University seemed like it came from a universe away. And the message it conveyed – that they would be delighted if she would accept the Research Fellowship on the terms they had discussed – as if it were meant for someone else entirely.

She knew who that person was. The one who had sat in that chair on Thursday, in that beautiful old college room, reciting some script buried deep within her somewhere. It had regurgitated itself quite easily, as had the studious and appreciative noises that streamed out of her mouth as they toured the Acoustics Department, where the labs made her previous college look like a kindergarten.

The email was kind enough to mention that they had been impressed she had used her short summer 'sabbatical' to trial some principles involved in her work 'in such a direct and engaging way in her home village', but they looked forward to helping her 'realise that vision in a more scientific manner and technologically sound environment.'

Shelley put down her phone and gazed across the Manor grounds. A more scientific manner and technologically sound environment seemed to be the last thing she wanted.

Another email pinged:

Congratulations! You absolute star! Just got out of another interminable fund-raising lunch with the Vice Dean, managed to winkle out of him that you were being offered the job. Here's to bigger and better things! I've always had the utmost faith in you. It's well overdue that you had it in yourself. Dinner tonight to celebrate? Marcel's in Winchester? Really push the boat out?

'*Lovely,*' she wrote back. '*But Pip's birthday today, Victoria cooking. Another time?*'

Russell did not reply.

The locked dining room was strewn with pound shop banners and balloons, completely incongruous in this grand space, but Pip was deeply moved and almost dropped the trout. That afternoon, he'd been treated to a cupcake tea with Ma, Bill and the foster kids, who had presented him with the drum kit T-shirt he had on now. As Bill had said, 'You'll be able to wear it again now, son.'

Everyone was rich in their praise of the trout and, with the remains of the wine and a decent amount of home brew, Pip was deeply aware of how unusually relaxed he felt. He watched as the others chatted and laughed and reminisced. They looked at him, they shifted their position, they looked into the light – when they remembered. And Pip smiled and sometimes he nodded. Like he used to when he was pretending that he knew what people were on about and was trying to be polite, to engage, to be part of it. But now it didn't matter if he was pretending or not; sometimes he would concentrate, sometimes he was just content to sit amongst it. It didn't matter that he didn't understand it all. He understood enough. He understood that these three people loved each other, they were comfortable, and they were connecting and reconnecting. And they didn't mind him being there. They were neither avoiding nor awkwardly inclusive; he was just there, with them. And he watched, and he listened, and a smile settled restfully on his face.

And he was OK...

He squinted up at the shifting patterns of light in the dining room as dusk fell. The high windows of the Manor caught and reflected the slightest change of sunlight on this fitfully cloudy evening. Shadows flitted over Victoria, Matthew and Shelley's faces. Victoria got up, closed the curtains and turned on the lights.

'You really must learn to make yourself at home, Pip...'

She came back with a Scrabble board. 'Aha!' she said. 'A true game of no disadvantage. Except, of course, my gargantuan vocabulary!'

And he really let himself go then, disconnecting his attention. Like taking off a tight pair of shoes that he'd been standing in all day, he sat back in the chair and expanded, diving under the surface of sound and letting himself drift in the quiet...

Victoria won, of course, but Pip secured one of the five games. An achievement that seemed to delight her more than her own victories.

But in the rare gaps between games and stories and mouthfuls, he glimpsed other shadows clouding Shelley's face. The smallest drawing together of her eyebrows, a longer intake of breath as if she was preparing for speech, her fingers rising momentarily and then falling back to the table as if she couldn't quite bring herself to raise her hand for attention...

'Congratulations,' she said as Matthew and Victoria retired to bed. 'We rarely get a game over Victoria.'

'It was a lovely night, thank you,' he repeated, preparing to excuse himself as well. But he sat back down, and looked directly at her. Like he used to when he really wanted to know what she wanted to say. Her acceptance of his story, this night, Victoria's accommodations, had given him the confidence to show it. 'Is there something up?' he said. 'Something you're not saying?'

Shelley hesitated, tracing the table with her finger.

'I got the job,' she said, idly stacking the plates.

'Oh, right. Well, congratulations.'

'Thank you.' The words were easy, but the voice was dead.

'Will you take it, then?' Pip ventured into the silence that followed.

'I don't know.'

'What would you do if you didn't?'

'I don't know that either.'

How many times had he seen those words on her lips lately? He knew her as someone so full of enthusiasm, ideas and passions, they were words that did not suit her.

'There's your problem,' he said.

Shelley nodded vacantly. She had never in her life closed a door without opening another first and the prospect felt very alien.

Pip decided on another tack, looking out of the window. 'This place is wonderful. It's really helping me hear the things that matter. I love it.'

'So do I,' she said. 'Always have. I wish I could stay, too.'

'Can't you?'

'I want to, I think. But what would I do? The festival failed. I don't have anything else to help Matthew, and I need a reason to stay.'

'Isn't that a reason?'

'What?'

'That you want to.'

She was staring at him now, as if she wanted to hear something else, but he was not speaking. He found it fascinating; it reminded him of what he did all the time. But he wondered if his attention was quite so intense. He'd have to think about that...

She blinked and her head flicked to the window as if she had been woken suddenly by somebody shouting at her.

'Yes,' she said, so quietly, as if she was answering, 'I don't want it.' A tiny smile of wonder inched up her face. 'I don't want it!' she repeated, loud and clear, springing to her feet, the smile bursting across her face. 'I don't want the fucking job!' She threw her arms wide and spun around. 'Ooh,' she snapped back, taking hold of the table. 'How strong is that home brew?'

'No idea. Somewhere between mead and meths, I'd guess.'

She laughed freely. 'Coffee?'

'In the drawing room? I've always fancied saying that.'

There was a renewed lightness about her as she brought the coffee jug from the kitchen, as if some switch had been tripped. It was infectious.

'I always wondered what's so great about this chair,' he said, bouncing up and down on Matthew's 'throne'.

'Apart from the fact that it's the only decent thing left to sit on in the room?'

'It is actually very nice, though.'

'Is it? I've never tried it.'

'Really? Ah well, bad luck, I'm kind of settled now. You can make do with a packing crate.'

'Is that right?' she laughed, put down the coffee, scooted round the chair and tipped him out of it. 'I don't think so!'

Pip slid from the chair, dislodging the cushions, from beneath which tumbled letter after letter. Invoices, final demands, council notices, solicitors' letters, unpaid insurance reminders, scattered to the floor.

42

OPENING LETTERS

Matthew strolled into the kitchen for breakfast. Victoria was sitting at the head of the table, staring down at a letter in her hands. The envelope was ripped open, which made him instantly nervous.

'Sit down, Matthew,' she said as he stood rooted to the floor. 'I think we need to talk about these, don't you?' Her voice was unusually quiet, and she looked a little older than normal. 'Shelley and I have been adding them up this morning. These,' she pointed to a row of paperwork lining the edge of the table, 'amount to just over £560,000.' Matthew swallowed hard but couldn't find any saliva. 'But this one,' she waved the letter in her hand, 'is for £3.2 million.'

'Wh... what is it?' Matthew stuttered, as if he couldn't guess.

'It's a foreclosure notice, Matthew, for a mortgage that Robert apparently took out in 1961, which I presume you knew about otherwise you would not have been able to *forget* to pay most of the interest payments for the last two and a half years! To an outfit called...' she checked the letter again. 'Aubrey Estates. Ringing any bells?'

Matthew barely nodded, the bell ringing like a death knell.

'Found in your chair with a haul of correspondence that would challenge the Post Office. Pip and Shelley did not want to upset you with the discovery. I, on the other hand, have no such misgivings.'

Matthew finally sat down as his legs gave way. 'Th... three million?'

'Unpaid debt does have a tendency to grow, Matthew. Inconvenient, isn't it? Or were you hoping it would just go away?'

'I was going to pay them,' he mumbled. 'Well, pay them something anyway, with the proceeds of the festival. I didn't ignore all of them...' he tailed off pathetically.

'Really? Just these then. Arrears statement. Another arrears statement. Default notice. Final default notice. Notice of claim for possession of the Manor. None of them so much as opened. And the pièce de résistance, your possession court hearing notice. This afternoon!'

Matthew went white. It was finally happening. He was finally going to lose it all.

'Shelley's gone to fetch Pip,' Victoria continued, regardless. 'She's going to sit with you and help fill out all the forms and then go with you to the Court. Pip and I will drive to Fortescues for the auction, and pray that we can get a decent price for the emerald drum kit in time to offer the judge a gesture of goodwill, in the hope that he might suspend the possession order. Then we'll go from there. But with absolute openness and honesty this time, we *must* know the extent of what we are up against... Are you hearing me, Matthew? Matthew!' He was already leaving the room. Victoria sighed and pulled herself to her feet. By the time she caught him up, he was walking down the hall towards the drawing room.

'Oh, no you don't!' she bellowed at him. 'Don't you dare get back in that chair, Matthew. I cannot do this on my own!'

Matthew had never heard such an admission from Victoria's mouth in his life. For a moment he just stared at her, before turning back to hurl all the cushions off the settle in the hallway, lifting the lid and scooping at the cavity below, like Beryl burrowing her shit in his rose garden, envelope after envelope flying past his legs to the floor behind.

'Oh, bollocks,' Victoria sighed. 'We're going to need another table...'

Pip had never touched the controls of anything quite like it in his life as he poked, flicked and pressed the antiquated knobs, buttons and pedals of Matthew's old Rover. The car was well past its best and only used to potter around within the Manor walls from time to time, or for extreme calls of duty, but they didn't make them like this anymore. Victoria was busy shovelling papers, crisp packets and dog blankets out of the passenger seat into a bin bag. Eventually, she gave up and squeezed herself on top of the remaining garbage; two toms and a hi-hat cymbal jammed between her legs.

'You do drive then?' she said.

'Yes. I know, people are always surprised.'

'Do not take me for one of them. I first drove with shot-deafened soldiers after the war, safest journeys I've ever had.'

'Nice to know,' Pip managed a small smile. 'Makes a change. The idea you have to hear to drive is pretty universal. Cheers me up actually, reminds me it's not me who has the limited world view.' He took off his shoes and chucked them in the back. 'It's been a while though, and this one is a bit *unusual*.'

'Does it go at all?'

'Let's find out, shall we?' He turned the key and it ignited first time. The clutch released, Pip's hypersensitive foot felt the instant the engine sprung into life.

'Excellent!' she declared. 'Yet I sense a flaw in this plan. I do like to talk when passenging and this presents a problem. If you are driving, you cannot see what I am saying.'

'Don't suppose that'll stop you.'

'Flippancy, Philip. Do you sign?'

'No. Why would I? I've never known anybody that does. I'd be talking to myself.'

'Hmm, well, I am a little rusty myself. Learned that after the war as well. Perhaps we should take lessons. What fun we could have behind people's backs!' Victoria tugged at an envelope wedged behind the seat belt clip. It ripped in half. 'I concede, however, that even that may distract you from driving if you have to look at my hands all the time.'

'Not really, highly developed peripheral vision. One of the other things my brain has learned over the years.'

'How about a mirror, then?' Victoria shoved the envelope in her bag and rummaged for her antique vanity case. She held it up in front of her face with a 'Ta-Da' smile. Pip laughed and wondered if she was deliberately trying to amuse him to distract them both from the inevitable trepidation about what might happen today.

'I'm flattered by your confidence, Victoria, but I really don't think I'm going to get much out of that. Tell you what, why don't you just talk anyway? I like the hum of it even if I can't hear what you're saying. And if anything really important occurs to you, there's always traffic lights.'

'Deal!'

They made it as far as the gate before the engine died...

Shelley and Matthew had been sitting outside the Judge's Chambers for an hour and a half. Increasingly alarmed at his worsening state, she was contemplating asking the usher for the fire bucket by the time they were invited in to the room. There were six empty chairs in a line in front of a long, thin table. The judge sat alone on the other side, looking like an accountant at the end of a very bad day; no gown or wig but a skew red tie that had caught quite a lot of his lunch.

'I apologise for the delay. We seem to be very behind today,' he smiled, gesturing to the chairs in front, but the politeness and the informality were lost on Matthew. He opened his mouth but appeared unable to speak.

There was still no word from Pip and Victoria at Fortescues. Aubrey Estates' solicitor, an impatient young suit with a very distracting twitch, made disappointingly swift work of his case. As Matthew sat mute and motionless, Shelley took over, passing documents as they were requested, with fluttered apologies that they were only forthcoming now, and doing her best to plead the case on behalf of a melting, mute, bankrupt Earl. She held back one sheet, absently folding and unfolding the corners, as she repeatedly checked her phone on her lap.

'And that one?' the judge prompted. 'Or are we making a paper plane?'

The screen flashed.

> Just made it! £185,000.
>
> Good luck!

Shelley grabbed a pen and scribbled £185,000 in the gap in the text, crossed it out and wrote £145,000. Please God, that must be enough. For the moment, at least.

The judge raised an eyebrow and passed the repayment proposal to the lender's solicitor. 'That seems like a reasonable offer, don't you think?'

The young suit didn't seem very happy about it, but since the sum covered the arrears owing, additional interest and two months' repayment of the remaining debt in advance, he couldn't reasonably argue.

The judge suspended the possession order on condition of an

initial payment of £145,000 and the resumption of timely payments in two months' time.

Shelley hugged Matthew, and he teetered to his feet.

'Thank you,' he croaked, finding a tiny voice at last. 'Thank you so much...'

Still wobbly, Shelley led Matthew to the water fountain outside Court Number 1, just as Russell came out of it. Wearing the battered and balding wig of his grandfather, which he always said won his cases, it was written all over his face that it had won him this one too.

'Shelley? What are you doing here? No trouble, surely?'

'Matthew's just had a little misunderstanding with a loan repayment, that's all.'

'I'm very sorry to hear that. You should have said, perhaps I could help with the proceedings?'

'It was all rather short notice, but it's OK, it's sorted now. I just need to get Matthew home. It's been a bit of a strain on him.'

'It looks it. Well, the blessings of a rare case in my local court and an early adjournment, please let me offer you both a lift at least.'

'We're waiting for Pip and Victoria to pick us up. They should be here soon.'

Another text pinged and her shoulders slumped.

'The car won't start, they're stuck in Fortescues' car park.'

'Well, *four* of you then,' Russell sighed...

'Driving without tax, MOT, or insurance, Pip? You do seem to like adding to your charge sheet,' Russell tutted in the auction room car park. 'No, no, before you say anything, Shelley, it's all safe with me. I'll get it towed in the morning...'

'What about that dinner then?' he said as he dropped them at the Manor gate.

'Another time, Russell. I think we all need to rest and recoup right now.' Shelley touched his arm and gave him a peck on the cheek. 'Thank you, Russell, you're a rock.'

'Yes,' he said, glancing out of the window at Pip, Matthew and Victoria. 'Aren't I?'

Matthew spent much of the next day at the kitchen table, opening letters. He was doing it very slowly, but he was doing it alone. Nevertheless appreciating the close proximity of Shelley and Victoria, who were huddled over Shelley's laptop at the other end of the table. Every now and again, one of them would look up and smile at him and his hovering hand would reach for another envelope. By the end of the afternoon, he had a full wastepaper bin and three piles – urgent, critical, and past salvation.

'Well, at least we know what we're up against now,' he sighed.

But there were two envelopes that fitted into none of the piles on the kitchen table. The first arrived this morning, special delivery from Aubrey Estates, offering to write off the outstanding sum owing and take on the rest of the estate's debts, as part of a *Contract of Sale* for the Manor.

It crumpled in Matthew's hand.

He took the second one, which Victoria had found stuffed down the side of the car seat, rising silently from his chair. Victoria looked warily at Shelley. She had covered the throne chair with red and white barrier tape since the court hearing, just in case. But Matthew just wanted to walk the grounds, alone.

He ended up at the Folly at ten o'clock that night, asking for an extra lesson.

'It helps, Pip,' he said. 'That's all.' He handed Pip the content of the second envelope.

An invitation to Stat's cremation.

Last Wednesday.

43

STAT COMES HOME

A gust of wind blew down the alley off Wardour Street and ricocheted Rex into the wall as he attempted to light another cigarette. Giving up and just sucking on the unlit butt, it took him a moment to put his feet back in the right direction. Adrift as he was, anchorless in the storm of his life, drawing on something that was no longer there.

He had nowhere to go but Stat's office; just wanting to sit there for the day, perhaps the rest of the week, perhaps until the rent ran out.

The room was warm and musty with years of cigar smoke ingrained in every fixture and fitting. Rex bit down on his cigarette butt and breathed it in instead. Sinking into Stat's oversized chair, it dwarfed him and only made him feel even smaller. His eyes roamed around the room at all the things he had seen a million times, but never really *seen* before: magazines, posters and papers everywhere; shelves and cupboards full of little oddities and memorabilia; pictures of Stat on the wall with Andy Warhol, Mick Jagger, and James Hunt. Always dishevelled, always with a cigar hanging out of his mouth, with a preposterously long ash that he always seemed to rescue just before it fell.

Well, the ash had fallen now.

Rex placed the urn on the corner of the desk, along with the papers that told him that he was supposed to have it. To have it all.

He had mutely left the organisation of Stat's funeral last week to his only remaining relative, a cousin named Sheila who Rex had never met. She had done it all without complaint, *before* Rex told her that Stat had willed all he had to him. His Soho flat, his life insurance, and his vintage Jensen Interceptor kept in a lock-up in Camberley. Rex promised to send her a cheque for the wake sandwiches as soon as the funds cleared. He was beginning to feel guilt in places he didn't even know existed.

Rex felt moisture drop onto his hand and looked up to the ceiling to nothing, before realising the drops were his own tears. He wiped his hand on the chair and then across his face, the papers on the desk blurring as he stared across all Stat's last preoccupations. Lists of venues with the band name at the top, each one crossed out; the Lumpwood Club contract and closure notice; and the Bedingford Opera programme. Rex picked up a venue list and tried to think which of them he could now buy a big enough share in to put the band on. To grace at least one of the stages that Stat had tried so hard to return him to. Perhaps even keep it going in his honour. But even if his bank account was soon to be unexpectedly full, Rex's heart had no currency to deal with anything in this room with his own name on it.

His eyes drew again to the stately home on the front of the Opera programme. Stat had circled the photo and scrawled beneath it: *This must not be allowed to fall.* Rex felt as if another gust had winded him, forcing him motionless in the chair. Stat's voice, which he had been struggling to hear all week, rang clearly through his mind. He remembered his words distinctly: 'It's a place where I'd like to end my days.'

Rex picked up the phone and made two calls. One to his AA Sponsor, and one to Bedingford Manor.

Victoria gave him very short shrift. Matthew was indisposed dealing with his bankruptcy after attempting to throw himself off the Manor roof, which she doubted his remarks had helped very much. Careless to Rex's stuttering distress, she hung up.

He emptied Stat's petty cash drawer and got on the next train from Waterloo...

Rex had never had cause to associate Basingstoke with any kind of existential revelation before, but there was a calmness settling in his stomach as the train passed onwards that he had not felt for a very long time, at least not without the aid of chemicals. Yet it troubled him today, as he could see no reason for it. He'd been to Hampshire before.

He recognised this very road in fact, as he stepped out of the station at Bedingford (which appeared to be nowhere near Bedingford, or anywhere else). His first wife lived here when he first met her, three weeks before their wedding in 1983. Or was it *that* road? There was the same level crossing and the slow rise upwards, from the quite big houses to the really big houses at the top. Rex briefly wondered if her father might still pop out of his mansion on the hill wielding a shotgun. The whole episode had lost the man his seat in Parliament after all, and a similar downward spiral into drink and disgrace as Rex's own a few years afterwards, as the *Daily Mirror* insisted on reminding everyone nearly forty years later. But since Sir Heston Wraysbury was now the knighted Secretary of State for the Environment, Rex supposed he had recovered a little better.

He walked on past the Bedingford village signpost, trumpeting 'Quietest Village in England'. No kidding, it was quiet. He could not compute this either; he had lived so long in the arms of the crowd. In his better days cloistered in offices, buses, planes and swanky houses like these; in his darker moments, shut in rehab, prison cells and mangy East End flats, where he rarely went out in case he was recognised. Or in case he was not.

Gates open and no old women with cameras and dogs, Rex passed quickly into the Manor grounds, realising he had not noticed much at all about the place on his brief visit before. Funny how he could remember a level crossing, a hill and a shotgun from four decades ago, but nothing here seemed remotely familiar after a matter of weeks. He was beginning to feel a little spaced out. Things were not making sense. He hugged the urn tighter, willing for the stability that was dead within.

'Rex, isn't it?' Matthew's voice broke through his journeying daze. It seemed too quiet and muffled for someone standing right in front of him. '*The* singer.'

'I'm... sorry.' The two short words echoed around Rex's head and he could not quite place them either. It was his voice, he thought, but he couldn't remember hearing it saying them before. Yet they repeated, again and again. Rex looked between Matthew in front of him and Stat in his arms and wondered why he could still hear them.

'It's really alright, you can stop apologising now... Oh dear, poor chap...'

And Rex knew he was crying again.

'What the fuck is he doing here?' Victoria demanded as Matthew led Rex inside.

'Perhaps some tea, Victoria? Would you mind?'

'Exceptionally bad taste, Matthew!' She turned to Rex and held open the front door. 'There's a petrol station on the Winchester Road. They've got a vending machine.'

Matthew shook his head with a knowing smile and closed the drawing room door behind them.

'Is that...?' he nodded towards the urn in Rex's arms.

'He wanted to come, you see,' Rex stuttered. 'Stat, he wanted to be here. I didn't know. Really, I didn't know very much.'

'Join the club.'

'Could he… perhaps… stay?'

'My goodness, of course! It will be lovely to have him back.'

'You didn't come to the funeral. I can't blame you after the way I behaved.'

'Oh dear no, believe me, it wasn't that. I would have done, we all would… Rex, I – probably *we* by the look of things – have done some very stupid things. I am trying to look beyond them, with help. Would *you* perhaps like to stay…?'

Matthew showed him to one of the habitable rooms on the third floor. Rex put the urn down on the windowsill and looked out across the grounds.

'Thank you,' he said.

Another two short unfamiliar words…

44

A DIFFERENT KIND OF WAY...

Mrs Burlington's great nephew was an independent financial adviser with a very tight mouth, a fast tongue, and eyes that pointed away from each other. Pip had no idea what he was saying. He didn't really know why he was here either, but Victoria had summoned him to this meeting and he was still rarely inclined to disagree with her. They were a team now, the four of them, she said, and he was even less inclined to disagree with that.

Pip tried to focus on the one side of the man's mouth that seemed the most expressive, resigning himself to relying on Shelley's notebook. She pushed another explanatory piece of paper across the table with a small, accepting smile. 'No. 3 – Art Gallery.'

'Preposterous!' Pip read the response quite clearly on Matthew's lips, his entire face and most of his body.

Having been briefed to find ways they could meet some of their obligations without resorting to the sale of the Manor, the cross-eyed financial adviser had taken the baton with relish. By his seventh offering, Pip was getting more than the gist of this 'conversation', watching intently as Matthew's teeth gritted and shoulders stooped a little more with each eager 'suggestion'.

'More tea, Mr Burlington?' Victoria attempted to slow him down, but Pip could see he was already poised for delivery. Chin lifted, eyes forward (well, one of them), lips pursed. Mr Burlington was clearly the kind of man who thought everything he said was a generous present for everyone else. Thoughts popped into and out of his head so fast they were already gift-wrapped.

'Isn't it the Glorious 12th of August in a couple of weeks? What about corporate pheasant shoots?'

'Specialist work, resource intensive, unpredictable income, and dangerous?' Matthew tutted. 'Fabulous idea.'

'Besides, we haven't got any pheasants,' Victoria added.

'Good point.'

'I'm sorry, your Lordship, but you are saying "no" to everything.'

'That's because they are all awful! And most of them require more money than they'll make. No! I'm buggered if I'm going to prostitute this place for country-house-by-numbers-weddings or the chance to get your head blown off by your customers!'

'National Trust?' Mr Burlington bulldozed on, undaunted; a man clearly convinced that lack of knowledge should never get in the way of a confident opinion. 'My wife's a member and they charge £3.85 for a bit of carrot cake. That could be very lucrative indeed—'

'No! Stop! I won't have this bloody nonsense a moment longer!' Matthew scraped back his chair. 'All I ever wanted was to keep this place going and become a proper music venue in time. If it's not going to be that, we might as well sell it. I won't listen to any more of this now.' His eyelashes wet with tears that would not fall in public, Matthew fled the room.

And taking his cue to leave was the first of the financial adviser's suggestions that everybody enthusiastically agreed.

Victoria returned from seeing him out and pretended to collapse in her chair. 'I've died of boredom. No flowers, please.'

'Can I send a card?' Pip laughed. Shelley didn't.

'Only if it's accompanied by a donation.'

'What now, though?' he asked. 'Might you really have to sell?'

'Well, I think it's...' Pip caught Victoria's mouth opening and tongue raised to begin the word 'likely', then registering Shelley's alarm, her lips closed around 'possible.'

Shelley thumped the table. 'All Matthew ever wanted was for people to enjoy the place and for it to sustain itself through music. I just wish there was *something* I could think of to help him, even if only to glimpse it.'

'Build him a sound and village-proof bubble and get Pink Floyd to play? The quietest rock concert ever!' Pip joked. 'What?' he added as Shelley stared at him.

'The quietest rock concert ever...' she repeated in a breath. 'Wouldn't that be what you experience when you go on stage?'

'Well, no, not really,' he laughed. 'I get all sorts of things. It's really noisy. Same as everybody else, I guess, just a different kind of way. I suppose it is a bit of a private experience.'

'Yeah,' she nodded distantly, a tiny light flickering in her eyes.

The quietest rock concert ever...

A private experience...

A different kind of way...

PART III

A BEAUTIFUL NOISE

? dB
…whatever you choose it to be

45

THE DAWNING OF THE DAY

Pip suppressed a yawn. This attention thing was very tiring. Matthew had been reluctant to leave his lesson and was still talking an hour later.

'It's got to go, Pip. I accept it now,' he said, sipping a home brew, staring out across the grounds from the Folly window. Pip knew he was lying, there was nothing accepting about the quavering in his tone and the lowered gaze of a whispered resignation. 'I've been such a fool, burying my head in the sand like this, hiding behind one daft scheme or another. None of them any better than that awful man's suggestions. I shouldn't have been so rude.'

'The opera wasn't daft,' Pip countered. 'It was completely logical. You chose opera to make the most money without amplification, right? And put it in the courtyard as a natural amphitheatre to spend the least money on staging, with a beautiful setting for the audience. Logical, not daft.'

'But none of it worked, did it? And now I'll never get to hear anything that I would want to—'

'What if you could?' Shelley hurtled in then, clutching pages of scribbled note paper. 'What if we *could* stage the music that you love, here in the courtyard?'

'You know that's impossible now, Shelley. On all counts. I can't hear it properly and neither the Council nor the villagers would allow it.'

'You're a very long way from silence, Matthew. And look what you've been learning here! So perhaps we could do it so you *can* hear it.' She turned to Pip. 'How *you* hear it. I've been thinking about it. A lot. All the things you're learning Matthew – to *look* more, to *feel* more – couldn't we take those concepts into a gig somehow? To model it on what you are, Pip. Turn the volume down, get the audience to see more, feel more... *listen* more.'

The flicker of light in Shelley's eyes quickly burned into a roaring flame as she gabbled a stream of consciousness, waving her scrawled notes and diagrams. It wouldn't really have mattered whether Pip or Matthew could follow everything she was saying or not. They were both dry logs to her glowing sparks and were bound to catch fire.

Pip felt the warmth of it first, excitement flickering from his stomach upwards, before he felt the need to dowse it.

'Yes, but you can't really turn a rock band down, can you? People wouldn't like it. Of course, you could do it so that it doesn't make their ears bleed, but certainly not enough to put it next to this village. Besides, isn't it in the Council's conditions that any performances have to be unamplified?'

'So what if we could direct the sound then, so people could hear it more directly, and they could even control what they hear? Through headphones, for instance.'

'Headphones at a rock concert?'

'They do it at silent discos.'

'I suppose so...' The flames were taking hold again. 'Could that work for a live gig?'

'Yes, I think so. I need to do some more work. But this is it, isn't it? This is my reason!'

Matthew had no idea what that meant, but Pip heard what she was saying: she was staying. And some other glow was taking hold of him now. He examined the feeling with his usual curiosity. It felt like... *hope*.

'Don't do anything for a couple of days, Matthew, OK...?'

Matthew never used to mind doing nothing. In a place like this, nothing didn't exist anyway. He paused from fruitlessly trying to nail planks of wood over the broken gate at the far end of the estate. Vera Swainsborough's pigs had been having a field day in the orchard for far too long. He wondered what it might be like to down tools, get in your Skoda and pop off to B&Q, before it was time for the match and the pub. Quite nice, probably. Matthew often had this fantasy of an ordinary life, in an ordinary house with an ordinary job, but in the end could never conceive of any life where he was not simply a custodian – of land and heritage. He was deeply connected to the air and soil of this small quarter of England's green and pleasant land. It wounded him deeply to contemplate that he had failed.

He caught sight of Rex standing amongst the plum trees, staring at Stat's urn in his arms, one leg cocked behind the other. Since he'd turned up at the door, tearful and apologetic and impossible to turn away, Rex had spent his days just wandering around the Manor grounds, occasionally coming to this motionless stand. Sometimes for minutes and sometimes for hours. The willow tree by the lake, the plum orchard, and the courtyard stage seemed to attract his vigils the most. And the mouldy old bedroom on the third floor, where Rex placed Stat on the window seat looking out onto the grounds, seemed to be the only place he put the urn down. Mathew had tried to talk to him, and Shelley took him food and tea and any number of items she hoped might encourage him out of his lost wanderings. Victoria had not yet progressed from viewing him as an arsehole.

Matthew watched him, in the distance, his vision unstoppably broadening across the rest of the grounds, trying to imagine how he could possibly cope if he was to lose something that he loved so much.

He would try again with Rex. Everybody deserved a second chance…

For Rex, this was no slow grief, creeping up on him as bits of himself fell away; this had been instant and usurping. Like looking through the Viewmaster toy of his childhood when it had got stuck on a new slide. Just like that small boy, Rex kept looking and looking, but there was nothing he recognised any more, and he could not move it on.

In those days, the toy had been glued to his face, always wanting more reels, more worlds outside his own. Worlds that one day he would see for himself, live in, conquer. In recent years, he too had got stuck on one frame, and that had glued fast to all of him. The moment Stat died, none of it made sense. Stat had been there all those years to get him what he wanted. Now he was gone, it wasn't even the shock and fear of having to get what he wanted himself, so much as not even recognising what that was anymore. Or even *who* he was.

The reel changed to that dusty hard shoulder of the A1, the first time he and the band had met Stat, all those years ago. And he could feel the rage rising, the frustration, the same tears pricking his eyes that he had had to hide behind the bonnet of the steaming van. It was always him. Always *him* sorting it out whilst the others, literally and metaphorically, sat on the sidelines, laughing and drinking tea and cider. As if none of it mattered. As if it didn't matter that they had to get there. They *had to* get on that stage. And he was the only one who could do anything about it.

Then Stat had appeared, got him somewhere, and cleaned up the mess behind. For forty-five years. Rex had welcomed it so viscerally. But welcomed became accustomed. Accustomed became expected. And expected, eventually, became demanded.

His eyes drew in to the plum orchard, the trees spinning slowly around him. Holding out a hand to steady himself on one of the trunks, a soft purple fruit dropped from a branch above onto the lid of the urn.

'I'm sorry...'

He lowered the urn onto the grass at the foot of the tree and sat down next to it. For a moment he stared at the plum, as if it too was as alien as his current existence and the words that he spoke. Leaning back on the trunk, half a dozen more fruits fell. He left the one on the lid of the urn and ate the rest, feeling the juice trickle down his throat like he'd felt nothing before, as he could feel the tears journey down his cheeks to his mouth to add their gluey saltiness to his meagre meal.

'I'm sorry...'

Now he was hearing it. Feeling something that, finally, made sense.

He began to sing, an old song of his childhood, *The Dawning of the Day*. And the sound took him home, to his voice. He had this voice. Stat knew that all along. How had it come to be about so much else?

Rex sat in the plum orchard and sang another song. And another, and another. The final notes stabbed him, but it was a comfortable pain, clean and sharp like the plum juice, not the dull ache of longing, guilt and loss he had been carrying since Stat's death.

Now, he wanted to *listen*.

He could hear drums playing in the Folly...

Rex knocked on the door to no answer, so he went inside. His calls went unanswered too, so he followed the sound upstairs.

The drummer stopped abruptly.

'Have we met?' Rex said.

'No, I don't think so.'

'You look familiar.'

He shrugged, putting his drumsticks away in their holder, his chest rising and falling in a rallentando of diminishing beat after what, Rex noted, must have been impressive exertion.

'No, don't stop, please.'

'I think I will, actually.'

'Pity.'

The drummer looked at him as his breathing steadied. No words, but clearly indicating it was still his turn.

'I've been singing today.'

'You're a singer, it makes sense.'

'Yes,' said Rex, the sides of his mouth quietly taking on life. 'It makes sense...'

'Ah, Rex. You've found our little den, then?' Matthew arrived for his lesson. 'Has Pip shown you our percussion collection?'

'No, we were just getting to know each other.' Rex glanced at Pip. He was still staring at him. 'I'd like to, though. Don't suppose you've got a bodhrán?'

'Yeah,' Pip replied simply.

'Can you play it?' Rex's eyes sparkled.

'A bit.'

'A bit!' Matthew guffawed. 'Ooh, let's have another lesson with the bodhrán, Pip! Come on, Rex, you'll like this...'

Pip turned into the corner of the basement to search the racks for the bodhrán. It was not so much that he didn't want to hear the conversation behind him, but that he knew what it was already and needed to be relieved of the obligation to join in. But he also knew that Matthew's animated chatter could leave him standing fiddling with accessories for the next hour if he didn't re-engage at some point. He turned, eventually.

'I knew a deaf drummer once,' Rex was saying. 'I mean, I didn't know him, saw him play once...'

Pip sighed. He should have taken longer.

'Hang on a minute, it is, isn't it? It's you! I didn't recognise you. You look... older.'

'It happens,' Pip sniffed.

'Blimey! Yeah, yeah...' the mist was clearing. 'Eighties retro festival in Finsbury Park last summer, you were headlining with Surface Tension. I was on a free pass from Alan, our drummer. He was way down the bill in some tribute band, bunch of shit... Jesus, man! What are you doing here living underground? You were fucking incredible!'

Pip looked to the ceiling, his foot beginning to race. He didn't want to hear this either. But Matthew had already taken the baton. 'Ooh, ooh, was he? Was he, Rex?' He clapped his hands together. 'I knew it, I knew it! He's good, isn't he? Oh, do tell! He won't really play you see, Rex—'

'Are you kidding me? Yeah, I remember now, the noise at the end! I don't think Surface Tension even had anything like that in their heyday...'

Pip's breath tugged suddenly and he couldn't force it out. He'd missed the cue. The thought had been a whisper, the image the blink of an eye. Up there behind his kit, the roar of the audience in the air, in the heat and vision and rhythm all around him. He couldn't breathe, the stillness exploding into chaos, the noise unbearable.

He dropped the bodhrán and fled. Up the stairs, out into the meadow, the exertion forcing the air back into his lungs. He ran down the hill to the lake and up again, as fast as he could, until the pain in his legs and lungs were all he could hear again...

'Are you OK?' Shelley had wanted to shout, seeing Pip

collapse on the ground by the lake, but she ran, standing in front of him as he sat panting, his eyes fixed on the sky.

'Trying to listen to the swifts,' he gulped the air. 'Can't hear anything. The other noises. It's too much.' He looked down at his paddling feet, his fingers tapping persistently on his thighs, and then up at her, as direct as all his gazes but she'd never seen that look before, desperately searching for help.

'Oh, Pip, what's happened?' She dropped to her knees beside him. 'I just saw Rex with Matthew coming out of the Folly. He said you were talking about a gig he'd seen you play. Was it Rex? Did he remind you of it all? Is that it?'

'Guess so,' he nodded urgently. 'Just came suddenly. Like I was there again, you know, on stage, I... Sorry, just had to get out.'

'Of course you did.'

'It's alright,' he breathed more determinedly. 'I'll be alright in a minute. Stupid. Sorry.'

'Yes, you will.' She touched his arm to draw his focus back. 'And it's not stupid, Pip. I can see it's very frightening. And it's no surprise the way you feel, how deeply these things affect you, the way you feel everything, with every bit of you.'

Pip squinted at her as if he had never made that connection before and was trying to test out its resonance.

'But it's OK now,' she continued. 'All that's over, isn't it? You don't have to do it anymore. You don't ever have to go on stage again if you don't want to. You've got a life outside of that now.'

'Yes. Yes. You're right.' He spoke in the short, sharp bursts that were the aftermath of such chaos. Even his lungs were tired.

'Memories can be so loud, can't they? But you don't need to listen to them anymore. Like you said, you're playing again now, that's all that matters. You don't need to perform.'

'No. You're right, you're right. Of course. Just play. Just play.' His fingers began to move faster but more rhythmically then, an intricate pattern in what Shelley thought might be 7/8.

'Perhaps you should go and play now? Hear that instead? Remind you of that instead? I'll get Rex and Matthew out of the way,' she smiled knowingly.

'Yes,' he nodded. 'Just play. That's all I need to do. Thank you...'

He looked from her to the sky.

And the swifts shrilled above once more.

46

HEARING AID

Rex shuffled into the dining room, clutching Stat's urn as usual.

'Do we have to have him here?' Victoria hissed.

'I think it might be good for him, Victoria,' Matthew replied, quietly. 'Besides, Shelley says he might have something interesting to contribute.'

'Interesting? I very much doubt it. The man's about as deep as a birdbath.'

Matthew (dangerously) ignored her and drew up an extra chair. 'Perhaps we can put Stat here,' he said. 'He was always so good at organising me, perhaps he'll provide some inspiration.'

Rex nodded and placed Stat on the chair beside him.

So the second meeting around the dining table this week quickly proved to be very different from the first. Matthew was saying 'yes' to everything. Ideas firing night and day, Shelley described in more detail her concept for what Pip had laughingly christened, 'Hearing Aid' – a rock festival on the August Bank Holiday weekend, with the music that Matthew wanted to hear, in a way that he could hear it; and the village could not. And, most importantly, an event that was a completely immersive experience for the audience, involving all the senses in hearing, in the way that Pip did, and Matthew was learning. There would be no amplification or PA, the bands would play with minimal stage monitoring, just to hear themselves. Every member of the audience would have their own private experience of the music via wireless headsets. The music would be complemented by as much visual and sensory stimuli as they could conjure, and be much closer to Pip's own experience of sound.

It would be the quietest rock concert on earth for everybody outside it. But for those inside it, as loud as they chose. The audience would be inside the music, using their ears, eyes and every part of their body to experience it. And their own individual volume, through their ears, would be completely in their control.

'What an enormously gratifying idea!' Victoria immediately re-engaged. 'Turning the volume down, but turning what people actually *listen to* up. My life's work! And full of possibilities.'

'Yes,' said Matthew.

'But people want live music to be loud, don't they? You want to feel it through the soles of your feet, right into your soul, banging your bones and quickening your heartbeat,' Rex chimed in with the longest sentence he had offered since he'd arrived. 'You want to be shaken by the speakers vibrating the air around you. I've made a career out of it.'

'Maybe, but which bit of what you've just said has anything to do with the volume in their ears?' Shelley replied, smiling knowingly at Pip. 'Or more relevantly in our case, the villagers' ears.'

'Yes,' said Matthew.

'Besides, if they're wearing headphones, they can choose that individually as well,' Pip added.

'Yes,' said Matthew.

'And if we get this right and provide enough other stimulus, perhaps they might find they need a bit less of it anyway. Protect their own hearing,' Victoria suggested.

'Yes!' said Matthew.

'Which might have done you a bit of good to learn in the old days, Matthew.'

Matthew said nothing.

'Yeah, right,' Rex retorted for him. 'It's like the fags, innit? We all know it's bad for us, but we're going to do it anyway.'

'Hmm, some of us, perhaps. Nevertheless, that could also be quite interesting to promote, could it not? We are calling it Hearing Aid after all.'

'Yes, great, why not?' Shelley said. 'Although we might have to limit our ambitions a bit, start small, just to see if it could work. We do only have four weeks, and without Stat...'

Rex put his hand on the urn beside him. 'He's here,' he said. 'He's here.'

'And I think he would like it.'

'Let's do it in honour of Stat then,' Victoria concluded.

Rex looked deeply at her. 'Thank you,' he said, then turned to Shelley. 'I'll get his carousel for you. Might be some useful contacts? Stat always understood that music can be just as much about what we see and what we feel as what we hear. But like most things in life, people pick one thing and focus on it at the expense of everything else.'

Victoria visibly huffed. The man didn't even have the decency to be a complete wanker.

'So,' Matthew perked up again, a gleam in his eye. 'Perhaps the headliner need not be a local band? Wouldn't Stat like that too?'

'I don't think we'd be much of a draw mate,' Rex said, something that would never have passed his lips before.

'But I loved your stuff, back in the day!'

'Did you? Well, that's nice, but "back in the day" is the operative phrase, isn't it? Mind you, that is pretty much all Stat has in his carousel.'

'So maybe we could make a thing of that too,' Victoria suggested. Shelley was delighted – this meeting was taking on a life of its own. Pip thought he might be delighted too, with the third of it he was getting.

'Well, I'd like it,' Matthew said. 'But what about the young people?'

'What's it got to do with them?' Victoria snorted. 'We'd be trying to save some very old things, by staging some other pretty old things, mostly for the benefit of a bunch of other old things. Why not be honest about it? Anyway, whoever said the young don't like old things? Look at these two, spending another evening with us relics.'

'Oi, oi!' Rex objected, with the first hint of humour since he'd arrived.

'I think we can cater for both,' Shelley smiled.

'Not teenagers obviously,' Victoria said. 'None of us has that much imagination.'

'And anyway,' Pip added, in the reasonable hope he had got the intention of the conversation at least, 'the only real difference between young and old festival-goers is that the young can drink *during* the day, not just at the end of it.'

'Right then, juice and smoothie bar!' Shelley giggled. 'I'm adding it to the list.'

'So then, why can't it be somewhere an old person can spend a day of music with a young one?' Matthew offered.

'Or a deaf person with a hearing one.'

'Lovely!'

'Or a live one with a dead one.' Rex patted the urn and brought the meeting to a temporary halt with that one. They all stared at him.

Matthew, however, was not to be derailed for long. 'Yes!' he whooped, bobbing up and down in his seat. 'Stat can sit in his office in the stables, like he used to. He would understand. This is exactly what I want to do with this place! We plant the seed next month and just grow it from there! And next year it will be the most fantastic multi-sensorial rock venue, all over the grounds!'

Matthew had that look in his eyes again. Victoria wondered if she shouldn't hose him down. She did sometimes wish that the Wolstenholmes would have some small staging post between the gutter and the stars.

But then again, she'd always preferred a rollercoaster to a roundabout...

Rex had been standing in the courtyard talking to the urn for almost an hour. Pip and Shelley were pacing out the stables.

'This is where Stat had his office, Rex,' she said, nodding towards the stable in the corner. 'Would you like to see?'

'That's his fountain pen,' Rex said. 'And his Mott the Hoople mug.'

'And you can still smell the cigar smoke,' Pip added.

'Can you? I wish I could.'

'I can't either, Rex. Pip has superpowers,' she winked.

It was lovely to see Pip so apparently relaxed and engaged again, throwing himself into every bit of this event and seemingly having something to say about everything. The last couple of days had seen him with a vocal performance worthy of Ronnie Corbett. It was getting like that, she noticed, as if he was slowly emerging. And emerging into something quite irrepressible. It filled Shelley with warmth and confidence.

Rex put Stat down on the desk. 'Mission control,' he said to the urn, in what was clearly a private joke. 'OK, I think he's up for it. Let's go through the carousel, see who might be available, identify the most visual performers.'

'That's you, isn't it?' Pip said.

And Rex, finally, smiled...

Yebut drummed his fingers on the dashboard of Alan's battered old splitter van.

'What's the matter with you?' Rex tutted from the double passenger seat, squeezed in next to him. 'This is lovely, this is.' He nodded out of the window as they sped out of a tree tunnel, the South Downs rolling in front of them. 'And we're nearly there.'

'Yeah but, we've already been two hours! I want the toilet. Why'd they have to build it so far from the M3?'

Rex looked at him and quietly shook his head.

'Yebut, you bellend,' Alan sneered from the wheel instead.

'What?' Yebut huffed. 'Twenty quid you gave us, said we'd be back by midday.'

Rex knew he'd lied about that, but the lie and the 'pocket money' were the only way he could persuade them to come and at least have a look at the place.

'I'll give you some more. Just relax. Enjoy it!'

'Yeah, yeah, very nice, very pretty and all that,' Alan piped up again. 'But I still don't know what's it got to do with us?'

Rex rolled his eyes. 'Were any of you listening? It's a beautiful venue and we can be a part of it. Help save it.'

'Why the hell would we want to do that?'

'Stat loved it here, and I know why now. They just need a break, so do we. No-one will put us on in anything bigger than function rooms now. So...?'

'Yeah but, we don't do opera.'

'Oh smart, Yebut.' Alan threw a peanut at him.

'Somewhat of an oxymoron,' Damon muttered from the floor of the van behind, whilst tying Benny's shoelaces together as he slept.

'Don't call me a moron,' Yebut pouted. 'He obviously means a Rock Opera.'

'Fuck off, we're not doing no Rock Opera!'

'Queen did it.'

'They did not!'

'What about Bohemian Rhapsody?'

'One song, Yebut, one song.'

'Yeah but, what about The Who then? *Tommy?* That was good, that was. "Down with the bedclothes, up with the—'

'For God's sake, Yebut, shut up!'

'Bunch of poofs anyway.'

'Who?'

'Yeah.'

'What?'

'What?'

'Who's a bunch of poofs?'

'Yeah.'

'*Who?*'

'Yeah!'

'Enough!' Rex finally attempted to redirect the piled up traffic. He'd never appreciated Stat more. 'Nobody is going to do an opera, rock or otherwise, OK?'

'Oh,' Yebut concluded, and that seemed to be all, a mellow blankness settling restfully on his face. Rex stared at him. It amazed him that Yebut could even count the four strings on his bass guitar, let alone bend them into such positions with such precision as to lift a whole performance on stage every night. But today, it made him smile.

'We do the best of our own stuff, plus some '80s classics, crowd pleasers you know, and we get to headline a full-blown bank holiday festival! And look over there, guys. You can just see the Manor in the distance. Can't you imagine the atmosphere?'

'Atmosphere, yeah...' Yebut breathed.

'Hang on a minute.' Alan was not the wistful type. 'Weren't they shut down for making a noise with an opera? How the hell are they going to cope with us?'

'Ah well, they've got this brilliant idea...'

Yebut's eyes and mouth widened steadily as Rex explained Shelley's plans, as if he were being read a thrilling bedtime story.

'That's genius,' he concluded.

'It's fucking bonkers,' Alan retorted.

'Yeah but, what a place to play, it's beautiful.'

'Yep. It is.'

'Thank you, Damon,' said Rex, a little surprised.

'Pussy,' said Alan.

'And we can stay here too, rehearse and all that?'

'You're not getting me staying in this backwater, mate,' Alan was still arguing. 'I'll do the stupid gig and a couple of rehearsals, but that's it. And I'm in the studio for the next three weeks with the Ceilidh band, so I'm not breaking down my kit every time. You'll have to get one here.'

'Yeah but—'

'It's OK, Yebut, sounds like consensus to me, and a spare drum kit is not going to be a problem...'

'You can let go now, thank you.' Shelley stopped her descent on the ladder propped against the Manor wall with her foot hovering over Victoria's head.

'Oh, yes. Yes, of course. All done. Safe and sound.' Victoria wiped her hands on her skirt and examined the red indentations left by her fierce grip. 'How strange,' she muttered.

'The village is eerily quiet again, isn't it?' Shelley said, surveying the gardens in view. Several of their neighbours were at work in them, but all hardly making a sound, as usual.

'Mmm, and I'm not sure I like it.'

'It all seems so determined, doesn't it? So purposeful. Everybody knowing what they're doing, quietly going about their business. Not like us, making it all up as we go along.'

'Oh nonsense, dear. Never attempt to judge other people's lives. It's like looking at a tapestry, it might look like it's got pattern and purpose, but you've only got to peek underneath to see what a fucking mess it really is— Good grief!'

All along the road, villagers stopped as an ancient splitter van rattled and banged its way up Trefusis Lane. Rex, squeezed into the passenger seat, gave a tight-lipped smile, half 'sorry' and half 'help me!' Alan jammed on the brakes and dixie horn at once, noisily reversing and leaning over Rex and Yebut to the window.

'Alright, gorgeous?' he bellowed. 'Busy later? We've got a little place up the road that we're sampling for a bit, sure we could make room for Grandma as well if you—'

'Fuck off!' said Victoria.

'Alan!' Rex smacked him with a prehistoric Reader's Digest road map. 'Have you no respect?'

'Respect for what?'

'This place, these people... Stat.' Rex hugged the urn tighter. 'Yourself?'

'You taking the piss? Take a look in the mirror, mate, and then talk to me about self-respect... Catch you later, darling!' Alan smacked the horn and screeched away again. Yebut waved from the passenger seat whilst Damon mooned at the neighbours out of the rear window.

'Well, that's blown it,' Shelley giggled at the Mexican Wave of mouth dropping all along the road. 'Now that really is going to cause trouble.'

'Excellent,' Victoria replied. 'This village is like cold custard. If you don't stir it up once in a while, it sets like concrete...'

47

OF COURSE YOU CAN'T...?

Graham Tweedle had a passion for noise abatement. Unlike the rest of Bedingford, however, his devotion was not to silence, but to the degrees of difference between it and sound. Graham had so painstakingly crafted the ability over the years to care about such minutiae of difference that he eagerly sought out any opportunity to display his gift. And *gift* it was, of that he had no doubt. A confidence burrowed into him from years of affirmation; his parents having been utterly mesmerised by him from the moment he first tottered on his nappied legs to switch off the hi-fi, to the day he received his membership to the Association of Environmental Health Officers. A seamless lineage between these events that, they claimed, 'made our Graham what he is today.'

Everybody else just put it down to bad luck.

This evening the 'gift' was being employed out of hours in the service of the Town Hall, but the duty lay lightly on him. Graham sat up in bed. The Noise Mitigation Strategy on his lap was, simply, perfection. There were even one or two acoustic elements he had never come across before. He licked his finger and turned the page, rubbing his thigh with the other hand. By

Page 15, he was fit to burst. Shelley had signed it at the end, and if she had included a photo, he probably would have.

Graham could feel a recommendation coming up. He would propose to the Planning Committee that the Stop Notice be lifted and planning permission reinstated for an experimental – no, 'nationally ground-breaking' (that was sure to press some buttons) fundraising concert in the Bedingford Manor grounds. This effort was more than worthy of such a reward, and he was the man to deliver it. Heroic. Of course he'd seen the little piece in *The Gazette* about that has-been rock star auctioning off a vintage Jensen Interceptor to help secure the future of that effort. And something about his bass player's employer being interested in supporting a prospective event. But a few media sound bites and a sponsorship from B&Q were nothing if the relevant permissions were withheld. Shelley would understand that. Shelley would know that it would be *he* who delivered the prize and saved the day.

He just needed to satisfy himself of a few details first...

Pip had spent most of the morning lugging drums and equipment from the Folly to set up at the Manor. The Edge of Darkness had made themselves at home in an abandoned room at the back of the house that was once a ballroom over a century ago. The cavernous space had holes in the floor the size of dinner plates and housed no more than a couple of moth-eaten sofas and a snooker table. Damon had therefore declared it 'perfect' and abandoned all his remaining resistance to staying. Even if he was having to share a bedroom with Alan. At least their mouthy drummer would not be making another appearance until next Saturday.

Damon and Yebut were arguing about which of the holes in the floor he was most likely to fall into, so that they could position the sofas over them, whilst Rex was trying to wrangle his tambourine from Beryl's mouth. The old dog had attached herself to Rex for the last few days, mooching round doe-eyed, begging for his bacon Wheat Crunchies and a small space on the sofa at his side. Clearly, she thought the tambourine was just another plaything.

Pip winced as Rex tugged the instrument from her jaws, examining the teeth marks and shaking drool from the bent jingles. Rex held it up with a helpless shrug.

'I'll get another one,' Pip sighed.

'Are you sure you won't join us?' Rex stopped him. The tambourine had always been an extension of his stage persona (or something like that) but he was having a hard time making it compensate for the lack of a drummer. Pip had already refused three times.

'Oh, that's a good idea!' Victoria sang, backing through the door with a coffee tray. 'Yes, please do get on with it, Pip, and save us all this elephant in the room avoidance.'

Shelley followed in with an extra microphone and a packet of biscuits. 'Victoria—'

'What's she talking about?' Yebut wrinkled his nose.

'Pip's a drummer, mate, that's all.'

'Are you?' Yebut breathed, as if he'd just been introduced to an astronaut.

'Yeah, but—'

'Oh, please God, not another one,' Victoria mock-grimaced. 'But, but, but... See how this tires me, Philip!'

'Sorry, but—'

'Oh really, young man! I simply do not see how such an apology can have the slightest degree of sincerity when it is followed so shamelessly by the repetition of the subject to which it purports to seek absolution in no further distance than the very next word!'

Pip sighed in exasperation. How on earth was he supposed to keep up with that?

'Victoria,' Shelley cautioned again, reading the pinching of Pip's face, although it was beginning to look more like anger than fear. 'That's enough. Leave him alone.'

'I'm only saying...'

'Come on, Pip,' Rex tightened the noose. 'Just help us out a bit here. You only need to keep the beat, play along a bit. Obviously we can't expect you to play our stuff—'

'Oh, can't you?'

'What's going on here, then?' Damon ambled back from the snooker table.

'Victoria and I are suggesting Pip stands in for Alan to rehearse, but he *says* he can't,' Rex concluded pointedly.

'Well, of course he can't,' Damon retorted. 'He's fucking deaf!'

'Oh, bravo!' Victoria clapped her hands. 'That should do it.'

Pip was already striding away. Vaulting over the side drums, he snatched up a pair of sticks, threw himself down on the stool and stamped on the kick drum pedal.

The Edge of Darkness didn't choose *Orion* as a set opener by accident, it always smashed the audience in two. And it was doing so now. Originally played by two drummers, The Edge of Darkness' USP in the 1980s, until the really talented one took up flying off balconies. By then, the band couldn't afford the manpower and just simplified everything for Alan to play on his own. But Pip didn't know that. He'd grown up on this stuff.

Yebut, delighted, scuttled off to pick up his bass. Rex started singing the last verse and by the time Damon and Benny shuffled out of their stupor to sling guitar over shoulder and plug into socket, the song was ending – the same way Pip had started it, with the drums.

He got up from the stool, threw down the sticks and walked out. 'I taught myself to play both parts when I was 12.'

Victoria caught him at the door, her hand on his arm. Pip looked as if he was going to shake her off, but he didn't. His chest rising and falling, he did not speak, but his focus remained on her face. She turned him into the hallway.

'That was an impressive performance, Pip, driven by spite. But can't you see that you don't play the way you do *in spite* of your deafness? But *because* of it? With your full attention. No wonder it's fucking incredible. *That* is what is fucking incredible.'

Still, he stared at her, listening hard, his breathing slowing.

'*That* is what you have to give, Pip. It does seem such a pity to keep it to yourself, does it not?'

His arm tugged under her hand. 'I've got to get another tambourine.'

'Stay with it, Pip,' she said quietly. 'Stay with it. Don't run this time...'

'Are you OK?' Shelley joined them in the hall, looking unusually crossly at Victoria.

'Pip and I are just having a little chat, Shelley. On our first dinner together, you may recall Pip, I reserved conversation on two matters for a later time. I think *this* may be that time... Oh, don't look so horrified, dear boy, the sex can wait. And I am heartily looking forward to it! Fear not, however, I know the discussion will be entirely theoretical. Cute as you are, I am 86 years old. Besides, I have little doubt you could be particularly well taken care of in that department elsewhere.' She flicked an almost imperceptible look at Shelley. 'If you could only have a little courage.'

'Did you just call me *cute*?'

'Excellent, I can see you are recovering yourself. But desist, both of you, in this compulsion to divert me. It is the word "courage" that is the operative challenge today. A few words more, Pip, if you please...'

. . .

'Alright,' Pip strode back into the ballroom and started moving the drums to the side of the room. 'I prefer not to be behind people, you know?'

'Yes, right, of course,' said Rex. 'So you can lip read my singing? Is that how you do it?'

And Pip realised in that moment that it didn't matter what he said, or did not say about his life, people would only hear the bits that matched their reality.

'Yeah,' he said, his body quietening. 'Something like that. But if it'd be OK to have some extra time with Yebut, that would be great.'

You could have lit a match on Yebut's glow.

'You play a bit fast though, man,' Damon sniffed.

'Sorry, it's how I remember it,' Pip replied.

'It's how I remember it an' all, but we tend to do things a bit slower these days.'

'Yeah but, do we have to?' Yebut ventured. 'Sounded pretty awesome like that, like it used to. We can keep up, can't we?'

'Well,' Rex smirked. 'I can.'

'You saying I can't?' Damon retorted.

'Of course you can't. You're fucking *old*.'

Damon snatched up his guitar. Pip sat down, raised his sticks and blasted into the song at the same tempo, and not a word more was said about it.

Except in Pip's head. 'It's OK,' he heard on loop. 'I am OK... This is OK... A few people is OK...' The mantra had rhythm. 'I can do this... I like this... I want this...'

I *want* this? That was new.

48

MARILYN'S CLARITY

Pip was smiling as he came out of another morning rehearsal in the ballroom, Yebut in tow fiddling with his digital recorder. 'Let me know anything I need to fix, OK?' he said, and Yebut bloomed.

It had always been Yebut's habit to record every rehearsal, every performance, listening back and making notes for improvement. It was his stability to be the best he could at something; there was so much of the rest of the world that he did not understand. The band just about tolerated it. Yebut was delighted to find someone, in Pip, who actually appreciated it.

'You look happy, going OK?' Shelley said, handing Pip the peanut butter sandwich that constituted lunch.

'Yeah,' he shrugged. 'They're good musicians, especially Yebut, they've chosen some fun songs and I'm enjoying it.' His brow furrowed for a moment, as if he was still working that out, but then he shrugged again. 'I guess that's OK.'

'I guess so,' Shelley smiled. 'Glad I've caught you, though. I had an email from Dad yesterday, moaning that his solicitor's heard nothing from Mum about the divorce. I take it she hasn't filled in the forms?'

'No, I don't think so,' Pip replied. 'They're still on the kitchen dresser.'

'I've been meaning to ask you. Is she OK? I saw you helping her the other day, with her arm in a sling.'

'Ah yeah, broken elbow. She's been a bit... accident prone lately. She didn't want me to tell you, otherwise I would have, I promise. It's not like... all the other stuff...'

Pip had been wanting to talk to Shelley about her mother for ages; just as much as he wanted to talk to Marilyn about her daughter. To tell her that Shelley was back, it looked like she was staying, and might she like to do something with that? But he hadn't found the right time, or the right words. How do you find the words to tell a mother that she criminally undervalues her daughter?

'The hospital said it was a good break, though. It'll heal well, they think.'

'Is she drinking, Pip?'

'Yeah,' he sighed. Well, he hadn't told her, she knew. No confidences broken, no trust destroyed.

'Anything else?'

'I don't think so.'

Shelley nodded slowly. 'Good.'

'Maybe you'd like to come round, talk to her?'

'Yes.'

'I mean, I can cope, don't get me wrong. I just thought you might like to, now.'

'Yes.'

'I could come with you, if you like, if it would make it easier, I don't mind—'

'Pip,' she laughed, waving in front of his face and pointing to her mouth. 'I said *yes*.'

'Oh, yep, course you did. Just letting the context override the moment, sorry.'

'Seems reasonable.'

The words were light, but Pip could see her mouth still contained something very heavy...

For three nights, or was it four? Marilyn had not slept at all. Lying awake, the divorce petition moved to her bedside table, engaged in a million silent showdowns with her estranged husband. Screaming at him for his infidelities, his desertions, his unaccountability. Berating herself for her inability to have done anything else with her life but believe and wait; and rage against the only person remaining – her daughter.

Like every evening for the last few weeks, the wine blurred the sharper details of her misery without blunting the weary bleakness of it. But at a certain level of drunkenness, a clarity of thought surprised her. She replayed family events, holidays, milestones, not inserting Horace's presence, as she had become so accomplished at doing, but seeing Shelley where he was not, and had almost never been. She hated herself for being so blind to what was really happening; too self-absorbed to think of the effect of his absence on anyone else. And she wept then for what Horace had done to her, by doing so little. But mostly, by default, what he had done to her daughter, by depriving her of her mother.

She recalled the last time Horace had been home for any length of time, leaning to kiss Shelley goodbye, pushing back a strand of her hair and making some comment about her beautiful ears, which always heard everything that mattered. He had put his finger to her lips then. How come she had never remembered that before? All she ever recalled was the praise, the indulgence. Had he silenced her daughter as much as she always had?

Marilyn threw off the bedclothes, went to the window and hurled her wedding ring out of it. She listened for its landing in the quiet dead of night, but found an unexpected relief that she heard no sound. She would not be tempted to look for it in the warmer light of morning. A temptation she knew would come knocking at her consciousness day after day, like the addict that she was.

She stumbled back to bed, knocking against the bedpost, a bruise appearing immediately, far more vivid than the wound she thought she'd incurred. Amazed at her own fragility, she suddenly glimpsed the fragility of it all. She picked up the divorce petition. Why had she not seen this coming? Her efforts for so many years to 'win' her husband and her marriage were irrelevant, raged against the opponent of his mammoth indifference. An adversary that could never be beaten and could crush her so ruthlessly.

If she continued to allow it. Which, in that moment, she decided she would not. She had fought back reflexively, throwing herself into the spite of ruining something that he cared about – the show, the applause. But the purpose and adrenaline before the Opera had long gone, and the cracks had opened up again, forging new pathways and splitting her in two. She could not win through spite, in the same way that she could never win through effort, doggedness, pleas, demands, or suet pudding. She would fight now with the only weapon that would work. The same one as his. Indifference. And when facing an opponent with such unaccustomed parity, the only thing to do is agree terms.

And this time, they weren't going to be his.

'I'll leave you to it then,' Pip said, hovering at the door of Marilyn's utility room. And he looked at Shelley with the greatest pull in his heart. How she moved him now, with only the slightest look, the smallest connection. She returned his focus, and he waited to see words, but none came to her lips. It mattered less these days whether words followed or not – the look this morning fully advertised her trepidation, her vulnerability, and only reminded him that he would do anything to prevent her being hurt. How long had it been since he had looked beyond his own hurt? Well, there had been enough of that. But now it was all about her. *Everything* was all about *her*.

Shelley had so much to think about at the moment, it was brave of her to risk the emotional disruption of another maternal rejection, and he turned to Marilyn, silently willing her not to give it to her. Marilyn blinked, almost as if she was hearing it.

'Sheldon, I am so very sorry. Can you ever forgive me...?'

Pip closed the door behind him, knowing that she would be alright.

They would be alright...

49

ALAN OUT OF THE CIRCLE

Graham Tweedle arrived at the Manor with his full artillery of monitoring equipment. Never mind that it was a Saturday, Shelley had asked him for a *personal* opinion, and that was his favourite sort. He followed her around the courtyard, lapping up all her plans, before setting off around the village to take some readings. He was disappointed that Shelley could not accompany him to her mother's house, but that was more than adequately compensated by her invitation to return for lunch afterwards. Lunch, no less! Besides, he had heard that Marilyn Harper was a lot less deranged these days. The evidence of her decapitating a whole shrubbery of gardenia on his way past had not entirely convinced him. Perhaps he'd just take his readings from the pavement this time. A little application of the Inverse Square Law would be more than enough for the remaining distance to her front lawn. These were *informal* readings after all, to put Shelley's mind at rest before he made his formal report to the Planning Committee...

'Blimey, has he finally gone?' Pip jumped down from the stage. 'I was beginning to think you might need rescuing.'

'Oh, I think I'd have managed another minute and a half or so. Needs must though, he will be very useful if he's on side.'

'I think it's fairly evident whose side he's on.'

'Thanks for that,' she grimaced. 'Are they done yet? Graham will be ready in Trefusis Lane in a few minutes.'

'Still waiting for Alan, stuck on the M3 apparently... Oh, here you go... Hi, nice to see you again.' Pip held out his hand to Alan beelining through the courtyard.

'What the fuck are you doing here?' he demanded with no overture, leaving Pip's hand hanging, and glaring up to the stage at his bandmates. '*I'm* the drummer in this band.'

'Yeah, I know you are,' Pip laughed. 'I've set your kit up for you. Hope it's alright.' He shrugged, smiled at Shelley, and left them to it.

'Why are the drums on the side of the stage?' Having hitched himself up on the makeshift platform, which seemed to have made him even more agitated, Alan paced between the instruments.

'Well, we've learned a bit in the last week, haven't we boys?' Rex said. 'We play more in a circle now.'

'So you've learned what, geometry?'

'Yeah but, it's really improved our rehearsing doing it this way, watching and feeling stuff, not just hearing all the mush. It's brilliant!'

'Shut the fuck up, Yebut.'

'Alan!' Rex stopped him, and wondered why he never had before.

'And we don't need to compete with so much volume,' Damon said. Everyone stared at him, dumbstruck at such an admission from their homicidally loud guitarist.

'Well, let's face it,' Damon continued placidly. 'We've played rock all the way from the mid-70s, we're all half deaf anyway. We're just in complete denial.'

'What are you talking about?' Alan retorted, the steam continuing to rise. 'I've got perfect hearing I have!'

'When it suits you.'

'What?'

'My point.'

'Guys, guys...' Shelley attempted to move things along. 'Maybe we could just make a start?'

'Alright, doll,' Alan barely looked at her. 'Wait your turn.'

Shelley opened her mouth to respond, but caught sight of Pip at the side of the stage, his hand on his forehead in the universal sign language for dickhead, and found herself laughing. Just like they had been when Horace arrived, sharing a private joke, an understanding without words. And remembering that things, people, that didn't matter, *really* didn't matter.

'Oh, but Mr Kent,' she said. 'You're the most important person on this stage. It's you and your drums that we need to find out about. It doesn't matter what they're doing.' She waved dismissively at the rest of the band, hoping it would not incite Armageddon. 'It's *you* we need to hear.'

Alan cracked his neck, his shoulders rolling backwards. 'Alright then...'

Rex could belt it out with the best of them, but Shelley knew his decibels would not be a patch on Horace. Without amplification, Damon, Yebut and Benny made very little sound at all. Shelley thought it appropriate karma if it would be only the drums that the village could hear, but even that was likely to be very faint on its own. And Graham Tweedle returned for lunch to confirm it. The whole 'performance' was well below permitted levels from Trefusis Lane and Yarnside Drive. They'd passed the first test, and his positive recommendation to the Planning Committee was confirmed, with the appropriate conditions of course. Matthew rolled his eyes from the wings. Another sixteen pages, no doubt...

Yebut was giggling like a schoolboy as the band tumbled off

the stage. 'Thanks, Pip!'

Pip looked quizzically at him.

'Poor Alan's gone for a nap. Came out of that dripping!' Rex elaborated. 'And swearing. He really doesn't like the speed we're playing now.'

'I don't think he likes *me* very much,' Pip said.

'Ah well, obvious, isn't it?'

'Is it?'

'He thought he was up for Tommy Wilson's stool. Wouldn't have liked you if you'd played in slow motion with hands like pig's trotters.'

'Oh right, I didn't know that.'

'I wouldn't worry about it.'

'I worry about a lot of things, but *he* isn't one of them...'

Graham Tweedle took Shelley aside and leaned in *very* close. 'I'm sure I can present it to the Committee on the terms we discussed, Shelley,' he, inexplicably, whispered. 'But there is still the small matter of the Parish Council. They are bound to object. As we have proved, an unplugged rock band is going to make far less noise than an opera singer and an orchestra, so they haven't really got a case. But Councillors will want to avoid any repeat of the disruption in the village last time and will be reluctant to overrule them, *if* they decide otherwise. I can't get involved, of course, but I will tell you that my colleagues have had pre-planning discussions with a development company who have... *alternative* plans for the future of the estate.'

'*What*?' Now he had her attention.

'More I cannot say, Shelley. I do not know the details and couldn't tell you if I did. But if your best hope of ensuring Lord Bedingford's continued tenure here is to make this event a success, then it will be up to you to persuade the Parish to support it, and not any potential alternatives. If you hear what I'm saying. There's an emergency Parish Council meeting on Wednesday evening, before Friday's Planning Committee...'

50

THE PARISH COUNCIL

Marilyn had summoned Pip and Shelley for time that neither of them could afford today. Pip to witness her signature on the divorce papers; Shelley to witness her tearing up Horace's version which they had conclusively replaced.

But it didn't look as if she would be letting them go.

'Harriet's not speaking to me again,' she said.

'Oh dear, I'm sorry about that Mum, but we are quite busy and the Parish Council meeting starts in an hour—'

'Oh, I don't care, stupid woman,' Marilyn waved her hand, dismissing both her old friend and her daughter's pre-occupations at once. Old habits die hard. 'She's aerated about the District Council supporting this "Hearing Aid" thingy. I just said that even a rock band fully plugged in and blasting through the entire village would be better than our beautiful Manor being turned into one of those ghastly country house hotels, and she went completely ballistic! The country needs stately homes that are lived in by people, I said to her, and preferably people descended from the original families. Without them, the buildings have no heart and soul, they are merely lifeless museum pieces, or seedy commercial honey pots. She said that would be just as well if the bloody Wolstenholmes *were* the original family, *and* if they had anything remotely resembling a heart and soul! Can you believe that? As for seedy, she said the place was no more than a drug-dealing den of iniquity these days, full of long hairs and no-hopers, and it was a disgrace for the village to allow it to continue—'

'Uh, Mum, we are in a bit of a rush – *country house hotel?*'

'Oh yes, of course, darling. That's the other reason I wanted to see you. Those pre-planning negotiations at the Council you told me about? High class corporate retreat apparently, whatever that means, with the coach house and barns converted to luxury apartments.'

'*What?* How on earth did you get to know all that?'

'I slept with Terry Pennington.'

Pip glanced at Shelley to check he had read that right. Her mouth dropped and stayed there so she looked like a paused video. He had then.

'You *slept* with Councillor Pennington?'

'Well, he wasn't a Councillor then... Oh, for goodness' sake, Sheldon, I don't mean this week. It was 1983!'

'Ah, before you were married.'

'Yes, of course before I was married. Although not before he was, which has turned out to be marvellous leverage! He's got me a copy of the plans, says I can pick them up tomorrow. His wife has her pilates at two. I'll go then.'

'Tonight!' Shelley sparked back. 'We must go now...!'

The chairs in the village hall appeared to be made of jelly. Pip could not get a hold on them at all.

'Do you ever sit still, man?' Rex complained. 'I'm going for a fag.'

'Where is she, though? It's about to start. Isn't it?'

'Not before nicotine o'clock.'

'Hang on!'

But Rex was gone, and Pip didn't have a hope now. He checked the door yet again, then started counting to fifty. Next time it would be sixty. He didn't look behind him more than once or twice a week these days. Perhaps the same principle of counting might wean him off looking at the door for Shelley's arrival. Come to think of it, maybe he should try it to wean himself of everything to do with Shelley. *One, two*... think about Shelley. *One, two, three*... think about Shelley. *One, two, three, four*... think about Shelley. Maybe he'd make it to a hundred. By the time he was 85. Perhaps he should try it in 7/8? That might be diverting... Look at the door, look at the door, *look at the door!*

Pip slumped in his seat, his eyes dropping to his relentlessly tapping feet, knowing that it was not the counting that had stopped him looking behind him, it was just that he had forgotten to do it. Better things to do. But right now, he didn't have better things to do than sit on his hands, looking at the door, praying for Shelley to get back with the plans before this bloody meeting started, and he would have to stand up in her place...

Rex stood smoking with his leg cocked against the wall as a young woman with a microphone approached him, tracked by a colleague with a camera. Rex's introspective face changed like a rubber over a chalkboard, his shoulders creeping back to the wall, his neck lengthening, his face uncreasing and the side of his mouth raising in an unspoken invitation that she was welcome to speak to someone who mattered.

But then he remembered, this wasn't his world. His world didn't really exist anymore, outside of the Manor ballroom, and there was no reason she, or anyone, would be remotely interested in his appearance in it. He looked away, closed his mouth around the remains of his cigarette, and pushed himself from the wall.

'Excuse me, Mr Trenton?' She strode towards him as he turned back to the village hall door. 'Wessex News. We'd be very interested in hearing your thoughts on the planning application under discussion tonight.'

'Yeah?' He turned, the performance muscles falling effortlessly back into place. 'I expect most of Hampshire would like to know what you're doing here an' all. A village planning application is hardly prime time, is it?'

She flushed. 'Well, we're a little short on... um...'

'Filler,' the cameraman grunted behind her.

'Filler,' Rex sniffed, grinding his cigarette butt with his boot. 'Well, let me tell you something...'

'Ooh, Victoria, quick, come and have a look at this!' Matthew squealed from the kitchen table, gratefully putting down his peeling knife and leaning into the tiny portable TV.

'I rather think I need not, Matthew, the volume you have that thing turned up.'

'But it's Rex, look! Goodness... the Manor, they're talking about us...'

'What is all this, anyway?' Rex anchored himself on his new hobby horse. 'You're standing here talking to me, not because of my own talents, not because I had more records in the Top 100 in 1983 than Bucks Fizz. We're both standing here today because a beautiful old landmark is going to rack and ruin and a tired old man tried to kill himself.'

Victoria and Matthew both winced.

'And this village wants to argue the toss about a few decibels for a few hours? It's a disgrace that this can be allowed to happen.' Rex's hobby horse saddle was proving extremely comfortable, as he sped from a canter to a gallop. 'And not only for this village. It's a disgrace for the country! A disgrace that we must all bear responsibility, with our pathetic "here today, gone tomorrow" attitude. A great injustice has been done to that man... the Most Right Reverend... uh, Honourable... Lord *of* Bedingford. It is about time we stood behind him, and all those like him. Stood up for our aristocracy, who have stood up for us for so many, uh... centuries... For Britain!'

Victoria looked at Matthew. 'What the fuck is he talking about?'

'Search me.'

It was doubtful if anyone in the entire country would really know either, but it was journalistic gold and the young reporter, previously considering sloping off down the pub, glued herself to Rex for the rest of the evening.

A bell rang from the village hall.

'Will you be speaking in favour of the application tonight?' she asked to camera.

Rex paused as if something of the utmost importance was dawning on him. 'Yes,' he said. 'I think I will. *This must not be allowed to fall...*'

'Oh, bugger,' Victoria said from the kitchen table. 'We're doomed...'

Pip had seen the bell ring and the remaining public were taking their seats. Faces from the podium glared at him and he realised his chair was clanging on the floor with the force of his bouncing leg. He checked the door for the hundredth time, willing Shelley to return. If she did not in the next couple of minutes, he was certain there'd be another empty seat in the row. His.

Rex sauntered in, followed by a young woman holding a phone in front of her mouth like a CIA agent, and an even younger man with a broadcast video camera. Rex winked at Pip, before taking a different place at the front of the hall. Harriet Pordage, in the seat next to him, looked appalled.

Quarter of an hour later, the minutes of the last meeting,

apologies for absence and village announcements dispensed with – and Pip melting through the floor – Rex turned in his chair and nodded at him. Pip closed his eyes, breathed in, located his voice and was just about to stand when Rex rose from his seat and did it for him.

'Ladies and gentleman, thank you so much for the opportunity to put the case for this application...'

The door at the back banged open and Shelley flew in, Marilyn close behind. She stopped as Rex stood on the podium, being recorded by Wessex News and holding the audience in rapt attention.

'So, in summary,' Rex concluded. 'I implore you to make Bedingford a place that is about something more than protests and bureaucracy. Your village is a beautiful, historic place, with a completely appropriate reputation for quiet. What more fitting setting to hold the world's quietest concerts? In this place so *understandably* concerned about sound, please let us have a little vision. And give Bedingford the reputation it deserves...'

Pip looked at Shelley, astonished at the thunder of applause. Some people were even on their feet. Their job was done. After that, 'threatening' them with Aubrey Estates' alternative plan for the village's showpiece Manor was merely pushing at an open door.

Harriet Pordage, and a few others, were out-voted 20-1.

'Good Lord,' said Matthew as they watched 'part two' reported on the late local news before bed. 'It's even better than Shelley said.'

'Is it?' Victoria twitched darkly. 'Did you see Harriet Pordage's face? I don't know why it never occurred to me before, but *Aubrey* Estates, Matthew? The mortgage creditors, the development company... The feckless rat-face that gambled away half the estate to your great-great-great-great-grandfather?'

'Aubrey *Pordage*.' Matthew's mouth dropped. 'It can't be them, can it? They wouldn't, *still*?' For a moment, Matthew's face had the confused, indignant disbelief of a child being told that Father Christmas doesn't exist. But then it assembled itself into something quite different. He stood up, his hands on the table.

'Well, that's decided it then. They can whistle for it. Because I will *never* give up now!'

Victoria smiled. At last. Her 74-year-old brother-in-law was finally coming of age.

51

THE KINDNESS OF STRANGERS

Morris and Tree were back. They had secured twelve retired or resting road crew for the bank holiday weekend, and the two of them would be there to do as much as they could in the meantime. They had also organised a collection from every band that Stat had even so much as bumped into in the last forty years, bringing with them an array of memorabilia to auction, as well as a redundant pickup truck, a mirror stage backdrop, and an old aircraft landing light rig. Matthew was quite overwhelmed. Since the Parish Council and the brief flurry of media that followed Rex's state of the nation speech, all sorts of offers of support had also been received from random villagers and county-folk – from free printing, to discount fairy lights, to pork sausages. Timothy Smollett was donating the Scout marquee; Marilyn was selling a valuable record collection, a wardrobe of clothes and a vintage train set (all Horace's); and Ma and the foster kids were planning a fundraising car wash on the village green on Saturday. The younger children were also making bunting out of recycled crisp packets at the local primary school. They were having lessons on listening to tie in with the event, and Matthew had promised visits from Pip and percussion in the new term. (He hadn't told Pip yet).

Apart from general meddling, Matthew had been put in charge of the grounds. It was a big and important job, they all told him, but he was comforted that so much of what he and the crew had prepared for the opera still had resonance with this new venture. He'd spent much of the spring laying a path through the small wooded area on the south side of the estate. And the picnic tables and covered seating in every nook and cranny around the woods, lawns and shrubbery were still there. None of it had got much use, since they'd never even made it to the interval of the first performance of the opera season but, Matthew hoped, it would have much better footfall this time around. The arrival of Morris and Tree only helped to build on what was already in place. Not to mention the hugely welcome return of the (sort of) retired, much-revered estate caretaker, long since let go when the money ran out. Bill had practically moved in.

It was all rather settling, and as he patrolled the grounds and the activity all around, Matthew was startled by the extent of what he could hear. So often his walks had become a time of regret for things lost: that he could not hear the chaffinches; that his knees ached; that there was no money to fix x, y or z; that he was on borrowed time with all that he saw around him; that the best of his life, including his son, had gone, and all that lay before him was debt and loss and being alone to the grave. But now he had been witnessing hope – Pip's abilities, experiencing the music he thought would be lost to him, in a new way; Shelley's tiggerish enthusiasm; people coming together to help him – he began to feel hope everywhere. He saw it in the anemones flowering for another year, the swelling fruit of his pumpkin patch, the dislodged roof slate that had miraculously righted itself in a windstorm on Wednesday night. The Manor could mend and renew. And so could he.

Then he noticed that his knees did not hurt so much; there

was a width in his chest and an expansiveness in his breath that reminded him what it was like to be young; he *had* a son and daughter here right before him; and the woman who had stood by him and guided him all these years was still here.

And a chaffinch chirruped in the hazel...

The newly found enthusiasm and generosity amongst the villagers did not, however, stretch everywhere. Harriet Pordage, in particular, was donating only her scorn.

'You seem very busy, Pip. *Elsewhere.*' Harriet cornered him on the first visit he had managed to her garden that week. 'It would appear, from what we heard at the Parish Council, that *you* are at the centre of this latest ridiculous venture at the Manor.'

'Well, I wouldn't say that, but—'

'I'm extremely disappointed, Pip. In fact, I would go so far as to say that you may have outlived your usefulness to me.'

'Oh, for fuck's sake,' Pip finally snapped. 'Do you know what? I don't like the way you talk to me – or anyone really – and I don't think I'm going to waste any more of my considerable effort in listening to it. So you can stick your bloody "usefulness" up your arse!' Victoria would have been proud of him. 'I quit!'

Harriet was shouting something at his back, he knew that much, but he kept on walking without the slightest inclination to know what it was, his feet and heart a little lighter than they had been when he arrived.

'You don't listen, do you?' Russell caught him in the drive as he wheeled away Bill's barrow of loaned tools.

Pip just laughed. 'You better believe it...'

Preparations for Hearing Aid were now in full swing, with more than a little hope over experience that the bureaucracy would, this time, allow it. Day by day, the draft of the advertising flyers lengthened, the list of potential participants growing. Shelley felt like she was on the phone all day, often looking across the desk to Stat's urn for confidence. So far, she had confined herself to *one* phone. And no cigar.

Rex was proving surprisingly helpful. He knew this world, these people, he spoke the language, and within the week they had filled almost all the slots for the Saturday line-up, and half of Sunday. It was beginning to look like a '70s/'80s classic rock revival, but it made Matthew happy and the visuals would certainly be there. Yebut too had thrown himself in. Whenever he was not rehearsing, he could be found around the grounds, (sponsored) toolkit in hand, ably demonstrating that you can take the man out of B&Q... Even Damon had his uses, a decade in a Spanish bar had taught him a hundred cheap ways with paella. Victoria was delighted to be off kitchen duty so often these days. Benny was not much more use than a doorstop, but at least he didn't upset anyone, and he'd usually wake up by the evening to entertain around the piano for those who had any energy left from the day.

But Harriet Pordage had been right – Pip was at the centre of it all. Hardly a thing was suggested, planned or decided without running it by him first. He still did not know quite how that was, but he did know that he thought of little else now. He wanted – *needed* – this to work. He hadn't felt so committed, so enjoined to a project in so long. And his body remained remarkably still. That was the real gift. That was real freedom. Perhaps this is where he should be then – behind the stage, out of the spotlight, making music happen in a different way...

There were, however, some backstage roles that it was really time to limit. Alan might have made his antipathy to Pip perfectly clear, but it was equally clear he was enjoying having his own personal drum roadie at the weekends, and the opportunity to exert as much superiority as possible that came with it.

'I told you!' Alan protested, some nonsense about moving his drum kit out of the light of the bay window.

'When?'

'Just now when I was adjusting the crash cymbal stand.'

'Right, when you were on the floor facing the wall,' Pip glanced to the heavens. 'Look, I know I'm a miracle worker. I converse with you, I play music, but don't expect me to answer if you can't even be bothered to look at me.'

'You hear when you want to,' Alan retorted.

Pip sighed. 'And how many bloody times have I heard that one?'

'Yeah,' Alan squared up, but his twitch betrayed him. Pip just shook his head and walked away. He had a sensory room to paint, a gong array to move, and three vintage congas to fix. He'd tried his best with the bloke but this had to be the last time he would subject himself to being in the same room as him.

'Wanker!' Alan called after him.

Pip raised his middle finger without turning. It was just a guess...

The next job on his list was checking the eBay shop he'd set up for any items in Robert's collection that they could bear to part with. He'd come to love every little item, every new sound and feel that he discovered in that room, and had to hope, like the rest of them, that they could keep the Manor going without losing all this as well – just as he had been given the opportunity to discover it, and to find the place where he should be. Besides, much of the collection was an integral part of their plans for the bank holiday event. Pip had begun to kit out a couple of the courtyard stables as sensory rooms, where people could wander around and look, touch, hear and experience new sounds and textures. Matthew and Victoria were even working on him to provide sound workshops, similar to Matthew's lessons – an idea that was starting to take root without a debilitating level of panic. Just a little bit of panic. So far.

'I've been thinking that I might even lead a workshop or two myself,' Matthew suggested. 'Beginners of course.'

'We're all beginners,' Pip said, and the idea settled a little further.

But he watched Shelley constantly. Hearing her, orchestrating everything, as full of dreams and 'impossible' ideas as always, ready to bring sounds to the world she had yet to discover. And he knew now, with no further doubt, that there was somewhere else he should be, too.

From the moment he met her, Pip had inched into love with only the tiny steps his broken spirit allowed. Now, with that spirit healing, and she at the heart of it, he plummeted.

Yet still his voice limped cautiously behind. The resonating chamber of his own body so finely tuned, he did not know what to do with all these new vibrations. Every time he thought about her now, saw her, heard her, a sweet cyclone tumbled around his head, stirring his chest, forcing breath deep down into his diaphragm. At one moment, the breath filled him with possibility – so much possibility his eyes widened. At the next breath a stab of fear – how would this be, this whirling out of control? His body, his thoughts, his reactions had been so out of control for so long, now that they were settling, could he bear this new onslaught? Could he tolerate this? Feel it?

Stay with it...

Shelley paced around the stable office, staring at the phone on the desk, and the most difficult call she had yet to make. She looked across to Stat as usual, but he couldn't help her this time. Outside, Pip was up a ladder triangulating the stage, Victoria was directing the Bedingford Women's Wheelers making flags from old curtains, and Matthew and Bill were re-planting the courtyard garden with sensory plants donated by Winchester Nurseries. It was such a hive of activity it filled her heart with the community of it.

But she was alone with this one.

Graham Tweedle drew up in a District Council van. He handed Matthew a letter, although he was looking past him across the courtyard to Shelley. Matthew's smile faltered, the letter wavering towards the inside pocket of his jacket. He held it out to her instead. She looked at him steadily, her hands remaining at her side. He nodded and opened it.

'The Planning Committee voted in support. The letter confirms the Council is minded to grant permission for the bank holiday concert,' Tweedle said, helpfully. Matthew was delighted – he didn't even have to read it! 'My Chief Executive is also rather taken with the idea and keen to support a regular event, if it goes to the plan you outlined, Shelley. Subject to a few points of detail, which the Committee wished me to discuss with you *personally*.' Tweedle licked a bead of saliva from the side of his mouth. 'The same level of noise monitoring will, of course, need to be in place throughout, and I will need to see the wireless headphone sets you propose to use. I have made myself available to you for the rest of the afternoon.'

Shelley was beginning to feel a little nauseous, but Matthew was already jumping up and down, hugging everyone in sight, including Tweedle.

'It's going to happen, Shelley! Finally, we might be on to something!' Matthew grabbed a shovel, waving it back and forth to attract Pip's attention, but he was far too engrossed to notice. That was the thing, Shelley knew, Pip had thrown himself so heartily into this venture, they all had. She would not be the one to make it all for nothing. Or to take that glorious smile from Matthew's face.

'Not quite there with the headsets, Graham,' she said. 'But it is... *in hand*. Could we come back to that?'

She headed back to the office, and the phone call...

. . .

There was a modest party at the Manor that evening to celebrate. Pip was delighted just bathing in everybody else's delight; he didn't need the words. Shelley, however, looked petrified. And he did need to do something about that. He looked at her for some kind of clue. She would not meet his eye. He *really* needed to do something about *that*.

'Got any more of those Wheat Crunchies?' Damon said, knocking back another tequila.

Shelley vacantly got up for the kitchen.

'What on earth is it with the Harper women?' Victoria tutted. 'More brains and talent than anyone else on the pitch and still compelled to make the half-time sandwiches.'

'Marilyn too?' Pip said, getting the intention, if not every word. 'Harper' and 'women' were amongst the easiest words for him to lipread.

'Yes, Marilyn too. She's a very fine singer, you know. Could have been a Montserrat Caballé by now, but she gave it up in favour of Horace's career.'

'Really?'

Well, he needed to do something about that, too...

Shelley returned with the last remaining packet of crisps and no noticeable change in her distance.

'So, what about these headphone thingies then?' Matthew said. 'We're going to need hundreds to make this work, aren't we? How are we getting on with that? I never thought I'd hear me saying this but I'd rather like to get the formal permission letter in my hands!' he laughed. Shelley didn't.

'Yes,' she said. 'It's sorted.' Pip's eyes narrowed. Her tone had certainty; her shuffling feet, twisted torso and clenched fingers, something completely different. 'Cambridge University has a partnership with Wahzuhören, the German audio technology giants,' she continued steadily. 'They're willing to discuss the loan of up to eight hundred headsets for research.'

'Cambridge University? Why on earth would they help us?'

'They wouldn't,' Pip said, staring pointedly at Shelley. 'Unless someone was on their payroll.'

Shelley nodded, still without meeting his eye.

'I've accepted a Research Fellowship in the Acoustics Department, starting on 1 September...'

52

THE EYES HAVE IT

Pip was startled to find that Mrs Burlington had invited the Winchester Hearing Loss Support Group to the Manor for tea. Particularly by the manner in which he found out, as Victoria trooped the lot of them into the Folly during Matthew's lesson that day. They shuffled in behind, sticking resolutely together, with practised smiles and resigned nervousness. All of them, Pip suspected, had, like Matthew, been stealth-bombed by gradual hearing loss in their middle and later years. Undoubtedly finding comfort and camaraderie in each other, but still finding their way through a new landscape of muffle and shouting, insecurity and isolation. New things were a worry.

But by the end of the afternoon, intrigued by Pip and charmed by Matthew, Hearing Aid had secured its event stewards and front-of-house staff. And most of them had also signed up for 'listening lessons' in 'the autumn term', as Victoria dubbed both.

Later, in the courtyard, she handed him a desktop academic diary. 'Thought you might need it...'

She must be able to see it, Pip thought – how much he was

going to need something to occupy him, come the *academic new year*. When Shelley was gone...

Damn, he'd been trying not to think about that. In fact, he'd been avoiding Shelley altogether since last night. A familiar panic rose in his chest; a new, uninvited trigger, but loss just the same. The world beginning to sway, he searched for something to steady himself, to hold on to for this additional, unwanted ride. He found it in another list of tasks to complete.

'Can you get that sound board across to the other side of the stage?' he said to Tree. 'And see if Morris can join me at the copse, we need more wood for the gong installation...'

Pip was asleep on the grass by the courtyard, exhausted by all he had done today. All those people, offering things, asking things, suggesting things, demanding things. And Pip, focused, attentive, trying to hear it, respond to it, deliver it, just by looking.

And all Shelley wanted to do, at the end of this day, was to lie down next to him.

The way he looked at her, she thought... sometimes... But he looked at everybody that way. He gave his full attention to everybody. She could see that clearer than ever now. In between her own manic tasks, she had watched him, his calm and confidence growing daily – directing people, enthusing with people, explaining, demonstrating – finding his feet in this glorious, mad endeavour. She could hardly get a minute with him these days. She had tried to speak to him this afternoon. There were things she needed to know for herself. He had smiled, a little, held up five fingers... But that five minutes never came. It never did anymore. She missed him.

Wouldn't it just be the way, when she was finally learning to trust her own judgment and know exactly what she wanted, that thing had grown wings and flown out of reach?

She walked away, to the next job on her list...

.   .   .

'Your Mother is proving difficult, Russell. Stirring up the villagers with these ridiculous "den of iniquity" claims,' Shelley said in The Huntsman's that evening. 'We even had the police round on Monday! Can't you do anything about it? You know how the media loves a bat and ball story.'

'Have we finally come out to dinner to talk about my mother?'

'No, sorry, actually I—'

'I've always done my best to curb her excesses, Shelley, you know that. Just as you have done with yours. Although I'm not sure I have the stomach for it anymore. Lately I am left wondering – particularly as you seem so intent on being anywhere else than where I would like you to be – what's in it for me?'

'Russell...?'

'Yes, Shelley, what is in it for *me*? My family wants something, my clients want something, *you* want something. I provide. Which one of them is different? What, *really*, is in it for me to continue for it to be you?'

Shelley breathed in hard. A slither of fright had passed through her chest as he looked at her. 'Actually, that is really what I wanted to talk to you about,' she said steadily. Even if she could not get what she wanted, it was long passed time to let go of something she didn't. And he had just made it a little easier for her. 'I don't think there is anything in it for you. I'm sorry, but this isn't working. I can't do this anymore, Russell...'

Six days to go and Shelley really did not want to spend three of them travelling to Munich and back. But the bigwigs at Wahzuhören wanted to meet her, squeeze some positive publicity, and ensure she was getting the right equipment to make the event a success (i.e. *more* positive publicity). Shelley was very glad of the last of those things – she'd been feeling a little lonely with this one. She wished she could take Pip with her, but even if she had been able to ask him, or even find five minutes where their paths crossed lately, it would have been inconceivable for both of them not to be on site this week. She was leaving him her tablet though, so they could video-call about the headsets she was choosing. If she could find him...

Bags packed and ready to go, she finally located Pip in the kitchen, hurriedly chucking together a cheese sandwich for supper.

'Hey,' she smiled.

'Hey,' he replied.

And that was all. Shelley knew it hadn't been that long since they'd been alone together, but suddenly the void seemed chasmic. Pip fixed his usual gaze on her face – focused, expectant, waiting for her to say something. She did not. She could not. Instead, she returned his gaze, straight into his eyes. And she realised in that moment that she had never done that before, not really, not for more than a second or two anyway; then she would look a fraction below or above his eyes, or almost anywhere else on that so familiar, beautiful face. Normally he might have looked away by now, unless she was speaking. But he didn't. And there was something so incredibly powerful about it, it caught her breath. She swallowed hard, but she could not maintain it. And she looked away.

'I'm sorry, I—' Pip sensed he had gone too far. She shook her head, and he watched her take a deep breath.

'Ah, thought I heard you down here.' Victoria appeared at the kitchen door. 'Russell Pordage is at the door, Shelley.'

'Russell?' Shelley muttered, vacantly. 'I can't—'

'Quite happy to show him straight out of it, of course,' Victoria bulldozed on.

'No, it's alright, I better...'

Pip had no idea if she said anything else or not, but it didn't look like he would have the chance to find out now.

Russell was standing in the hallway with an armful of pink lilies, beaming steadily at Shelley. His eyes moved briefly to Pip as he passed to the front door. He nodded, losing none of his determined smile. Shelley suddenly felt a little seasick, set adrift between two worlds, and finding no voice for either of them.

'Well, good luck in Munich,' Pip said, his smile as determined as Russell's. 'And sorry again about... earlier.'

Victoria had made it up the stairs by now and chugged down the hallway, sending waves of disapproval billowing across the room. 'Where is Pip, Shelley?' she demanded. 'Why has he left without saying goodbye?' Shelley stood mute, looking through Russell to the closed front door. 'I see,' Victoria nodded. 'I see...'

Russell held out his uncollected bouquet. 'We need to talk, Shelley—'

'How delightful, Russell. Let me take those for you.' Victoria whipped them from his arms. 'Pink is quite my favourite colour this week, and they'll hide a particularly ugly damp patch in the dining room. I'll be there for a little while if you need anything, Shelley. But I expect you'll want to keep things *short*. You do have an early flight tomorrow, do you not...?'

Matthew had kept the Council's permission letter in his breast pocket like a talisman for the last three days, as if by some process of osmosis it would continue to warm his heart with the truth. Shelley had been in Munich only a matter of hours but had already emailed to confirm Wahzuhören's sponsorship and loan of equipment. Printing the email out and strutting round the grounds showing absolutely everyone, Matthew was beginning to find a new love for correspondence.

Everybody wanted to celebrate this last uncertainty cleared out of the way, but still the atmosphere was muted. Nothing could stop them now, they all knew that. It was really going to happen. But they also knew, like any band in the wings, the waiting was nearly over and any minute now they all really needed to 'perform'.

Pip sat with Matthew and Victoria, nibbling sandwiches and sipping at an unaccustomed glass of cheap fizz, on one of the shrubbery picnic tables. Alan was back, and The Edge of Darkness were preparing to do what they always do with any kind of performance limbo – go down the pub. Pip declined. He needed to be with Victoria. He needed to hear something other than the swell of adrenaline laid bare on him, now this event was almost upon them, and the grinding despair of his own thoughts about what lay beyond it. However challenging they could be, he missed Victoria's speeches. The orator and the deafened, and their own unique symbiosis of language that spanned the gap between them.

But the three of them ate in silence.

'It's marvellous, of course,' Matthew finally spoke. 'But it's not the same, is it? When she's not here.' He absentmindedly flicked crumbs off his trousers. One by one. 'I know I encouraged her to go back to London, but I wasn't myself then. It will be awfully hard when she leaves for Cambridge, won't it?'

Pip got up. This wasn't helping at all...

The noise in the right side temporarily hushed as Rex led the group into The Huntsman's Arms. He glanced around the faces swivelling towards him. Half of them turned back to their drinks and conversations, but the other half started clapping. And it was like fairy dust to Rex. He rose a good couple of inches, smiled graciously, and took a bow. It quickly became clear that he would not be buying anything that night.

Pip shuffled his feet, regretting allowing himself to be bullied into coming after all, but he had a face like a wet weekend, apparently, which would not be tolerated. Alan, who had just arrived for the rest of the week from Essex, looked pretty regretful about it as well, but since he had made his way straight towards Rosamund Pordage and a group of women in jodhpurs in the corner, at least Pip would be free to choose anywhere else to sit.

He was momentarily cheered by the sight of Marilyn sitting with Timothy Smollett, Dr and Mrs Page and the other half of the polo club, especially as she was sipping a glass of mineral water. 'Oh!' she said, flushing beetroot as Rex sat down beside her, and she remained speechless for at least ten minutes. Pip had never seen that before.

When he had suggested to Marilyn last week that she sing something at the festival, she had simply burst into tears. He thought then that it had been the right thing to do. Looking at Rex now, animatedly introducing her to the charms of soft rock, he was sure it was. On so many levels.

Pip watched as spirits soared and glasses clinked, but the remains of his own flagging spirit were soon dissolving into the senseless cacophony all around him. The place was impossible. He could not keep up with any of the conversations and the distorted mush of noises all around him was completely disorientating, like someone turning on twenty TVs at the same time and asking him to make sense of one programme. Not that he could remotely concentrate on anything since Russell had joined his sister and made himself at home in the midst of the polo club/rock band combo. Darkness descended over Pip every time he looked at him these days. There was a modicum of guilt involved – Russell had secured his liberty and a decent bit of income for a while, the least he could do was think nice thoughts about him. But watching him now, holding court, a leading actor with the extras in his orbit, made everything inside of Pip tighten. Especially as he was pretty sure he'd seen the word 'Cambridge' on Russell's lips twice already...

The bell rung. Paradoxically, Pip seemed to be the only person to hear it, taking some glasses to the bar and, gratefully, preparing to leave. Landlord Mick sighed as another whinny of horsey laughter cut through the chatter of the still full pub. 'That's the trouble with living in Bedingford,' Mick nodded towards the privileged rabble in the corner with a weary half-smile. 'It's full of people who live in Bedingford... Come on you lot, haven't you got second homes to go to?'

Pip gave him a sympathetic smile. He'd long since had enough himself. The effort of trying to decipher anything Cambridge-related that was passing between Russell and his sister had given him a headache, never mind the amorphous battering he was getting from everywhere else. A stranger at the bar seemed to be speaking to him. Pip squinted with the effort to tune in. The man sploshed down his pint glass, with the ubiquitous pub demand, 'What you looking at?' Pip's lungs tightened, the words instantly transporting him back to the same demands in prison: *What you looking at, deaf boy?*

He was getting it wrong. It was time to go...

He sat for a moment on the pub wall outside. The air was still balmy, the sky mesmerisingly clear. He needed to feel the warmth of it, and an empty space that was brighter and more enduring than the one opening up inside him. He kicked his feet against the wall.

'Leaves a hole, doesn't she?' A voice murmured at his side.

'Sorry?' he said, looking up to see Russell standing over him.

'Missing Shelley, no doubt?' he, sort of, repeated. 'I most certainly am. I doubt, however, that she is missing you.'

'Yeah, I doubt it as well,' Pip replied. 'She's got far too much to do.'

'Not quite what I meant. She feels sorry for you, you know,' Russell shrugged, leaning on the gatepost next to him. 'But I think it's becoming increasingly difficult for her. She told me last night that she suspects you're in love with her, and it makes her sick. It's the way you look at her, she says, she finds it disgusting, but she's too nice to say it. I think that may be why she told me, actually, because I, as you've probably guessed by now, am not.

Not that it really matters. I'm favouring a spring wedding in Cambridge, and I doubt you'll be invited.'

It was the most terrible blow that Pip felt as hard in his gut as if Russell had kicked him there. Winded, he could no longer speak, his body pitched as if the ground had disappeared beneath him. All he had left, the fantasy of her, disintegrating into the night air. A fantasy that he held as closely to him as the fantasy of his musicianship. *One day...* He had long since given up any real notion that Shelley could feel the same way about him, exactly as he had given up believing that his body and mind would ever quieten enough to allow him to perform again. But the fantasy endured. One day, one fantasy day, he would have them both.

And he was good at it. He was used to making sense of his world with only a certain amount of reality, and the rest using memory and imagination. The constant direction of his attention had embedded her features so surely behind his eyes, and her voice so clearly in his head, it was as if the imaginary conversations were real memories he had stored, carefully wrapped in acetate on the top shelf of his mind, and all he had to do was take them off the shelf and press play. Like he might an old tape recorder, every night he rewound them, pressing play repeatedly, until he fell asleep. It kept him there, sleeping, until the reality of the dawn. A reality that was always less than he wanted, but it was something.

Now he had nothing. To know that she could actually feel *that*... that ugly, piercing word. Like fingernails on a blackboard, he could not bear to hear himself think it. And not for his past mistakes and lies either, but because of the *truth* of the matter: the way he looked at her. The way he must always be looking at her. How could he ever have considered that he would not be? Everything he could never say to her must surely be in his eyes.

'*She feels sorry for you.*' Those other ugly words twisted their blade in his gut. Of course she does. That's the other thing that hearing people do.

And Shelley was supremely hearing.

And supremely incapable of speaking her mind...

Russell watched as Pip ran down the road towards Yarnside Bridge, wondering if the momentary satisfaction was enough and, unusually, suspecting it was not. After all, Pip was going home alone, but so was he. Especially after what Shelley had *really* said to him last night. He still had work to do...

Musicians, crew and horse riders tumbled out of the pub, Rosamund conducting her friends towards Glebe House. 'Come on home, Russell,' she said, drunkenly tugging at his sleeve. 'I've promised the polo club a glass or two of your XO.'

'Oh,' Russell sighed. 'I don't think so. You go on.'

'Yeah, I know what you're thinking,' Alan sloped up, following Russell's dark focus across the bridge. 'He's an annoying little prick, isn't he? I'll have that drink with you,' he winked at Rosamund. 'I could tell you some stories...'

Russell turned his head to the eager stranger beside him.

'Well, perhaps just the one then...'

53

NOT ALLOWED TO LOOK

Shelley had texted to say she would be a few minutes late – there was some problem with security at the Wahzuhören factory door. Pip was relieved. He'd never done this video call thing before and it gave him a moment's more orientation, as well as avoidance. He did not know how he was going to see her, how he was going to hear her, let alone find anything to say, ever again.

He stared at his own half of the screen. For years he had become so accustomed to studying himself from the inside, the outside was not something to which he paid that much attention. It was a curious thing to be looking so intently at himself on the screen now. It felt unnerving, and he hoped that the direction of his focus was not quite so undressing to everyone else. The anxiety rose again. Russell's words last night had so brutally reminded him that it obviously was.

But what was he to do? He had to see to hear. How could he listen if he was not allowed to look?

'Hi, Pip. You made it then?' Shelley looked tired as she clicked into life before him. But his eyes remained on himself, sometimes moving to the corners of the screen, brushing past her face quickly. 'Just in *time*. I've been *over with* the chief engineer testing headsets all day. But we think *we're done now*. It all has to go through the *University* unfortunately, so I'll have to drive up to *Cambridge* on Friday to pick them up. Another *job*, all we need, eh? *Bloody nuisance*.'

The few intermittent words and the accompanying non-audible sigh were all he got. He could not look at her.

'Are you *OK*?' she said.

He nodded.

'I *don't think* this is working, is it? Perhaps the sound is *bothering* you...? Pip?' He glanced at her. 'Do I need to make myself clearer?'

'Uh uh,' he shook his head quickly and lowered his gaze again.

'OK, this *obviously isn't working*, is it? I'll let you off,' she smiled briefly. He missed it. 'You can *go now*. I'll do the best I can *without you*. Thanks anyway, I think we've got the *right outcome*. I'll see you back in Bedingford on *Thursday*.'

'Thursday,' he repeated vaguely, and her eyes narrowed. He immediately read annoyance and returned his focus to the corner of the screen, missing her concern.

'I think we probably both need some *sleep*. Hope you're *OK* though and have a *good night*. Lots to do *for the weekend*. And I've made *a decision*.' She waved and his roaming eyes headed back to her briefly. 'Pip, can you see me properly?'

'Yes.'

'When I get back, I think we need to talk some more.'

'Yes.' His eyes dipped again.

'Are you sure you're *alright*?'

'Maybe after the gig then?' he hurried. 'Let's just get through this the best we can. I... I'll do my best.'

'I know *you will*,' she said, her brow furrowing again. 'You always *do*.'

'Goodnight then.' And he clicked himself off. In his place, a faceless, silent avatar, who she no longer had to pity or put up with. But her beautiful, expressive face burned into the screen, he could look directly for one more secret moment and tell her he was sorry, he loved her with all his heart and he did not know what to do, but he promised to himself that he would leave her in peace as soon as the concert was delivered. His own heart, broken, he would deal with as some kind of appropriate retribution.

For the so many things he had got wrong, 'getting ideas above his fucking station' – the memories of the past still screamed so loud. But most of all, for failing in the thing he always thought had been his greatest skill.

Listening.

54

NOBODY WILL EVER HEAR

Shelley had back-to-back meetings tomorrow, otherwise she would have merrily laid into the mini-bar. But, it seemed, more to silence a storm than to clink glasses with the calm she had hoped from sharing a productive day with someone important. There was still so much to do, and she was struggling to keep up remotely. And there was something wrong with Pip. She realised again how much of her confidence about the coming weekend came from him. She just hoped they would both last.

She lay on her hotel bed, picking at a packed salad, two chocolate bars and a butterbrezel, debating that improbable urge she had sometimes to talk to her mother. Wondering, this time, if perhaps Marilyn was becoming a version of motherhood she might come to recognise...

'Hello, Mum. Are you busy...?'

Shelley cleared away the supper debris and climbed into bed, her mother's parting words embedded in her head. But this time because they were worth taking root. The call had been long and cathartic. Marilyn was bored, and so delighted that she had called, which opened a whole box of opportunity. As usual, the balance of listening to talking fell firmly in Shelley's court, but she didn't mind. She heard things she had never heard before. Marilyn happily ranged across the full spectrum of (largely Horace-related) rages and anecdotes, disappointments and glories; from Horsham to Covent Garden, from Hampshire to Las Vegas. And as she did so, the solid core of Shelley's frozen inadequacy began to thaw into an unfamiliar fluidity, with the realisation that she was, and always had been, the strongest person in that house.

Perhaps then, she might have the strength to do all that she had to this weekend, as well.

She had talked too, a little. Marilyn had invited it, eventually. She was happy, she ventured to admit to her mother, at the Manor. If she could only stay there.

And if she could only have...

'You've always heard everything so clearly, Sheldon,' her mother said. 'But sometimes you just have to find your voice. Go,' Marilyn concluded. 'Trust yourself and speak your truth. If it is there, you will hear it, if you listen properly. And if it is not, walk away. Do not live your life in service to a man who cannot give it back.'

Thursday night, one more to go, and Pip went 'home' to Ma and Bill's shed. It wasn't his home anymore, but it was where he wanted to be tonight. The cold and sparsity seemed somehow appropriate. He wouldn't be able to avoid Shelley over the weekend, of course, but the longer he could hold out from seeing in her face what he had already heard, the better. He knew he would not sleep much anyway. He tried the fantasy to put him to sleep, but other words kept getting in the way. He stared at the dark wood roof and mouthed his own, but stumbled. He did not know the words of love. So much of what he heard in his head was echo from the past, and so much of what he spoke from his mouth was muscle memory. Ma and Bill had shown him a kind of love – a solid, safe kind – but he had never heard the words. And he did not know how to hear them now. He knew the sound of *I*, the sound of *love*, the sound of *you*. But he'd never formed the words together. He tried it now, and he did not know if he was doing it properly. Usually so confident in his speech, he might as well have been trying to speak Chinese.

'I love you.'

Feeling each word, examining the resonance in his throat, the width of his mouth, the movement of his lips, and the memory of his voice in his head, which still spoke so clearly.

But nobody would ever hear him say them now.

55

SOMETHING VERY PRECIOUS

Inspector Foster got the call personally this time, but Sergeant Riordan was having none of it. His careless boss knew full well he was allergic. The last thing he needed was another fruitless trip to Bedingford with the added companionship of a sniffer dog. He'd be puffy and streaming for hours, and for what? He'd bet his last doughnut it would be nothing. Again! The last six calls with 'reliable information' of drug-dealing at Bedingford Manor had turned out to be so flimsy they were barely worth a visit from the PCSO. It was ridiculous. What was wrong with this village? The station would be a laughing stock before long, and Riordan knew he would not be the only person in the Hampshire Constabulary to consider that, never mind the alteration of the National Park boundaries, it was about time Bedingford was discreetly moved into Berkshire.

Besides, he was never going to get a promotion at his age anyway, and so what? Riordan looked around the office, his colleagues, the routine he knew so well, in one of the last remaining community stations that hadn't been sold off for budget cuts. What was so wrong with where he was? And he wondered then, how many other people in the world wasted so much of their lives dreaming of places they'd hate if they actually got there...

However, on her first visit to Bedingford Manor, it turned out that the dog had a very distinct brief. The call this time had been persuasive *and* specific.

'Any drums here?' Riordan's young (and apparently more ambitious) colleague asked at the Manor door, the dog and handler by his side.

'Ha! Take your pick!' Matthew managed to laugh whilst restraining Beryl from sniffing the poor spaniel to death. 'In the old ballroom at the back, perhaps...? Oh, um, wait a minute!' Matthew's stomach thudded with the sudden recollection of where casually letting people in with no forethought usually landed him. He galloped his way down the hall, holding onto Beryl's collar, and slid into the ballroom behind her.

'These yours, sir?' The officer asked Alan, sat at his drum kit by the window. Alan nodded, not entirely breezily, but the dog was already heading for the *other* drum kit. The one on the *side* of the room.

'Oh dear...' The young police officer picked up the snare drum at which the dog stood furiously wagging and panting. Beryl went ballistic. Matthew could barely contain her. The officer shook the drum uncertainly, clearly wondering what he should do next in the interests of not looking a complete idiot. 'Are *these* yours?' he said to Alan, buying time.

'No,' he smirked. 'They're his...'

Pip was busy in the courtyard. He had heard nothing. Sometimes it was just the way he liked it. But now the noises were coming thick and fast: Alan pointing at him out of the window; the police officer beckoning him in; the matching thud of his heartbeat and his feet up the Manor steps; Matthew trying to bundle Beryl into the dining room; his drum kit with another dog sat, tongue flapping, next to it...

In a flash, Pip took in two tiny things – the snare stand was off-centre, and there was the faintest hint of perfume around the kit. Not one of Shelley's usual scents – the cinnamon or coconut that he knew so well – this was the much more floral fragrance she had worn only once, as far as he could remember – the day of Horace's arrival, the dress rehearsal. On auto-pilot, his spirit rose. She must be back from Cambridge already... And then it crashed. The dog remained manically wagging at the snare drum. Pressure was growing in Pip's chest now, the heat rising, the back of his neck stiffening, his breath getting shallower and shallower, the thoughts chasing each sensation. He could see the officer asking questions, Alan handing him a drum key...

'Oh dear, oh dear,' the officer said, prizing open the drum head and holding up a fat pouch of white powder. Pip stared at him; he seemed to be in slow motion. Once again, his world had taken a wrong turn, and the lurch was nauseating. He stood paralysed, his tongue stuck in his mouth, his breath held prisoner in his body. Pip could no longer look, but he knew all the words the officer was speaking now.

'You do not have to say anything...'

He could not breathe. He didn't think he could say anything, ever again...

Shelley felt calmer than she had in days. It had been an unwanted trip to Cambridge this morning, hastily organised, but the drive back was a joy; the small hire van stacked floor to ceiling with eight hundred industry-leading wireless headsets. She kept looking at them, overspilling onto the passenger seat. Her mood made all the lighter knowing now that, whatever the consequences, she would soon be relieving herself of the heavy bargain she had made to get them.

Her unconscious smile spontaneously inched further up her face as she turned into Trefusis Lane. Everything they needed would be on site now, and she was delighted to have had such an easy journey *home*. She needed the time. She had a lot to do. And a few things to say.

Where was that man? When she'd got back from Munich last night, Pip was nowhere to be found. But he had to be at the Manor now, and wherever he was, that was her first port of call.

A police car drew up to the Manor gate. She stopped the van to let it out to the road. Pip was in the back seat. He turned and stared at her out of the rear window, and her smile froze. He had taught her a thing or two about hearing in the last few weeks, and she could see that he was silently pleading, his lips slowly drawing together in her favourite way, because it looked like a kiss. *'Why...?'*

Shelley tore back into the Manor and straight into Victoria, putting on her coat as if it was battle armour. A kilogram of cocaine had been found in Pip's snare drum, she said, but she'd been tying bunting in the barn with Marilyn and the Women's Wheelers so knew nothing more. Matthew was failing to jump-start the Rover, with a lump hammer, so Marilyn had gone to fetch her car so they could follow to the police station to find out.

Shelley ran down the hall and burst into the ballroom. The Edge of Darkness were mid-song. She wrenched out the guitar plugs. 'What do you think you're doing? Why have the police taken Pip? Why aren't you doing something?'

'Like what?' Damon sniffed. 'What can we do about it? We've still got a show to do.'

'A show to do?' Shelley spluttered. '*He* is the show! Haven't you worked that out yet?'

'Anyway, it was funny,' Alan sniggered, taking the opportunity to get up for a drink and another much needed rest. 'I guess that's just what happens when a dog biscuit turns out *not* to be a dog biscuit.'

'What did you say?'

'Don't worry about it, love, just a private joke.'

'A private joke, really? *How* private?' The rage rising, Shelley could feel herself beginning to shake as she turned to Rex. 'Do you get it?'

'No.'

'You?' She turned to Yebut, who shook his head blankly.

'You?'

'No.' Damon and Benny completed the ignorance.

A trickle of relief was immediately drowned by a tidal wave of fury. She spun back to Alan.

'Well, it looks like it's just the one of us that does then, doesn't it?'

'I haven't got time for this.' He brushed her away like an annoying speck of dust. 'We've already wasted an hour with the fuzz here and then explaining it to the old lady.'

Alan strode back to the drums, but Shelley grabbed his shirt-sleeve. 'Well, you can "waste" another few minutes explaining yourself to me then, can't you? I know exactly what you are talking about! And you are coming with me to the police station, right now, to tell them all about it.'

'Shelley, what is going on here?' Victoria said, having only just managed to catch her up. 'Tell them what?'

'I think we've just found out who was responsible for Pip going to prison, Victoria! And I wouldn't be surprised is behind this farcical arrest too. *He* planted drugs in Pip's snare drum. Twice!'

'Oh, hang on, hang on, I ain't planted no drugs nowhere,' Alan scoffed. 'A dog biscuit hardly counts, does it? And that was only a joke, take him down a peg or two on that tour. He'd have got off, you only have to look at him! Not my fault he was stupid enough to do a runner.'

'Are you serious?' Rex gaped.

'And you're not pinning this one on me. Suppose I might have given someone the idea...' For a split second, Alan's cocksure posturing wavered, as if this had only just occurred to him. 'But that's all. It's a good story!' He immediately recovered himself.

'Besides, he deserves it, jumped up little twat, always going round like he's the bee's knees or something.'

'Are we talking about the same person?' Victoria sniffed. 'Or even cohabiting the same planet?'

'Oh yes, Victoria. That's Pip all over, isn't it?' Shelley exploded. 'What a fucking show off! Nobody can be in any doubt about his confidence, can they?' She lunged at Alan with a fury she had never felt before. 'You absolute cunt! Have you no idea what this has done to him?'

'Who did you tell this "story" to?' Rex joined in. 'And please don't tell me you gave them a drum key as well!'

'I don't have to listen to this,' Alan turned away, but Rex grabbed him.

'Well, if you're not going to tell us, you're going to tell the police.'

'Whose side are you on?'

'Oh, for God's sake Alan, you... what she said.'

'Sheldon, darling, you're back!' Marilyn trundled through the door then. 'I've brought the Clio.'

'Right, get in the car!' Shelley tugged at Alan's sleeve.

'I'm not going to the police!' he retorted. 'Especially not in a Clio.'

'Then we'll just have to get them back here then, won't we? We can tell them what you've just told us and maybe they'll have better luck with who they cart off this time!'

'Don't be ridiculous, I'll deny it. I'm not that stupid.'

'Yeah but, you're *quite* stupid.' It was the smallest of voices as Yebut pointed to his digital recorder. The colour drained from Alan's face and he lunged for the microphone stand. Rex got there first, grabbed the recorder and threw it to Shelley whilst the rest of them shunted Alan out of the house.

Rex held Alan's wrists as he pulled the front seat forward and bundled him into the back of Marilyn's car.

'Give me the keys, Mum,' Shelley demanded.

'It's alright, darling, I'll drive.'

'You're too slow! Give me the keys!' She grabbed them from her mother's hand.

Victoria was already lowering herself into the passenger seat.

'Get out of the car, Victoria.'

'Certainly not!'

Marilyn elbowed Rex out of the way. 'Excuse me, Rex, but this is personal.' She jumped in after Alan, wedging him on the back seat, with her hand on his crotch. 'You move and knob junior gets it. Do I make myself clear?'

And so the three women drove off with their valueless cargo, to rescue something very precious indeed, to each of them.

56

TRUTH IS ALL WE NEED

Alan virtually pleaded to be taken in by the time Marilyn and Shelley hauled him into the police station, Victoria behind, prodding him up the steps with her umbrella and generously educating him on what kind of man he was. Now he was bleating like a lamb in the interview room next door. The commotion had been loud enough for the whole station to hear. Almost.

Pip stared blankly at the walls of the custody cell downstairs. The bright white tiles reflected back at him in their silent nothingness. He felt displaced, two worlds colliding. How had it all come to this *again?* This fine short summer, when he was beginning to be reminded of all that he had, all that he was capable of. Able to listen again and finally starting to hear something worthwhile. Could he really have got it so wrong?

His body pitched into chaos, words in his head tumbled over each other. He could hear nothing that made sense. Like a herd of wildebeest pursued by a lion, they thundered past in every direction, impossible to catch hold of or halt. He could not bear the return of all of this. His hand pressed against the wall, his head to the cold stone tiles, he felt the sharp edges of his voice echoing into the dead, empty room. The words were unfamiliar. 'Help me...'

In reception, Sergeant Riordan was patiently trying to explain that Shelley could not see Pip, so there really wasn't any point in wearing out any more carpet with her frantic pacing.

'He's refusing communication again anyway,' Riordan said. 'But we've called for the duty solicitor and Mr Stent is on his way.'

'Frederick Stent?' Victoria retorted, banging her umbrella on the counter. 'I'm surprised he can find his way to his own home of a night, let alone ten miles down the M3. Excuse me, I wish to represent Mr Berry.'

'You retired from the bar twenty years ago, Countess,' Riordan sighed.

'And this is significant, how? Please convey the choice to my client – me, or the pasty-faced conveyancer from Basingstoke. Victoria Wolstenholme QC will do, no need of the Countess, thank you very much.'

Sergeant Riordan rolled his eyes. What was it with this bloke that city barristers seemed to be falling over themselves to represent him?

'Ask him if he noticed anything different in the ballroom today,' Shelley cut in.

Victoria tutted. 'I do have some small experience of defendant investigation, thank you, Shelley.'

'Ahem,' Riordan thought he should remind them who was doing the investigating, but Victoria's pin sharp gaze quickly convinced him it wasn't worth it.

'Yes, yes, sorry, of course,' Shelley gabbled. 'But Pip, his senses you know, he notices things—'

'Quite. And your fidgety enthusiasm for the truth is most gratifying. As I am sure it will be to Pip. Excuse me Sergeant, on our way, are we...?'

. . .

Victoria had never seen Pip like this before, so reluctant to raise his eyes to her face. A hot lump appeared in her stomach and she was reminded just how much she had come to love that quality of attention over the past few weeks.

'Truth, Pip, remember?' she gently raised his chin with her hand. '*That* is all we ever need. I have been fully appraised of the matter of the dog biscuit, for which my sincere condolences and heartfelt fury.' It comforted her that he nodded faintly.

'Little it matters now...' His voice, when it came, was a fragile and delicate thing.

'Ah, no,' Victoria waved her finger. 'It is of the utmost significance and will, at last, be enough to bring this whole sorry business to a close. I wonder, Pip, if you have ever considered what you might do if you were to find out what kind of amoeba stuck a dog biscuit in your snare drum in the first place? Should you be tempted to commit a real crime, our *other* drummer is next door and is at this moment disclosing to the police to whom he has also spoken of it. And to whom he recently loaned a drum key. I shall be pleased to create a disturbance whilst you go in there and make mincemeat of him... Excellent, I have your full focus once more.'

'Alan?' Pip mouthed, forgetting or unable to speak. 'Are you sure?'

'Admitted it himself. Shelley made certain of it and the delightfully eloquent Yebut recorded it.'

'Shelley?' he squeaked.

'She is also most anxious that I ask if you recall anything different about the ballroom this morning?'

'She's *here*?'

'Yes, of course. Would you doubt it?'

'Yes, apparently.' Pip looked totally lost now. 'The perfume...'

'What perfume?'

'That was the only difference I noticed. Apart from the

moved position of the snare stand, there was a very faint perfume. She doesn't usually wear it, but it's definitely one of hers.'

'Well, I can't believe that. What is this perfume like? Can you describe it?'

'I know the scent. It was in Marilyn's garden, big white thing under the lounge windowsill, before she took a machete to it.'

'I see. Well, let's ask them, shall we?'

'Marilyn's here as well?'

'Indeed. The pair of them driving poor Sergeant Riordan quite mad, I should think.' She fixed him with the sturdiest of gazes. 'And *that*, if nothing else, Pip, *is* what matters.'

Riordan appeared at the door. 'Everything alright? Mr Stent is here. Is he speaking?'

Pip turned to Victoria, his eyes set on her face, and another lump appeared in her throat. From the earliest moments of their meeting, Pip had always been so confident with their conversation – they had both made it that way. Now she was reminded of the reality of it; the difficulties that his confidence in close quarters obscured. Of course he could not understand the sergeant, across the other side of the room in a darkened doorway. And he was looking at her to tell him, with a face full of trust.

'Yes,' she said, swallowing the unexpected emotion and steadily returning his gaze with a small, gentle smile. 'He is speaking. And I think he might have some interesting things to say...'

Pip breathed hard and grabbed for something solid in the vortex of messages and vibrations he was feeling, and found it, as so many times before, in Victoria's words.

Truth is all he needed.

He fixed his eyes on the familiar officer.

'I have not mentioned it before, Sergeant, but I am deaf,' he began, as steadily as he could. 'I rely mostly on lipreading to understand, and I would appreciate your help to ensure that I do. I am also pretty frightened. This has happened to me before and it makes me very... agitated,' he tried to pin down the maelstrom. 'When I feel these things, it interferes with my ability to hear. So please could I ask you and your colleagues to write down everything you say from now on, and that Victoria remains with me during any further interviews. I do not know anything about these drugs, I have nothing to hide, and I *will not* allow this to happen again...'

'He says the snare stand was about ten centimetres off centre and there was a very faint perfume,' Victoria reported back in reception. 'I asked him what it smelled like and he said the big white flowers that used to be in your garden, Marilyn, under the lounge windowsill.'

'The gardenia?' Shelley and Marilyn said together. They looked at each other. 'Horace?'

'Apparently you've worn it once, Shelley. Pip thinks it's yours.'

'Ah no,' Shelley snorted. 'Hate the stuff. I've palmed all Dad's gifts off on... Rosamund... for years.' She ground to a halt, dumbstruck.

'Rosamund Pordage?' Victoria prompted. 'Matthew said she came to the Manor looking for you last evening, to offer her help at the weekend. No doubt the credulous man gave her free rein of the place while she waited. Which, I now assume, she didn't?'

Shelley was not listening. 'Oh... no... no, he surely can't think...' Her face melted, remembering that look from the back of the police car, and that single mouthed word, *'Why?'*

'No!' She sprung to her feet and made a run for the custody suite, but was quickly intercepted by the duty desk officer.

Marilyn pulled her away.

'Keep your head, Sheldon, we have work to do...'

. . .

Rosamund was on her way out to town. Morris and Tree were exceptionally helpful in diverting her. And the back seat of a two-door Clio was exceptionally helpful in detaining her.

Still, Shelley slapped her. 'How could you do something like that?'

'Mummy told me to!' Rosamund wailed.

'Oh, don't be absurd,' Marilyn retorted. 'You're thirty years old! What kind of idiot child listens to their ridiculous mother at your age?' She glanced at Shelley whilst poking Rosamund like a boxing cat. 'So, where is she?'

'You won't get her,' Rosamund pouted. 'She's taking a break at the Geneva lake house. She'll be at Southampton Airport by now...'

Harriet was three passengers away from the security gate when her feet slid from beneath her. She gazed up to the biggest man she had ever seen, one trunk-like arm securely around her, his other hand holding a family portrait. Apparently satisfied, he stuffed the photo in his pocket and she was now being moon-walked backwards through arrivals and into the back of an old friend's car.

'Thank you, Tree!' Shelley cheered, as he folded himself into the passenger seat.

'Harriet Pordage!' Marilyn shrieked, pinning her against the now extremely crowded back seat. 'You're nicked!'

Shelley sped away. Rosamund burst into tears. Harriet appeared unmoved.

'Oh, put it a sock in it, darling. It's a first offence, you won't be gone long.'

'But they're *your* drugs, Mummy!' Rosamund bawled. 'You got them at the Law Association party!'

'Don't be ridiculous, darling. What a thing to say! Who on earth would believe that? Especially as *you* took them to the

Manor. But don't worry yourself, Russell will sort it all out. He always does, doesn't he? Even if he has to take the blame. We can say it was his idea anyway, can't we?'

Marilyn stopped wriggling and gaped at her.

'What kind of mother would do that to their children?'

'And you think I'm taking lessons in parenting from you?' Harriet snapped back. Shelley jammed on the brakes and she flew forward between the front seats, her face straight into Tree's elbow. 'Yes fine, take me to the police station, I'll have you for assault!' Harriet rubbed her colouring forehead. 'I have no fear. *My* children know which side their bread's buttered. Russell always does as he's told...'

Russell was being escorted to the desk when they arrived back at the police station. Shelley stared at him and then at the sergeant.

'Just assisting with our enquiries following Mr Kent's interview,' Riordan said, helpfully indiscreet as usual. 'Oh,' he glanced past her to Harriet and Rosamund being dragged in behind, one under each of Tree's arms. 'It's a family party, is it?'

'You two-faced, lying prick!' Shelley charged at Russell. His lips tightened, looking between her and his family. He shrugged lightly, a flash of sadness in his eyes, as if two-faced-lying-prickdom was an open door he'd walked through a long time ago and had clicked shut behind him with a deadbolt.

'Ah, good. You're here already, Russell,' Harriet smirked. 'I've no doubt you'll clear all this up.'

Mother and son looked at each other, a hundred conversations playing out in silence. Shelley stepped back as she watched their faces, the edges of her anger dissolving into a weary sorrow. For so many things, and so many people, for every truth left too long unsaid, and every warning gone unheard whilst listening to the wrong person.

Locking eyes with Russell, she knew now how she would like to conclude this. She pressed play on Yebut's recorder.

Harriet's voice may have been muffled by road noise, but it was clear enough for her son. Steely eyed, his focus narrowed, and he turned to the counter.

'Yes,' he said as steadily as any courtroom summation. 'You're holding the wrong man. The drugs belong to my mother, and she arranged for them to be planted. I regret that my sister and I may have given her the idea for *where*, and that Rosamund – like me – is fool enough to "do as she's told", but that is all.'

'Good God, Russell, you throw anyone under a bus to get what you want,' Rosamund grunted, looking darkly at Shelley and, habitually, taking her mother's arm like a kicked dog who fetches your slippers.

'Oh? And I wonder where I— we,' he corrected, 'get that from.'

'That's enough, Mr Pordage,' Riordan suggested. 'We'll interview you in private shortly. You don't need to make a statement in reception.'

Russell glanced at Shelley and then returned his eyes to Harriet. 'Oh yes, I think I do... And I would like it on record that my mother was also responsible for the disruption of Bedingford Opera, charges I believe including public nuisance, trespass, and criminal damage of the festival sound screens. She also gave a false witness statement regarding alleged stolen property the last time Mr Berry was arrested.'

'For God's sake!' Victoria exploded at last. 'Don't you ever stop? It's our home! For *three hundred years*! And this is our family. Do you not care who you use to ruin us?'

Harriet ignored her. 'Russell!' she barked. 'You know you are talking nonsense and you will say that on record, do you hear me?'

'Yes, I hear you mother, it's very hard not to, but I am not listening anymore. People who listen to you tend to get things *wrong*...'

. . .

The station reception quiet again, Marilyn was quieter still.

'I am sorry Victoria,' she finally spoke. 'I think perhaps I have never considered that the Manor is in fact somebody's *home*. And, perhaps I have also never acknowledged, a place that provided a home for my daughter, when hers was... not ideal.'

'Matthew has always said that the Manor belongs to all of us.'

'I see that now and I am sorry.'

'Accepted, thank you.' Victoria smiled graciously, as the three Pordages disappeared to the custody suite.

This was turning into a very fine day indeed...

Pip was exhausted. Led back to the counter, he felt like a struck bell, vibrating to discordant resonances he did not recognise. Nothing made sense. Marilyn took his arm, a benign quietness on her face, and no words on her lips. Shelley, his gentle Tigger, her movements slow, a fury in her eyes, her body tight as if she were a balloon blown up too far, collecting his bracelet and neck chain from the desk, her voice a blunt, staccato, unhappy sound. And Victoria, high notes, fast, her mouth sprinting from one thought to the next, talking nonsense as far as he could make out... Who *were* these people?

Victoria climbed (ambitiously) into the back seat of the car next to him. She was still talking. His bankrupt gaze brushed over her face, to Marilyn turning towards him in the passenger seat, to the rearview mirror and Shelley's eyes, moist, looking back at him. He could not see her mouth. Had she spoken? He did not think so, but it wasn't disgust he was hearing in her eyes. Disconnected and light-headed, he did not know what it was. Struggling to focus, he tried to tune into the comforting rumble of the road, searching for a restful space to understand, to work it out. But with the uncharacteristically descant harmony of Victoria demanding the attention of them all, it would have to wait. She still had not stopped talking by the dual carriageway.

'Look at me, Pip,' she insisted. He squinted at her and the relentless nonsense that he could not grasp. 'I simply must tell you about Shelley in the ballroom. What a spirited performance! It was really quite something. You should have seen her! Isn't that right, Marilyn? Like a mother lion, she was. And is that word yet permitted on the BBC, Shelley?'

'No, never.'

'See how fucking far we have come in my 86 years? Do you know, however, I have never yet had occasion to let the word *cunt* pass from my lips? Oh, until then. Mmm, I rather like it—'

'Victoria?' he finally murmured, a chink of light breaking through.

'Yes, Pip?'

'Shut up...'

57

ELEPHANT SHOES

'So much to do...' Pip's heavy eyes roamed the Manor hallway, the whole place heaving with activity, people coming and going, words and notes and rhythms waving in and out.

'Not for you, young man,' Victoria said. 'Just a nice hot bath and a lie down for you, I think. It will all still be here when you're rested. Why don't you take him upstairs, Shelley? I'm sure you could lend Pip your rooms for a while, could you not?'

'Yes,' Shelley replied resolutely. 'That is exactly where I would like him to be...'

By the time they got to her door, Pip's exhaustion was mutating into agitation. Trying not to cry, or scream or shout, his teeth gritted, elbows stiff at his sides, as if they were armed guards keeping prisoner all that was held tight within him. But he was home now and it was all roaring to be released.

He glanced around him, afraid that this was very much the *wrong* place to keep the cell door closed. The room was full and lived in. The walls looked freshly painted, a 'new' set of curtains with an Oxfam tag sat on the chair by the window, a battered old chest of drawers stood on newspaper, sanded and undercoated, with a tin of lilac paint and set of brushes on the floor.

His eyes narrowed. 'Aren't you leaving for Cambridge on Tuesday? You don't look very ready to go.'

'No, I'm not ready at all.'

Pip fought to remain silent whilst his whole exhausted body screamed, *'Well, don't then! Stay with me! Stay... with... ME!'*

'I don't want to go, Pip,' she was looking at him so directly now, demanding his focus. 'I've never wanted to go, but I really don't want to now.'

He sighed, pushing his hand through his hair. This was torture, and he had to put a stop to it.

'Oh, here we go again. Then why are you?' he demanded, rather more forcefully than either of them was expecting. 'Why don't you just get on with it, for once, and stop asking everyone else to make up your mind. Especially me. I can't do it anymore.'

'Pip...?'

'Look, I'm sorry, this was a bad idea,' he hurried, knowing that any means of holding himself together was fast becoming undone. 'I shouldn't be here. I gotta go.'

'No, please don't, Pip...' She caught his arm. He shook it off.

'Stop it! Can't you see what this is doing to me? You, with the great empathy for all suffering creatures, can't you see *this*?'

'Pip, I'm sorry, I... You want me to go?'

'*Want you to go?* Are you fucking crazy? Or is it just me?' The room spinning a little, he stabbed the words like a bee sting, knowing that he would leave them behind, pulling his insides out with them. 'Of course I don't want you to go! But not for whatever reason you're doing it now – saving Matthew, saving the Manor, saving your mother, your dream job, or your fantasy sound world! But this...' His head dropped, his voice disappearing to a whisper, his palms raised in surrender. '*This* very real, flawed and lost, hopelessly in love bugger of a one here. So *please*, stop asking me to help you make the decision.'

'What did you just say?'

'Oh, you're the deaf one now, are you? Don't make me say it again.'

'I think you said something I... I wasn't expecting.'

'I know that!' he retorted. 'Don't you think I know that? It wasn't supposed to happen. Look what you've done now? Now I've got nothing left, not even my pride. Nothing at all...' His voice faded into a hopeless sigh. 'What does it matter?'

'But, Pip—' Suddenly her face filled with a kind of wonder and a delighted smile broke across her face.

'Oh...' Pip screwed his own into despair. 'You... I never thought you... How could you? Don't you dare laugh at me!'

He turned away from her now, desperately fighting tears of exhaustion and humiliation.

'Laugh at you?' Shelley instantly sprung back. 'How the hell could you think I was laughing at you?' Her vehement tone quite shocked him, but he remained turned away. She grabbed his arms and spun him back towards her.

Pip did the only thing he could then. He clamped his eyes shut.

'Don't you dare stop listening to me, Philip Berry!'

Pip's closed eyelids twitched, as if he were compelled to look at a sunbeam which he knew would blind him.

'Sometimes the voice is enough, obviously! More fool me, I've let mine go a bit quiet in recent years. But are you hearing this?' She took one of his hands in both hers. It flinched and tugged, and it broke her heart how he continued to expect something so different from this reality. She held onto it. 'And this...' She placed it on her heart. The muscles in his hand loosened and his eyes blinked open a fraction, so tentatively, a deep sense of bewilderment, close to fright, drinking thirstily for explanation. 'And this...' She reached up to touch his face, circling her hand to the back of his neck. His eyes drove through her. 'And this...' She touched her lips to his, so gently, so briefly... 'OK? Get the picture?'

Pip was staring quite disturbingly now, his mouth open without a word.

'No?' And she kissed him again, strengthened by the collapse in his resistance as his mouth fully engaged with hers now, so needily, so directly.

'Completely clear?'

The moment was an age.

'Elephant shoes, Pip,' she mouthed with no sound. 'Olive juice.'

His jaw dropped further, staring down the bridge of his nose as if in some kind of fearful suspension. He shook his head, as if none of this was quite getting through. However that could be.

'I love you,' she said, a third time.

'No.'

'Yes,' she replied instantly. 'Yes. I have never wanted to go, you know that. I've never wanted to leave all this, Matthew, my home. But I decided in Munich that, more than any of that, I just could not leave... *you*. I will be in deep trouble when I tell them, I know that, but I decided that I was going to stay here to try to... interest you.'

'Interest me?' he squeaked, as if he could not possibly have read that right. 'But what about the wedding?'

'What wedding?'

'Russell, a spring wedding, he said.'

'He said that?'

'He said a lot of things.'

'Well, people who listen to Russell tend to get it wrong,' she echoed darkly. 'What else did he say?'

'The way I looked at you, he said, you found it... disgusting,' he hurriedly mumbled the word, as if he could not bring himself to hear it again.

'*What*?' Shelley's jaw dropped. 'Oh God, Pip, no!'

'So you... don't?'

'Of course I don't!' she choked. 'It's how you listen to me, isn't it? How you've always listened to me. That's the main reason I had to stay, to try and get it back!'

There was something very strange happening to Pip's body now, a whole new kind of electrification. And he grabbed her, his hand to the back of her neck, pulling her forward, pleading with her in that open kiss. The final unlocking of all that physical and emotional tension, dramatically pouring out of him, he was shaking, and then he was crying.

'Oh God, Shelley, love me! Please God, love me!'

He sunk into her arms, and she enclosed him completely. And there could be no further doubt for her now. She could touch it, feel it and hear it – one and the same thing – as if he was reaching in and drawing her into him.

'I will,' she whispered. 'I do.'

58

CUSTODY

The gates set to open at midday, the music starting at two, everyone had a job (or fifty) to do and everyone was in place. Well, *almost* everyone...

The Chief Constable of Hampshire Police – Mrs Burlington's granddaughter – had 'decided' that local officers needed a little more time to 'investigate' Alan's story. He was therefore spending 23 hours and 59 minutes in a police cell. Rex was satisfied with that. Victoria was delighted with herself for arranging it. Pip, exchanging kisses and unspoken promises with Shelley every time they ran past each other, couldn't give a flying fart where Alan was.

'Is the fabled Mrs Burlington coming to this gig then?' he grinned instead.

'She would, dear,' Victoria replied. 'But she's 102 and dances like a carthorse...'

Pip lay on the grass behind the barn, out of view of everything and everyone. Taking a moment to stop, to rest, to drink in a little quiet before the inevitable onslaught of noise. He hadn't really thought about it amidst the whirlwind of preparations, but would it be too much? All those sounds at once, all day, transmitting through all his channels? Hearing people selected their sounds, only focusing on one channel at a time. If they were listening through their ears, half the time they were oblivious to anything else around them. Or they chose to look rather than listen. He saw it all the time, people being in a space, having a conversation, but looking somewhere else, often at their phones. How was it possible for them to really know what was going on? How is anyone really connecting with anything, or anyone else? Few people seemed to have the patience to stop, slow down, focus. Being deaf had forced him to.

He opened his eyes and smiled. That was really rather good, if you let it be.

He glanced over to Shelley, up a ladder fixing something to the sound desk riser. He would cope today. Today, he could do anything.

Besides, wasn't that the point of this event, after all? To give people a glimpse of what it was like to do it *differently...*

59

HEARING AID RULES

LISTEN

ENJOY YOURSELF

BE CURIOUS

PAY ATTENTION

From the ticket onwards, there were only four 'rules' for the Hearing Aid weekend. Reminders were everywhere. Banners crackled and flapped with the words, and the setting was alive with the movement of both sight and sound.

With the Winchester Hearing Loss Support Group as stewards, from the moment people walked through the gates they had to think about how they communicated. Badges reminded them to slow down, speak clearly, and face each other. Visitors had free rein of the estate and there was something in every nook and cranny to watch, touch, or hear. Matthew and Bill, with Pip as consultant, had arranged the grounds into 'rooms' – the lake, the meadow, the woodland, the barns, lawns and terraces – room to breathe, room to stretch, room to touch, room to watch, room to listen...

The sensory stables were a highlight, full of Robert's percussion to explore, and sounds to hear and feel. Pip and Matthew's listening workshops were fully signed up within half an hour. Elsewhere, in the Scout marquee, there were hand, foot and head massages, meditations and dance workshops. Clowns, magicians and mime artists passed through the grounds, and student actors in outlandish costumes burst into impromptu sketches and routines. For those visitors who didn't mind a little exercise there was a guided walk down to the lake, one of the quietest places of the estate, during which they were encouraged not to speak but to communicate, if they needed to, in any other way. And instead, to listen to everything around them, as much as they could, with every part of themselves, unfettered by the disruption of anything anybody else had to say.

The lawn was ringed by tastes and smells. As well as the hog roast, bread oven, vegan curry van and beer tent from the opera, the Women's Wheelers had been promoted to a bunting-strewn barn, serving tea in vintage china with homemade biscuits and cakes (all sampled by Pip). The Scouts and Guides turned up this time with their barbecue, along with the Rotary Club tombola and the Parish Council produce stall.

And then there was the music. The courtyard – the stage and focal point – a feast for the senses. Colours, movement, bunting, banners, lights and magic. With none of the traditional stacks of speakers, the sound was transmitted wirelessly to the audience's headsets, immersing them in the music and enabling them to choose their own personal volume and experience. Panels on the sides of the stage played images that moved to the music. A local cartoonist drew along live during some sets, his creations projected onto the panels, whilst a sign language translator and two performance artists provided visual interpretation during others. The opera seating gone, the arena floor was layered with lighting pads, wired to the sound desk so that the lights moved and changed to the beat of the music. And a small area at the side enclosed vibrating floor pads, which small groups could try for ten minutes at a time for an extra stimulus. If they could get Pip and Matthew out of it first...

The grounds buzzed and flowed with people relaxing, laughing, engaging with all that was around them, passing in and out of the Palladian arch from one band to another at their choice all day. The afternoon stage was graced by an eclectic mix, from Winchester Community Choir, to the best of the acts from the Lamb and Flag off the Mile End Road, minor '80s chart bands, and anyone in Stat's carousel who was currently underemployed, doing a favour, or just plain curious. The audience grew with every one.

Rex and Marilyn closed the afternoon session with a rendition of *Barcelona* which really took the lid off the crowd. Marilyn was almost knocked from her note by the power of it, feeling something stirring inside of her that she'd forgotten existed.

And when Rex took her hand for the final soaring notes, it was *two* things.

Shelley glanced towards the west wall as the applause and roar of approval showed no sign of diminishing, never quite able to let go of the responsibility, and the nagging doubt that it would all go tits up with just one too many decibels. Of course, they had done everything they could to limit the volume coming from the stage; they had not really considered the volume of a crowd's pleasure.

She peered over the audience to the archway where Graham Tweedle had been dispensing headphones (and 'advice') all afternoon. Stuffing his face with organic sausages and garlic mash, he closed his laptop on the afternoon's monitoring.

The crowd funnelled back to the adventures beyond.

So far, so good...

60

TRUST

The Manor uplit and the courtyard glowing as the sun dipped in the sky, the evening acts were getting progressively more well-known and accomplished. Just as The Edge of Darkness were getting progressively more twitchy. Of course they wanted all the bands to be good. Just not *that* good.

And now they had another fight on their hands. As soon as Alan had walked back through the door, Yebut decked him. Yebut had been wandering around ever since, staring at his coloured knuckles with childlike awe, as if they had taken it upon themselves to avenge the last twenty-two years of spite and bullying.

Alan went down like a skittle and had been in the St John Ambulance tent for the last hour. He seemed alright at first, until he started muttering about being at the Reading Festival in 1979 and moaning about the price of a pint of Watneys Red. And now they were carting him off to the County Hospital.

'Now look what you've done!'

'Yeah but—'

'Leave him alone, Damon.'

'Yeah? And what the fuck are we going to do now?'

It was obvious to everyone. Except Pip.

'Oh no,' he said, his hands up, backing away. 'No, no, no, you crazy... I can't!'

'Oh, stop saying that, we know you can...'

Victoria slipped away and knocked on the window of the St John Ambulance. 'Come straight back once you've dropped him at A&E, would you? We'll organise a taxi back for him. Make sure to tell them it's *not* an emergency...'

Shelley arrived at the stage edge, breathless and panting. She had run all the way to the Folly and back to fetch his own drumsticks. The crowd was waiting and thoroughly warmed up. Pip, however, was on fire.

'Oh God, Shelley, what the hell am I doing?' He sat quivering in the darkness on the floor behind the stage. 'Look at me, I can't hear anything above all this!'

She took his shaking hands and placed his drumsticks in them. 'I know. But I also know that you can.'

'I want to. I want to. But something happens even when I think about it. Look, I can't even hold the sticks properly!'

Rex, Damon, Benny and Yebut re-appeared, crowding round him, question after question that he could not follow: Did he remember all the songs? Should they shorten the set list? Perhaps try a couple of numbers, just to see how it goes? They started with their once legendary drum solo – did he want them to pull that one? Shuffle the set? Start just before the verse?

'No.' *What the f...?* Pride had disconnected his mouth from his brain again. But he could hear no more. He got up and walked out on stage.

'Hang on a minute...!'

The stage in darkness, and assumed to be a technician, no-one noticed Pip sit down on the stool, his hands on each drum.

Shelley followed, crouching by him. She put hers on his. 'What can I do? What do you need?'

His eyes roamed the stage. 'One in-ear monitor, lots of Yebut, vocals, but no guitar or keys. And have we got time to move the drums to the side?'

'We'll make time,' she smiled and squeezed his fingers around his sticks, signalling to a stagehand before she disappeared back to the sound desk...

Everything checked and ready, Shelley looked out over the heads of the audience, to him, sitting alone at the side of the stage as the landing lights rose. He just looked so small there, fiddling around with the stool, fingering the sticks, studying the kit, studying, studying, studying. The focus, the barely concealed alarm. Her stomach tumbled. He wasn't the only one in need of the fire bucket.

Then he raised his head. Yebut was there beside him, turning a stage lamp onto himself. Never in the spotlight, Yebut stood wordlessly ensuring that he would be seen. They looked at each other and Pip, finally, nodded.

The audience had grown to capacity now. Shelley turned on their headphones. The sample music played into them again, a voice reminding them of the instructions on their control packs. Matthew was squeezing his way to the front, to the nearest this event was ever going to get to a 'mosh pit', whilst Victoria settled herself into her red velvet chair, at Shelley's side on the riser behind the audience.

'Ooh look, there he is!' She scrambled to her feet again. 'Pip! Cooey!'

'Victoria, sssh!'

'Apologies.'

The crowd shuffled and fiddled, settling in anticipation. And then there was hush as Benny placed his hands on two keyboards, and one fat, lush chord swelled into everyone's ears.

It seemed to go on forever...

Until... BANG! The drum 'duet' of *Orion* hurled out from the side of the stage, not going too much further, but weaving over the bass notes and powering through everyone's headphones at once. Jolted to attention, the audience stood mesmerised as the lit floor beneath them went wild. Shelley thought for a moment she was going to faint, all that nervous energy fizzing into the most excited engagement. Victoria's eyes found Matthew. He turned instinctively to look back at them both – the team that they were – sharing the relief and the wonderment. And everybody else? Well, what did they know that this resurrected band's drummer was, this minute, being spirited down the M3 in the back of an ambulance? Whoever noticed the drummer?

But by the end of the first number, nobody could have failed to, really. He was bloody everywhere...

Yebut remained steadfast, facing Pip from the moment he walked on stage, exaggerating the cues with his eyes and his fingers on the strings, mouthing the odd hint. Let Rex, Damon and Benny play to the audience – he knew where he needed to be. But they, too, were looking back at Pip as the song ended. He hadn't really emerged in that last ten minutes, but now he was returning their gaze, scanning them all. He looked a little like a kid at the top of a rollercoaster... and then he smiled. A kind of energised smile, but with a touch of bewilderment. Like he didn't quite know either...

Starship's *We Built This City* was a master stroke as a second song. Cranked up by the rhythmic powerhouse of the opener, the audience joyously settled into familiarity, singing every word. Rex momentarily stumbled. Without the deafening volume that was normally present on stage, he could hear the audience singing back to him more than he ever had in his life. Like a battle cry with everyone on his side, the noise was life-saving. And he threw himself into it. Once, in 1983, he had made an ill-fated fall into the crowd, an act of faith which had ended with him being dropped in the fifteenth row and breaking his collarbone. But for fourteen rows, it had been heaven. Just as it was now, hearing every word from the crowd en masse, he felt like he was being carried on the wave of it.

Only some knew the special significance of the song, as Rex leapt and strutted, sweeping an arm across the courtyard towards the twinkling Manor walls, ending it pointing at Matthew, *'We built this city on rock 'n' roll...'* Matthew was crying; he knew he was saved. They all were.

The backing vocalist in the shadows was surprising, too. Marilyn was having the time of her life.

And for Pip, the song gave him a moment to breathe after the exertion of *Orion*, to just sit back on the beat and hit hard, allowing his concentration to relax a little, to understand what he had done, what he was continuing to do. And to look out, for the first time. *People.* So many people. It was hardly Wembley, but he had not seen so many people in front of him since that last night in Belgium. The electricity started to spark. He made himself look at them. They were just people. Re-focusing on the sound travelling from his sticks through his body, he realised it was never the people he was afraid of. It was himself.

And *this* is who he was, who he had always been. But now no longer fighting to hide the unhideable, nor tightening around the anxiety of a life he could not fulfil, nor running from an audience he could never please. A new sound had crept into him whilst he wasn't looking. A softer sound of acceptance.

He looked to the back of the courtyard, Shelley on her riser, hands on the sound desk, but eyes on the stage. And that glorious love-for-life smile, beaming its spotlight on *him*. Had he really done something to deserve that? He could bathe in that smile for the rest of his life. And a flash memory of the night before reminding him that he might just have been invited to –

dissolving all the other memories that had shouted something else for so long – Pip felt something unfamiliar growing in his chest. A readiness to let go of something held too tightly for too long, a welcome release of a heavy weight. He was not sure what was happening to him. He glanced around the band, all looking to him to start the next song, smiling at him too. Yebut nodded.

Trust.

The band reeled off one '80s classic after another, including their own. The audience even lapped up a couple of their lesser-known numbers – which most of them were, if they were honest – it did not seem to matter. Uninhibited by being unable to hear the clapping, singing or shouting of anyone else, the audience clapped and sung and shouted and danced with abandon. Pip played every number like it used to be – how he remembered them – but also how he heard them now, with every bit of his body. As if the music had taken possession of it and was playing through him, the spaces within him opened up, clear and resonant, the sound of him flowing outwards through the audience to the horizon, where *she* stood...

Three encores, and it was all over. Pip got up from his stool. His fingers curled quietly around his drumsticks and the stage was solid beneath his feet. The audience moved and roared, but he was still.

Then something else came bursting into life, as if the release of the performance had obliterated any inclination to control the volume of his own desires. He swung the microphone boom over the drums and screamed into it.

'I love you, Shelley Harper!'

He was not lost. He had been there all along...

. . .

Backstage, Pip was being handed round like a pass-the-parcel. Shelley watched quietly, delightedly, from the side until they'd finished with him. He was pink, his shoulders rising and falling with the effort of drawing in enough air to feed his electrified body. A heat coming from him, you could almost see the steam rise. Chest expanding, eyes so wide and alive.

And then they were on her. Both their faces exploding into a big dipper gape. She screamed at him as they threw their arms around each other. 'You did it! You did it! And Jesus, Pip, did you do it. That was—'

'Yeah, don't say it... fucking incredible!'

And then he screamed too, swinging her around the emptying courtyard.

'So, do you want the job?' was all Damon had to say. But it kind of said it all.

'Only if it's part-time,' Pip replied, his eyes never leaving Shelley. 'I've got a lot to do here...'

61

LISTEN

Matthew stood alone in the old library, looking out of the window on the debris of the night, watching a streamer flapping in the breeze shouting the words, 'Pay Attention!' He smiled. For once in his life, he thought he might have.

The library looked the same as always as he turned and gazed at it, floor to ceiling. But it sounded different. The whole Manor sounded different, as if it were whispering sighs of relief, and the words 'hope' and 'future' that Matthew had been trying so hard to hear for so long. Mostly in the wrong places.

So many people had told him today that, never mind the music, the grounds had been a revelation. A multi-sensory playground, which could surely be a visitor attraction in itself...? Consultants, creditors, well-wishers, naysayers, and cross-eyed financial advisers had surely missed that one. Of course they had. He had needed other people to teach him that.

They were all in the drawing room opposite. He could hear the music, the laughter, the loving; the hallway vibrating to the sound of the people he loved, each – *finally* – having found what they most needed.

And it was a beautiful noise.

He wandered to the library door and looked in across the hall. He was the very heart of this place, but he wanted these moments apart. To pay attention. To *listen*. To hear it all. The room was full of the musicians and crew, actors and dancers and therapists of the day, spilling out onto the terraces whilst there was still a little warmth in the night air. He could hear the swells of activity, the rise and fall of gathered conversations. He watched them for a while before seeking his familiar faces.

Rex, sitting in an open sash window, smoking, enigmatic and aloof, like an introspective teenager on their first day back at school. And just like that man-child, the distance lasted only until someone affirmed his significance, asked him a question, paid him attention. Two minutes later and he was in the centre of Marilyn and the stewards from the Winchester Hearing Loss Support Group as they lapped up rock 'n' roll tales of life on the road. In the heyday. His and theirs.

Victoria sat nearby in the quietest corner, teaching Yebut to play Scrabble. It was not clear which of them was coming off worse. Until she convulsed in laughter, upended the board, sending tiles flying everywhere, and sprang up to teach him the jitterbug instead, *Wake Me Up Before You Go-Go* booming from Morris' makeshift stereo.

And Pip and Shelley... Oh, goodness me, well, they *were* busy!

It was the best of conclusions to a set of conclusive bests. Victoria had found a new lease of life, in the hope of security for the Manor and everyone in it, including Robert's memory. Rex had found his new audience. Shelley had found her voice and her vocation. And Pip had regained his courage, and pride in his ability. Free of the real disability: his silence.

And the two of them had found each other. Running past him now, out of the room and up the stairs hand in hand, Pip looked back at him, dropped his mouth and crossed his eyes in an unspoken disbelief at his good fortune, before taking the steps two at a time to catch up with his destiny. Matthew held his thumbs up, nodded and smiled, a deep and grateful smile. This was all their doing. The boy who had taught him how to listen, and the girl who had loved him enough to make it all possible. His children now.

And yet. *And yet...*

Tears pressed behind his eyes. He breathed in hard and located the remaining hole in his heart. It was always there. So many years spent doing his utmost to avoid it, ignore it, or obliterate it, tonight he would just feel it. He flattened his back to the wall and pressed his palms against it.

Amidst the volume, he would hear the remaining pain himself, alone, in silence.

The doorbell rang. He felt it quite clearly.

'Bloody fog at Sydney. I've missed it all, haven't I?'

'Edward...?'

THE END
of their beginning...

YOUR OPINION MATTERS!

If you have enjoyed A Beautiful Noise, it would be tremendously helpful if you were able to leave a review.

The publishing industry is tough for authors right now and reviews really do help bring my books to the attention of others who might enjoy them.

Review on Amazon via your order page, or via the link at www.samjcollins/reviews

THANK YOU VERY MUCH!

And I hope you will join me on another adventure soon...

ACKNOWLEDGMENTS

If you've got this far, first I'd like to thank *you*. I was once told by a wise old author that anybody who reads the acknowledgments in the back of a book is either expecting to be mentioned in them, or has really enjoyed the book. Whichever you are, you have my deepest gratitude. Brewing this story for many years is both a huge pleasure and a frequent challenge; having people read and enjoy it is the greatest privilege of all.

I don't think I'm being too controversial to say that the publishing industry is a pretty difficult place for authors, especially new ones. So I am very thankful to have found Mostyn March Publishing as my true home, enabling this story to be published without compromise. Nobody's going to retire millionaires, but we've done it fairly, with creativity, commitment and integrity.

Sincere thanks to my wonderful Advance Reader Team whose support was an invaluable confidence-boost and undoubtedly kicked me up a gear: Helen Barrow, Sarah Beaton, Chris Brinklow, Liz Brinklow, Katrina Copping, Nicky Dyer, Angela Green, Trish Gamble, Jess Geoghegan, Maura Hubbard, Sue McCreeth, Sue Murdoch, Claire Page, Helen Thom, and Anne Boyere (who was there at the beginning of this publication journey and whose fabulously nutty children's stories really deserve a wider audience).

Thank you to those who have shared their experience of hearing loss. To my fabulous lip-reading classmates, and in particular our esteemed leader, Helen Barrow, who never fails to make every week full of warmth, fun and education. (Join in at www.lipreading.me.uk).

To all the musicians (including the twats) I have known over the years. Massive respect to two drummers in particular: Phil Collins, who is not in the best of health anymore, but has been a huge inspiration to me for most of my life. Thank you for all you have given over the years and I wish you comfort, love and happiness in your retirement. And the marvellous Dame Evelyn Glennie, whose lived example and mission to *teach the world to listen* has been a particular inspiration for this work. There are few problems in this world that better listening could not improve, and I very much look forward to further supporting the work of the Evelyn Glennie Foundation (www.evelynglennie. foundation).

To my family. Mum and Dad who are not here to see this – they wouldn't have liked the language, but would have been delighted, nonetheless. My wonderful sisters Jane, Maggie and Karen and brothers Chris and Pete, who are still the most interesting people I know. And to Mike, and all the Victorias of this world, who have faith in us when our own is sadly lacking – thank you. After all these years, you are still top of my charts.

Finally, this is for the 1 in 5 people you will meet today who will be working hard to hear you – the vast majority of whom do not use sign language, or have a drum to bang, but quietly fly under the radar, doing the best they can in a (differently) hearing world, relying on adaptation, technology, patience (yours and theirs), tenacity and courage. I salute you all!

ABOUT THE AUTHOR

Whatever my other shortcomings, unlike Eric Morecambe, I have spent most of my life coming up with words and putting them in the *right* order. I've written practically everything in my time (some of it voluntarily). After 20 years in Whitehall, producing anything from public pamphlets to troublesome Government Ministers' speeches, I am now completely feral as a self-employed writer. (The commute is better, but the boss is a right cow).

I suppose the thread that runs through my writing is 'what lies beneath' – the things we do not say, the truths we hide. In fiction, as in real life, I am most interested in our flaws and fears, and our honest struggles with the, largely unseen, psychological and emotional challenges of this life. I have become a bit of an expert in fear over the years – I am a lifelong sufferer of anxiety, and have a PhD in stage fright. Both are a profound inconvenience, but it does, perhaps, give me a deeper understanding of people, and I am drawn to writing which balances plot and character with plenty of insights into our human condition. My characters are flawed and lost, but they evolve and find their way – in the end – with a little help, and a little humour. Whatever *their* shortcomings, I like to bring them to a place of hope.

In that, I am a great believer in the healing power of humour, and a little larger-than-life escapism. There is always room in my books for both, and always room in my life for a Downton Abbey or a Richard Curtis film. And the best self-help book I have ever read is by Jimmy Carr.

When I'm not writing, I sing, play the drums and grow vegetables. I live in rural Herefordshire, on the border of England

and Wales, with my partner and a deaf cat called Malcolm. I am currently learning Welsh and lip reading. Neither has made any impact on Malcolm.

Get in touch or join my VIP Club for free content and to be the first to know about new books, events and promotions:

www.samjcollins.com

I'm listening!

Printed in Great Britain
by Amazon

50146559R00254